Outside(Inside) In(Out)

Outside(Inside) In(Out)

Nihara Krausé

Copyright 2010 © Nihara Krausé

ISBN 978-1-4457-7635-4

This novel is a work of fiction. Names and characters are the product of the author's imagination and any resemblance to actual persons, living or dead, is entirely coincidental.

All rights reserved. No part of this publication may be reproduced, stored in a retrieval system, or transmitted in any form or by any means, electronic, mechanical, photocopying, recording or otherwise, without the prior permission of the copyright owner.

Cover photograph by Jodie Krausé

Contents

Chapter 1	My World	1
Chapter 2	On the Move	13
Chapter 3	The Mystery of the Knickers in the Bin	21
Chapter 4	G-Spots and Pit Stops	33
Chapter 5	Alice in M(a)y(a) Land	41
Chapter 6	The Undertakers	49
Chapter 7	New Beginnings	59
Chapter 8	Friendship and Frigidity	69
Chapter 9	Endings	79
Chapter 10	Van Morrison	91
Chapter 11	STDs	99
Chapter 12	On the Wall	111
Chapter 13	Breaking Point	117
Chapter 14	Flight, Fight, or Freeze?	131
Chapter 15	Predator	139
Chapter 16	Shopping for Love	151
Chapter 17	Lighter than Air	163
Chapter 18	What Goes around Comes around	173
Chapter 19	Pink Elephants and Bearded Goats	191
Chapter 20	Friends	211
Chapter 21	Mata Hari	217
Chapter 22	Hot Air	227
Chapter 23	Confession and Atonement	237
Chapter 24	Moving in Circles	241

Chapter 25	Brown Snow	247
Chapter 26	'Man Ahoy!'	259
Chapter 27	Eat As Much As You Can	271
Chapter 28	Misfit v. Miss Fit	283
Chapter 29	A Walk in the Park	295
Chapter 30	Hostage	305
Chapter 31	Kicking Butt	329
Chapter 32	White Noise	341
Chapter 33	The Best Thing since Wheat Bread	353
Chapter 34	Outside (Inside) In (Out)	365

In Suffolk

24 July 2006

He lies on the floor of his bedroom, gasping in pain. The packets of pills lie scattered around him, the vacant blisters resembling numerous accusing eyes. His stomach cramps again, and his knees jerk up in pain. He wants to retch, but he can't. He swivels his eyes to where, propped on the table, lies the note. He has checked its existence a number of times, but he needs to do it one more time. Yes, it is there. His eyes blur, and his head jerks back violently. Another spasm, and then another. He waits for the pain to end. The envelope that houses the note is addressed 'To Maya.'

Prologue

There is a world under my feet – the world of the underground 'tubes.' Think about it, and it seems bizarre: that underneath our 'over ground' lives is an underground city, teeming with life. People in this underground city are solitary, compartmentalised in their own personal space bubbles; they rush like atoms, colliding against each other, but they don't acknowledge their exchange of energy. Each is wrapped up in their own world of experiences. Each is intent on getting to their destination, in isolation.

Not many like descending into this domain of Hades. Some experience breathlessness, palpitations, or dizziness; at the extreme end of the spectrum, they may gasp for breath, their accelerated intake culminating in major panic attacks. They believe they are unique in this suffering. To share it would make them vulnerable, like a mollusc exposed to salt.

Our age-old instinct to survive is conditioned deep in our brains. So keep moving, and do not burst the invisible shield that divides and separates. Make no eye contact, and hope and pray that the tube does not stop in a tunnel, or worse still, get blown apart by a terrorist attack.

Why am I so fascinated by this underground world? Perhaps it mirrors me. I, too, have an underground world – a cavern into which I am afraid to descend. My experiences, like tube passengers, compete to remain compartmentalised, trying to ignore each other, trying to negate the impact they may have, the links they could make. Trying to propel me to a destination, where?

Chapter 1

My World

May 2006

My name is Maya, and I am twenty-six years old. The meaning of my name, I am told, is 'illusion.' 'How appropriate is that?' exclaimed a teenage friend a long time ago. I live on the outskirts of London, as I have done on and off since my birth, away from the internal intimacy of the centre. The same teenage friend also accused me of being out of line with others' views of me. They say I look 'striking,' I hold out that I'm rather ordinary-looking. They think I'm confident; I disagree, but here's the biggest difference: they accept me.

'Mummy, what's half-caste?' I asked when I was six. She didn't answer me, but for a long time I thought it meant something that was incomplete. 'Mixed race' is no more comforting, but mixed I certainly am, and the blend is often in conflict. Just as both the sun and the moon exist within the same body of blue but are not often seen together, my Asian and Caucasian genes coexist warily, while raging within me is a tug of war for domination.

About a month ago, I made a discovery when I was sorting out some storage boxes under my bed. Well, I made out they were a discovery, but I've known all the time that they were there: my diaries from over the years. No great discovery should go by without record of it, and I duly felt that I should attempt to review them and collate them into one volume.

'I have plans to make a travelogue of my life,' I airily told a work colleague one day. 'Isn't everyone supposed to have a novel within them?'

I never verbalised the real reason, which was the hope that through this, I might collate myself.

This thought has been an amazing instigator of avoidance. I have become expert at finding other things to do. Here's my problem: I fear that when I start to explore, I may have more baggage than found at Heathrow and Gatwick airports put together.

So I have exhausted myself with various tasks until I am finally ready to face the issue. The fact is, I need to do this, because I am about to make a major change in my life that involves someone else, that involves being *part of,* and belonging is what I have longed for all my life.

When I wake up this morning, I know that this is the beginning. I make myself comfortable and close the drapes in my living room to keep out the seductive sun. I unplug the telephone and make sure I will not be disturbed. I settle on my velvet sofa, which is threadbare but comfortable. My old blanket, a childhood comforter darned and softened by years of use, covers my knees and feet. I take out my new notebook, feel its thick pages tentatively, and lay it on my lap along with my long-coveted fountain pen.

I open the first journal, started when I was eight years old. I see my neat, schoolgirl's cursive writing and read the first few lines…

I love my beautiful Mummy…

I read, recall, and then write on the first, pristine page of my notebook. I want to combine the diary entries of the past with my adult memories and reflections.

My mother, Diane, is beautiful. I am certain no one else in the world compares. I love her lion's mane of golden-brown hair, which her pride never lets me feel. This is her recipe for luxuriant hair, which she wrote down for me and which I stuck in my diary:

Ingredients:

Sandalwood powder
Rainwater
Jojoba oil
Vinegar
Chamomile shampoo

Instructions:

First, mix sandalwood powder (it has to be pure) with warm water, preferably rainwater, into a thick paste. Next, apply it onto your scalp. It's messy, but it cleans the scalp and hair. Leave this gooey mixture on the scalp for at least ten minutes, after which run a diluted version of the mixture through the hair, moistening with some jojoba oil. Rinse with two parts of rainwater to one part of boiled, cooled, water. If rainwater is unavailable, just use boiled, cooled water. The water will run brown and gritty. Now wash with a mild chamomile shampoo and finish with a dash of vinegar for an iridescent shine. Then leave to dry naturally.

As I transfer her recipe, I wonder where she got it from since it is far too exotic for her background, but then, my mother has always been a woman of contradiction.

Daddy says that Mummy is prettier than Barbie.

My mother has hazel eyes surrounded by long, curling eyelashes, and her mouth is wide and generous. She has a perfect figure, even though she doesn't think so, and long legs – 'Barbie legs', I suppose.

My mother was born in Surrey, the daughter of a high court judge and an ex-model. From the stories I have heard, she grew up wilful and rebellious, courting a string of unsuitable boyfriends and constantly getting into trouble. She went to finishing school, got expelled for smoking marijuana, and then travelled abroad for six months, backpacking with a friend – common now as a gap-year activity but not so acceptable when she was young.

My father was considered one of the most unsuitable of all of her boyfriends; to her father in the early days, he was 'one of those Asians'. He wasn't rich, but he was clever – although my grandparents would say, 'They have to be clever, academic achievement is prized in their culture.' Or 'Their horizons are never broadened to include anything but study.' In defiance my mother married him, but she was restless, especially when, with time, he became respected and liked by both her parents.

Mummy is always so quick at things.

My mother wears impatience like perfume. She rubs it on her pulse points in the form of rush, got to keep on the go.

'Maya,' she screams, 'this bed should have been made up hours ago! For heaven's sake, get these clothes off the floor – and whilst you're doing that, you might as well bring any washing you have downstairs. Oh, and don't forget to change your towel and flannel – and when did you last have a new toothbrush?'

She often skids in her haste to complete the many things she wants to do – no, the things she feels she has to do. 'Got to clean the silver today,' I hear her mutter. 'Got to weed the garden and call a plumber for a quote.'

I am caught in her frantic whirl to sort out the house. Then she rushes around, occupying herself with activities outside the house. I never see her stop for a moment, not even when I watch television in the evenings or when she tucks me into bed at night.

I like it when Mummy plays with me, but she can't always do this because she's so busy.

'Goodnight, Maya,' she says, tucking my bedclothes around me whilst she picks up a book from the floor and puts it on the shelf, smoothes her hair, and rubs a picture frame to check for dust. (As I got older, I realised that her manic behaviour had a purpose, and that was to get away from her demons, the black ninjas of depression, who pricked her when she was busy but dug out her very core if she was still.)

Occasionally I glimpse her darkness. When she is cooking, I see despair in her face or hear a break in her voice when she answers a question I have asked her. Sometimes I see her staring blankly at the wall. Once, when I come back inside from playing in the garden, she is seated at the kitchen table, her head in her hands.

'Are you okay, Mummy?'

She stares wildly at me, her eyes wide and unfocused. 'Er, yes, yes, go and do your homework,' she mutters as she stumbles to her feet. 'I've got a lot to do.'

Sometimes I feel something hard in my tummy and at the back of my throat. It hurts and makes me want to cry.

All this time, I reverberate in harmony with her. I rush around being ultra busy and deny any sadness I feel. For me, as for her, these feelings are forbidden, because they emanate from a shameful kernel within.

When my mother isn't rushing, she tries to drown herself in alcohol. At times, it works.

Today is my Mummy's birthday.

I am so excited, because I have saved up to buy her a special lamp with beads on it for her dressing table. It has taken me about two months to save the money, which I have earned through doing household chores, and I have wrapped it up carefully, first in tissue paper, and then in some beautiful gold wrapping paper. Early morning, when I wake up, I run upstairs to her room and give her the present. She looks so sad in bed that I stop for a moment. For a minute, I think, *is it really her birthday today?*

I sang 'Happy Birthday' to Mummy.

'Thank you,' she says as she takes the gift. She opens it. 'Thank you,' she says again. 'It's lovely and so useful.'

I have a heavy feeling in my chest, and my tummy gets hard and hurts again. I make my way slowly downstairs. It is only seven in the morning, far too early to rush to school. I sort out my breakfast and sit down to eat. No one joins me, but that is not unusual. I wash my bowl and get dressed. I sit in my room until it is nearly time to go downstairs to leave. I hear the postman drop the letters in the box, my father close the front door as he leaves for work, and the neighbours argue as they always do about who should take the rubbish out. When I go downstairs and collect my schoolbag, my mother comes down. She is a different person. Her face glows, and there are little beads of perspiration on her upper lip. She smiles. 'Come on, then. The birthday girl wants to go out,' she trills, her voice higher than usual. Her eyes gleam. 'Let's celebrate by beating the traffic, shall we?'

Sometimes Mummy smells funny.

'Happy birthday, Mummy,' I say again when she drops me off at school, and she smiles.

'Yes, indeed. Happy birthday to me,' she sings.

Things don't always resolve themselves in this way, however, and sometimes I am frozen in the headlights of her rage. 'Maya, you forgot to collect the newspaper on your way back today!' she would scream. 'Can you do anything on your own accord without being reminded?' Or 'Why can't you focus on a simple request? Am I asking for too much?'

On rare occasions, her anger tips into the physical. She throws a glass of water at me when we are sitting at dinner because I am not listening to her. Another time, she throws two plates on the floor. After one argument with my father, she kicks and dents the door on the refrigerator. Once – and only I know this – she puts her fist through the bathroom window.

Mummy cut her hand today.

I fear these times, but I am also mesmerised by the rhythm of them. They have been part of my environment from the womb onwards; they are my jungle drum; they are me, and without them I am incomplete.

On the other hand, my father, Ruwan, is, to me, what dreams are made of.

My daddy is the best dad in the world.

He is the three kings rolled into one – kind and loving, good and wise, fun and talented. His love for my mother is unconditional.

I own a plasticine machine. It is a precious possession, even though I outgrew it years ago. It looks like an engine, onto which I can fit a wheel, which has a shape cut out. I then feed the plasticine into the machine and press down a lever to squash it, and out shoots a pliable worm in the shape I want. I love this machine. I love the way I can impress upon the soft stuff my desires, only to be able to roll everything into a ball again and remould it.

My mother does the same to my father. 'You should wear these trousers,' she says to him. 'They'll flatter you. You look too thin.' He wears them when they next go out. 'You should go on a diet,' she tells him. 'You have quite a stomach showing.' Another time she says, 'Don't have a drink with Colin after work. He's a waste of time.'

A few days later, she invites Colin home to dinner. 'We need to cultivate some friendships for your dad,' she tells me.

I, too, am my mother's plasticine shape, green and circular one day, red and triangular the other. I have been moulded and remoulded. It is a task that completely absorbs her and totally confuses me, although I can accommodate being flexible, malleable to please her.

My hair is long now. I want it to be the same as Mummy's, so I can use her recipe for beautiful hair.

'I like short hair,' says my mother, observing a newsreader with a new haircut on the television. 'It's so chic.'

I'm going to surprise Mummy and get my hair cut short.

I secretly arrange for my father to take me to the hairdresser down the road. He leaves me there whilst I sit through my haircut with a happy, fluttery feeling in my chest. I can hardly recognise myself in the mirror when it is all over, and neither can Daddy for a moment when he comes to pick me up. 'It's very nice, darling,' he says as he pays. I am so excited.

My mother opens the door when I get back. She takes one look at me and laughs. 'Oh, Maya, what an awful style to choose,' she says. 'I know many people wear their hair short these days, but short hair is gamine and long hair is so feminine.'

How fast does hair grow? I want it long, really soon.

Whilst my mother propels herself into activity to get away from herself, my father propels himself into activity to prove himself. Improve study, work, achieve at work, and work at achieving more, study about how to work at achieving more, the combinations and permutations of self-propulsion are extreme. This has meant him selling his soul to his employers. They ask the impossible of him, and he always delivers – why not? After all, he asks it of himself.

So this is our system, my father, my mother, and myself.

*   *   *

I finally give in to the sun, which has been making a valiant attempt to shine through my drapes to remind me of the world outside, as well as the demands of my stomach. I have not eaten anything since breakfast, and it is now well past lunchtime. I put down my diary, stand up (my limbs stiff from sitting in one position), and hobble to the kitchen to put the kettle on. On the table I can see my shopping list of groceries I need, another list of people to ring, and a book related to my work in engineering that I have been trying to finish. I make myself a sandwich and a cup of tea. I will permit another hour of the past before I let reality impinge upon me.

I turn on the alarm so that I don't over run my allocated time, settle in another chair, and pick up my diary again.

In Suffolk

25 July 2006

The letter addressed 'To Maya' is still lying on the table where it was placed. The radio alarm turns itself on at 5.00 a.m. The radio announcer sounds unusually loud in this quiet room. No one wakes up to the sound. By 8.00 a.m., sun rays peep inquisitively at the paisley-sheeted bed, still unmade with no occupant in it. They then make their way around the room, first lighting up the wardrobe and then the cobweb on the far corner wall. A wicker laundry basket has unwashed clothes, and in one corner books lie neatly stacked, their spines lining up as do the books on the shelves. There is a satchel made of worn, brown leather in the corner. The rays hesitate and then grow bolder. They lighten up more areas and brighten the middle of the room. There lies what looks like a pile of clothes, but a protruding arm is lit, and then a foot. Whatever is there is motionless. The sun glints on something shiny near the arm: it could be a mobile phone. It looks as if the arm is pointing to the far corner, where near the bed is a side table. The sun shines a little longer before it turns away. Everything is still.

Freddy, in London.

24 July 2006.

Freddy kept pacing between the kitchen and his bedroom taking stock of things around him as he did so. He did this repetitively as he waited for what seemed an eternity for Jackson to be back home. Where was he? He checked his new mobile phone for messages – nothing. He sent Jackson his fourth message of the day and started his worried pacing again taking large bites of chocolate from his special stash. He tried to listen to a new CD but it was no good, he couldn't concentrate. It was unusual for Jackson to be inconsiderate and not to inform him of his whereabouts, and more than that, Freddy urgently wanted to discuss what had been on the news all day.

The news was all about the three bombs that had exploded in South East England in the morning. 'Several terrorist groups are claiming responsibility,' announced the news reporter 'but the bombers remain unidentified.' The news reports further stated that all the explosives were made from easily available materials and were placed in public places: a railway station, a shopping centre, and a government building. 'The extent of damage to people and property is still being assessed, but since they all exploded in the rush hour, the death toll is estimated to be high.'

Freddy went back to his room and turned off the T.V. He put on his music and made himself finish the work he had been doing. When he finished it was late. He wondered if he should make himself something to eat but he wasn't hungry. As always, the chocolate he had eaten earlier sufficed. He checked his telephone. No messages. Freddy started the agitated walking between his room and the kitchen again. Suddenly he cut short his striding when he heard a noise emanating from Jackson's bedroom, and stiffened. He slowly made his way to the kitchen and picked up a sharp knife. He edged towards

Jackson's door. As he got closer, he thought he heard the sound of sobbing. Freddy was puzzled. As far as he knew, Jackson wasn't home, and anyway, crying was not something associated with him.

He quietly pushed open the door to Jackson's room, knife poised and was startled to see Jackson face down on his bed, his shoulders heaving. He put down the knife. For a moment, Freddy's conscience, which he had been trying to dampen, resurfaced, and he firmly pushed it down. He approached the bed and sat down heavily on the side. 'Hey, Jackson,' he said, 'I know it's grim, but work is work, you know. You can't blame yourself.'

Jackson sat up, reached over to a box of tissues, and blew his nose. 'What the fuck are you talking about?' he asked, looking confused.

'The news?' questioned Freddy, whose turn it was to be puzzled. Really, Jackson was behaving in the most incomprehensible manner.

Jackson looked at his friend. 'I couldn't give a shit about the bombs,' he muttered. 'I just wish they had exploded in me.'

Chapter 2

On the Move

Maya, Mid 1980s

We are moving again.

A multitude of experiences expand and explode within my awareness as we drift through a myriad of countries due to my father's job, throughout my early life. We move from home to home, town to town, country to country, a group of nomads. I do not like the upheaval. Like a leaky paper hole puncher, I leave little circles of myself everywhere, like spasmodic confetti. I have to say goodbye to my homes, to my friends, to schools and routines. This is very hard. At first I do it with tears streaming down my face and a pain somewhere near my heart. With time, I become more practiced in the art of making an ending. I float through experiences and relationships, never letting myself engage. I still experience pain, but it is now nearer my stomach and not in proximity to my heart.

One of my first moves occurs when I am about five years old. I have just started at my first school. I am shy. My teacher, Mrs MacDonald, a large Scottish woman, bears down on me. 'Maya, what a lovely drawing of a cat,' she says. I have drawn a duck, which is yellow, with an orange beak. 'Now, your desk is here, with Ben and Laura.'

I sit down, glancing timidly at my two companions. They are fighting over who sits on the less scribbled chair, and they barely glance at me. I stare at my metamorphosed duck-cat. After much tussling, Ben and Laura sit down, still not acknowledging my existence. Soon they are squabbling again, Ben kicking Laura and Laura grabbing all the crayons on the table to scribble on his drawing.

'Children!' Mrs MacDonald bears down on us. 'Children, this is quiet time, not noisy time. Now let's see what's happening here. Hmmm. Maya, why don't you move to that table over there with Alex? I'll put Charlotte between Ben and Laura.' Oh, the ignominy of it. Chastised for a crime I have not committed, I move to another table. Alex and the others move to give me space, giggling.

I want to have a lot of friends.

I don't get to know Mrs MacDonald or Ben or Laura or any of the others, because during my first term at school, we move to Belgium.

Moving country is like starting a new relationship. First there is excitement and hope, the need to explore, and the curiosity to find out everything about it. There is a thrill with each new discovery and a gorging on new tastes, sounds, scenery, and experiences. There is reaffirmation of how wonderful it is, how blessed one is. To bond with something, it seems we need to see its good side exclusively but as with relationships, in time that passion subsides. The beginnings of indigestion set in, and you start to notice, oh, such little things. Like an ardent lover who sees for the first time the lack of symmetry in his loved one's face, you notice the lack of warmth and friendships, the loneliness, the repetition of the same pattern of interactions, and bit by bit you get disillusioned and you start to contrast your current life with the past. You may even start to grieve for what you left behind.

I don't like school.

I don't fit in very well at my new school. I am tall for my age and sound different. There are not many mixed-race children around.

'I don't want to attend any of the evening functions,' my mother announces at breakfast, early into our settling in.

'I think it'll be a good thing for us to do, Diane,' responds my father.

'Well, you'll have to do it on your own, then,' says my mother, decisively adding, 'Take it from me that I'll also not be joining the women's coffee mornings, the charity cake sales, and the Tupperware parties.' My father says nothing, and I puzzle about why adults want to exclude themselves from such enjoyable-sounding experiences.

No one has asked me over to play yet.

At school I am quiet and uncertain. I am the unwanted new baby in a family that is already tired of an excess of children.

'She's strange,' I think I hear them whispering. 'She's not like us.' I pretend not to notice, but within me, my anger and upset ebbs and flows, breaking on the borders of myself in little frothy bubbles, so that when I go home I am in a bad mood. I stamp around my room, and occasionally I grab the soft toys on my bed and fling them on the floor. I embed my fingers in the bedspread and make little holes that I then tear slowly into bigger and bigger holes. Once I even scribble on a wall, on a part that cannot easily be spotted by the side of my bed.

There are more brown faces in England.

I start to notice differences in groups of people around me, and one day I ask my father what immigration means. He reads some facts to me. 'The emergence of Asians in Britain stretches back to the foundation of the East Indian Corporation in 1600,' he quotes, 'although there was an influx of Indians, Bangladeshis, Pakistanis, and Sinhalese since the 1950s in response to the demand for post-war labour. The troubles in East Africa meant further migration of groups of Asians to Britain in the late sixties.' It all sounds rather dry to me.

All I know is that by the time I was born, Asians were integrated into the British population mix in the same way as curry formed part of the national diet – albeit, according to my father, transformed from its original composition, with turmeric, curry powder, and sultanas, to make dishes such as Coronation Chicken. So when my European classmates ask the standard question, 'Where are you from?' and when I reply, 'From England,' and they laugh, I am puzzled.

Where should I have come from?

My parents are initially pleased with their decision to move. 'This is good,' my father would say to my mother, 'life away from the bustle of London and its pollution.'

'The shopping is much better here,' says my mother, 'and the food. As for the standard of education, well, I never would have thought I'd say it, but even that seems better.' She doesn't mention some of the difficulties she faces.

Mummy is very tired. She stays in bed every morning.

Out of bed she is a tightly coiled spring, pacing the kitchen while drinking large cups of strong, black coffee. I tiptoe around her, trying not to ignite her temper. When we get in the car, I notice a film of sweat on her face, her hands shaking as she negotiates her way out of our drive. She follows the same route to school every day, whether there is traffic or not. One day, when she has to follow a diversion due to roadwork, she has to stop the car and get out for a while, her breathing erratic, and her muscles all tense.

'Bloody roadwork,' she mutters to herself, 'bloody school run. Some bloody life.'

Mummy doesn't talk to any of the other mothers she meets. She stands away from them, waving me on. I wonder if she is shy like me.

One day after school, she says, 'Those mums look so smart and immaculate.' I fumble for words. I want to tell her that she stands out, and will even in rags, but I am tongue-tied and then worry that she will think my silence is agreement.

She struggles with household chores, at having to cook meals from scratch. She tended to rely on frozen and tinned food in England.

Apparently custard – real custard, that is – is not made from custard powder but with eggs. Ugh!

As time goes on and we move again and then again, my mother takes to not wanting to get out of bed in the mornings. I have no idea how long she remains in her room. All I know is that on many afternoons, when I get back from school at about three o'clock, she is in bed, drowsy but not always asleep. I creep into the house and prepare her a little tray of food – some toast or a hot buttered croissant and a cup of tea – and take it to her room. Sometimes an eye mask covers her eyes; sometimes she is staring up at the ceiling as though slowly tracking the progress of a meandering fly. I gently place the tray on her lap and prop her up with some pillows as if she were an invalid, and she munches on half a piece of bread or delicately sips her tea. 'Maya,' she says, 'I can't eat this toast, because you've made it too crisp.' On other days, she shudders. 'The toast is so soft, it's soggy,' she says. 'Take it away. It's awful.'

Some days, when I bend towards her to place the tray on her lap, or to prop her up, I can smell wine on her breath, and on others, I can smell the heady aroma of extra-strong mints, sent to us from England by my grandmother. I say nothing, but I am driven to investigate under her bed or in her wardrobes when she is out of the room. Guilt shrouds me when I do this, but I usually come across several empty wine bottles. Sometimes I take them to a large dustbin down the road, and at other times I leave them there and find that she has cleared them a few days later. The strange thing is that she never seems to suspect when I spirit the bottles away.

Unpredictability is characteristic of my mother. Quite suddenly, when she feels that her calorie intake through alcohol is interfering with her ability to maintain her trim figure, she makes herself get out of bed, stop drinking, and start to exercise.

> *Mummy exercises all the time. She says she has to, or she will make lard in her body. I hope I don't make lard when I am older. It sounds horrible.*

I have always been struck by the similarity between the words exercise and exorcise. For my mother, it is to exorcise that she goes to the gym, pushing herself as far as she can go to try to rid herself of the demons within her, as well as to punish her weak flesh for expanding. She spends hours upon hours in the gym or joins several exercise classes, back to back. I know this, because I come across gym timetables with two, sometimes three classes in a row that she has bracketed. Sometimes she writes comments on slips of paper like, 'Did well today, and lasted for four hours in the gym.' Or 'pathetic, no more than two hours today of endurance! I hate the curse.' I sometimes see her doing push-ups at home in the bedroom at night or sit-ups that seem to go on forever. She exorcises herself at every possible opportunity. When watching television, she moves her legs and exercises her ankles, and when cooking, she probably works her pelvic floor. She tends to prefer to walk or to run rather than to drive; she climbs stairs rather than use a lift. The stigmata of these events mark her for days.

> *Mummy's feet were really sore today, and there was blood on her socks.*

Her stigmata are angry, red wheals on the backs of her ankles from the scuffing of her shoes, occasionally bleeding when her feet crack from extra effort; blisters on her toes; sore muscles that she gratefully dips in a bath full of Epsom salts; calluses and blisters on the palms of her hands from pushing weights that are too heavy.

Once she rids herself of her excess weight, she lapses again into lethargy and despair, taking up her revolving love affair with her bed for hours on end. The long periods of sleep fuel her flatness, the flatness prompting further depression and the depression inducing more sleep. Soon the cycle is as familiar to me as day turns to night.

My father makes no comment on my mother's behaviour. Instead he talks to me about achievement. 'If you don't achieve in life, Maya,' he says, 'you never know if you have proved yourself. Have a goal and focus. This is the best advice I ever got from my parents.'

Once he talks to my mother and me about his feelings of being uprooted as a child when he moved to the UK, aged nine, with his family. 'I was so sad,' he says 'to say goodbye to my friends and extended family. When we first moved to London, I especially remember waking up and not smelling the temple-flower trees outside my window, or hearing the cries of the street vendors starting their day early to maximise selling their wares. I even remember the bed sheets felt different. Tougher, rougher cotton, not the delicate and fine cotton of the sheets back home, beaten into submission by the washer-people or *dhobis*, who dashed them on the rocks to clean them, and then when we lay them on the bed, they smelled of cinnamon.' He looks so forlorn when he recounts this that I start to cry, my mother stands up and walks out of the room, and he stops talking.

*   *   *

I stop writing and put away my new journal for the day. I plug my telephone back in, and it rings immediately, as though it has been waiting for me to give it life. It is Bella, a great friend and colleague of mine from work, who is aware of my current task. 'Well,' she asks, 'what have you found out, then?'

I hesitantly reply, 'I think we were lonely.'

In Suffolk

4 July 2006

He had been staring at the television for the past three hours without absorbing anything. When he got up, his limbs felt stiff and unsteady. The televised audience laughed at something that Davina McCall asked the Big Brother *contestant she was interviewing. The room reverberated with their noise, but never had he felt so detached and alone. He was so listless that he could barely put one leg in front of the other to get to the kitchen, where he poured himself a glass of water. His throat felt very dry from the medication he was taking.*

His thoughts suddenly whirred into action. This happened sometimes – absolute apathy followed by a short period of intense brain activity. He shuffled to his bedroom and stared at the bed, neatly made but not enough; he would rearrange it again, straighten the pillows and refold the sheets. On the bedside table were the packets of pills. He read the back of one of the packets compulsively and then picked up another and did the same. He felt completely detached from everything as he worked out how much time he would have before he made the call. Once he'd run over the calculations several times, he shuffled back to the living room. He slowly lowered himself onto the settee and stared again at the soothing repetition of the television screen, his personal lullaby.

Chapter 3

The Mystery of the Knickers in the Bin

Maya, 1980s

Today is a rainy day, in contrast to the day I read my first journal. The patter of raindrops is a soothing constant outside. I settle myself comfortably with journal number two and my diary.

We are going back to London now. I am really excited.

We have a three-up, two-down, semi-detached, shared-drive house with a small garden on the outskirts of London. It is a pleasant neighbourhood, with rows and rows of similar, redbrick houses around small patches of green. Poplar trees line the streets. They are pleasant to look at in the summer but are painfully contorted when pruned down to their arthritic, knobbly branches by the tree surgeons working for the local authority in late autumn. Several little mini-roundabouts join the roads. It is a learning driver's paradise for practicing negotiating roundabouts and reversing around the kerb. My school is on a parallel road, a long road with several rows of raised humps affectionately nicknamed sleeping policemen. About a five-minute walk away in our small shopping parade are a newsagent and grocer, together with an estate agent and an undertaker.

I hate that place. It's so creepy.

The undertakers are housed in a squat, whitewashed building with a discreet name sign and a long, rectangular, blank window with blinds festooned across it. The building looks like a hearse. The blank bareness of the windows mirrors the emptiness of the clientele inside: the hollowness of grief.

I always cross to the other side of the road when I have to pass that building.

I am neither excited nor unhappy about where we live. I love my bedroom, which is the same size as my parents' room. I choose a deep lilac hue as my wall colour, much to my mother's dismay.

'How about a pale shade of blue?' she asks wistfully, but I am firm. I want bright lilac, like a newly opened Iris before it is bleached by the sun. The colour is my only concession to frivolity: the rest of the room is Spartan, with a desk and a matching pine chair, a bookshelf, and my bed, which has plain white bedcovers.

I love reading.

I discover books when we move back to London. What I enjoy most is that the world of words allows me to be in a place where I can be myself, or be parts of other people, and always feel completely acceptable. I visit the local library, which is a ten-minute walk away, and pick up my allotted number of six books per week. I read everywhere. Books are useful, not just as an entry ticket into a fantasy land, but as a way of excluding me from others.

Why doesn't anyone like me at school?

Integrating becomes difficult again. I am not familiar with the class work, the structure of the day, or the attitudes and interests of my peers. I find the breaks the hardest. Immediately the bell rings, everyone rushes to play outside. I don't know which group to join.

Some of the girls asked me to play a game of hopscotch today, but when I hopped, I fell down.

'Where are you from?' they ask me.

I don't like packed lunches.

I make my own lunch, since my mother is in bed when I leave home. I make Marmite or cheese and tomato fillings for my sandwiches, but I don't really like them. I would much rather have cheese and chutney or peppered salami, but I don't take these, in case the other students see them as strange. I don't register that school dinners are stir-fried noodles on Mondays and curry on Wednesdays. I go to great lengths to pretend that anything Asian is not to my taste, commenting on how difficult I find it to digest spices or wrinkling up my nose at the smell.

I hope no one finds out that my favourite meal is the rice and curry that Daddy cooks every Friday.

I eat quickly in the first ten minutes of lunch and then wait to see if anyone will ask me to join them to play. I pass the time nonchalantly looking around the dining area, scanning the food facts chart on the wall (which I know by heart already), and watching people out of the corner of my eye as they seem to approach me but then veer off in another direction.

I carry out this waiting game for about two months, and then I find that I can disappear discreetly into the school library or somewhere else quiet to read my book. I have to time this well. I cannot go missing from my classmates for too long, because the girls on lunch duty may question my absence. I am lucky. In all my time at that school, I am never found out.

I don't like the toilets at school.

I don't like the smell or the fact that the toilets are not that clean. I am intrigued by the odd scribbles: 'Rosie loves Max' or 'Amy and

Natalie – best friends forever.' These are my first introduction to graffiti. I become fixated on the fact that there is a large gap under the door and that someone may peep at me.

I decide to resist the use of the toilet. Lunch breaks now become even harder to endure. The fact that I sometimes have to seek refuge in a toilet to read, particularly if a teacher happens to be in the library, makes self control difficult. Occasionally, I wet myself and then panic.

I am so wet I drip! Ha! Ha!

I take to hiding a spare pair of pants in my school bag and secretly find ways of changing, throwing my wet knickers in the bin in the toilet. I have to be clever about cutting off the name labels from my pants. After about six consistent months of this, the cleaner notices the knickers in the bin. The subsequent report is handled by having the teachers ask us various questions. I am not caught, but my supply of pants at home starts to dwindle. I start putting the offending articles in plastic carrier bags and discreetly adding them to the wash at home.

*   *   *

I had forgotten about the knickers-in-the-bin mystery and giggle when I remember that there were two occasions when I had no underwear because I had forgotten to bring in a fresh pair.

I put down my pen and stretch. Whilst amused, I am also vaguely uncomfortable. Does this indicate some deviance in me? Should I tear out these recollections?

*   *   *

I think there is something wrong with me. I don't like myself, and I don't like school.

I watch the children pick on an obese child in the class. They hunt in packs, and they have no mercy, ripping out the innards of the child through their bullying.

I don't like the children in my class.

Take Susie, for example, who is very overweight. I could like her, but I am a coward, and so I can't admit this. I observe Susie consumed by fear, gulping down her feelings. I watch as they tease her, jeer at her when she changes for swimming or PE, and jostle and push her unnecessarily. They do not want to sit next to her, they hold their noses when they walk past her, and they never invite her to play.

I don't like my teachers.

The teachers carry out their own torture.

Today Mrs Wilkinson, our class teacher, asked Susie to come up and write words high up on the blackboard.

High up, so that the class can snigger at her huge bottom as it jiggles up and down, as laboriously she writes the words on the board that she has been asked to spell. As she raises her arm to write, her sleeve pulls back so that her flesh spills over in folds and wobbles. Once her sleeve splits all the way around as she reaches up to the very top corner of the board, and the laughter of the class echoes down the corridor, so that the teacher from the next class comes in to find out what the noise is all about. When he returns, he tells his class the reason behind the commotion, and their peals of laughter echo back to us. Stoically Susie continues with her tasks, and Mrs Wilkinson continues to choose her to be the scribe.

Mrs Phillips, our games teacher, is the worst. She picks on Susie continually. On Sports Day, she gets Susie to take part in the 500-metre race. Susie's cheeks get redder and redder as she huffs her way around the circuit, her laps continuing twice after everyone has finished. Mrs Phillips insists that the next race cannot begin until Susie finishes.

Mrs Phillips also devises a dance routine for Sports Day, the British equivalent to cheerleading, I suppose. We are to wear swimsuits with grass skirts. It is a very hot summer, and Mrs Phillips wants our outfits to reflect a South Sea Island theme. She provides the fabric and gives us instruction on how to sew the costumes. 'Susie,' she says in class, 'Come in front of us all so that I can demonstrate how the skirt should be made.' Susie goes up and stands in front of the board. Mrs Phillips gets out her measuring tape and measures Susie's waist size, not once but twice, and then writes down her dimensions on the board for all of us to see. She then measures out the length of cloth needed. 'You will all need a lot less fabric, of course,' she tells us.

She beckons Elizabeth, the most petite girl, to the front of the class. She makes her stand next to Susie, and she measures Elizabeth's waist, raises her eyebrows, and then writes the dimensions on the board next to Susie's dimensions. Susie says nothing as she walks back to the sound of giggles. Elizabeth grins widely as she goes back to her desk and then whispers something to her neighbour, who bursts into laughter.

On the day of the performance, Susie looks a fright. The swimsuit reveals rolls of thick adipose tissue along her arms and neck and in solid wave formation around her chest and waist. The skirt exposes large, cellulite-covered thighs, which brush against each other. Any rhythm or gracefulness that Susie might possess is taken over by extreme self-consciousness, so that her movements are jerky and awkward.

Whilst I look on and pity, contradictorily I fear the part of me that wants to join the pack. I squash these thoughts so that they join my other suppressed emotions, mainly anger, which I hide under a developing insouciance.

* * *

I stop writing and feel very restless. I still have trouble in expressing anger; instead I sabotage anger through indifference.

I go out for a while to calm myself. I trudge along muddy paths in the common. It is still raining, and a light patter of water falls gently on my hair and shoulders. My short leather boots are the worse for wear as they squelch in puddles. Not many people are out in this weather, although I spot the occasional dog walker or dedicated jogger. It takes me ages to release the tension in my shoulders and neck. Finally, I walk back home, my muscles spent. I have to go for a dress fitting in a few hours.

As I let myself back in, I see my open journal, and I cannot resist it. I sit with my hair dripping and my feet damp. I start reading and writing again.

*   *   *

The Principal told us about the 'lost register' today.

'We are hoping to start a register of lost items, no different from the lost property office,' she announces, 'but this time, the register is purely for students of the school who find lost items and return them to the office. The names of the students returning the lost items will be read out aloud at assembly.'

I am really excited about the idea. I start scouring the school grounds every lunch break, spotting the occasional eraser or hair ribbon and gleefully returning them to the office, gladly spelling my name to the bored secretary filling in the entries. The first time we have assembly, I can barely breathe until the end, when the principal reads out the list of names and when I hear mine I nearly faint with pride. I want to hear it repeated again. Soon, I become a recognition junkie. I start searching for lost property in earnest, and sometimes when I can find nothing, I hand in some of my own things, like my favourite pink hair band, or my little blue fluffy purse.

Greta, Marissa, and Laura have all claimed my things as theirs.

The month of the project is possibly one of my happiest at junior school. I am bereft when it ends and even take a few more things of mine to lost property immediately after, with the vain hope that my name may still be read out, but it never is.

*   *   *

I put away my journals when I realise the time. My hair has dried in curls on my head. I glance at my watch, and I realise that I have no time to make my hair look tidy, or to put on any make-up. I grab my handbag and rush out of my flat. I cannot afford to be late for this dress fitting, since this will be the most expensive outfit I have owned to date. I also fear the response of the seamstress, an upright French woman who reminds me of a ballet teacher I once had at school: stern, and a stickler for rules.

'You must not put on any weight if you want me to make a dress for you,' she tells me firmly at our first meeting. 'You must be on time for fittings and always wear the same brassiere. Make sure it fits you properly and that the straps don't sag. Payment will be due in instalments and no later than ten days from the invoice.'

She terrifies me, although I have seen a softer side to her when I have complied passively with her demands to stand straight and be pinned. I get in my car and drive through London traffic as fast as I can.

When I return home, it is late, since I have also had a quick dinner at the local Chinese. I am restless, and I realise that I want to continue to read, although I have to go in to work tomorrow. I make myself a large cappuccino and settle down in bed with the next journal.

*   *   *

Today is my birthday, and I have a present of a book of poems and a notebook. The poems are a selection of verses for children, written by poets both modern and old. I love poetry. Here is a poem I wrote when we went on holiday.

Never the same

*I watched a house burning
And tumbling to the ground,
Its roof all charred and blackened.*

*I watched a river flowing and
Peacefully gliding along,*

*Until someone threw in a pebble
And its rhythm became all wrong.*

*I watched a little night fly
Playing near a light,
And when the switch was turned on,
It frazzled out of sight.*

*I watched some ants in a sink
Foraging here and there
When someone opened the gushing tap
And ants floated everywhere.*

*I watched and watched every possible thing,
and in the end I find
It's never the same, there's nothing left,
Not even in one's mind.*

This is my escape. Reality is different. Every morning when I wake up and I make my way to school, I don a necklace of fear. It lies tight against my neck, each bead a measure of uncertainty, apprehension, a need for acceptance. How I wish it would break, or that I could make each bead tumble and disappear through the cracks of the wooden floorboards. Instead, it tightens against my throat, making me husky at times and freezing my voice at others.

I try to face fear through distraction. I have seen my mother do it. I do not have her energy for physical release, so I invest in my ability to absorb. I start learning, but this is no mere focus on learning and revision; this is assimilation in a major way – study binges. I gorge on knowledge, regurgitating it as a bovine chewing its cud. If the fullness is uncomfortable, making my eyes red with exhaustion and my head hurt with knowledge, I do not complain. I want to overdevelop my intellect and eradicate emotions – I want to be a walking brain.

Soon I am different at school for another reason. I am Maya the swot, the peculiar, geeky girl who keeps herself to herself, digs her nose in books, or comes first in class. I do not understand much about group dynamics. My hope is that by being quiet, I will remain invisible. What I know now is that within a group, a person who is quiet draws as much attention to herself as someone who is very loud, and that the attention she usually receives is negative attention. I am an easy target to project badness onto, like a lightning conductor grounding others, charring myself.

My poems become prolific, and my grades at school improve even more. My misery grows in proportion. I have moved from feeling, albeit for a brief moment, that there is light at the end of a tunnel, to a belief that there is always a tunnel at the end of any light that shines down on me.

Jackson, in London

2 March 2006

Jackson emerged from the depths of the subway into pale sunlight and strolled down the road, his hands tucked nonchalantly into his pockets. His eyes darted around, looking for unmarked police cars. He was used to being vigilant. Apart from two convictions for burglary, he had the sort of face that made people suspicious, especially the police. He needed to keep out of harm's way, because distributed among his clothes was cash totalling twelve thousand pounds. He also had tucked in his jacket a small but lethal knife, and in his backpack, some hash and three Ecstasy tablets, another knife, a pack of chewing gum, and the remaining half of a rosary, which had once belonged to his grandmother, and which he carried everywhere as his good luck charm.

He arrived at Acacia Road and slunk down the road to Number Ten, and having looked once over his shoulder, he inserted his key and entered. Ten Acacia Road was a hostel that housed a variety of young people of dubious background. It was not uncommon for residents of the hostel to be subjected to occasional drama, whether between some of the residents or with the police, and today was not a day that Jackson wanted any interaction with a member of the constabulary.

He walked up the bare stairs and unlocked the door to his room. Freddy was sitting on his bed and looked up expectantly.

'Deal went through,' said Jackson. 'I got the cash.'

Freddy let out his breath. 'Did we have all that was required?' he asked.

'Pretty much,' said Jackson. 'They seemed to know what they wanted, even though they looked like amateurs. I just sold them the stuff and left really quickly.'

'They paid in full?'

'Absolutely.'

The two men looked at each other and grinned. 'I reckon we celebrate and rustle up more business?' said Freddy.

'I think I may already have another deal,' said Jackson.

Freddy looked at him expectantly. 'Roll on with it,' he said. 'The sooner we can move out of this shit-hole into a proper house, the better. You wait and see, Jackson. I'll maintain that house to a standard that will make you proud.'

Chapter 4

G-Spots and Pit Stops

Maya, 1989

Grandma Phillips, my special grandma, is lovely – really, really lovely. She is the kindest, best grandma in the world. I wish I could live with her.

Having been forced by my grandfather to give up a lucrative career in modelling to become a housewife, my grandmother conceived my mother with some difficulty and, it is said, after my mother was born became obsessively focused on maintaining her house and her daughter. My grandfather was her audience, and she always endeavoured to please him. She needed his approval. After all, the way she received validation was through other people's opinions about herself. The ramp had been her magic mirror, where she had relied on responses to her silent question of 'People, people, in the hall, who is the fairest of us all?'

When my mother was young, how she looked became my grandmother's replacement career. She was, however, thwarted by my mother's unwillingness to co-operate.

'Leave me alone,' my mother would mutter sullenly when my grandmother admonished her for not dressing well enough. 'I dress the way I want to.'

'But Diane, you would look so much smarter with a scarf, and that jumper is far too baggy. I have a wonderfully soft cashmere cardigan that would look wonderful on you.'

By the time I was born, my grandmother had grown older gracefully and had come to need less affirmation.

Grandma is never critical of me. I love her stories. She is like Scheherazade in Arabian Nights.

'Did I tell you that I modelled evening wear at the Savoy?' she would start, and I would immediately sit down, hands folded on my lap, entranced to hear her story, even though this was one that I had heard before.

'Tell me,' I would invite, starting to visualise a grand hall in an elaborate hotel.

'Well, they were Franconi's designs, and very few models got to work for him. I wore his best creations and was always on stage towards the end of the collection. How fast we had to change, and what wonderful accessories we got to wear!' She would sigh and stare ahead, recalling her past rapturously. 'Then there was another time he sprayed me in gold leaf. All of my body, face, and hair were covered. I got the most hideous skin reaction the following day, but the papers said I looked like a Greek statue.'

She filled in important details about my past: for instance, how she met my grandfather (having ballroom dancing lessons), about what sort of a little girl my mother had been ('She looked so sweet and angelic and yet she was such a naughty little girl'), and, most importantly, facts about me ('Oh, you were adorable, Maya, and such a good baby') and how like my mother I was when I was younger.

'Did Mummy and I really do that in the same way, Grandma?' I would ask incredulously.

'Oh, yes, indeed, you are two peas in a pod.'

When I was with her, my negativity about myself dissolved, and I felt part of a unit. When I left her, I felt bereft. She was my umbilical cord to belonging.

Grandma is a wonderful cook.

Having lived for years on cottage cheese, salad, and egg-white omelette, my grandmother now truly appreciated good food.

Today Grandma made bread. She kneaded the dough, that distant look on her face when she concentrates, eyes narrowed, mouth pursed up. We then made small, plaited bread rolls, some with poppy seeds and some with sesame seeds on the top. We also made baguettes, which we both ate immediately they came out of the oven, without any butter, just tearing chunks with our hands and shoving them into our mouths.

Sometimes we would roll pastry, ice cakes, and make lasagne, each dish baked with a dollop of her special love and care.

I can always conjure up the many smells associated with my Grandma. Her Chanel No. 5 perfume and her face powder are favourites, but what I associate the most with her is a mixture of vanilla, warm, crusty bread, and strawberries. Her smell and the smell of food often intertwine, so that when she makes me a packed lunch, I can smell her when I open my food. I can also smell her wafting from the bread counter at our local supermarket and when I cook a dish I have learnt from her at home. I smell her in the rush of air that emanates when I open the oven door.

I also connect various sounds with her: the stirring sound when she makes my hot chocolate, her spoon quickly tapping the edges of the mug to mix the cocoa, and the frothing noise of the milk whisked separately in a jug. I connect to the whoosh of her wooden spoon when beating cakes and, endearingly, the slight slurping noise of her drinking her tea.

Grandma is very particular about her tea. She never uses tea bags, and she always has to drink from a china cup.

'Mugs are for peasants, Maya,' she says. 'They alter the taste of the tea.'

Grandma's Tea Ceremony

Warm the teapot with hot water.
Obtain fresh tea leaves, preferably, the best orange pekoe Ceylon tea.
Drain the pot and add a spoon of tea leaves – one for each person drinking and one for the pot.
Pour in hot water, just before it comes to the boil.
Brew to the strength desired, stir, and pour.
Garnish with a slice of lemon – remember, milk kills the taste of tea.
P.S. Used tea leaves make excellent compost and can also be placed under the eyes in muslin bags to lighten dark patches or soothe puffy eyes.

In contrast to our relationship, her relationship with my grandfather is a roller-coaster ride. At times she clucks around him maternally, making sure he eats well or has enough cleaned, ironed shirts for the week. At other times, she is savage with her tongue, attacking him about his hopelessness. She is not discreet. I remember hearing about a coded topic she brought up often, which, I never knew then, was about her unfulfilled sex life.

'I miss not experiencing the, er, you know, final peak,' she would say.

My grandfather would look uneasy. 'Do we have to discuss this again?'

'Yes, of course we do!'

'I try. I can't be blamed if I cannot find your so-called G-spot, can I?'

'How can you find it,' she would ask, giving him a dark, glowing look, 'when all I am is a bloody pit stop?'

When Grandma and Grandfather argue, I try to disappear into my head. I dream my favourite dreams where I am a ruler of a tribe, who is loved and adored, or that I am a brain surgeon, admired by the world.

This strategy usually works very well, and I can fade out of the scene, so that when they suddenly remember my presence and focus on me, they have to say my name a number of times to make me come out of my reverie.

These types of battles really do confirm to me why I don't want to grow up. To me, 'groan-ups' are aptly named. It also makes me confused about relationships.

Why do groan-ups want to be with each other when they fight all the time?

* * *

Startled by the vividness of the description of my grandparents' relationship I stop writing and notice that it is after two in the morning. Do I regress into the same pattern of variability in my own adult relationships? As tired as I am, I continue.

* * *

Grandma often cooks for my grandfather after they fight.

Usually, aggressive interactions with my grandfather produce the most wonderful of dishes, the most elaborate and succulent of meals. The time taken for peeling, chopping, dicing, slicing, and stirring becomes foreplay, with some sadomasochistic banging of pots and pans and sharpening of knives for added thrill; the time taken for cooking, baking, and roasting becomes, oh, that delicious wait just before the point of no return – and then the ingestion, that first mouthful, and the next and the next until the smells, tastes, and sensations peak.

On these ceremonial occasions, I am banned from the kitchen, and instead I am asked to either complete my homework or to read aloud to my grandfather. This second task is tedious to both of us.

> *I don't want to read out loud what is in my books, since to me they are sacrosanct. Reading out loud feels almost as bad as undressing in public.*

My grandfather doesn't enjoy this duty either. I know this, because I see a look of long-suffering patience cross his face, and I haven't forgotten the time I was reading *Little Women*, involved in one of my favourite parts of the book, and heard gentle snores emanating from his armchair.

'I never listened to my daughter read,' he tells me gruffly, and once he adds, after I think he had drunk a few extra glasses of port, 'I see no reason why we have to go through this charade. Your mother frittered away her education, and so, I am sure, shall you.'

However, we are both obliged to comply with Grandma's command, so influential is she in our lives.

> *Grandfather never hugs me, cuddles me, or talks to me. Daddy says that he is not really a 'child-friendly' person. I don't think he is an 'anyone-friendly' person. When I am with him, I act stupid. I can't stop stammering, and I usually never do that.*

*　　*　　*

Tired and tearful, I reach out for the box of tissues by the side of my bed. I remember my grandmother telling me once that my grandfather could only relate to people through his work. I now think that she was right. A clever barrister who became a fair and respected judge, he saw a person in the way the legal system requires you to see them – two-dimensional, guilty or not guilty. There were no *possibles* or *maybes* with him – no shades of grey. With his great intellect, he couldn't figure out why his daughter had turned out the way she had, why she had not furthered her education, why she didn't have a high powered job and most of all, why she had decided to throw away her life to live with my father and bear him a child. As far as he was concerned, she had a good upbringing and opportunities for education, and there was no excuse for why she didn't use them.

I picked up on my grandfather's polarised way of thinking very early on in my childhood, and this created a gulf between us. My belief that he thought I was an idiot made me act increasingly like one when I was with him. Luckily our encounters with one another were brief. He spent most of the time after his retirement playing golf, advising young aspiring lawyers on various legal matters, and writing books.

My grandmother was lonely. Just as she was my link to intimacy, I was her link to unconditional love, and so we did things together, never sensing either my mother's or my grandfather's silent envy at our closeness.

* * *

I finally give in to my exhaustion. At four o'clock in the morning, teeth un-brushed and make-up still on, I go to bed clutching my worn blanket in my arms and fall into a deep, motionless sleep.

In Suffolk

28 July 2006

The heavy, stillness of the room is shattered by the intermittent bleep of the telephone indicating that it's battery is about to cut out. No one stirs to pick it up off the floor. About half an hour later, there is some noise outside: footsteps along the path, and then a ringing of the doorbell.

A commanding voice shouts, 'Is there anyone at home?'

Ring, ring, ring.

The flap of the letterbox is open because there is some mail blocking it.

'Mail not picked up,' another voice comments.

'Don't state the bloody obvious, mate. Let's go and see if there's a neighbour who has a key,' says the owner of the commanding voice.

There is a pause, and then the footsteps recede.

A cat lazily crawls across the garden and sits down on the lawn to purr, while a squirrel, disturbed by the previous noise, frisks down a tree trunk and sits up on its haunches. Everything looks calm and normal.

Chapter 5

Alice in M(a)y(a) Land

Maya, early 1990s

My routine hasn't been calm or normal and I haven't written for about a week, although I have craved the inner peace it instils. I have been rushed off my feet at work, since I only have six more weeks before I take a three-month sabbatical.
Today is Sunday, and I have cancelled lunch with Bella so that I can have a free day. Soon after breakfast, I start writing.

* * *

I don't think I am going to like being eleven.

I go for my annual sight test, and I am told that I have to wear glasses. ('I knew you would ruin your eyesight with all that reading in the dark,' says my mother). However, this disastrous news is overshadowed by the inclusion of Alice in my life.

Everyone knows Alice but I have never been her friend because she is one of the cool girls. She always says what she thinks. I want to be like her.

Alice is not one of the most popular girls in the class. She is abrasive and confrontational. She incites extreme reactions from others, so that she either has a little following of admirers or a group of enemies. I belong to the former.

Today Alice argued with a dinner lady for serving her a piece of chicken that was not hot. Yesterday she called a teacher a 'stuck-up witch' because she did not choose Alice for a part in the Christmas play.

About a week before my birthday, we are asked to compose a poem about our head teacher, Mr Newell, who is about to retire. 'The best poem will be chosen to go into a remembrance book, which will be presented at his farewell,' says our class teacher. 'Now I would like you all to work in pairs on this project.'

Alice is allocated to be my partner.

There have been other class projects where we have been put into pairs or small groups, but this project is different. It is to create a poem – easy for me, not so easy for Alice. We also have ten days to complete it, so that should school time not permit, we will need to meet after school.

I've been invited to Laura's house and to Sophie's house to tea this year. I didn't say anything when I was there.

'Well,' says Alice, 'I hope you're good at this, because I'm crap.'

Once I get to know Alice, I realise that swearing is characteristic of her, but now it both shocks and excites me.

'Um, er, I'm not sure, er, but I would like to, er, um, try,' I give a self effacing shrug.

Alice and I approach the project with enthusiasm and, unusually on my part, with considerable confidence. I have an idea how we can incorporate a witty yet touching account of the headmaster, using a mixture of writing styles to indicate our grasp of the beginnings of our exposure to English literature at school. I am chatty and bubbly, not quiet and hesitant as usual, and a lot more relaxed. We sit down to discuss ideas, and I take the lead. We discuss how long the poem should be, how we should present it, and what message we want to get across. Soon the invitation that I have been longing for happens.

Alice asked me to come over to her house today.

'Oh, yes,' I say, thrilled, and then, because I don't want to appear desperate, 'I think I'm free to do that.'

Alice's house is a detached property, on a road of similar-looking detached properties. It is double-fronted, and I am impressed by the stone lions that sit on either side of the pillars on their driveway. There is a green in front of her house too. A red BMW sits on the drive, and Alice nods towards it.

'That's my mother's car,' she says flatly. 'She must be home.'

We enter the house though the side door and go into the kitchen. In the middle of the kitchen floor is a free-standing unit, with pots and pans hanging from the ceiling above it.

Alice's kitchen looks like those featured in magazines.

There is a large vase of lilies on the table, and their fragrance perfumes the house.

Alice's mother, Eloise, doesn't work. Her father is an accountant in the city. Eloise is sitting in the living room when we enter, reading the afternoon newspapers. She looks up when we walk into the room and gives us a smile.

'Hello, girls,' she says.

She is a thin, tired-looking woman with melancholy eyes; she is dressed in a twin set and pearls. She looks older than her years, in the way that women over forty-five do if they have no weight on their face. The melancholia in her eyes is, as I later find out, due to years of marital difficulties with Alice's father. They have three children, and within their seventeen years of turbulent marriage, Alice's father has apparently had a succession of affairs, starting off, as most men do when of a certain age and of a certain professional status, with his secretary; moving on to the woman who lived two doors down the road, to the wife of a family friend, and (the latest scandal) to the twenty-year-old daughter of their general practitioner. Alice is aware of all the details and recounts them with relish.

'My father's therapist has told him that he involves himself in 'Madonna/whore' relationships with women.'

I have absolutely no idea what she means.

Alice is really clever.

'What's a therapist?' I enquire.

'It's who, silly. They both go and see some person whom they can talk to about how angry and upset they feel about each other, and she then gives them advice. We all went once, and it was awful. We had to sit in this room in a half circle, and this woman, who had very curly hair, unshaven legs, ugly shoes, and long earrings, asked us all questions about ourselves and about how we felt about each other. I think she got a bit cross with me because I wouldn't answer at first and kept staring at everyone's shoes. I then got the giggles and set off my brother, Andrew, but she ended up saying that we all needed to learn to talk to each other. Duh!'

Will Mummy and Daddy stay together forever? I don't think they talk to each other.

'My two older brothers, Andrew and Colin are fucking horrid,' continues Alice.

'Why?' I ask, almost disappearing into my head when she swears.

'They just are,' says Alice. 'You're so lucky to be on your own, although I'm usually on my bloody own. When they come back from boarding school, Father does exciting things with them, like cycling and hiking.'

Alice swears a lot in front of her father. He doesn't tell her off.

Alice excels at sports, and she can name all the footballers in the major British football teams. She is not interested in pop stars, jewellery, or make-up. She dresses in her brothers' cast-off clothes – jeans or trousers and shirts or sweatshirts – and she never goes out without a baseball cap. When things are bad at home, she finds fault with people, reacts without the slightest provocation to something that is said in passing, and falls out with friends just as quickly as she can make friendships.

When we complete our poem, Alice gruffly tells me that it is 'fucking marvellous' and that our class teacher would be 'taking the piss' if she doesn't select it. She also acknowledges my efforts with magnanimity. I shrug my shoulders nonchalantly, but I am really pleased.

Of course, the poem is chosen – I had known it would be. Not only is it selected, but it is printed on the opening page of the farewell book to the head teacher, and is also used in the programme for the school prize giving. Alice's father congratulates her on her shared success. I am there when he does it, and I can see Alice glow. From then on, we start spending more time with each other.

*   *   *

I am interrupted by a knock on my door, and I open it to my landlord.

'Just wanted to discuss your leaving plans,' he says, adding, 'I'll need to take a full inventory before the release of your deposit.'

I can see the pound signs in his eyes and take on board his warning, which really is a preparation for not getting my money back, even though I know that I have maintained the property to a high standard. Keen to get back to writing my diary, I open the front door wide for him to step out, and he looks rather surprised, since I am sure he is expecting me to put up more of a resistance to his proposal.

Sighing, because I had hoped it would be a quiet day, I go back to writing.

*   *   *

I had my eyes tested today.

The optician tells me that I will have to wear spectacles. He is an elderly man wearing glasses. Why do all opticians wear glasses, and why do all dentists have perfect-looking teeth?

I need to wear glasses. The optician told Daddy, and I cried. I wonder if he could have got it wrong. What if I didn't do the test properly? When he asked me if the red dot or green dot looked clearer, I really wasn't sure.

We choose frames, tears still rolling down my cheeks. My father gently squeezes my hand.

'Do you want to come back and select them another day?' he asks.

'It's best she chooses them today,' says the horrible receptionist, who is also wearing a pair of glasses.

I cry all the way home from the optician's, my vision blurring even more.

'When you can wear contact lenses,' my father says, giving me a little hug, 'we'll get you some. I was three when my parents were told that I had to wear glasses.'

Mummy didn't say anything when we got home. She must be cross with me.

Jackson, in London

9 March 2006

Jackson felt cross and out of sorts. Although he had told Freddy they may have another deal this wasn't proving as straightforward as he had hoped. He was also bothered because Freddy wasn't talking to him at the moment, since they had had a minor argument. The idea that Freddy was displeased with him always made him uncomfortable, since although Jackson would never admit it to his face, Freddy was the second most important person in his life. Things not going according to plan agitated him and made him feel jittery in an uncomfortable way. Jackson was used to living on adrenalin. He craved it, he needed it. He hated being bored, over stimulation was far preferable. In Freddy, he had a soul mate.

Jackson met Freddy when they were both sleeping rough outside King's Cross Station in London seven years ago. He and Freddy were both around sixteen at the time, and Jackson had been pleased to put as much distance as he could between his stepfather, or 'the Bastard', as he called him, and himself. He was fed up with feeling the impact of the Bastard's belt across the backs of his thighs and his fists punching him in the face. He was also weary of seeing his mother's black eyes and bruises every time she stepped in to take the blows meant for him. Being away meant saving his mother from a beating. The last two incidents with the Bastard had been the deciding factor. Whilst recalling the penultimate occasion still made Jackson wince, the final and trigger event leading to him leaving home was when the Bastard came home full of beer and spirits and Jackson knew it was coming and that he could do nothing to prevent it.

'Jackson!' screamed the drunk 'Get down here, you scum!'

The punch landed full on his nose with an excruciating crunch.

'Stop it!' shrieked his mother as blood spurted on Jackson's shirt. 'For God's sake, Ray, leave him alone!'

She doubled up as the kick landed in the middle of her stomach.

A red mist rose in front of Jackson's eyes. His fists rose automatically, and his right hook nearly lifted Ray off the floor when it landed clean on his chin. Ray went out like a light.

'Oh, God, Jackson, what have you done?' screamed his mother. 'Quick, get out of here before he kills you.'

Jackson grabbed the money she gave him, picked up a towel to clean his nose, gathered some of his clothes from the washing basket in the corner of the room, and turned towards the door. He went back to his mother.

'I'm going away from this place to London, but I'll be back for you, Ma,' he muttered. 'Just make it easy and poison the bastard, won't you?'

That was seven years ago, and Jackson had not seen his mother since, but he knew he would see her soon. She was the most important person in his life, and he would go rescue her after the success of the next deal.

Chapter 6

The Undertakers

Maya, early 1990s

I want to be rescued of feeling such embarrassment. I am so self-conscious wearing glasses at school. I feel like a snail pulled out of its shell being subjected to daylight.

I wore my glasses to school today. Strange, no one said anything.

My friendship with Alice progresses. She sits next to me at lunch and then asks me to join her after, sometimes to help her with something she has not understood so well in the class. I listen earnestly to her opinions. She doesn't like Maggie, because she is so high and mighty; have I seen what Lucy has done to her hair? 'Isn't India fat? Perhaps she is competing with Susie.' Or did I see how John kicked that football into goal? Did I see the bruise on Charles' shin after he got into that fight with Mike? Usually, her comments about the girls are scathing; about the boys, admiring. My participation in these conversations is to agree. I am just thrilled to be included.

Will Alice still be my friend tomorrow?

Panic is now also my best friend. It's my breathing that first changes, becoming short and shallow, so that I worry whether I will be able to take in enough air. My hands then start to feel clammy, and my heart races and pounds. Often the first thing I have to do once I get home is to run to the toilet to relieve myself, since my bladder has constricted and lost its ability to hold onto a volume of liquid. Sweating profusely has become a way of life on these walks back home, and my mother often shrivels up her delicate nose and comments on the start of teenage hormones affecting my glandular system.

I start to have frequent baths. I wash my hands obsessively and shower at least twice a day. I scrub my body hard as I shower, rubbing layers of soap into my skin with a pumice stone, so that the lather clogs the drain. Although the primary reason for these ablutions is to halt any body odour, a small part of my brain wonders if this might also lighten my skin. As time goes on, and my washing becomes more frequent and fierce, my skin rebels against the soap and breaks out in large dry patches, but the colour is disappointingly still tattooed on me. The palms of my hands are red and sore with the scrubbing. Impressed with an advertisement on television for a deodorant that promises dryness throughout the day, I buy myself some when I next pass my local parade, still avoiding the undertaker's.

Going to school every morning brings on a further spate of symptoms, which often delay me from leaving the house in time for an early start at school.

I want Alice to be my friend forever.

When I see her and she remains cordial towards me, my breathing miraculously returns to normal, and my high body temperature abates.

I want to do really well at school.

Transfer to senior school becomes my main goal. I spend as much time as possible revising. This includes summarising whole texts into understandable and memorable chunks. I practise old science papers until I can formulate an answer from the wording of the first sentence. I test and retest myself.

The fact that I am permanently in my lilac bedroom when I am at home does not appear to concern my mother, who is exorcising again. My father is abroad for six weeks. I miss him.

Daddy now goes away on his own for work, and Mummy stays with me.

When I finally get my exam results, I am thrilled with them.

I have got a scholarship to the best private girls' school in our area.

My parents mull over the implications of this offer for days. My father is keener than my mother and ultimately resolves the dilemma. He consults me before the final decision is made, the place is accepted, and I am to start in my new school the following term.

* * *

I stop writing to ponder over my mother's hesitancy over my school offer. Had she been concerned that it was a school similar to her own school and that I wouldn't fit in, or was it that she was jealous of my father's obvious pride in me, when her own father's approval was not so easily won?

* * *

When I go to school the day after my offer, I hesitantly tell Alice about my future plans.
'I think we should form a secret pact of friendship before it all ends so that we will remain friends forever,' she says surprisingly.
I am thrilled.
'Let's meet down by the shopping parade after school so that we can buy some sweets from the shop to seal our deal,' she suggests.

I am at the stipulated meeting place at the required time, pocket money in hand. She is there about ten minutes later and looks very excited.

'We have to follow the rules of membership to the friendship club,' she says.

It is the first time I have heard of it, but I nod.

'Before I buy the sweets, I need you to close your eyes and take an oath of friendship.'

I obligingly close my eyes.

'I have brought a blindfold to make sure you don't peep, Maya,' she says as she tightly binds my eyes and swirls me around. She then pushes me forward four or five steps, or maybe it is more; I am not sure.

'All right, now repeat after me. Friends are shit, I don't like them one bit. Friendship sucks; it's all a load of sodding muck.'

'What do you mean, Alice?' I wish the soft blackness I am staring into would dissolve so that I can look at her face to make sure she is joking.

'You want to be initiated, don't you, Maya?'

'Yes, Alice,' I repeat the phrases, blushing at the point when I have to swear.

I feel her gently guiding me to sit, and then she places my hands behind me. Something holds my hands together.

'Have a good time in your fucking new school; Maya, and hopefully this ceremony will help you never to forget me?'

'Of course not Alice.' Things are suddenly looking up again, and I try to still the fearful voice within me that started making itself heard a little while ago. I smile at her, or at least where I think she is standing, and wait for her to release me. The sweet shop beckons. There is no response from Alice.

'Alice? Alice, take this off now, please.'

No one answers. I can hear people walking past me, so I know I am not alone. She must be around, or else they would question why I was here, wouldn't they?

'Alice?'

Uncontrollably, I can feel the pressure of tears behind my eyes, and I try to restrain them from flowing. I will not show her that I am rattled by what she is doing. Perhaps this is part of the test too. I sit there passively for ages. My hands feel uncomfortable, and what initially seemed soft around my wrists now appears to have a tighter grip, as I struggle surreptitiously to release my hands. It doesn't work.

I sit there a lot longer, until it dawns on me that Alice has left me. She is not patient, and she would never wait as long as this. People continue to pass me by, which puzzles me. Why are they not stopping to rescue me? Hesitantly, I clear my throat.

'Can someone please untie me?' I ask, the next time I hear footsteps. I hear some falter and others stride past. I repeat my request a few times, my voice more tremulous with each request, before I hear footsteps coming towards me.

'Can you please release me?' I ask again, and this time I can't stop the tears from rolling down my cheeks.

Suddenly my blindfold comes off, and my eyes alight on a pair of polished shoes. I look up at an elderly Asian gentleman on his way home from work.

'Have you finished your charity collection now?' he asks. I mutely stare at him. He gestures to a board that has been placed next to me.

'Charity Collection,' it says in large letters. 'Student collecting money for the blind and disabled in India. Please give generously.' It is in Alice's writing. There are some coins on a plate next to the board.

I am still too paralysed to respond, although there is a word storm in my head. I try to tug my arms free, and I suddenly realise where I am. She has sat me down on the low wall in front of the undertaker's. I am tied to the posts of their railings, and as I look, the empty windows glare at me. I open my mouth to scream, but somehow my breathing has gone ragged again, and I feel my head spinning. I try to say something to the kind man, but before I can, I find myself falling into a sepulchral pit of unconsciousness.

When I come out of my faint, my hands are untied and I am lying on the pavement. A few commuters surround me. They ask me where I live and what made me decide to collect for charity in this way. Someone also asks me who was supposed to come and release me. I stare at them and then struggle to get up to my feet.

'I live just five minutes away,' I say faintly. 'Thank you. I'm all right now.' I notice that the Asian man who took the blindfold off me is still there.

'Thank you for releasing me,' I say to him, and slowly I back away from the undertaker's. 'I'm going home now.' He accompanies me without saying another word. I feel safe with him, even though he is a stranger. Once we get home, he gives me an eccentric little bow and hands me some coins. I stare at him, puzzled.

'Your charity collection,' he says, and I instinctively grasp the coins and stumble into our house. How apt of Alice.

No reference is made to this experience when I go back to school the following day, but Alice is distant and indifferent. The tables are reversed. She is now in control, having rejected me, rather than me leaving her. We are no longer friends; instead she has a new friend, whom she introduces to everyone as her 'best forever' friend.

*   *   *

I stare, blurry-eyed, at what I have written and feel the increased rate of my heartbeat and wince at the fluttery feelings in my stomach. Why was Alice so horrible to me? My diary says that I thought it was because I had offended her by letting her down. As an adult, I realise that it was because she didn't want me to succeed. Desperate for her father's attention and approval, she could only turn against me when I achieved something she couldn't have. Her choice of tormenting me as the 'charity child' further showed her inherent prejudice of me, the mixed-race scholarship girl.

Why was I so attracted to Alice? Was I so starved of friendship that anyone would do, or did I receive something familiar from her? Was Alice, to me, a mirror of my mother?

*   *   *

I thought Alice was my friend, but how stupid I was. Friendships always end. I wish my nightmares about the undertaker's would end. They are so strange, because I not only see pictures in my head every night, but I always smell lilies, like the ones that were in the vase in Alice's house that first day I went over there. I want my nightmares to stop.

In Acacia Road, London

16 March 2006

It was a clear day, and Freddy rolled another joint as he trudged through the park. It was early for him to start smoking, but he needed to relax, having woken up feeling wired. He never slept well and was often disturbed by a recurrent nightmare. Last night had been particularly bad, and he'd got out of bed feeling agitated and alarmed. He was pleased however that he had made up with Jackson from the week before; he didn't like it when they had their minor fall-outs. He mulled their latest deal. He had to give Jackson credit for his persistence and ingenuity, what they had achieved over the past year surpassed his wildest expectations.

Freddy grazed his hand over his chin and winced as he ran over a cut. The light in the communal bathroom in the hostel where they lived was so poor, and the mirror so begrimed, that he found himself ending up with a headache due to having to squint whilst he shaved. He tried not to look at the cracked bath or the graffiti on the walls as he went out; he wanted to ignore how they represented his current, stained life. He kept getting dragged back into squalor, and he wanted to get out of it, for good.

Freddy found his thoughts drifting to his school days, something he usually never thought of. What was the story that his English teacher had once recounted? A story about a Greek goddess... Percy something? Persephone – that was it. From what he recalled, it was all down to greed, because she was tempted to eat four pomegranate seeds given to her by the lord of the underworld, and her punishment was to return there four times a year. Well, poverty was his underworld and crime his pomegranate seeds, but their current venture held the key to release. The way things were progressing, they would probably only be in the hostel for another month, and as he'd said to Jackson the other day, he would be more than pleased to move out of Acacia Road. Flats flattened you; well, they squashed him, anyway and kept him as low as the lowlifes that lived there. He had no worries about sharing with Jackson. They were friends, and they had a history of surviving through adversity.

Freddy's first meeting with Jackson was when he was at his most destitute. He had run away from home, and he had been sleeping rough for about a month and was struggling to get by. He had decided to wander near King's Cross Station to beg. He had been there for a week, but the takings had been far less than he had hoped for. In desperation born out of hunger, he seized the opportunity to pick a purse out of an open handbag. At first he couldn't believe what he had done, and he stood still, with the purse in his hands.

'Put it away,' hissed a voice, and in a dream, he quickly tucked the purse in his sock. Chaos occurred around him when the woman realised that her wallet had been stolen. In what seemed like seconds, the police appeared.

'Here, hide it here,' whispered the voice again, and Freddy saw an arm beckoning him to a low wall near him. 'Put it in here,' said the voice, insistently now, and Freddy tucked the wallet between two loose bricks. 'Now walk with me,' said the voice, and Freddy started following the walking quilt that rose in front of him. It was not a moment too soon, because the police were starting to stop and search. He avoided being caught, and it also meant he could retrieve his takings later in the day, once the chaos had died down.

The walking quilt was Jackson, and their friendship cemented rapidly. They worked as a team, picking pockets efficiently, and when they wore out possibilities in an area, they moved on to fresh pickings. After a couple of years of living rough they moved to the hostel in Acacia Road. They always kept in touch, even when Jackson went to the Isle of Wight for a year to work on a building site and Freddy served a short time in prison for assisting in a burglary. Over the past year, their business dealings had become considerably more *ambitious, and here they were now contemplating their biggest moneymaking venture.*

Freddy smiled to himself. He was no longer wired. He felt chilled. He threw the end of the joint into the bushes and quickly walked through the park, eyeing the various desirable houses they had earmarked as possibilities to rent, past the local shopping parade, and on to his meeting with Jackson.

Chapter 7

New Beginnings

Maya, 1992

My new school is situated on a very desirable residential road. It is a big red brick building about a thirty-minute walk from home; it has its own swimming pool, theatre, and health club. The classrooms are light and airy, the laboratory well equipped, and the gym large. It is very proud to be the only school in the country where the canteen serves organic food as an option (parents pay extra in tuition fees for this), and there is a cornucopia of extracurricular activities and clubs. Most importantly for me, the toilets are clean.

Before the start of term, we are invited to an induction day for new students and their parents. My parents are nervous.

'I'm not going,' says my mother a number of times before finally deciding that she will join us, after all.

She tries on a dozen outfits before we leave, parroting all the common woes of modern-day women – she is too fat, her hips look huge, her hair is not fashionable enough, she looks old, she doesn't have a new pair of shoes... The list is endless, and with it, her discontent rises, as does her anxiety and her disillusionment regarding herself, her marriage, and her life, until it all bursts into anger and attacks on my father. *He* isn't dressed well, *he* looks scruffy, *he* is looking as though he is developing a tummy, and *he* snores and keeps her awake, so what does *he* expect of her looks when she has been up half the night... She does the plasticine bit again, gets him to change a number of times, ruffles his hair, and then slicks it down again. I wait for my turn, but she leaves me alone.

We are late when we finally get there. The principal has already begun her welcome speech. We cannot find three seats together, so – symbolically – we sit on our own, spread out among a hall of strangers.

The head talks about the virtues of the school and lays down the rules for both girls and parents: no holidays are to be taken in school time (glare at parents); no senior girls are to dye their hair (glare at front-row girls); and so on. The speeches go on for an hour, and then everyone troops to the small hall for drinks and nibbles, graciously provided by the Parents' Association.

I join my parents in the main hall. Small talk is not really our style. I can see my mother checking out who is wearing what, my father checking out who has the friendliest face. Finally, a jolly parents' representative comes to rescue us.

'You need some *labels* with your name and year,' she says concernedly, the label distributor obviously not measuring up to her expectations. She is back soon, sticking tags on us. My mother has never changed her maiden name – another difference between us. Her label gives her my father's surname. The mislabelled name angers her, and she embarrassingly points this out to the now not-so-jolly parent representative.

My father, initially hesitant, moves around the room, searching for parents with daughters in the same year, and introduces himself. My mother stoically stands steadfast. My heart pounds and my palms are sweaty.

'Hello, Maya. I am a Year Seven teacher,' says a tall individual approaching me whilst holding out her hand.

Is it rude to clean your palms on your skirt before shaking hands? I do anyway.

'Let me introduce you to some girls in your year. It will be nice for all of you to get to know each other before school starts.'

I am whisked off. They all look very well groomed.

'Hello,' says a blonde girl. 'Where are you from, then?'

'Oh, from Woodbury Park School,' I say, thinking that they will now know I come from the state school system.

'No, silly,' says the girl. 'I mean where are *you* from?'

* * *

I have been dedicating myself to the present over the past three weeks. Plans for my forthcoming wedding have taken over and keep me away from my goal of writing, although it is this very event that has given me the impetus for self-discovery.

My parents' best intentions to help in the wedding cause further delays. My mother telephones me every morning, questioning me on whether I have completed the most trivial of matters or excited about a new idea she has thought of that she is sure I should incorporate. Since her ideas don't always coincide with mine, I find myself, as always, in a quandary, part pleased about her involvement and part irritated by her plans not coinciding with mine. My father has not been very well over the past few months, and I am perturbed by his apparent frailty, panicked by dreams of him not being there for my wedding, even though there is no logical reason that I need to believe such a catastrophe.

As a family, we had to attend Grandfather Phillips' funeral only two months ago. It was a sombre and grand affair, organised in style by Rhona, his current wife. It would be hypocritical of me to pretend to be grieved by the loss of this distant man, but his unexpected gesture of bequeathing me his inheritance has left me dumbfounded.

* * *

I don't think it was worth working so hard to get into this school.

It is fatiguing settling into a new school.

Some things at this school take a bit of getting used to. The book-lined halls are pleasant enough, but the portraits of stuffy old men and women on the walls – scholars or governors from the school's past – send a shiver down my spine as I catch their painted eyes, so disapproving of me do they look.

I sit on my own for lunch, since I am not on the organic option for food, like most of the girls in my year, and during my free time I usually disappear into the library for 'research' purposes.

I struggle with academic work for the first time in my life. I have been top of the class as far as I can remember, with no one posing any huge challenges. The first time I have my English essay marked and realise that I am tenth in the class is devastating. Even in maths, which has been my forte, I am fourth.

I have my first period when I am travelling back home in the bus from school.

I've been sick all week: aches and pains and a sore throat. In the bus, standing, holding onto the rail, I felt a violent cramp in my stomach, so sharp that I got all sweaty and thought I was going to faint. I didn't want anyone to notice. Then I had another cramp, and like in some of the books I have read, I bit my tongue, because I didn't want to scream out aloud. It was like the whole of the inside of me was tying itself up in knots.

I stagger out of the bus at the next bus stop, where more schoolchildren rush to get in, and fighting the urge to throw up; I make my way to a low wall near the bus stop to sit down. I sit there for a while, hoping my head will stop spinning, whilst bus after bus grind to a stop and then take off. They discharge the contents of their innards onto the pavement or admit more passengers in a ceaseless, monotonous rhythm. I can't stop shivering.

I decide to walk home. The walk is probably about fifteen minutes. I stop every time I have a stomach cramp. The pain is spaced out but sharp, like someone twisting my intestines around my bladder and then letting them go.

Maybe I have appendicitis. Two girls in my class have had theirs taken out, one because it needed to and the other because her father is a surgeon and apparently told her that the appendix is a useless part of one's anatomy, just there to collect all the rubbish, and so can just as easily be whipped out before it causes any trouble.

I decide to detour past my grandma's instead. It will only add another twenty minutes to my journey. A man passes me by, walking hurriedly, and looks back over his shoulder, staring at me peculiarly before he goes on. Someone else rushes past, giggling. The pain makes me light-headed.

A mother with a child in a buggy passes me, and then she hesitates and stops.

'Excuse me,' she says. 'I just thought I'd let you know – your uniform is dirty at the back.'

'Thank you,' I reply, glancing behind me. There are reddish, rusty stains streaked all along the back of my skirt.

'It must be from the wall I sat on,' I begin, but she is gone.

I stagger to the railway station, get on the train, and finally arrive at my grandmother's house.

'Hello, poppet. What's wrong?' she exclaims.

I burst into tears, burying my head in her welcoming arms. 'I think I've got appendicitis. My stomach really, really hurts, and I feel sick.'

'Oh, baby, let me see. Come into the kitchen, and I'll take your temperature.' As I stumble towards the kitchen door, she exclaims, 'But Maya! What have you got on your uniform?'

'Oh, it's nothing, Grandma, just marks from the wall I had to sit on when the pain was really bad.'

Grandma is so clever. She told me what the stains at the back of my dress were, and she made me change my stained pants for blue silk ones of her own. She then wrapped me in her perfumed dressing gown whilst she washed my skirt and made me some hot chocolate.

We have a chat about puberty. I realise that I have had an hour at school being informed about this, but that I somehow excluded myself from listening to it, because I thought it just wasn't something that would apply to me.

'I don't want Mummy to know. She'll be cross with me.

My grandmother thinks otherwise. 'Your mother told me when she had her first period,' she tells me, untruthfully, I think. 'It's a celebration, Maya. You are now a woman.'

I stare at her. 'How can you say that, Grandma?' I burst out. 'It's awful. I'm sure no one in my class has it, and it's something I'll have to put up with forever. I hate it.'

'I missed many years of having a period due to being so thin when I was a model,' she says. 'Now because of this, I have osteoporosis. It's a horrid condition, Maya, because my bones have thinned out like rice paper and break easily. I was so relieved when my period came back, but it still took me ages to conceive your mother.'

Since I don't respond, she resorts to bribery.

'I want to buy you a present,' she says, 'but I can't do that without Mummy finding out.' I give in.

My mother is in a good mood when I get home. She has started seeing a cognitive therapist for her depression. The therapist is positive and supportive, and my mother likes this. She tells me that cognitive therapy accesses and examines the negative thoughts that are the foundations of depression. To access the basis of your depression, 'think it, and then ink it' is the initial main instruction. My mum is enjoying writing down her thoughts, expressing outwardly things that she tries otherwise to suppress. Bits of paper, scribbled in rough before she copies her organised thoughts into her cognitive diary, litter the desk.

I tell her that I have started my first period. The statement is bald, and I can hear it reverberate around the room and rest on my reddened cheeks.

Mummy was busy and didn't look up when I told her.

One of the things I have noticed about depression is that you can act but not react. You can also act but not interact. I think being this way protects Mummy from feeling any more than she needs to. Depression is a state that she accepts, a comfortable, old coat to wear. I miss her connection and notice that the absence of this prevents me from interacting with myself.

Grandma says that I should celebrate being a woman. I don't want to. It's horrid being a grownup.

My mother never mentions the subject again; however, she buys me a box of sanitary towels occasionally, which she adds to her basket at the supermarket. She never tells me it is for me; she just leaves it in the bathroom cabinet. I don't like what she buys, and so I get my own sanitary wear, but to please her, I use some of it. Of my worry about the irregularity of my periods, of the cramps and the headaches I seem to get in conjunction, I say nothing. Nor do I mention how bothered I am about the spots that appear on my face just before my period is due.

My grandmother is true to her word and takes me shopping.

Grandma took me to the jeweller's in the shopping centre today. At first, I couldn't choose between a necklace, a bracelet, and a ring, because I liked them all. I finally got the necklace, which is silver with a little heart, and she put it on my neck before we left the shop.

She takes me to buy my first bra. We choose two, one in white and the other a pale pink, both very fetching, lace and ribbon. These acquisitions are the only silver lining, as far as I am concerned, in my experience of 'becoming a woman.'

I hate my monthly cycle. I take to excessive washing and showering during these times, because I am disgusted with the mess. I find it difficult to sleep. At peak points during my cycle, I dream vividly. It is always the same dream.

I am in a coffin in the window of the undertaker's. I am their new mannequin, and a notice is on my neck, advertising their services. The tie on the notice holds me back. It is a noose, but only I know that, and so I cannot struggle or escape, because I will die if I do so. In my dream I can't move; my muscles are heavy, but my mind races, planning escape routes all the time. Passers-by throw roses at me, the thorns of which scrape and prick me. One passer-by stops and peers through the window. She is jeering and laughing at me. 'Hello, Maya,' she says. 'You finally got to be where you belong.' It is Alice, and at this point I always wake up shivering and really sweaty.

It bothers me that I don't know whether anyone else in my year has reached puberty or how they experience it. I am not usually included in the changing room gossip, so all I can do is to try to guess who might be going through what I am. As time goes by, it becomes more pressing for me to find out, because I don't want to be the only one, yet again, to be going through a new experience. I worry about what I should say at school if I have stomach cramps during PE or, worse still, if I stain myself at school.

My toilet visiting behaviour now swings to another extreme. When I have my period, I act as though I am prone to incontinence, excusing myself to visit the toilets frequently, obsessively checking that there are no leaks.

I try to set up conversations with some of the girls in my year who look like they might be wearing a bra or those who have acne, but I have little success in finding out more intimate details about them. One day, I impulsively reach for the telephone, and before I know it, my fingers dial Alice's number. My hand trembles as I hold the receiver and my heart sinks when I hear her voice on the telephone, because she is in one of her cold and distant moods. Time has not changed my response to her.

'How are you?' she asks insincerely. I can sense the impatience in her voice.

I mumble an answer. 'How are you?' I ask in return.

She says, 'I'm very busy at the moment. I've masses homework to do.'

I suggest, bravely for me, that we meet up.

'I'll phone you, sometime,' she says.

I ring off disappointed but also annoyed with myself; her hesitation hasn't escaped me. Friends are dispensable to Alice; I should know that by now. She doesn't hoard people or things, and discarding comes easily.

Alice never contacts me again; she is admitted to an adolescent mental health unit for the treatment of depression fairly soon after we speak. It coincides with her parents' marital break-up. I hear from a mutual friend that her father had moved out of the family house and announced to Alice and her mother that he had a baby with his current mistress. It had been a complete shock. He had said that he was fed up with living a duplicitous life when he had a baby daughter that he loved, and whom he wanted to spend time with. Alice cracked up fairly soon after.

In Suffolk

28 July 2006

The peace that had descended in the garden is broken. There are voices at the door again.

'No luck with the key. Apparently he was very reclusive. Well, strange in the head or cracked up was what they said, and that it wouldn't have been his style to give a spare key to anyone.'

'Let's ring again,' says his partner, and the doorbell is rung twice. An inquisitive blue jay sitting on a nearby tree hops closer to the officers, seemingly unafraid.

'Anyone home? Sir, please open up. It's the Police.'

Silence.

'Okay, let's go for it, then. One, two, and three...'

The door creaks and flies open easily, so that the force of two burly shoulders sends the officers hurtling into the room.

'The door wasn't locked. That's strange.'

'Never mind the lock, just smell the stench! I think we'd better be ready to call in emergency services.'

The two officers enter the flat, cautiously easing their way through the hallway. They enter the bedroom and then halt in their tracks.

Within minutes, the crew needed on a crime scene arrive.

PC Reeves picks up the letter by the bedside.

Chapter 8

Friendship and Frigidity

Maya, 1993

Things are changing at school again.

One day, when I am sitting in the canteen, eating my non-organic sandwich with chips, Nora, the 'appendix-less' surgeon's daughter comes to sit with me.

'The organic stuff is awful,' she says, by way of an explanation.

We tentatively strike up a conversation. I am reminded of Alice and how our friendship ended, and so I do my best to remain disengaged. The ache to belong has faded, and if anything, I now long to maintain my privacy, to stay out of those elusive circles rather than try to step in. However, she is amusing and witty, and bit by bit, I thaw. We start spending our lunchtimes together.

Nora has everything.

She has wealthy parents and a beautiful house, she has been to the best of schools, she travels abroad on holiday twice a year, she learned to ski when she was four, she is an accomplished pianist, and she speaks fluent French and German. A cleaner, an ironing lady, a landscape gardener, a fitness instructor, and a yoga instructor visit her home, a minimum of twice a week, to 'improve' her mother, who does not work but who supports her busy husband's social schedule. Her mother also plays tennis, attends various charitable fund-raising functions, and finds time to pop into the nearest alternative health centre for a Reiki treatment, or to be 'Rolfed'.

What is this thing called Rolfing that Nora sometimes mentions? It must be something Australian, like learning to play the didgeridoo.

Imagine my disappointment and chagrin to find out that Rolfing is a type of massage.

Most of all, however, Nora's mother enjoys entertaining in grand style. To help her create culinary masterpieces, she has, through the years, enrolled in a variety of cookery courses. She has completed the Prue Leith course; she has attended the Mosimann Academy, where she followed both courses offered by Mosimann himself; she has enjoyed the Raymond Blanc L'école course; and according to Nora she was predestined to attend the Cordon Bleu special cookery course.

The upshot of this is that Nora and her father and older brother are the guinea pigs of lavish four-course meals on a regular basis.

'I can't bear it,' Nora confides over our lunchtime discussions. 'It just shouldn't be allowed. Most cosmetics are not tested on animals. Why can't Mother's cooking be shunned in the same way? Beauty without cruelty, they say. Well, meals sans Cordon Bleu should be our motto.'

Along with all of these admirable and glamorous details, I consider Nora to be blessed with enviable looks. She is tall and lanky with the most beautiful eyes: a piercing blue in colour and fringed with long lashes. Her hair, which has natural blonde highlights, is cut short, cropped close to her head, yet her high cheekbones and her elfin face carry the severe hairstyle well.

She does not eat lunch at all when she joins me, and on the rare occasions she does, she picks on a few salad leaves. I don't notice.

Our time together lasts only the lunch hour. When the school bell rings, heralding the afternoon block of lessons, we go our separate ways. What I don't realise in my innocence is that I am providing Nora with a way of avoiding eating lunch at all – organic or otherwise. When I get to know her better, I learn that avoiding eating is Nora's ultimate goal.

When I am with Nora, I sense a battle within her: a tug of war about pleasing and not pleasing, about her perceived goodness and her innate badness; a tug of war between the excess around her and the poverty within her, about the greed that she sees around her and feels within her, and the fear that this will never be satiated. It creates chaos within, like a million voices singing different tunes, in different pitches, to different beats.

Our lunches continue, and slowly Nora starts to lose weight. I still don't notice. I am too absorbed in myself, too much of a novice in relationships.

I am tuned into depression: that I can sense and deal with down to minute nuances, so that I can pick up, from the frequency in the airwaves when I enter our house, what my mother's mental state is. I then modify my own reactions, just as a weathervane points out the direction of the wind.

The other girls start to notice Nora's loss of weight and whisper amongst themselves at lunchtime. I assume they are whispering about me, because when I walk past them, they stop. They often stare, and sometimes they mutter things under their breath, but I can't decipher what they say.

One day, when Nora and I are at lunch together, our form teacher comes up to us. This is unusual –teachers usually don't come to the lunch halls.

'Nora,' she says, 'you shouldn't be sitting here. Your parents pay for an organic lunch.'

Nora is unfazed, as are many of the privileged when they are rebuked, since they are unable to see themselves as being put down.

'I prefer it here, Miss Watson. The food tastes nicer.'

'Maya, I'm sorry. Please, could you excuse us whilst I have a chat with Nora?'

A flashback I try to quell is there at the back of mind, like vomit you are trying to swallow back in your throat. Traces of the bile rise.

When Miss Watson asked me to move today, I suddenly remembered Mrs MacDonald, my old teacher from nursery school. This random thought then popped into my head. Other people do bad things, but I get moved.

I can no longer continue with my lunch. I leave the hall, a fine mist in front of my eyes.

Later that day in class, I find a note from Nora. 'Meet me after school in Orchard Road,' it says. This is a small road close to school. I wonder how Nora plans to meet, since she is usually picked up after school by her mother. When we meet, she gives me a hug. A deluge of tears immediately courses down my face, saturating my school coat. Nora is aghast and awkward.

'Oh, Maya, I'm sorry,' she says. 'Why are you upset?'

'I'm sorry for getting you into trouble.'

'You haven't. She wanted to sit next to me to make sure I ate, and look.' She triumphantly digs into her pocket and brings out the remains of a sandwich and some chewed pieces of apple. 'This is what she thought I ate, silly cow.'

I stare at her.

'Look,' she says, 'she wants to sit with me for the rest of the term, and she wants to do it in your dining area, so that the others will not see or suspect anything. That means we can't be together at lunch anymore, but shall we try to meet after school?'

I nod, overwhelmed. My damp coat is the only testament to a previous grief. Nora is to tell her mother about 'choir practice' after school, and we are to meet here.

Lunch hours become solitary again, but I don't mind. I am part of a duplicitous plan.

Nora and I meet every other day after school. We sit on a low wall, near an overhanging creeper, and chat.

Our conversations take on deeper overtones. From having talked about the music we like, we move onto discussion about our families. I tell Nora about my father, his intelligence, his passion for work, his gradual isolation from my mother and myself. She tells me about her father, who is well known in his field but whom she never sees, about the fact that she thinks he is gay, because she once saw him kissing another male doctor.

I am shocked. How can her father be gay? We puzzle about men's emotions and wonder how they show them to the outside world. My view is that they just over involve themselves in work to cope. Nora is convinced that they convert their feelings into sexual urges so that they are resolvable. Actually, that is my interpretation of what she says. She believes that they have no feelings whatsoever – not of the type we are discussing, anyway.

'They are just walking penises,' she says, and we both giggle at the image this depicts. Part of my laughter is to cover my embarrassment. I don't think I have ever said the word 'penis' out aloud. Hearing it makes me want to disappear into my head, in the same way I do when my grandparents argue, although now I am more interested in listening to what they say, because I can understand some of it. I am also uncomfortable, because I know that Nora is wrong. My father is not like that. However, I am too shy to contradict her and too gentle to withstand her force.

I tell Nora about my mother's depression, Nora tells me about her mother's loneliness and obsession with weight. I tell Nora about my mother's exercise routines, Nora tells me about her mother's exercise routines. This generates another discussion. Are a lot of women closet exorcisers? Do most women control their mood by controlling their weight? Nora is not so keen on this discussion. I can see that, so we never dissect it in the same way that we do our discussions about men.

One day, when we are sitting down and talking in our usual way, Nora interrupts me.

'My brother's stupid. He's made some moves towards me.' Her face is blank, expressionless. 'I was six years old and he was thirteen the first time, and then he tried to repeat it two years later.' She shudders suddenly, and I tentatively put my arm around her shoulders.

I am pleased that I am an only child for once.

'I've never told anyone, because everyone thinks he's amazing,' she says. 'He's successful at whatever he does. He's just got a place at Oxford to read medicine.'

'That's not fair!' I burst out impulsively, and she looks at me gratefully.

'I don't think that he should be a doctor either,' she says, misreading my outburst, 'especially with his paedophile tendencies.'

Are we permitted to say that word in conversation?

'You know what, Maya?' she continues, with a wry grin. 'I am holding onto this information to ruin his career, should I need to at some later date.'

The negative energy she puts into this statement terrifies me. It reminds me of Alice's vengeance. Nora imparts all of this information to me in a flat, unemotional tone, as though she is discussing a television programme or a book she has recently read. She is emotionally detached and unaffected. I express and experience her emotions for her.

'What about now?' I enquire.

'I lock my door every night when he is home, in case he thinks of surprising me,' she says. I shiver as my imagination runs away with me.

I ask her if she has had a period, and I am delighted to hear that she has, although they have stopped recently.

'I'm pleased,' she says. 'I hate all the mess. That's why I'll never have sex either. I think it's disgusting.'

I make a little sound of protest, but Nora doesn't hear me. 'Women only put up with men and sex because they have to, not because they want to,' she continues. 'Don't do it, Maya.'

I don't agree with Nora's views, but she is too strong to stand up to. Instead, I write her a poem called 'Frigidity' (I looked up the meaning in the dictionary), putting her views of men and sex (and pretending that I share them) on paper. What does the poem say? Well, she says it's horrid to lie next to sweaty skin and smell unwashed teeth. She says it's disgusting that skin rubs next to skin – think of all those dead cells. Well, that's the kind of stuff I put in, but I don't think it's horrid at all. It's all part of acceptance and belonging, but I'd better not tell her that.

Nora takes a copy of the poem and sticks it on her bedroom wall.

*   *   *

My present self stops to ponder Nora's views on sex. I suspect that my friend would still share the same view, and I feel sad that she has such a persisting negative opinion of attachment. Is this what anorexia is, a restriction of intimacy? What does this say about our relationship with each other, my need to belong versus her need not to? There are so many questions and so few answers. Are we just mirror images of the same?

*   *   *

Throughout this time at school, Nora continues to restrict her eating, although there is now a battalion of teachers who hunt her down at mealtimes and a school nurse who weighs her regularly. She never finds out about the many litres of water Nora drinks before she is weighed, so that sometimes she has to climb on the scales very carefully, in case the water, which sits just below her throat, comes up in one big rush.

Her parents are concerned but think she will grow out of it. Her father has asked one of his friends, a psychiatrist, for his opinion. He has recommended a short stay at the local private psychiatric hospital – according to Nora, apparently to 'fatten her up.' 'Think of gavage and geese for foie gras, Maya,' she tells me wryly.

My goal this year is to be top of the class.

Lunchtimes without Nora are lonely, and so I eat the minimum and then rush off to the library. My studies improve, and my position in class is never less than third and always top in maths.

My short and intense liaisons with Nora after school give me a heady feeling, rather like having an affair. I feel bad and happy all together.

On parent-teacher meeting day, my parents make one of their rare visits to school. They are both awkward and anxious when they meet my teacher.

'We would like to propose that Maya go up a year at school,' the teacher says.

My parents are delighted. I hesitate.

'Can I think about it?' I ask. 'I mean, it is a great honour, but I don't really know if... I mean... I'm not really sure about it.'

'Of course you can think about it,' says my teacher, 'but I must inform you that your scholarship is more likely to be extended if you listen to the school's advice.'

'We will be guided by you,' says my father.

Everyone thinks I should move up a year. All I can think of is that I won't be with Nora. Why is it that when I'm in, I'm moved out?

In London

7 July 2006

Jackson collected all the materials on the list. He chuckled inwardly. We're in, he thought. As far as he could see, they were on their way up, since they were already onto their second assignment as suppliers of certain ingredients. He knew all too well what they went up to make, although he disaffiliated himself from thinking about this, as he did from thinking about other matters. This time they were increasing their price to thirteen thousand pounds, and that was all that concerned him.

Jackson had been dreaming about ways of making plenty of money since the day he left home. He yearned to buy a house that would not only have space for Freddy but also for his mother. He fantasised of being able to hire a hit man to kill his stepfather, but his best dream was to go to the Bastard's home in a flashy car, enter the house, and tell a cowering stepfather that his mother's days of suffering with him were over. After this deal his hopes could become a reality. In the years Jackson had been away from home, he had painstakingly put aside money from every job he did into a fund to rescue his mother.

He packed the last few items into his backpack. It was the anniversary of the London tube bombings, and the radio he had switched on broadcast a smattering of news items about it. One of the pieces of information he heard made him give a wry grin. *Such major destruction at such a small cost*, said the expert being interviewed, *since the cost of assembling the bombs could total as little as eight thousand pounds.*

BBC NEWS

Four suicide bombers struck in Central London on Thursday 7 July 2005, killing fifty-two people and injuring more than 770.

The co-ordinated attacks hit the transport system as the morning rush hour drew to a close. There were four bombs: three on the underground trains and one on the bus.

Of the fifty-two people who died that day, thirteen were on the bus. Twenty-six died at Russell Square station, seven at Aldgate, and six at Edgware Road.

The bombs were constructed using materials that were readily available and that required 'little expertise' to turn them into explosive devices.

Freddy turned up just as he was about to leave. Freddy's job was to obtain the ingredients, whilst Jackson met up with the customers. They had unspoken respect for each other's contribution to their success.

'I checked out the details of the purchasers again,' he said to Jackson. 'Definitely genuine. I will be in the Fox and Ferret as agreed.'

'Make sure you get me a drink, then,' said Jackson. The adrenalin rush was on, and he could feel the racing of his heart and the tightening of his gut. He gave Freddy a thumbs-up sign and stepped out, feeling the heat of the sun rush to warm him. He raised his face to the halcyon skies and smiled. It was going to be a wonderful day.

Chapter 9

Endings

Maya mid 1990s

Summer holidays have started.'

We are experiencing a warm summer this year, with occasional rain. The streets are clear of the usual rush-hour traffic, since they are not clogged up by the school run, and the pace of life is calmer. The clotheslines in the gardens, which are usually in hibernation in the winter, are laden with newly washed clothes, and the sounds of lawn mowers whirr in the air. At the weekends, the little green in front of our house teems with children, and the ice-cream van sometimes makes two trips down our road. I settle into a routine of getting up late, completing various chores around the house, and then doing something on my own or with my mother. She is at a crossroads regarding her treatment, now that the euphoria of self-expression has died down. It is far more comfortable to be drawn to the familiarity of her well worn coat of depression. The payoff for changing versus remaining where she is does not stack up for her.

She has started exorcising again until her feet blister and her ankles are chafed and red. When I sort out the clothes for washing, her sports socks are stained brown with blood from tired and cracked feet.

Occasionally, we go down to the shops together, a journey we make by tube into the West End, or to the large shopping centre close to us, or we go to the cinema to see a film. I love these outings, because we are doing what 'real' mothers and daughters do. We don't say much to each other during these trips, and we always end by going to my grandma's house. I savour this ending, in the way that I enjoy eating the cake first and the icing last.

My grandmother looks forward to these visits as much as I do. For her, it is yet another opportunity to try to bridge the growing chasm between herself and her daughter. My mother frequently runs out of motivation and desire to do much with me, and the onus of responsibility for making the summer holidays an enjoyable time weighs down on her, like the heavy weights she bears at the gym, except devoid of the accompanying pleasure.

She knows that a visit to my grandmother's house will make things easier on both of us. My grandmother willingly provides the energy and impetus lacking in my mother, by cooking for us and making elaborate plans for the week that is to follow, often not noticing that my mother barely eats what she cooks nor seems enthusiastic about her plans.

'When will Father be home?' she often asks, the only time she shows some animation, but he is barely there, arriving just before dinner, so that he can eat and retire to his study with a book.

I think my mother married my father because he seemed accessible, because she had no reason to believe he would abandon her, as she felt her father had. He had proved her wrong.

I miss Daddy so much these days. He is away for such long periods of time.

My father has been promoted at work again, but with it is a price tag. I still haven't got used to him being away, and I grieve every time he goes; and every time he gets back, I greet him with a heart full of intense expectations, inevitably never fulfilled, and therefore I am always disappointed. Our communication becomes telegraphic, and catching up on our ongoing development with one another becomes arrested, as we have to 'update' on each another's progress when he is there, whilst time stands still when he isn't – like children who go to boarding school do with their parents. Adjustment to maturing on both of our parts is difficult, as is orienting to the changes this process causes. I think I am losing him, and each separation underlines that loss.

We grow to be more formal with one another. We discuss world matters or new scientific discoveries. To project a unity onto something neutral seems safer. He never asks me about how my mother contends with difficulties in his absences or about my relationship with her. He casually mentions school but veers away from conducting any awkward discussions about friendships or how settled I might be.

I don't like breasts. They are awkward, painful, and uncomfortable. They make you noticed and slow you down when you run. They jiggle under shirts and bounce when you move. Maybe I should bind them like they did in history, and then they wouldn't get in the way.

Having been proud of the two bras I acquired with my grandmother, I am now embarrassed by them. They are too small, but I am discomfited by the process of having to make a new acquisition, so I continue to wear them by cutting the band at the bottom to allow for more space. I also focus on the slightly coarsening hairs that sprout from my underarms and my thicker, corkscrew pubic hair.

I am not sure, about my feelings towards my underarm hair. My mother is forthcoming in her views.

'All women should shave under their arms,' she says, as she gives me one of her razors.

My initial reaction is to resist and to tell her that in Europe, only one in six women shave. I know, on the other hand, that women in Asia over pluck and wax and shave most of their body hair. I want to make her identify with my 'other' hidden side – *her* side – but I stay mute.

I also find that being a teenager gives me emotional vertigo. My moods soar and plummet with constant regularity. In fact, my emotions pulsate in a similar way to my breasts.

The same feelings that drove me a few years ago to tear holes in my bedclothes, or pace up and down my bedroom, are frequently present – but how to express them now? There is a schism within me. Internally, I am awash with variability; externally, I am calm and collected. I take to biting my nails, and now and again I develop an annoying twitch near my left eye. My outlet of words is invaluable.

On being a teenager

I don't want to stay in one place.
I want to
move.
I want to run through the
vast
expanse of time.
To feel sensations against my
body,
evoking in me strange
desires.

I want to
scream
and laugh
until sweat and tears pour down my face.
I want to
reach out, but also
drum my naked legs on new-cut grass.

I want to
move,

to break all barriers connected with
my body
and feelings.

I want to be
free
of all of these strange and unexplainable
desires
that I suddenly feel.
I want to
move.
To be free of this
body,
which shackles me.

I start to take an interest in clothes. My grandmother flourishes on this news. 'Let's go shopping,' she says as she hastily grabs her purse.

We window shop in boutiques and pop into the many clothes shops on the high street. Her trained eye seeks out garments that I never would have spotted. Her taste is impeccable. She mixes colours like condiments, throwing in exotic and dramatic touches to otherwise ordinary wear.

'What do you think of these?' she asks, eyes gleaming with delight, holding up pale blue jeans. I dither, whilst she is never at a loss, pouncing on an outfit like a terrier on a rat, shaking it out of my clasp if she doesn't agree, or nodding delightedly if she thinks I am developing an eye for fashion. Chic or classic, modern or individual, she adjusts to the style with the fluidity of mercury.

When we went shopping today, Grandma suggested we stop for coffee and cake as usual but a little earlier than normal.

'Are you all right, Grandma?' I ask, grudgingly acknowledging that she is older than me and that we are not partners in crime. 'Not bored, are you?'

'Of course not, sweetheart,' she replies, 'just a bit tired, but nothing to worry about.'

We joke our way to a cafe to order our regular snack: a Bakewell slice with a pot of Earl Grey tea for her, and a slice of the 'cake of the day' with a cup of hot chocolate for me. We chat, my grandmother commenting again, as she always does, on the lack of fine porcelain teacups and how tea doesn't taste the same from the thick, white china cups that are used in most cafes.

'Dishwasher friendly, I expect,' she says.

'I like them,' I tease.

'You can't mean these mini birdbaths,' she retorts. 'They're so thick and ugly. We're becoming used to being served large portions, encouraged to drink a pint of tea or coffee instead of a delicate cupful.'

Once we finish our tea, atypically Grandma proposes we go back home, cutting short a little extra shopping. We get the bus back to her house, and I leave with a basket of goodies for my parents, all cooked by my grandmother, but not before she gives me a huge hug and I give her a similarly generous squeeze. Briefly I bury my nose in her neck, nuzzling my most favourite part of her, and drink in the feel of her, like a marshmallow against my skin.

'I love you, sweetheart,' she says. 'You're the most wonderful girl, and I love spending time with you.'

Later I speak to Nora on the telephone.

'I'm bored, bored, bored,' she complains, having just returned from a trip to the Algarve, 'and you probably think I'm an ungrateful, spoiled brat to say that.'

'How was your holiday?' I enquire.

'Mega boring!' she exclaims. 'We stayed in the villa of one of my father's patients, which had a swimming pool of its own and was very close to a golf club. My father spent all his time on the golf course, whilst my mother spent her time having beauty treatments or tennis lessons.'

'What did you do?' I enquire, immediately feeling out of place.

'Oh, I was on my own most of the time,' she informs me airily. 'My brother initially refused to come, and then he consented to under parental pressure – worst luck – but luckily went off and did his own thing every day too.'

'So what sort of things did you do on your own?'

'Well, I read a number of books, and then I set myself the task of exploring the surrounding area on my own. That was great. I walked for miles and had no one on my case.'

'What about the place itself?'

'Oh, the same as any other place we go on holiday.'

We arrange to meet up at the shopping centre later in the week.

That evening, my mother is in a good mood. My father is back from one of his long periods of work abroad, and they have a glass of wine as they cook together. I eat with them, and then my parents decide to watch a film on television, which is rare too. I go upstairs to read, feeling strangely put out.

It is close to midnight when the telephone rings. I don't hear it. I am in bed, fast asleep. It is my grandfather, who is cheerfully greeted by my mother. Her husband is back with her, and now is her father finally making a connection too? However, an avalanche of ice encases her as he urgently summons her to the local hospital.

'They think your mother's had a stroke,' he says. 'She's being taken to hospital by ambulance, and I'm about to leave with them.'

My mother staggers out of the house as though punch-drunk, my father initially offering to stay with me whilst I sleep, and then changing his mind rapidly when he sees her state.

My recall of that night is hazy. I remember my father shaking me awake, I feel his closeness and his warmth, and I remember him telling me to get dressed because we have to go on an urgent journey. Existing in the margin of a dream, I respond by pulling on the jeans and sweatshirt I have lying on the floor and following him downstairs. In my mind, I dream that my mother is pale and sick, but when I get downstairs, she is there, on her feet, ashen-faced but not sick. Who, then, is this urgency about?

We get into our car, the familiar smell of car upholstery and air freshener enveloping me, the feel of a few bits of paper and a sweet wrapper on the floor, comforting. My father's raincoat is neatly folded in the back seat. My parents don't say a word during the drive. I think I must doze in the back of the car; I have no clear recollection of the journey. I plummet into the heavy slumber of an adolescent and awake when my father gently shakes me. My mother is not in the car when I blearily sit up, my mind still locked in the basement of sleep.

'Maya,' says my father. 'Maya, we must rush. We need to find out how Grandma is.'

Grandma? I thought Mummy was sick. I stare uncomprehendingly at him as he says to me, 'Maya, darling, Grandma's not well. She's been brought in an ambulance here, to hospital. Grandfather Phillips is with her, and Mummy's just run in. Come on, let's go and see how she is.'

My lungs solidify, and I try to surface for breath. I can't do it, and instead I fall further into a thick, heavy treacle of uncertainty, which hurts my solar plexus and makes me gasp. I double up in pain, and I fear for a moment that I will never breathe again. When I realise that I can retain some oxygen and my limbs appear to function, I open the car door. It is an unusually mild night. A smattering of light raindrops accompanies me as I run as fast as I can, following my father through the swing doors of the Accident and Emergency Department, a childhood prayer, a safety mantra rushing through my mind, repeatedly.

Please, God, let her be all right. Please, God, I'll be extra good. Just let her be all right.

They are in a waiting area with other wounded people. In the air are the smells of antiseptic, infected body secretions, and the tiredness of waiting. It is busy, as Accident and Emergency Departments always seem to be. My eyes are drawn to the middle seam of the balding, brown carpet, to the patches of bare plaster on one of the walls that needs whitewashing.

My mother steps out of a corner seat when she sees us. With her is my grandfather, who also stands up and carefully makes his way towards us. He looks impressive, well attired, and masterful in these dingy surroundings. To me, they both look like shadow puppets behind a screen. A part of my brain screams, and a part of it is paralysed. I know they will unite when the screen is pulled back, and I don't want it to. I register that my grandfather is holding my mother's hand, and I note the pain in their eyes.

'She died in the ambulance,' says my grandfather.

I soundlessly mimic his words. *She died in the ambulance.* Then a scream tears out of me. 'My Grandma just died in an ambulance!'

* * *

I have stayed in the present over the past two weeks. I have used the excuse of winding down at work as the reason, but I know that I have to face up to my grandmother's death. Until now, I have avoided that. I have tried to move forward, making as much effort as possible to condense the pain. It has been the only way to manage.

Nearly thirteen years on today, I still have no clear recollection of the events that followed that night, or the time immediately after. What I do know now is that a part of me died that night too: the child who had permitted herself to be nurtured and be dependent, the child who had believed that people you adore are with you forever.

I was not permitted to see my grandmother. Instead, my mother sent me home with my father, and I went straight to bed, for once, my mother's panacea of sleep welcoming, beckoning me into an ebony crater. I descended in its bottomless elevator gratefully. The following morning, my father spoke to our GP, an elderly man who had known my mother since she was born, who told him that I was too young to confront death.

    I wish they had asked me. I would have liked to have held her, rested on her marshmallow neck just one more time, and told her that I loved her. I would have braved my fear of visiting an undertaker, just for her.

In Suffolk

29 July 2006

PC Reeves happily entered the police station resisting the urge to whistle. He was in love with Susannah Martin who taught art at the local primary school and had never been as content. I love my job too *he thought affectionately as he went through the rotating from doors.* Can't believe I've been here two years, but Suffolk, with its leafy areas and well-mannered residents, suits me down to the ground. I don't like London, I know that from my training there – all that frenzied, violent energy with so much exposure to the dark side of human nature, corruption, death, and despair. Here, the most ferocity I face is the occasional domestic fallout, although Ipswich town can get busy at the weekend, mostly with drunken brawls and petty thieving. *He gave a wry grin when he realised his musings weren't applicable to the current time. The bombings had been exceptional and perplexing. There appeared no reason whatsoever to target the area other than to make a statement.*

He made himself a cup of tea and then went into the office he shared with five other officers, and pulled out a box file with a sheaf of papers pertaining to the latest case. On top was the letter he had picked up from the dressing table.

PC Symmonds passed by his desk. 'Love letter from Susannah, mate?' *he asked jocularly.*

The officers were familiar with Susannah's penchant for sending PC Reeves perfume sprayed love notes and handmade cards.

'No, no, suicide note,' *said PC Reeves, adding hastily,* 'Current case – not from Suz, of course.'

He carefully tore open the note. It contained one sheet of densely written paper. He summarised the main facts. 'He wants Maya to know that she's special and that he wants it all back. He wants to stop being a burden to his parents. He is unhappy and has been a loser, but he wants to try to turn his life around with her help. She's the only one who can save him, make him feel whole. Without her, life is not worth living.'

Chapter 10

Van Morrison

Maya mid 1990s

With some trepidation, I sit down to write again. Arrangements for the wedding have taken over all my spare time, but I also know that I have been avoiding reading and writing about this period in my life. I know why, and perhaps this quote that I once read and kept describes it best: 'Death is not the greatest loss. The greatest loss is what dies within us when we live.'

* * *

Today is the day after Grandma died. Daddy took me to her house, because I wanted to go there. Mummy is with grandfather, sorting out things.

My grandparents have always lived in Surrey, in the house that my mother grew up in. It is a large, detached Georgian property flanking the commuter belt favoured by bankers and city workers. The journey by car is long, veering through country roads flanked by trees, or driving through small villages studded with select boutiques. I doze on my way there, but I am wide awake when we arrive. My father parks his car on the drive usually occupied by my grandfather's Bentley, and we make our way to the front door, my father having been given a key. We say nothing to each other.

I enter the house and make straight for my grandmother's bedroom. It is luxurious in the way that I have always thought a film star's bedroom would be. It has an azure carpet and powder-blue wallpaper embossed with a tiny silver pattern, and to complete the cerulean theme, there is a four-poster bed with misty blue voile drapes and four pillows fluffed up at the head, with my grandmother's special orthopaedic pillow on the right-hand side. The bed-head has an ornate silver pattern on the fabric, which, when I was younger, I thought resembled the scales of a myriad of fish, or a host of heavenly shooting stars. The room smells of her Lily of-the-valley drawer liners.

I sit at my grandmother's dressing table, a beautiful piece of furniture made of walnut wood, with a polished base and a large mirror with cleverly concealed lights. I look at her many creams and potions that are arranged symmetrically on the table. There are rows of containers: day and night face cream, anti-wrinkle cream, under-eye cream, camouflage cream, blemish cream, tinted moisturiser, body cream, elbow cream, dry skin cream – there is no denying that my grandmother loved her emollients. There are large decorative jars for her dressing table; small, sample-size jars, which she kept for her handbags; designer-made, elaborate containers mixed with simple ones bought at the market. They represent her: my grandma.

'Do you know, Maya,' she once said to me over tea, 'according to Professor what's-his-name, all these luxury creams are no better than the most basic and cheap ones. Just think of that: Ponds face cream at two pounds is the same as my designer cream that costs eighty-eight pounds. Am I extravagant to still buy expensive creams when I know this fact?'

'No, of course you're not, Grandma.'

I make her appear and evaporate for over half an hour that day each time I open the various jars on the table, so that I am left with a fusion that was her. Tears tumble down my face, mixing with her makeup, leaving slimy snail tracks along my cheeks.

When I finally stand up from my place at the dressing table, I notice a rust stain on my grandmother's dressing stool. How strange; my period has started mid-cycle. I hesitate, not knowing what to do, but only for a moment. Even in her absence, she comes to my aid. In her bottom drawer I find some press-on towels she keeps for me for emergencies. Next to the box are two photographs of me: one on my own, the traditional school photograph, my serious face staring at the photographer on the other side of the camera; and the other is of the two of us in front of the British Museum.

I stare at this photograph for a long time. I notice how bright the sun is in the photograph and how happy we look. I can feel how tight her arm is around my waist and see the pride in her eyes, and for a moment, I feel like a bar of Aero chocolate, full of happiness bubbles. Then the bubbles all burst, and I am dragged into a vortex of emotions. I wish I could only hold onto happy memories, but they slip away from me, like the albumen of an egg through my fingers. I seize some of her pots of cream and her favourite lipstick and run downstairs to my father.

'Daddy, we've got to make sure that Grandma has her make-up,' I announce urgently. 'She wouldn't want anyone to see her without.'

'Of course, Maya,' he says.

'Daddy, you don't understand,' I screech frenziedly. 'She needs to have it now. There's not a minute to lose.'

My breathing quickens, and I feel the first wave of a panic attack. He holds out his arms, and as I rush into them, I feel myself trembling all over. After about five minutes, very slowly my breathing starts to echo his own deep, evenly spaced breaths, and my trembling ceases. He kisses me on the forehead.

'Go back and see what else has to be done,' he says. 'We'll sort things out with plenty of time. I promise no one will see her without her make-up.'

I go to the kitchen.

Grandma had baked some biscuits. They were still on the cooling racks, to be filled with jam and dusted with icing sugar. She had been making the biscuits for me.

I hadn't noticed the sounds of her kitchen until now. The sluggish-sounding tick of the kitchen clock and the humming of the refrigerator are usually drowned out by the music from her little radio on the side, or by the sound of her voice. The radio is quiet now, almost as if out of respect for her. There is a buzzing from the aerator in the little fish tank in the corner, where she has kept numerous goldfish for me since I was three years old, and in which swims Phishy, our current joint pet.

I look around the kitchen, memorising the little touches that represent her. The salt-dough figure I made for her when I was six years old still hangs on the wall. I see the fine hand paintings of fruit she bought on holiday in Thailand; a pile of cookery books on the shelf, one titled *Erotic Foods;* and a small picture of Ricky Martin in concert (she fancied him rotten), stuck with a magnet on her notice board together with a note in her handwriting saying, 'Buy vegetable stock cubes.' It's silly, really, to think that I need to memorise them. They are branded in my memory, just as the layout of her bedroom is, or the way in which she arranged her clothes and underwear by colour.

I turn to leave the kitchen, and then, acting on an impulse that I can't understand, I rush to where the biscuits are and stuff two of them in my mouth. Immediately my tongue tastes the sweetness, I feel like Judas. My legs carry me automatically to where the bin is, my mouth opens, and I spit out the masticated remnants of the two biscuits. Once I have spat out as much as I can, my legs carry me to the sink. I rinse out my mouth over and over, drink some water, and stick my fingers down my throat, trying to make myself sick. Nothing comes out. I straighten up, feeling light-headed, and look around the room for the last time. I go back to my father and nod my readiness to leave.

*   *   *

I stop writing, quite disturbed by reading what I've written. I had forgotten the incident with the biscuits. Had I wanted one more opportunity to consume what was left behind? Why, then, did I feel so guilty and have to expel so violently what I had ingested? I don't really want to read what follows, but I know I have to. With a sigh, I take up writing again, but only after pouring myself a large glass of wine.

* * *

Today is Grandma's funeral, and it's been raining all day.

I wake up to a deluge of water around me and feel that Nature is in accord with me, comforting me with her tears. My body has decided to weep too. Blood has seeped out onto my mattress in the night. I wake with my bottom resting on a large rust-coloured stain. The emotional tension within me has become so pressurised that it has had to release itself.

I wish Grandma was here to tell me what's wrong with me.

I wear a pair of black trousers and a white shirt. My mother is wearing a new black suit.

I've never seen Mummy in a hat.

We make our way to the church in silence. I find myself shivering and wish that I have my winter coat on. The funeral is well attended, the church is full, and the ceremony is formal. I gaze at the coffin lying in the front, completely covered in flowers. My grandmother was not the type to say no to flowers. The coffin is surrounded by masses of wreaths of all colours. The smell of lilies, jasmine, camellias, roses, orange blossoms, stock, and stephanotis mixes with that of incense.

Do churches burn incense at funerals to cover the smell?

The coffin looks so small. A note from me has been put inside by my father. I had sat up for most of the night, thinking about what to say. Corny as it sounds, how do you say goodbye to someone you love?

I am jolted out of my reverie by the sound of my grandmother's favourite song. In her usual unorthodox fashion, she has requested that Van Morrison's 'Bright Side of the Road' be played at her funeral. Finally, the waterfall that has been cascading within me sneaks out a small spray. An icy hand of panic squeezes my heart, and I suddenly realise that she is gone. I will never see her again.

In London

7 July 2006

Freddy felt several waves of panic as he scanned the pub anxiously, his fingers tapping an agitated rhythm on the table. Jackson was five minutes late, and that made him feel jittery. He wanted the deal to succeed, but most importantly, he wanted to see his friend, so that he could be sure he was safe.

He was immediately reassured when out of the corner of his eye, he glimpsed a familiar jacket push its way through the door, and Jackson tipped into the pub, looking somewhat dazed. Again, distributed around his person were packets of money; 'Thirteen thousand pounds, to be exact,' he wanted to shout. He saw Freddy seated in the corner, and true to his word, in front of him were two full pints of lager.

'Okay, mate?' asked Freddy, his fingers still tapping frantically, and Jackson nodded. It took effort to contain how he felt. He sat down gingerly and downed half his lager.

The pub TV was on. The mood was sombre as grieving relatives and friends attended a service to remember those killed or hurt by the tube bombs a year ago. Jackson gulped the rest of his beer and then walked over to the bar and bought two more pints, which he brought over to the table. The two men found their gaze drawn magnetically back to the screen, where a number of 'experts' were now giving their view on why such crimes had been committed. Someone from the Muslim mosque spoke about martyrs in Islam.

'You know what, Freddy?' said Jackson suddenly and loudly. 'I think martyrdom is about self-esteem. It's when your opinion of yourself is at its lowest and you need a public way of feeling better about yourself or mass punishment so you can absolve yourself.'

'Yeah,' said Freddy uncomfortably, his drink still untouched. 'Let's go, mate.'

Jackson drained his drink and looked at Freddy. Heady and euphoric, he had no intention of leaving until his friend heard him out. 'Another thing, Freddy,' he said, 'the Bastard my mother married used to work for London Underground.'

Freddy looked at Jackson in surprise and with some alarm. Although they had shared a variety of experiences over the time they had known each other, they had never disclosed any information about themselves. They especially didn't talk about their pasts. To Freddy, history was redundant.

'What an arse-hole,' continued Jackson. 'Wish he was working on the tubes now. I would plant a fucking bomb on his train myself.'

Freddy spilled some of his drink, as he carefully placed his tumbler on the table. He lowered his voice. 'Careful, mate,' he whispered. 'Come on, let's go now.'

'I can't wait to see his face when I visit them,' Jackson announced, still rapturous over their success. 'I'll show the ponce.'

Freddy got up abruptly. 'Come on, Jackson, let's go,' he said urgently.

Jackson followed him out of the pub. Soon he would see his mother. He couldn't wait.

Chapter 11

STDs

Maya, mid 1990s

I can't wait to see Nora after the holidays. Our meeting point is at the Broadway Shopping Centre, a medium-sized mall frequented by schoolchildren due to the large number of music shops and cheap accessory shops housed within it. I barely recognise her when we meet, since she has become so thin. I notice how sparse her hair is, and then the large, silver bomber jacket she is wearing. I recall seeing the jacket in the window of Gap Kids not that long ago. I realise the bomber jacket is not large; it is Nora who is small. She has shrunk, so that her head looks disproportionately large on her shoulders. Her hands have also grown, sticking out at the ends of her stick-arms. She has silver clips in her hair. Wrinkled skin adheres to her bones. Her face lights up when she sees me.

'Hi, Maya,' she exclaims, hugging me tightly.

This instinctive show of human contact is the trigger needed to burst the dam that has controlled my tears since the funeral and my body spasms with the force of my grief. She hugs me awkwardly, and her jacket acts as a sponge and absorbs my tears. After a while, my violent outburst ceases, although I continue to sniff and occasionally hiccup. Nora suggests that we go somewhere more private and invites me to her house.

Why do I always seem to choose friends who have houses so much grander and better than mine?

Nora lives in a huge double-fronted house in the best street in our area. Purple wisteria clings onto the brick-fronted façade, whilst the front garden has a mass of beautiful mature trees and shrubs, as well as flowering plants. She gives me little time to see the house, opening the front door with her key and whisking me upstairs to her bedroom, but not before I have sniffed space and wealth.

Her bedroom is white and extremely tidy. She has a stack of compact discs and a pile of films, all aligned perfectly and arranged in alphabetical order. A work desk with a computer stands in one corner, a tidy bookshelf above it. Her papers lie in a neat pile, her pencils are all sharpened, and her pens are primly arranged in a desk tidy.

On the wall are some beautifully framed, colourful posters. My eyes focus on them immediately, so striking are they in contrast to the purity of the rest of the room. I later find out about the artists. The most dramatic of these paintings is above her bed, a nude titled *Danäe* by Gustav Klimt. It is a sleeping redhead curled up in a foetal position, her thighs drawn up, dimpled and appearing large from the angle drawn. Near her desk are two smaller posters by Egon Schiele: the first, titled *Female Nude on a Coloured Blanket*, is of a much thinner woman, also asleep, but this time in a more open pose. The second, titled *Nude Back of a Girl with a Long Braid* is of the back view of a slim girl, perhaps the same model as in the previous picture, the figure masculine and square, the shoulders set and pointed. Disproportionately muscular calves bulge on her. Near Nora's dressing table is a small, oval-framed Schiele, apparently titled *Madonna*. An abstract figure of a woman is highlighted against a murky brown background. The face of a child is embedded on her body, positioned close to her left breast.

* * *

Reading this description brings back Nora's room vividly to me now. I hypothesise that these pictures help me to understand Nora, particularly the *Madonna*. To me, that picture reflects an adult and her inner child, appearing to separate, but in reality struggling to merge. The sombre background, brown, like faeces, reflects the sordidness and filth she felt around her, no matter how white, how clean, or how tidy she was. Nora's obsession with the female body and its contours at all angles and sizes is another theme. I can see why they predominate in the bareness of her room, in the way that the same idea predominates in the bareness of her self.

*　*　*

It is now Nora's turn to be vulnerable. She talks in a way that she has never done before. She is unhappy. She because she says she saw her mother nude, straddling her personal trainer in the bathroom a week ago. She tells me that she has noticed that her mother is unusually happy when he is around, and that she had seemed eager to get back from her holiday to recommence her fitness routine. Apparently her mother's favourite saying this summer has been 'There is only one letter that separates fab from flab, and that's L for labour.' Nora snorts sarcastically as she recounts this. 'More like L for lust,' she says.

'My brother was a freak when we were away,' she says. 'I hated the fact that my mother persuaded him to come with us. Do you know, I sometimes wonder if she knows and does it to torture me?'

'I'm sure not, Nora.'

She shrugs. 'There was no lock on my bedroom door in the villa, but I jammed a chair under the door handle every night, so that it couldn't be opened.'

'Did anything happen?' I ask, eyes wide, and for a moment Nora looks at me peculiarly.

'He went off to find *local talent,* and he said that he ended up meeting a couple of Portuguese girls on the beach. He told us at breakfast that he shagged them senseless.'

'What did he mean by that?' I ask, my eyes round with curiosity.

'Oh, you know,' she says, shrugging. 'He had sex with them.'

'He said that to your parents?' I exclaim.

'Oh, yes, and my father told him to make sure he had adequate protection, so that he didn't end up with an STD.'

'Nora, what's an STD?'

Nora snorts. 'It should stand for "stupidly tired dick" in the case of that prat, but it really stands for "sexually transmitted disease." The two of them are constantly talking to each other in abbreviated medical jargon, now that my brother is reading medicine.'

Nora and I had an amazing afternoon. We watched programmes on television and ate popcorn - or rather, I did, since Nora nibbled on about five pieces, which she made last for ages because she chews so slowly. We wrote silly messages to each other and danced. When I told her it was time to leave, Nora kissed me. She kissed me on the lips. I just stood there and let her.

When I get home, my mother is putting away dishes in the kitchen. She has been drinking. I can tell from the way she looks, and if I stand close to her, I can smell the alcohol on her breath. Her face looks blotchy, and her lipstick is too red, so that it makes her lips pout like they have developed some virulent disease.

'Where have you been, Maya?' she asks.

'At Nora's.'

'I hope you're not outstaying your welcome,' she mutters.

'No, Mum. Nora asked me to stay.'

I find out that my father's parents are making their annual visit to see us today. No wonder my mother is nervous. My father's family have been open in their disapproval of my father's choice.

Grandfather and Grandmother de Silva are general practitioners in Hertfordshire. They are fiercely proud of their professional status. When they were young and 'at home' in Sri Lanka, there were limited choices of careers that carried social acceptability. They could choose between being a doctor, a teacher, a lawyer, or an accountant. Any other profession meant you had fallen between the cracks and were a failure.

They saw their son, my father, with his career in biochemical research, as a failure. Yes, he did have the title 'Doctor' because he had a PhD, but that wasn't the same. They constantly brought up in discussion all the efforts they had made for my father's education, their move to the UK, the sacrifice of their specialist hospital careers in Sri Lanka for general practice in the UK, the funding of his education, the higher rate of fees they'd had to pay for an independent boys' school as compared with the independent girls' school his sister went to (and yet *she* had became a 'proper' doctor), the lack of family holidays because of the costs of fees… the list was endless. When they would start on this, which they did with constant regularity, my mother would leave them with my father and take me to the kitchen, where she would hold her nose and say, 'Oh, the smell of burning martyrs!'

When my mother was out of earshot, my grandparents became personal. 'What has all our hard work been for? All for nothing!' they would exclaim, dramatically shaking their heads. 'Ruwan, you have completely ruined your life by marrying *that* woman.'

My father would then ask them to please be civil to his wife when they were in his home, at which request Grandmother de Silva would give a long-suffering sigh. Then my father would excuse himself to see if my mother needed comforting.

'What a wife! Why did Ruwan have to imprison himself by marrying a depressed English alcoholic?' my grandmother would moan when he was out of earshot.

They had no regard whatsoever for my mother. They had refused to come to my parents' wedding and had also refused to see me. It had been at my father's insistence that they acknowledged me at the age of three years, following which they consented to making their annual visit to our house.

Daddy's parents usually visit us just before Christmas.

These visits galvanise my father and mother to tidy the house, wash the curtains and carpets, shine the windows, weed the garden, and even wash and polish our car. Even with all this effort, I have never seen Grandmother de Silva impressed.

When she first visited us, she commented on what a provincial part of London we lived in. Once, she commented on how small our living room looked with such large chairs; another time, she muttered, 'Do you know, it's so strange, but I always have backache after visiting you. Did you buy your settee from Ikea?'

She usually tells us about her daughter, my aunt's house, how she has redecorated her living room and how bright and airy it looks, or what an impressive car they have.

'It's so important these days to have a safe and *solid* car like a BMW, isn't it? Not a flimsy Japanese type,' she would say, whilst my father's flimsy Japanese type could be viewed on our drive, through the windows, from where she was sitting.

Another tradition of this grandmother is to bring some of her old crockery and cutlery with her 'as a gift' and to suggest that we eat tea from these.

'What a stuck-up, condescending old bat,' my mother mutters, infuriated, in the kitchen, 'bringing her rubbish pieces of crockery to eat from. Does she think that our plates are contaminated?' She bangs the plates and cups on the counter and once smiles when the rim of a cup chips.

These grandparents have little interest in me. In fact, they are the only people I know who notice the 'invisible' part of me, the part that is my mother, and they make no bones about expressing their dislike of it. Of course, they are delighted by my academic success – 'Just like her father, just like our side of the family,' they mutter. The rest however, – no ambition, no personality, the way I look, my supposed moral code – no, that is my mother, and it is not approved of.

The timing of this visit is unusual, because they have come to pay their condolences to my mother. They want to do the right thing. They hadn't come to the funeral, since they wouldn't want to accept my mother publicly. My mother is extremely nervous, because this time they are visiting with my father's sister and her dentist husband, who have never been to our house, met my mother, or seen me.

I help my mother prepare the food. She has two glasses of wine as she cooks. She is very speedy in her conversation, like a tape being fast forwarded. My internal mood gauge shifts to be in line with hers. I too talk at a faster pace and rush around arranging chairs that have already been arranged twice.

My father comes home early from work. My mother is exasperated by his slightest move. She is so tense that her responses come out in brittle, snappy reactions and sharp, barbed criticism. The mood in all of us is of wired explosiveness.

At the expected time, Grandmother de Silva invades our house, followed docilely by her husband, my aunt, and my uncle. She briefly clasps my mother's hand. *I can be gracious towards someone who has experienced bereavement,* says her body posture, even though she has some difficulty in saying something positive about my dearest Grandma.

'She was quite a well-known model in her time, wasn't she?' she asks, the comment together with the accompanying sniff, carrying with it her hidden prejudice about people who use their physical attributes to make a living.

My mother nods, stands up abruptly, and excuses herself to get some food from the kitchen. I rush to help her. As I enter the kitchen, I catch her gulping down another glass of wine.

'Why are you so quiet today?' she snaps at me, and she sends me off with a tray of sandwiches. As I leave, I hear the sound of her pouring more.

My aunt talked to me today. She seems friendly, but I wonder if I think that because she looks like Daddy, just shorter.

'What sorts of subjects do you like at school?' she asks.

'Oh, maths and science mainly, especially physics,' I say. 'I also like English, because I love to read.'

She smiles. 'So do I,' she replies.

Her husband doesn't say much, but I can see his eyes following me when I stand and when I bend down to place a tray on the coffee table. He is tall and attractive in a dark, 'Latino' way. His hair shines faintly, as though he has used hairspray on it. His trousers, which also reflect a faint sheen, are cut straight and look ever so slightly tight across his crotch.

When my mother comes back into the room, I galvanise myself into small talk. This is, of course, to please her, but also to try to cover up the fact that she is drunk. I regale them with tales from my school. I answer questions about my academic progress. I look suitably modest when my father tells them that I have been promoted a year. They are impressed. The academic reputation of my school is well established.

After I feel I have performed to my parents' satisfaction, and once my aunt starts talking about her speciality, obstetrics, I ask to be excused and go into our TV room, which is tucked away at the back of the house. As I leave, I can hear my aunt talking about a complicated clinical procedure, and my grandparents' animated participation in the discussion. I hear my mother's forced and inappropriate laughter and cringe.

Once in the TV room, I flick through the television channels. There is a children's television programme on, and I aimlessly watch it. I look at the time and calculate how long they have been with us: one and a half hours.

They always leave after two hours.

My uncle enters the room. 'I was en route to the cloakroom,' he says in a conspiratorial whisper, 'and then I thought that I would come and see what you were up to.'

He hesitates at the door, looks behind him briefly and then comes and sits down very close to me – so close that if I turn my head to look at him, I can see his nostril hairs. He has definitely used hairspray. It is the same type as the one my mother occasionally uses. My nose twitches, and I wonder if I am going to sneeze as I usually do for aerosols.

'I used to watch this programme with your aunt when I was a kid,' he comments.

'Oh?' I respond.

'Yes, our parents were family friends, and we've known each other since we were seven years old.'

'That's interesting,' I say, and I cringe at how inane I sound.

He looks at me slyly. 'She was an awkward, gawky kid at your age, your aunt. Not pretty or mature like you.'

My heart started pounding.

I don't want to show him that I am uncomfortable and a little scared. I notice a thickening of his voice and a fine layer of sweat on his brow.

'You,' he says suggestively, 'are like your mother – extremely gorgeous.'

He pretends to flick something off the settee but then casually places his hand on my thigh. He is staring at the television as though nothing is happening. His index finger starts drawing little whorls, so subtle that I would have to take my mesmerised eyes from the screen to confirm this. I can hear his breathing quicken. He rests his other hand on his lap, over the bulge of his tight, shiny trousers.

'I had just finished watching a programme about STDs before I tuned to this channel,' I say. My voice comes out in a squeak.

His fingers stop, and his hand rises slowly and is suspended in mid-air above my legs. 'What's that, then?' he asks as he rests his fingers, five predators, on my lap again.

'It was about sexually transmitted diseases. We learnt about them at school, and my mother and father were talking about it at breakfast with me today.'

'Bloody hell!' he says, moving away from me and lifting his hand off his crotch. 'I didn't think your father had it in him. It must be the influence of your mother. Some sexy lady, isn't she?'

I stand up unsteadily. 'It's now four o'clock, the time when Grandfather and Grandmother de Silva leave,' I mumble. 'I'm going to say goodbye to them.'

My shaky legs carry me out into the living room, and as I leave, the sneeze I have so wanted to emit explodes out of me. I go into the living room, and I can see that my prediction is right. They are standing up, preparing to leave. My mother looks as though she is ready to faint, and my father is gaunt and pale.

I dutifully say goodbye. My uncle comes blundering into the room. His erection is visible through his shiny trousers. He kisses my mother ardently, shakes hands with my father, and then casually bends down and kisses me on both cheeks. His kiss is rough, purposeful, and I think I feel his hand brush against my bottom. I sneeze again and excuse myself to get a tissue. When I return to the living room, they are all gone.

> *I slept badly last night. I felt so strange. My nipples felt sensitive when I touched them, and in the night I woke up touching other parts of my body and felt a weird wetness between my legs. I thought I had started bleeding again, but when I went to the toilet to check, there was no blood. I feel bad.*

On a London Bus

7 July 2006

'That was bad, Jackson,' said Freddy as he stared at Jackson, whose gaze did not meet his eyes. They were on the top deck of a bus, heading back from the pub, towards the mainline station. *'You've got to watch what you say,'* he hissed when Jackson continued to look the other way.

Jackson glared at him belligerently. *'You know what, Freddy?'* he said. *'I've done that all the time I've known you, but today, when I should be fucking ecstatic, I feel like fucking shit. So if I want to talk to you about my stuff, I'll fucking well talk to you about my stuff.'*

'I didn't mean with me, you Wally. Just watch what you say in public, and keep your voice down.'

Jackson lowered his voice and looked Freddy in the eye. *'Since we did this deal, all I can think of is going and rescuing my mother from that shit-arse of a man. I know I'm getting closer to being able to do that, but every minute that passes is a waste of fucking time. When I think of her having to endure him it just makes me want to kick something. I meant what I said about wanting him dead.'*

Freddy was quiet for a moment. *'You know, Jackson,'* he said, *'my foster parents weren't all that great either. I mean, they treated their pet hamster better than they ever did me. They didn't want me, just what they earned from having me, and I never wanted them. I ran away several times, starting at the age of seven, only to be found each time and returned to bigger and more brutal punishment, until the last time, the only successful time. That was the time I met you. Strangely, I've never wanted* them *dead. It's me. I've wanted to die.'*

Jackson took his eyes off his friend and looked out the window pensively. *'If you die, you don't get revenge,'* he said quietly. *'I want mine, and I want to see it happen, maximum impact. Every time we sell this stuff and we hear of a bomb blowing up somewhere, I dream that he's there, being blow up into a million pieces.'*

Freddy shrugged his shoulders. *'That's where we're different,'* he said. *'Every time there's a bomb, I dream of being there. I never told you, but last year, after the London bombings, when you were away on that job, I purposely took the tube several times. I travelled the length and breadth of the tube map, hoping and hoping. It would have been so easy, but it never happened.'*

A woman, laden with shopping, climbed to the top deck and sat in front of them. She scratched at her swollen ankles as she settled herself. She was talking animatedly on her phone to someone and didn't give the men a second glance. Jackson and Freddy got off at the next stop.

Chapter 12

On the Wall

Maya 1990s

It's strange to go back to school. I feel different again, because I don't think anyone at school has lost someone close to them.

I am new again.

I wish I could go back to my old class.

You don't deserve to be here is what I think the new class thinks of me. I rise to the challenge and start up my binge reading. I sit in the library after school, pondering over reference books and journals or carrying out literature searches on the computer, so that whether it's an essay for English, a piece of research for history, or an experiment for biology, the effort is huge and the outcome a mini masterpiece.

We have resumed our normal rhythm at home, but we never refer to the loss of my grandmother. Once, I see some of her clothes in my mother's wardrobe, and I am startled and betrayed. Has Mum been sorting out her clothes without me? Why have I not been given something of hers as a keepsake?

I have three main worries, and I will list them in order of significance. Worry 1: Will I forget Grandma? Worry 2: My period. Worry 3: Strange happenings in my body.

The feelings I have about Grandma's sudden loss proliferate like a cancerous growth in me. At the same time, I panic if memories of her appear vague. Fear of disloyalty tightens its circle of thorns around my head, and some days I wake up with a terrible headache from its grip.

My period is vengeful, and I am drained by its persistence.

The feelings I experienced in my body that night after the encounter with my uncle keep recurring, and I notice that on some nights, my hands explore secret parts of my body, always with the same consequence: that strange wetness that worries me.

My meetings with Nora continue to be clandestine. I'm not sure why, although I have a suspicion that it is because Nora likes secrets. They make her feel powerful. We continue to meet after school. We sit on the low garden wall of a house down a quiet lane, where we know no one is at home and where we will not be spotted. We can be quiet or chatty.

Nora sometimes kisses me goodbye on the lips. I never react.

One day, Nora asks me over to her house after school.

'My mother is away on a self-awareness course,' she says. 'Our housekeeper's at home, but she won't bother us.'

This time, I get to see more of her house, which I find extremely impressive. Many sculptures and paintings adorn the living room, which is in rich wine and gold colours with wood-panelled walls. The conservatory is probably the size of the whole of the downstairs of our house, glass paned, with orange and kumquat trees in ornate pots. There is a home gym with many pieces of severe steel gym equipment, and there is a games room that houses a full-sized snooker table and a table tennis table. It all looks pristine and unused: another showroom in a show house. Looking out into the garden, I can see a swimming pool and a hot tub. Huge koi and other carp swim lazily in the large ornamental pond that runs through the house and into the garden. Large lilies and oriental lotus float in the water. The magnificent and opulent surroundings dwarf me and make me realise the vast difference between Nora and myself.

Nora puts her hand on my shoulder. 'I hate all of this,' she says sincerely. 'I hate large. I would much rather live in a small, cosy home.'

I say nothing. This is my usual response when I disagree but don't have the confidence to verbalise it.

'Let's watch a movie,' she suggests.

Her room is the same as before; if anything, everything looks even more precise and ordered, but that is possibly because I am contrasting it with the mess that is in my room. The only new touches are a vase of rosebuds on her dressing table and an 'Abdominiser', one of those sit-up machines to tighten stomach muscles, housed discreetly in the corner.

We start watching the movie Nora has recommended. She is in a playful mood. She keeps flicking my hair from time to time or pinching me playfully. When she does this, I gently hit back at her, and when we finally tire of this game, I rest myself comfortably on one side of her, my head resting on her shoulder, her arm around my waist.

To be close to Nora is the most normal thing in the world to do.

Halfway through the film, Nora's arm brushes past one of my breasts. I feel a frisson of excitement pass through me. I turn my head slightly, and she kisses me full on the lips. It is a long, lingering kiss, gentle like the brush of a cobweb against my skin, desperate like a caged animal longing to be free. I respond like a limp piece of spaghetti. I say nothing, do nothing. I just wait. Very gently and slowly, her hands travel downwards, tracing a route from my face to my shoulders and then descending into areas that no one travels but me. Her fingers enter intimate areas, and she starts to gently rub me, up and down, round and round.

I don't really know what she wants to do, but it feels comfortable. I am a detached observer in this situation. The monotony of what she is doing surprises me, since I am not sure how I am supposed to respond. After a while, it starts to hurt a bit, and I also get restless about missing the film, and so I arch my back and gently move her hand away so as not to hurt her feelings.

'Was it all right?' she whispers.

'Yes,' I say. What response is she is expecting? I go back to leaning my head on her shoulder and watching the film.

* * *

I stop writing. I remember telling a boyfriend about this experience a number of years ago.

'Do you think you might be bi, or that Nora is gay?' he asked me.

'No,' I replied honestly, 'I can truly say that there were no sexual feelings of that sort connected with what happened. Yes, what Nora did make me feel strange, but I never thought about it in a sexual way in the context of our relationship, let alone extrapolate it to others.'

That was the only occasion when something like that happened between Nora and me. It made me feel less alone and, I think, less ugly. I am pleased that I have read this bit. I can finally differentiate between the exploitative incident with my uncle and my innocent episode with Nora.

Nora and I are still the best of friends, and she has agreed, although under considerable pressure, to be my bridesmaid. I have a feeling that Nora might react adversely to a discussion about what happened. Whatever my interpretation of the situation, I think she may have another, more negative interpretation, and I know, as most of my discussions with her, that ultimately it will be her view that wins. I still permit her to overpower me. It is our pattern. I have also now got the confidence of being in a loving relationship, and an awareness of my sexuality, which I am not sure she does. She is single. She is still awkward about any discussion of emotions. I decide not to concern her.

In Suffolk

31 July 2006

PC Reeves knew he was worried because his good mood had dissipated and was replaced by concern. He was currently preoccupied on two accounts: one was personal, the other work related. On the personal side, things with Susannah seemed to be getting more serious, not a bad thing on its own but he wanted to be sure if the time was right for him to broach on confirming this. Usually his timing was lousy – either too serious and soon, or too laid back and late. I don't want this relationship to be affected by my poor sense of judgement, *he thought,* I wish mother was around so I could ask her. She would have helped me get the timing right.

He pressed his fingers against his temples. 'Do you guys want me to help you out with anything before I deal with the complications of this case?' *he asked the other officers in the room who were all much busier sorting the aftermath of the bombing. He was secretly relieved when they gave him the thumbs up to continue with his case. He gave a heartfelt sigh. He had still not had any success in identifying the Maya for whom the letter was for either.*

PC Evans, *a young, new police officer entered his office with a pile of boxes disrupting his reflections.*

'Got these from the house,' *he said succinctly.*

PC Reeves *stared at the pile. The boxes were full of high-tech cameras and telephone bugging devices.*

'They're spy cameras,' *announced PC Evans excitedly.*

'Why would he have wanted those?' *PC Reeves asked aloud.*

'I think these tapes might reveal more information,' *said PC Evans, digging into the box,* 'also these detailed diaries. I reckon he was a blackmailer.'

'That puts a completely different light on things!' *exclaimed PC Reeves, looking worried.* 'I wonder, was Maya one of his victims? What might her involvement be in all this and is any of this connected with the bombings?'

Jackson 1996-1997

Jackson's father moved out of home when Jackson was fourteen. His sexual involvement with the eighteen-year-old girl who worked as a waitress at his local pub meant that he had a very public reason to be kicked out of the house by Jackson's mother. The eighteen-year-old was the daughter of the pub owner. After she moved into the bed-sit his father was lodging at, the pub owner banned Jackson's father from ever stepping into his pub again. Jackson missed his father terribly, especially since he never made an effort to see Jackson or to telephone him. Jackson was dead to him. The pub owner's two sons, who attended the same school as Jackson, made sure that Jackson's life was made a misery. Just as Jackson's father was excluded from the pub where he had spent most of his time, Jackson was ejected from his peer group. With time, Jackson adapted. He learned to grow a tough hide of invulnerability around himself. It was difficult initially, but Jackson was soon to learn that although being left out by friends was painful, as was being abandoned by his father, being separated from your mother was the worst.

When Jackson was fifteen, he came home early to find confetti on his driveway and a strange man in the house.

'Jackson, say hello to Ray,' said his mother, who was looking surprisingly happy and youthful in a new pink dress. 'I met him at Bingo two months ago, and we got married this morning. Ray, say hello to your stepson.'

Ray was a possessive man. He didn't like his wife thinking of anyone else but him. He didn't like his wife looking after anyone other than him either. He went about systematically ensuring that he kept Jackson well apart from his mother. 'Divide and rule' was his policy, and it worked every time.

Chapter 13

Breaking Point

Maya, mid 1990s

I have some new school friends, and I'm trying my best to stay included in the group.

There is Francesca, who is serious and conscientious. Amanda, who is the tomboy of the class, is generally forgetful but bright and vivacious. She is the sports captain and ultimately wants to be a sports commentator. Leah, who is dreamy and eccentric, excels in English, because she likes it, and in nothing else, because she is not motivated to. I am surprised when one day Leah says, 'Really, Maya, contrary to popular belief, you are quite approachable, aren't you?'

Me? Unapproachable?

We are worked hard at school to ensure that the results of our first set of public exams are good, since they will affect the school's reputation and desirability. We are brainwashed into good performance.

I got my mock exam results today; they were good, but I am so sad.

Nora has been fighting a fierce battle with food. Her weight has been plummeting gradually, and on the day I get my results and I seek her out, I am told that Nora has collapsed at school and that she has been rushed to casualty.

I have a sudden rush of the bile of emotions in my mouth, the same aftertaste of the panic and fear I felt the night Grandma died.

I go over to the school secretary's office to check on whether she can inform me about Nora's health. She is not prepared to tell me much.

'Nora's in a stable but serious condition,' she says.

'Where is she?' I ask forcefully. 'What does stable but serious mean?'

The secretary stares. 'You'll hear more when we have information we can share,' she says haughtily.

Angrily I turn around and leave, and then, acting on impulse, I go over to the school nurse's office, feigning nausea and stomach pains. She takes my temperature, which is, of course, normal, but since I am persistent in my claims of feeling nauseous, she agrees to leave me with a bowl in the sick room, which has darkened drapes, a comfortable chair, a bed, and, most importantly for me, a telephone.

Ten minutes after the nurse leaves me to tend to the usual mixture of minor ailments from children, I am on the telephone. I obtain an outside line (I have learnt how to do this from Nora) and call her home. Her brother, Nick, picks up the telephone. He sounds distant, unapproachable, even aggressive, and I nearly ring off.

Does Nick think that I've helped Nora to get worse?

'How is Nora?' I ask.

He snorts. I experience a pang of sadness when I hear him do this, because it reminds me of her.

'She's being tube-fed at one of the medical wards at St Matthew's Hospital.' He takes a malicious delight in telling me.

This is the largest hospital in our area, about five miles from the school. It is where Nora's father works and also where my grandmother was rushed to on her final journey. Nick goes on to add that her electrolytes (what are they? I must make a note to read up more about *Anorexia nervosa*) are so low as to be nonexistent and that she has only just been prevented from going into total organ failure.

Apparently her body mass index (something else to check up on) is also extremely low, and although she was weighed two weeks ago, it seems that because she has been 'water loading' before being weighed, as well as wearing heavy clothes with weights in her pockets, her weight has been registering as much higher than it really was. Because of this deception, the crisis in her physical system had not been detected when it should have been. No blood tests were taken for ages because the nurse was persuaded by Nora's verbal arguments.

'Professionals can unwittingly collude with anorexia by buying into the same denial and not monitoring the individual thoroughly enough,' says Nick loftily.

Just like all of you, I think but don't say.

He continues, 'The silly cow was making her condition even more serious by water loading. Her kidneys are not in a good state, and obviously everything went into overdrive today.'

'Do they permit visitors?' I ask hopefully.

'Not at the moment,' he replies. 'She is sedated so that she retains her nasogastric tube.' He adds that visitors possibly will not be permitted for a while, since they were talking of starting an incentive programme for social contacts once she was on the Eating Disorder Unit.

'What do you mean by incentive programme?' I enquire, confused.

'Oh, well, you know, the chances are she'll start refusing to eat the recommended amount of calories whilst on the ward, and they may try to encourage her by setting up a reward scheme. The most likely rewards they would use are visits from friends.'

I am stunned by this piece of information. I might not be able to see Nora for a while. Worse than that, the only people she would be seeing are her family – not much incentive to get out of her sedated state for that, either. In a wry part of my brain, I find the fact that I might become a reward amusing.

'Who can I speak to so that I can keep up with how she is?'

He gives me the ward details rather than offering to keep me updated, but then he also dashes my hopes by saying they probably wouldn't give me information on the telephone, since I wasn't family. 'I don't know if she'll remain where she is for physical stabilisation,' he adds uncertainly. 'She may be transferred to private care once she is medically fit, or she may be transferred onto the Eating Disorders Unit in another wing of the hospital. My father is trying to sort out funding matters with the hospital managers.'

I put down the phone in shock. Surely it had only been another game that we teenagers play?

I never thought anything like this would ever happen.

I have totally believed in the strange disconnection that is part of adolescence, between what we do and their consequences. I think of that ordered and neat bedroom of Nora's and visualise those beautiful paintings on the walls. I remember her generosity and kindness and how she was able to hold me when my world fell apart when my grandmother died. I swallow back a lump in my throat, just as the nurse bustles in.

'Oh, you are looking a bit peaky,' she says. 'I've tried to contact your home to see if someone can come and pick you up, but there's no one there. I see from the permission form your parents have filled in that you are permitted to go home on your own. Do you want to stay here until you know one of your parents is home, or would you feel more comfortable being at home straight away?'

My antennae for sensing trouble go into overdrive. It is unlikely that my mother is out. Why is she not answering the telephone at home? I get out of bed, and as I stand up, I feel the unexpected rush of rivulets of blood down my thighs and on the floor: droplets of my life on display. The nurse brightens: finally, a diagnosis.

'It must have been your period causing you all this bother,' she says. 'Come on, I've got some sanitary towels, and I'll help you to clean up.'

Her fussing over me brings back memories of Grandma, and I bite my lips hard and stare up at the ceiling to stop my eyes from spilling their tears. The nurse, noticing my withdrawn state, fusses over me more.

Before I leave school, I go to collect my books from my locker. The classroom resounds with the voices of the various girls discussing their results. Francesca bounds up to me to compliment me. I look at her puzzled for a moment. What is she talking about? Then I remember we have had our mock exam results. Leah makes her way towards me, and I purposely avoid her as I go up to my teacher to ask to be excused. I try not to think about the hurt look on Leah's face as I rush out.

My walk back home brings back poignant memories of Nora. I pass the wall we sit on, the hedge with the flowers we surreptitiously pick on the way. I keep walking and go through the park and past Acacia Road, which my father has told me to avoid en route home, since there is a large hostel housing 'dodgy' people.

On my way, I pass a man selling roses by the traffic lights. They are reduced to two pounds a bunch, since they are wilting. On impulse, I buy my mother a bunch with my lunch money.

I let myself into the house. The door is not double-locked, so my mother must be home. Everything is quiet. I go to the study, as I always do, to leave my school bag. I notice some photographs on the table. Curiosity draws me closer. There is a pile of photographs of my mother when she was a child. Many feature Grandma and my grandfather. Lying next to it is a scrapbook. I put the flowers down on the table and look at the photographs curiously. A thick red line has been drawn across my grandfather's face in one, a thick red cross on his face in another. Flung on the floor is a thick red marker pen. My mother obviously made these lines today. What does it mean?

I go into the kitchen. It looks pristine, except for some unwashed crockery in the sink. This is unusual; our kitchen is usually in disarray unless my father or I tidy up. I make my way to my mother's bedroom. Her door is ajar, and I timidly knock first and then push it open. A scene of chaos hits my eyes. She has opened all of my father's wardrobes and pulled out all of his clothes. They are dumped on the ground. Some of his trousers have been cut into shreds. A broken bottle of his aftershave sheds its contents in a desultory drip-drip fashion in a corner. She has thrown her make-up on the ground, and powder, blusher, creams, and perfumes lie in psychedelic disarray on the carpet. The telephone by her bed has been wrenched out of its socket and lies drunkenly on its side. For a very brief moment, I wonder if we have been burgled, before my eyes fix on the bed.

I found Mummy in bed, snoring, with two empty vodka bottles by her side.

She had been writing some letters when she passed out. I pick up the sheets of paper and put them in my pocket. I go into autopilot. I plug the telephone back into its socket and call the ambulance.

My legs started to shake, and my stomach felt full of butterflies. I telephoned Daddy's office and got his answer-phone. I collected all the clothes that were thrown around and put them into a big rubbish bag and shoved them in my wardrobe. I cleaned the mess as best as I could and quickly emptied the bin. Then, even though I didn't want to, I called my grandfather.

A woman answers the telephone. I am sure that I have dialled the wrong number, but I ask for him anyway. Surprisingly, she doesn't tell me it is the wrong number. Instead she asks me who I am. Before I give her my name, I repeat who I have called for and I ask her who she is. My spine straightens and stiffens brittle like caramelised sugar.

'Oh, I am a family friend of Bill's,' she tells me frostily, repeating her request for my name.

She's a family friend of my grandfather's? What friend is this? What family? I have a hunch that she is connected in some way with my mother's current state.

'I am a family member of Bill's,' I tell her, like I too am staking a claim to him. 'I am his granddaughter, and I have an emergency to report.'

Her voice warms immediately. 'You're his granddaughter? You should have said,' she replies with a coy laugh. 'Maya, isn't it? It's such a beautiful name. I've heard so much about you. Anyway, an emergency, you say? Well, I better not hold you up, then. Let me get your grandfather on the line.'

I am brusque with him; I want it to hurt. I tell him that I am waiting for the ambulance to come and take my mother to hospital – *the* hospital (I say the name out loud for maximum effect). I don't tell him that she is in a drunken stupor. I also withhold from him my opinion that the chances of her going to hospital may be negligible.

'I think she's unconscious,' I say deliberately.

'What?' he exclaims.

'I've got to go. I can hear the ambulance on its way,' I say untruthfully and ring off. Let him and his 'family friend' stew for a while.

The ambulance arrives promptly.

What if this was the same team of paramedics who tried to save Grandma?

The ambulance men ignore me and go about their task. It is as I suspect. They check her out, recoiling from the smell of her breath.

They check the room. I am pleased that I have put away the innards of her distress.

'Is she on any medication?' they ask me.

'No, she isn't,' I reply.

'Can you show us where the medicine cupboard is?' is their next request.

They look through the contents and seem satisfied that there is still a nearly full pack of Paracetamol and an unopened pack of Nurofen Plus. They don't know that I have already checked.

'Can we check the bins?' they ask me.

'I've already done so,' I inform them, catching them by surprise.

'What have you searched for?' they ask.

For empty packs of medication, their blistered spaces ruptured, for bottles of poisonous substances. To check if any other lethal chemicals have also been imbibed with that overdose of alcohol, or, my deepest fear, whether there is a suicide note.

'Oh, I thought I'd check if there were any empty bottles in there,' I say.

They look at me in an almost embarrassed way. They pity me to have such a mother.

'She'll probably throw up soon,' they tell me indifferently. 'Better keep this disposable bucket handy and plenty of water to rehydrate her.'

Their negative reaction to self-inflicted harm is clear. I think they would have been much more supportive of a rampaging psychotic schizophrenic with murderous intent. The prejudice that exists about addictions is huge. People, including professionals, often see managing an addiction as within the control of an individual. I don't think my mother's addiction is within her control. It is a parasitic entity that has grown within her, poisoning her with its vitriolic appetite.

I am not defending her; after all, I too have often shared in their same condemnation. My frustration at her not doing anything about it is always with me. That is why I'm so sensitive to feeling helpless and try to short-circuit this feeling if I ever experience it.

My mother stirs and comes to, vomiting violently, as predicted. The ambulance men question her for a while, although they get no coherent answers. They linger indecisively. I understand that they may be worried about leaving me, sixteen years old, alone at home with her. I am about to reassure them when the doorbell rings. It is my grandfather. He looks distinguished as always, tall but portly, his voice rich and creamy as a Swiss *pot au chocolat*. He walks in and takes control of the situation straight away. The ambulance men, virtually bowing under his command, back away and then leave, informing him of the signs to look out for in an emergency. Any negative inference that is made by the more courageous one of them, any hint at how helpful a referral to a psychiatrist might be, or a referral to the Drug and Alcohol Team at the hospital, is silenced with a glare. He is Judge Bill now, not Joe Public. They leave hurriedly after checking my mother one more time.

When they have left, my grandfather carefully folds his Barbour and places in over the arm of our settee. He then methodically places his hat over his coat. He has kept his over clothes on until the paramedics leave, almost as though staying in full attire gives him greater stature. He is used to wearing robes in court, after all. He looks very seriously at me. I square my shoulders. I am in the witness box, and the cross-questioning is about to start.

'Has your mother been drinking a lot recently?' he asks. 'Have you ever seen empty bottles of alcohol around the house? Do you know why she has drunk so much today?'

I assume the blank, glazed stare of youth. I am not going to let him get under my skin. That is what they do in court, and then the validity of a witness is lost. I answer his questions briefly and obtusely.

'I don't know why she drank too much today.' (My fingers cross in my pocket, the tips touching the pages of her letter.) 'And I haven't seen empty bottles around the house.'

For once, I am pleased that my complexion is as it is, since it makes it difficult to spot my awkwardness at having to lie. I don't care whether he believes my answers, but I am not prepared to say any more, and I can see that he knows it. He sighs and goes into the kitchen to get some water for my mother to drink. She is very much awake by now and is calling out for me. When he is in the kitchen, I hurriedly go to the study, put her scrapbook away, and slip the two defaced photographs into my pocket. I don't want him to find out his contribution to what happened today. That will give him too much power and inflate his ego even more.

I put the flowers I bought Mummy straight in the bin.

I go upstairs. My mother is lying pale-faced on the bed. Her forehead has beads of sweat on it, and she doesn't smell too good.

'What happened to me?' she asks, bewildered, rather like Alice in Wonderland who deliberately drank from a bottle labelled 'Drink me' without questioning, and was then surprised at the consequences.

'You haven't been well, but you're better now,' I say, caught off guard. I have no idea whether my mother wants to be confronted with what she has done.

My mother suddenly sits upright in bed, memories flooding back. She desperately looks around her, not knowing if she has been found out.

'I put the bottles in the bin,' I say, 'and cleared all the clothes and makeup. The ambulance men had to know about the number of bottles, for your safety, but I've told no one else. Daddy doesn't know anything at all yet, and Grandfather knows about the drinking, but doesn't know how much.'

My mother rests back gratefully and then sits bolt upright again.

'Grandfather!' she exclaims. 'What does he know?'

Before I can brief her, the man walks into the room. My mother gasps and then lowers herself back onto the pillows helplessly. To give him his due, he is good. He sits on the side of my mother's bed, gingerly, but nevertheless the nonverbal cues he gives by the bridging of personal distance are good. He picks up her right hand and gently traces the veins on the back of it. My mother lies there woodenly, shocked by this sudden display of closeness and warmth by her idol.

'I know things have been hard for all of us since your mother died but I hadn't realised how hard it has been on you. I mean,' he says, averting his eyes slightly, 'I suppose I have been somewhat selfish in expecting you to organise everything and in expecting you to look after me, along with the running of your own family and home.'

I can see the game he is playing. He is manipulating the blame onto the loss of Grandma. I suddenly realise that it's not the dead who make it hard to adjust to your loss; it's the living.

My mother says nothing. She stares at him wordlessly.

I can no longer bear his duplicity. On my mother's face is the same expression I have seen on my grandmother's when I used to escape into my daydreams. It is a yearning, a longing for some sort of fulfilment. It is also an expression of love. I am strangely cold, and my legs have started trembling again. I get up and leave the room, and neither of them even notices that I have gone.

I make my way into my bedroom and impulsively do something that I haven't done since I was a child. I carefully get into my wardrobe, sit among the hanging clothes, and let my mind drift into a secret place, a make-believe land that I used to visit when I was very young. I suppose I must have been influenced by *The Chronicles of Narnia*. The space in the wardrobe is very cramped. What felt like a cosy place to a seven-year-old is uncomfortably claustrophobic at my age and size. A stray shoebox digs into the small of my back. I shift my position, and as I lean on my side, something in my pocket rustles: my mother's letter. I get out of the wardrobe and pull the sheets of paper out of my pocket. I hesitate only for a second. I have to find out the cause of my mother's current distress.

It seems that my mother had gone over to my grandfather's house early this morning (unusual for her, which is why she caught him out), and Rhona (the 'family friend') had been about to leave. According to my mother's notes, it had been obvious that she had stayed the night. This shocks me. Had she slept in my grandparents' bedroom? Surely not in their bed!

The telephone rings. It must be my father. My grandfather picks up the receiver before I can get to it. I go out of my room, onto the landing, to hear what he is saying.

'Yes, yes,' he says, 'just a small panic after a little accident on Diane's part, but everything is absolutely fine now. You have nothing to worry about.... Yes...' He lowers his voice slightly. 'Well, it has been a strain on her after Louise's death.... A delayed grief reaction.... No, no need to telephone the doctor.'

My father asks for me, and my grandfather calls out from the top of the landing. I want to deface him. If I had a can of spray paint, I would graffiti him; perhaps that would obliterate him and his smarmy pass-the-parcel-of-blame game. I grab the telephone, and because I know that my grandfather has the other receiver up, I want to shout, 'He's guilty!' but of course I don't.

'All is well. Nothing to worry about, Dad,' I reassure him. 'Mummy doesn't need to go to the hospital. The ambulance men have dealt with it all.'

'We must talk on my return, Maya,' he says. 'I'm looking to get a flight back later tonight. Are you sure you're all right to deal with things on your own?'

'You mustn't worry, Dad. I can manage perfectly well,' I say. 'Finish what you have to do. Just get back, I think Mum would love to see you.'

'I'll see you both soon,' he says. 'By the way, Maya, have you got your results?'

What does it matter how well I do, when Nora's in hospital and my mother's heart is broken?

'They'll be out sometime later this week,' I lie.

*   *   *

I collect my diaries and pensively put them away. I had forgotten the details of this event, and re-experiencing it now makes the grown-up me puzzle about why I involved my grandfather in this sorry happening. As I put away my fountain pen, it comes to me that I sensed my mother's longing for her father just as I knew the yearning I had for mine. As Euripides said, 'The gods visit the sins of the fathers upon the children.'

I also think about the two emergencies I faced that day; Nora and my mother, one an excess of control, the other a serious lack of control, yet both causing huge amounts of self-inflicted devastation. What is the fundamental factor that imbalances the spectrum of self-regulation and control? Is it such low self-worth that you either deny nurturance or over-give to yourself? All I know is there was always a lack of fulfilment in what they both did to themselves; it was compulsion with empty gain.

In Suffolk

2 August 2006

PC Reeves was thoroughly enjoying his evening with Susannah. They dined at a pizzeria and then saw a film. PC Reeves always chuckled when Susannah chose what they would see at the cinema, because for a quiet, demure teacher, she had unusual tastes. Apart from enjoying reading the most gruesome of murder mysteries, she adored action movies. PC Reeves loved her even more for this. He had never told her that he preferred to watch something more thoughtful. He now sat back in his seat and rather than watching the big screen watched discretely the varying expressions on her face. He also anticipated her little screams at the exciting bits or her clutching his arm at times of suspense. He treasured these moments so much that when they left the cinema had someone asked him what the film was about, he would have been hard pressed to answer.

They walked to her home after the movie; several passionate goodnight kisses later, he reluctantly turned down her offer to stay the night. Sadly, he had work to complete before the night was over.

He finally tore himself away from their mutual embrace, trudged home, changed from his jeans into his uniform, and was at work in twenty minutes. He entered the building he knew so well, said hello to the officers on night duty and buried himself in his office. Sighing, he got out the many boxes of tapes and firmly made himself stop thinking about Susannah. He made himself a strong black coffee, the first of many, and settled down to a late night's work.

Chapter 14

Flight, Fight, or Freeze?

Maya, late 1990s

I now have a predictable routine. I make myself a strong coffee, and I sit on my bed and write in my diary every night. It's a comfort, and it makes up for the poems I no longer write. My only fear is that someone will find my diary and read it. I would just die if they did. Things are hard for me. I miss Nora and I worry about her. I have no regular news on her progress. To not think is the only way to deal with my concerns over her. I worry about my mother too. That's hard to cut off from.

My mother has started attending regular Alcoholics Anonymous meetings and individual therapy. My father is supportive of her attendance. My grandfather is not.

'How can you even think about attending meetings with a group of losers?' he asks, outraged. 'AA is for people who wake up in the morning reaching out for a drink. As for individual therapy, the outcome of analysis is paralysis. Totally bloody useless exercise.'

'I want to do this,' retorts my mother, 'and as usual, you criticise me. Are you afraid of what I might find out? Who might be to blame?'

'I knew it!' he exclaims, enraged. 'Blame – that's what this society wants everyone to do. Blame it on others, and conveniently forget your own contribution to this whole bloody mess.'

My mother looks at him, eyes glinting dangerously. 'What exactly is it that I have contributed to this mess?'

'There you go again, deliberately needling me. There's nothing that finding a job and putting your brain to work won't do. That's been your problem throughout. You can achieve, but you've never wanted to, and in the idle time that you have, you find other useless tasks to occupy yourself with.'

'That's your solution to everything!' my mother explodes. 'Get a job, and the whole bloody world will fall into place. Well, whilst your job was apparently solving everything for you when I was growing up, it wasn't solving anything at all for me.'

'No, and whose fault was that? You kept getting yourself into trouble. That's what you're doing all over again. You are deliberately setting out to annoy me by doing what you think I disapprove of.'

'Well, you're wrong,' says my mother, but she is shaken. She retreats behind her usual mask of indifference. She will hide her need for his acceptance, his approval, and his unconditional love.

My mother also starts a course of antidepressant medication, although this is a secret even to my father. Antidepressants imply failure, and she cannot be that revealing, even to him. I know because, much to my shame, I continue to check the stocks of potentially harmful substances in the medicine cabinet and snoop around her room when I can, making sure that there are no more empty bottles hidden in the crevices of the mattress or in her cupboards, and no sharp objects: small metal nail files, sharp scissors, or pointed tweezers are all risk assessed by me.

I can sense that my mother's feelings towards attending AA meetings are ambivalent.

'I just can't fit into groups very well,' I overhear her telling my father. 'I can't and don't want to do it.'

'You're an only child,' I hear my father say. 'You've no experience of shared activities or of competition. Give it a bit longer.'

I have never thought of it in that way. Is that my problem too? I mull over it for a while and then dismiss the thought. After all, it's not me that doesn't want to belong to a group - I don't have a group that wants to accept me.

I try to clear my mind of such distractions, since it is serious study time ahead.

I just can't revise at the moment. I am jumpy most of the time, and I watch Mummy incessantly. Sometimes I feel on edge, almost as though I'm being followed. Sometimes I think I can see 'it' just behind me, and I then get very scared.

I start to feel tightness in my chest and shooting pains in my right shoulder. I'm sure something is wrong with my heart. Sometimes I can't take in a deep breath, and then I panic. At times I am light-headed, and I keep experiencing trembling of my leg muscles. I feel tired all the time, and yet I find it difficult to sleep, often waking up in night sweats, which make me start my obsessive showering again. At night, I think of my grandma, and I wish she were here. I put my arms around my pillow and try to imagine it's her softness and warmth that I bury my head in, but its polyester filling remains inanimate and without consolation – nothing like her cosiness at all.

My thoughts rush through me like an express train gone amok. Is, for example, my heart going to stop? Am I going to be able to take in my next breath? Why can't I focus? Am I going mad?

I'm worried about Mummy. Has she got cleverer at hiding her drinking? What if it gets worse and everyone knows? I hate thinking this, but I might as well admit it – it's another stupid reason for people to think I'm weird. Why does she have to be so embarrassing?

I read in the newspaper about a bomb going off in a theatre in Central London. Luckily the theatre was evacuated after a tip-off, so no one was hurt, but the journalist writing the article elucidates, with vividness, the extent of the bomb damage. He describes the fallout, the affected areas extending over several hundred metres. The article says that it will take years to put right the damage, some of it to things that are irreplaceable. Depression is such a bomb. I am part of the fallout, as is my father.

As I slouch around at home, living in a twilight capsule of part academia and part anxiety, my aunt and uncle come on a visit of their own to see my father. It is their second visit to us and the first time that they have come without Grandparents de Silva.

Daddy's family somehow seem to know when Mummy's at her lowest.

We're all surprised that they've decided to visit us, and I'm also curious of the reason for why they've come on their own.

'Could you please check on whether the living room and the kitchen are clean for later today?' my father asks me on his way out to work.

'Maya, I wonder if we have any biscuits or cakes to serve them,' says my mother.

I take both these suggestions as requests from them to make sure the visit goes well and spend my morning cleaning the house and baking a cake.

They arrive on time. My aunt looks young and attractive in a pair of jeans, her hair held back with a tortoiseshell hair band. My uncle is also casually dressed, in khaki trousers with an open-necked shirt revealing a hairy chest. His hair is immaculately in place and has the same sheen. My noise twitches as I go forward to greet them, and I can feel the familiar scratch an allergy creates in my throat as I resist the urge to sneeze.

My mother joins us for a brief moment before excusing herself, saying that she has a terrible headache. I can see the disappointment in my father's eyes and try to make up for it by being as good a host as I can. I make them tea and bring them wedges of my cake to eat. I try not to acknowledge the fact that my uncle's eyes follow me around the room. I find that I cannot meet my aunt's eyes, although she hasn't made much effort to talk to me today. I feel guilty; as though I have betrayed her, and my uncle's constant endeavours to meet my eyes make me feel like I am part of some cheap conspiracy.

Once they have munched through the first slice of cake, my aunt says that she is worried about her parents' health and future. 'They are now one year away from accepting voluntary retirement,' she states, 'and I would like to see that their future is secure.'

'That's their responsibility,' says my father flatly.

'Ruwan, they invested in our future by going through hardship when we were young,' my aunt argues, 'and so I think they merit our involvement now.'

'What sort of involvement are you proposing?' my father asks.

She tells him that she would like to invest in buying a large house for herself and to convert part of it into a self-contained flat for their parents. As she describes her plans and the type of house she thinks would be worth developing, the purpose of her visit becomes clear. She has seen a property that she would like to buy, and she would like my father to invest in this venture with her. My father says nothing, and I can see the disappointment in her face as she continues to press him for an answer.

I share in my father's discomfort, and so it's almost a relief when my uncle asks me if he can have some more tea. I excuse myself to go to the kitchen to fill the kettle, leaving behind me a silent room, although as I enter the kitchen, I can hear my aunt start on a litany on the value of parents. I gratefully rest against the kitchen counter after I refill the kettle.

Before my next coherent thought, my uncle is in the kitchen, standing very close.

His breath was disgusting. It smelled of stale onion.

'I thought you might want some help,' he whispers. His arm 'accidentally' brushes past my breasts. I feel the start of the heavy beating of my heart. He moves to stand behind me, reaches around, and squeezes my nipples.

'Let me help you,' he says, another waft of onion coming my way, and he lowers his face as though he is going to kiss me on my neck. I shakily move away from him, pretending to get a spoon. He drifts closer, and I find that he has trapped me against the kitchen counter. My legs shake, and my heart increases its pace.

Daddy could have walked in.

'Sexy skirt,' he says, and his fingers drift down towards my legs, making light strokes on my thighs as I try ineffectually to stir the tea in the teapot. Into my head pops a stupid line, which I later berate myself for: *All the better to tantalise you with,* it says. To my frustration, my voice has deserted me.

When my uncle did what he did today, I split in half. My head was desperate to stop him, but my body wanted to find out more. I am such a slut.

His fingers are now more insistent and make their way up my thighs and through the elastic legs of my knickers, until he cups my bottom with both hands. His breathing is heavy, and his voice is thick. He presses his body forcefully against mine, and I can feel his penis hard against my thigh. He starts gyrating his hips, rubbing himself up and down along me, whilst his fingers probe deeper. I have a sudden vision of the dog next door making a similar movement against the leg of his owner, and the crudeness of the image helps me to detach myself from him. I grab the tray with the pot of tea and the clean mugs and rush out of the kitchen into the room where my father and aunt are.

My father looks up in brief surprise at my hurried entrance and then resumes his conversation with his sister. I dump the tray on a side table, not even noticing that there is only one mug on it, and say that I have heard my mother call out to me. I excuse myself and avoid going downstairs again until my father calls me to come and say goodbye. When I reluctantly come down, my aunt looks disappointed; obviously my father has stood his ground about not supporting her in her plans. My uncle smiles at me.

'Perhaps Maya can come and spend some time with us one weekend when she's finished her exams?' he suggests. 'There's a new bowling alley opened up near us. I'm sure she'll enjoy trying it out. It'll be a good excuse for us to see what it's like too. Won't it, my dear?' he says to his rather surprised wife.

'Oh, of course, Maya,' she says, 'any time.'

I climb wearily back upstairs. I am shivery, like I have a fever. I stare at my bed for a moment and then slowly make my way downstairs again; because I know that first I have to help my father put away the dirty cups and plates in the kitchen. I cannot bear to go close to the kitchen counter where I last stood with my uncle.

My father senses my reluctance and says that I can go back upstairs to complete my homework, and so I find myself sitting down in front of my desk, trying to revise. All I can focus on, however, is the touch of my uncle's fingers on my nipples, the feelings that shot through me when he added pressure, and at this image, a wave of nausea suddenly hits me. I stumble to the toilet and get there just in time to throw up violently.

Once I have brought up most of the contents of my stomach, I get in the shower and turn on the water. I make it very hot and as powerful as I can tolerate. I stand there for what seems like ages, letting the water pierce me like a thousand needles and scald my skin. I take the body brush that is in the shower and methodologically scrub my legs, calves to thighs and thighs to bottom. I scrub and scrub until my skin is red and sore, trying to remove the memory of his fingers from my thighs. I do the same to my breasts. When I finally step out of the shower, my body is so sore that to dry myself with the towel is agony.

Even hot water doesn't sterilise me. I still feel dirty.

I go back to my room and see my skirt on the floor, together with the blouse that I was wearing. I rummage in my drawers until I find a large pair of scissors and cut my skirt carefully into thin strips. I also cut my knickers into strips. I then collect all the strips and put them in a bag. I place my shirt on top. I never want to see any of these clothes again. When I next go downstairs, I take the bag with me and put it in the refuse bag outside. I make sure it has been collected by the dustman when he next empties our bins.

Every time I remember what happened in the kitchen, I find it hard to breathe.

The pains in my chest get worse, and I am convinced that I am about to die of a heart attack. I am too afraid to tell my parents, but I secretly write a will. I leave my books and poems to Nora and everything else I own to my parents. I put all my journals in a bag and pin on them instructions for their destruction. It is explicit in the instruction that no one should read them. I try to take them to the dustbin, but I just can't bring myself to throw them. I ask that my ashes be buried with my Grandma.

I wish I could, in a heartbeat, freeze a moment with her.

Chapter 15

Predator

Maya late 1990s

I go away for a short break. It's a bit silly when I have so many tasks to sort out before my wedding, but I also have some leave that I have to use up. The love of my life can't join me, since he has various deadlines to meet, and so I take my diaries with me and end up sitting in the bed of my hotel room from early evening, catching up. There is urgency in me to complete this record of myself, and I give in to the feelings I have tried to bury for so long.

* * *

I am worried. The whole of my revision period has been so hard because I have not been able to stop thinking about Nora. I also have so many dreams of Grandma. I had my first set of exam papers today, and just before the exam started, my heart felt like it had stopped. My head felt full of fuzzy, useless thoughts. Just before the papers were given out, I thought I would faint. I finally managed to start writing, but I don't know if it made sense. I just want to go to bed and sleep. I miss them.

Once the exams are over, I try to contact Nora. I telephone the hospital and am put through to various wards until I find that she is on a medical ward, because she has again, to be fed through a nasogastric tube. Nick told me once that she always resisted this type of feeding by trying to pull out the tube when she was left on her own, so unsurprisingly, she remained heavily sedated.

'When can I come and see her?' I ask every time I telephone.

'No visitors except for family at the moment,' I am told consistently.

I send Nora a card urging her to get better soon. Worried that it will be read to her by hospital staff or family, I keep my sentiments brief and neutral.

Once I finish my exams, some of the panic symptoms die down. This is a relief, although I continue to be over vigilant of my mother.

My mother has become hyperactive. She whitewashes the house and then redecorates it. She tidies the loft and throws away years of family history. She bags my old baby clothes, books, and clothes she never wears and deposits them at our local charity shop. She scrubs, polishes, and cleans. It is not unusual to be woken up at six in the morning to the sound of the vacuum cleaner. She continues to exorcise.

Shopping also takes on a new dimension. Do they call them shopping complexes because that's what they give you?

Mummy often hides her bags of shopping at the back of her cupboard. Mostly she buys and returns; sometimes she wears what she has bought, but in little bits so that Daddy doesn't notice.

Once she buys five pairs of shoes, all within a space of half an hour; on another day she buys six jumpers, all the same style, just in different colours, binge buying. Once she starts, she cannot stop.

*   *   *

I'm sorry to say that I too appear to have acquired this penchant for shopping. Maybe it's not in the excess that my mother had all those years ago, but I'm also attracted to the lure of the shops and the goodies they vend so provocatively. I too desire the quick fix that acquisition offers. What does it anchor in me, I wonder? Maybe it makes me feel effective? Alternatively perhaps it makes me feel I can acquire, through external means, uniformity with everyone else?

*   *   *

When my mother goes out, I go into her room to check on her supply of medication. I eat less and sleep badly. I am woken up most nights by nightmares. I dream of my grandmother. In one dream, we are in a boat together, and it's dark. The boat rocks comfortably, and I am content. I doze, and when I wake up, my grandma is asleep. We are passing land that is barren, with some carrion scattered around. It's all empty. I look down at myself, and I can see within myself a reflection of what is outside of me. I too am empty, with dead bits of body decomposing within. I speak to my grandma urgently, because I'm afraid of what's happening to me and I want to point it out to her, but she doesn't reply. I reach out to wake her and to tell her to listen to me, and as I do, she shrivels up, slips from my grasp through a hole in the boat, and is lost. I don't want her to be in the murky water or in that desolate land that I am passing through, but I can't prevent it; I can't stop her from slipping away. It doesn't matter how much I search; she's gone, and I know that when I next find her, she will be at the undertaker's down the road.

I wake up in a bath of sweat, clutching my chest and gasping for breath.

During the day, the enemy I battle against, and the predator that causes me to panic, lies within me and is my fear of losing my mother. I find it hard to believe that what has happened with her was an accident and not premeditated, and that the only substance she has used has been an overdose of alcohol. I want to make sure that there wasn't an intention to die. Because of this, I'm very relieved when I overhear a telephone conversation my mother has with her sponsor from AA.

'What I wanted that day was some time out, I hear her saying. 'I just wanted to stop my world from moving on for a short while, so that I could catch up with it.'

I don't go out. Whilst I convince myself that I am doing this to keep an eye on my mother's welfare, I know that I have hidden intentions. The first is to appease my conscience, which keeps up a constant ringing in my ears, like a bad case of tinnitus that tells me I must be to blame for my mother's depression, and that this is one way to atone for what I may have done. The second concerns the fear that overwhelms me when I step out of the house: a fear that is inexplicable but instantaneously present and which immediately brings on my panic symptoms and breathlessness.

I went to school today to pick up my results. I've not been out of the house much recently, and when I stepped outside, I felt really panicky. The walk to school seemed so far that I wasn't sure if I would be able to do it. Everything seemed noisier and brighter.

I wonder whether to call in sick, but can't bring myself to, and I finally get to school, having had to stop along the way a number of times to reorient and reassure myself. I notice, as though for the first time, the size of the large brick building where my school is housed and the vast number of girls teeming around. The whole environment is over stimulating after the lonely existence that I have been leading, and the tightness in my chest gets worse, and I feel the beginnings of the tingling in my fingertips that herald panic feelings. I escape to the toilets to calm myself, and when I appear less perturbed, I make myself join the others, knowing that I have broken into a sweat and that my stomach is doing cartwheels. The pounding of my heart is thunderous. As I open the envelope with my results and scan the contents, my breathing goes erratic. I have got all A-star grades, but I do not process this, because I am suddenly enveloped in a soft blackness, and I feel myself falling.

When I come round, I am walked to the room belonging to the school nurse and asked to lie down. The nurse keeps dabbing my face gently with a damp cloth and then thrusts a glass of glucose in my hand when she sees that I am fully aware of my surroundings.

'Drink,' she commands, and I gulp down the orange liquid. 'Now, what was that faint about? Overcome by your good grades, were you?'

Her shrewd eyes appraise me, and then she walks to the door and closes it.

'Now, Maya,' she says, 'I don't know what's been happening whilst you've been on study leave, but you've lost some weight, and you look very pale. Do you want to tell me what this is all about?'

Her voice and manner are so gentle and caring that my verbal floodgates open, and I talk and talk. I tell her about my grandmother's death, and how my period has kept occurring relentlessly. I tell her about my mother's drinking and about my dread of a repeat experience or worse, of my terror of my mother killing herself. I tell her about my panic attacks: how they overwhelm me and control me, the ropes of anxiety making me a marionette to their wrenches. I tell her that I miss Nora, and this final statement makes the tears rush down my cheeks and form a little puddle on top of my jumper. I omit my experiences with my uncle.

This chaotic outpouring is a breakthrough for me. Nurse Taylor listens without interrupting. She then explains what has been happening to my body. She normalises my reactions by explaining that my body's defence mechanisms are currently working too efficiently and that this has been happening because I have faced so many adverse events. She explains that without anything real to defend against, what I am feeling are the end products of this ongoing physiological reaction in me, with negative consequences. She reassures me that I am not having a heart attack. I start to like and respect my body, the way she describes it to me. After all, it is looking after me rather than letting me down. What is more important is that she explains that the feeling of not being in my body is normal. I am not going mad! It apparently happens when anxiety levels are very high. She encourages me to start to think more about myself and to practice going out frequently, so that I face my fear and learn to conquer it. She asks me to try to detach from looking after my mother so intensely, because she needs to learn to look after herself. Best of all, she tells me that she will arrange for me to go and visit Nora when visitors are permitted.

I leave the room walking on air. The knowledge and understanding of my physiological state moves me out of a Rip Van Winkle condition of ignorance to dawning insight.

To say that one discussion and the learning of some anxiety management strategies have put right my symptoms is, of course, a trivialisation. Avoidance is the root of anxiety, and I will need to face my fears to eradicate the symptoms, but I am on step one of the ladder, since I have moved from reacting to reflection and from abstaining to action.

With inner confidence, I go back and talk to my classmates. Leah is initially quiet, reluctant to engage in an interaction that would cause another rebuff, and I can understand that. I have been behaving like Alice, and I know how that hurts. We are all proud of our achievements, and for the first time I have no feelings of difference when I go to lunch with them.

I finally go back home, happy not only because of my exam results but also because I have found an inner sense of security in myself and in my friends. My parents are delighted with my performance. My father rewards me by taking me to the optician's for my first pair of contact lenses. I can think of no better gift.

* * *

I am jerked back into dealing with matters pertaining to my current life by my mother's surprise sojourn to my home. She has never come to visit me on her own before, and so I am astonished when I answer the entry-phone and find that she is standing outside, waiting to be let in.

My mother still looks too young to have me as her daughter. She is wearing a blue dress with some ethnic jewellery. She balances on high shoes, much higher than I would ever wear. Her hair is shoulder length and stylishly fashioned.

'I'm trying out a variety of hair styles for your wedding, and this is one of them,' she informs me, putting several bags of shopping and her shocking pink raffia handbag on the floor. 'Now, get me something to drink before we talk.'

I obligingly make her a cup of tea, still rather mesmerised by her presence.

'Maya,' begins my mother, 'I have to tell you that Daddy's in a state about your wedding.'

I bridle instantly. 'What do you mean? Are you saying I'm asking for too much? Anyway, Daddy never gets in states.

'Well, he does now,' she responds, and for a moment I catch a glimpse of a wobble in her chin as she lifts her face upwards to the ceiling, as though to hold back tears.

My initial irritation subsides, and I experience an awful sense of foreboding. 'What do you mean?' I question moving closer to her.

'Well, you know he hasn't been very well recently,' she begins.

'Yes and the doctors said he needed some rest and that his pressure needed to be monitored.'

My mother takes in a deep breath. 'Well, they now think he may have a very early stage of Parkinson's disease,' she says.

'Parkinson's disease?' I know my face is ashen. 'Not Daddy! Surely not Daddy!'

'Well, it's only very early, and he has no shakes at all. He just gets very tired when he does a lot and is convinced that his right leg drags a bit,' she says.

She digs in her bag and thrusts a pile of paper towards me. 'I got this information off the Internet. It's very informative and hopeful. You know, nothing needs change for years, if at all.'

'What can I do?' I ask, my first instinct being to rush to my father and comfort him.

'Nothing at all at the moment,' she says. 'I expect he wants to tell you himself. What I wanted to say was that he's worried about walking down the aisle with you, and of his leg not permitting him to do that. Now, will you tell him that this isn't going to happen?'

'How can I? I don't know that.'

'Maya, your wedding's in two months time. How can Daddy be affected so soon?' she reproves. 'Anyway, don't most fathers worry about walking down the aisle without making a mistake?'

I stare at her, hating her strength and matter-of-factness, until I see that she has tears in the corners of her eyes. Taking a risk, I go over to her, and I am relieved when she opens her arms and hugs me.

There is a long silence between us.

'Do you know,' she says, 'this has made me realise how I've always seen your father as a pillar of strength. I think I've taken that for granted, and I only hope the stress I've put him through hasn't hastened this.'

My instinct is to comfort her, to deny her role, but a part of me is angry, especially since I have been going through the process of collating my life and noting the effect she has had on me.

As though reading my mind, she continues, 'I hope I haven't upset you too, Maya.'

I pull out my new journal, and I read aloud some of the paragraphs pertaining to her. I read them with dramatic effect, because I am frightened about my father and angry with her, and saddened for the teenager that was me. When I finish, I can see that she is horrified by what she has heard. She cries in earnest. 'I'm sorry,' is all she can say for the first half hour. 'I'm so sorry.'

I have vented my anger, and my emotions subside. I can now acknowledge a generosity of spirit towards her, and we spend all evening in discussion. I warm towards my mother, because she is strong and decisive. She is clear that I mustn't rush to support my father through his crisis, as I have done throughout my life with her.

'This is a task for Dad as an individual and for us as a couple,' she says. 'This is your time, and we'll support you in whatever way we can.'

Mummy gave me something unforgettable today. She told me that my feelings were important, and for that, I truly love her.

Jackson 1996 -1997

It was clear from the beginning that there was no love lost between Ray and Jackson. The first day that Ray moved in, he removed Jackson's toiletries from the bathroom. When Jackson woke up in the morning, he nearly fell over a cardboard box outside his door. In it were his first bottle of Eau de Cologne his mother had bought him for Christmas, his toothbrush and a tube of toothpaste, his hair brush, his shower gel, his deodorant, and a toilet roll. A note lay on top of the items. 'Move your stuff downstairs,' it read, and at the bottom, it said, 'and buy your own bog roll from now on.' Jackson shrugged and carried the box to the downstairs cloakroom, which had a toilet and a small hand basin. There was no mirror over the basin, so he didn't brush his hair that day.

When he went to the kitchen to make himself some breakfast, he found the cereals he ate every morning not in their usual place. Ray was sitting where Jackson always sat at the table.

'You can put the food you buy for yourself in the box in this cupboard,' Ray said, barely glancing up from his paper and vaguely gesturing to a low cupboard where Jackson's mother kept the dust cloths, furniture polish, and floor cleaner. 'Oh, and I've also left a box in the fridge for you to put your cold stuff in.'

Jackson turned his back on Ray as he digested this information. Being fourteen he had never had to buy his own food, but if this was what was required of him, he would comply although he would need some money from his mother to do this. As if he cared. Food had never been that important to him anyway and if it meant he just ate his school dinner that would do him for the day.

Over that week, Ray systematically marked his territory. Jackson woke up most mornings to nearly trip over something of his that had been left outside his bedroom door. One day, it was his stereo player; the following, his CDs. His dirty laundry was piled outside his door with the address of the closest launderette and some coins on top. His mother no longer had time to talk to him, and he gradually started to withdraw from joining in any activities at home. On Sundays, he roamed the streets, once even attending a morning church service; anything was better than the stifling atmosphere at home, where his bedroom had become his whole world and his possessions were around him in boxes.

A month after moving in, Ray informed Jackson that he would have to work for his pocket money. He handed him a list of daily duties and said that he expected rent once Jackson stopped school, which he believed to be at the age of sixteen, since education was for 'poufs.' Seeing his mother in the garden hanging out the washing, Jackson questioned her about her participation in the plans concerning him. That evening, his mother's left eye was purple and swollen.

'I walked into the base of the washing line,' she said when Jackson, horrified, asked her what had caused it. That was the moment Jackson named Ray 'the Bastard.'

Over the next few months, the Bastard methodically started the process of breaking Jackson down. If Jackson approached his mother or even made eye contact with her, she sported a mystery bruise later that day. Unable to control himself any longer, Jackson asked the Bastard why he was so pathetic as to hit a woman. That evening was the first of many that Ray took a belt to Jackson, and then, when Jackson's mother begged him to spare her son, he used his fists on her.

'Just remember, it's your fault entirely,' Ray said to Jackson. 'Your mother's pain is your fault.'

Chapter 16

Shopping for Love

Maya, 1996

Where does 'fault' lie when someone develops an eating disorder? Is it society's pressure? Is it vulnerability within the individual or their family? Is it a peer-related issue or a biological one? There is no 'fault' and no one factor, but a veritable stew of ingredients that assemble in a lethal, simmering combination to create the complex enigma of an eating disorder.

* * *

I finally got to visit Nora today. She has been in hospital for five months.

We meet in Ward J2, which comprises a number of bedrooms leading off a narrow corridor, a large dining room, and a meeting room. I am ushered in there. Two small windows adorn one wall of the room, from which hang some metal blinds. The walls are covered in the magnolia paint so favoured by the National Health Service. The carpets are threadbare and add to the colourless feel of the room by being a nondescript brown. Two 'compulsory to the National Health Service' Monet prints hang on the wall opposite the windows, and one of them is very crooked. I have to conquer the urge to straighten it when my eyes catch it – an old habit of my grandma's that I too have acquired. There is a rack with some out-of-date magazines, and a listless plant on the window ledge. I can't understand why her parents, with all their wealth, haven't opted for a more luxurious private suite, because this is in such contrast to their wealth.

After about five minutes, a nurse enters the room and asks me to follow her to Nora's room. My friend is in one of the end rooms, sitting on the bed, tapping her foot, and looking very restless. Nora is not expecting me; the school nurse, with the consent of Nora's family, has arranged it so that it's a surprise.

I find it impossible to describe the rush of emotions I feel when I greet my friend. We hug each other hard. She holds me tight. I am gentle, worried that I might break her.

At first, I didn't know what to say.

She too is rusty in social interaction. I go into performance mode, and start by regaling her with stories about various teachers at school.

'Miss Jenkins is on maternity leave,' I say. 'No one knows who the father is.'

Miss Jenkins is our eccentric art teacher who wears tight, short, uneven-hemmed skirts and black lipstick.

'I'm very surprised,' says Nora. 'I was so convinced that Miss Jenkins was lesbian. Maybe she and her gay lover have gone for artificial insemination.'

'Oh, Nora, don't be outrageous!' I laugh, knowing my friend's penchant for drama connected with anything sexual.

'What about Mr Thornton? Is he really having an affair with Mrs Moon?' she enquires.

'As far as I know,' I say. 'Ayesha is convinced that she saw them kissing after a school function.'

I tell her about the new friendships I've made and about how horrid I've been to Leah.

One thing I really like about Nora is how she just listens.

We talk about school for ages.

'Is the swimming pool still as cold as ever?' she asks, and I shiver theatrically when I tell her that it is even worse than before, and how Alex secretly dropped a clean tampon in it one day, to make sure the pool would be closed for cleaning and that we wouldn't have to dive into its freezing depths. Soon the awkwardness disappears, and I stop performing. We talk about pop music; she has a radio by her bed that she can listen to and is up to date with the charts. I tell her about the extension being built onto the Broadway shopping centre so that it can house a multi-screen cinema, and about the closure of one of the more popular clothes shops in the high street. She tells me about her family's reaction to her hospitalisation and her fears of what the next step of her treatment programme might be.

I take a good look at her as we talk. She still looks frighteningly thin but is less pale. Her head is now more in proportion to her body – less of the 'lollipop' that anorexic patients are accused of looking like. I notice that her arms are very hairy, and she follows my eyes and shrugs her shoulders.

'One of the side effects of low body weight,' she says casually, 'is more body hair to trap heat. If you think my arms are bad, you should see my tummy – ugh! Anyway, apparently it will all drop off when I can retain my body temperature, which is, sadly, when I gain weight. What a choice – hairy as an ape or fat as a grub.'

'Don't talk to me about hair!' I exclaim. 'I've eyebrows that look like moustaches.'

'Let's make a deal!' she exclaims enthusiastically. 'When I get out of here, let's go and get your eyebrows done, and I'll get my nose pierced.'

Nose piercing is the fashion at the moment. My grandfather says they are a hideous contribution of Asian culture.

'Why do you want a nose piercing, Nora?'

'Oh, I've been reading about the history behind the tradition, and I'd like to make a statement about being different.'

'Is there a history of significance?'

'Well, apparently nose piercing originated in the Middle East around four thousand years ago but was not popular. It gained popularity when it was brought to India in the sixteenth century. Indian women have a nose stud, usually worn in the left nostril.'

'I know that, but why the left?'

'Well, according to this article I read, this spot is associated in Indian medicine with female reproductive organs, and the special chain that joins nostril to earrings in Indian weddings symbolises fertility and sexuality. Apparently a nostril piercing is also supposed to make period pains less and childbirth easier. I'm going to get my right nostril done, though, because all the fertility stuff's useless for me.'

'Nora, you'll have to let my grandfather know about all of this. He just thinks it started with the hippies who travelled to India in the sixties.'

'Tell him he's behind on the scene, Maya. This part of Asian culture has integrated into British and world fashion. Even Janet Jackson appeared on stage with a nose-to-ear chain.'

I so love Nora. She not only makes me think, but she also makes me feel like I belong.

There is a knock on the door, and Nora is brought a milky drink and some crackers with cheese, which she has to have whilst the nurse waits. She is not permitted to go to the toilet for at least an hour after she has eaten.

'Could you please leave Nora on her own whilst she has her snack?' the nurse politely requests, but Nora says quite firmly that I should stay.

The nurse hesitates but then reluctantly agrees. I feel honoured, because I know that this is a hard thing for my friend to do. I wait awkwardly whilst she eats, not sure if I am supposed to be quiet so that she can concentrate on what she consumes, or whether I should chat to her so that the situation feels more normal. Since the nurse says nothing, I too remain silent. Nora drinks and eats slowly, chewing very slowly and methodically, and gets through the biscuits and the drink within her allocated time. The nurse locks up the toilet adjacent to Nora's room so that Nora can't get rid of any food she has consumed, leaves out a bedpan, nods to me, and goes and sits on a chair just outside the door – far enough not to eavesdrop on our conversation but keeping Nora in her sight in case she tries to get rid of what she has eaten and drunk through vomiting or exercise.

There is a short silence when she leaves, before Nora asks me casually about my exam results. I feel instantly guilty. I have been dreading this question.

How cruel that I can continue with my life when Nora's has temporarily stopped.

I modestly lower my eyes as I mumble my grades. However, her response is as warm as ever, and she bounds over to give me a hug.

'I knew you'd do well,' she says. 'You lucky thing – you've done your exams a whole year earlier than anyone else, and I'll have to do mine a year later than everyone.'

She sees the serious look on my face and smiles. 'Don't feel bad for me,' she says, reading my thoughts as usual. 'This is my way of saying I'm spread too thin.'

I give her a wry smile. How symbolic can some illnesses get? I tell her that I have to go soon, and we start to discuss her future treatment plans.

'I hate being in here,' she tells me. 'I feel they're pillaging the essence of me and there's even worse to come.'

She is following a stabilising and reorienting programme preparing her to be a day patient. She has to learn to adhere to a calorie-controlled eating plan at home and to show that she can maintain this eating plan and thereby her weight. This plan has to be maintained when she goes home, starting with the weekends only. Once she has shown she can do this, she will be sent home for longer periods of time, until final discharge. Nora tells me how she hates attending any of the programmes, because there are other girls and a few boys, all diagnosed with some form of major eating disorder, who are all either trying to recover or in recovery, and who make her feel guilty and bad about herself, particularly because she is ambivalent about her intentions. They are, of course, according to her, all thinner than herself.

I try to cheer her up, but her description of being 'pillaged' sticks in my mind. Is this really the only way forward for Nora? Does she have to have to lose herself to move on?

As I stand by Nora throughout her arduous process of recovery, I see that what is the essence of her at this time is also the essence of anorexia. It is a terrible condition that infiltrates you like a tapeworm and then houses itself within you, sucking you dry, moulding you to exist in a parasitic relationship with it until you can no longer differentiate between yourself and the illness. From what I see, anorexia is juxtaposed with steely doggedness upon you and is usually the dominator; you cannot detach yourself from it without fortitude and ambition and significant outside help.

Whilst Nora gradually follows her treatment programme, I start preparing for the final part of my education. I have decided that I would like to stay on at my school and that ultimately I would like to complete a degree in engineering. Why, I do not know, except that here am I, yet again, hoping to be in a career where I will be in a minority (at the moment, it is a male-dominated field) and where I will have to focus on facts and figures, far distanced from emotions. No one else from my school is applying for the course, but this time I don't mind standing out.

Just as I resign myself to a tedious time ahead and a year passes swiftly by, suddenly, out of the blue, something really exciting happens.

I'm afraid to write this down, because I don't want anyone to read it but, if I don't record it, I think I'll explode. I've met someone called Mark. Our meeting was so random. I was at the supermarket, shopping for some weekly groceries, and he was the man standing behind me in the queue.

How can I describe him? He is tall, just over six foot, I think, and cute. He has blond hair and green eyes. When he saw me looking at him, he smiled. I left the shop before him, but we then stood at the bus stop together, and he smiled again. Why did I smile back and say hello? I don't know, because I have never, ever done that before.

'Hi,' he says, 'I'm Mark,' and he transfers his shopping to his other hand so that he can offer his right hand to shake mine.
'I'm Maya.'
'Maya, your name suits you.'
We move away from the bus stop, and by mutual consent we start walking, and as we do, we pass a café. He hesitates for a moment before suggesting we have a coffee. I hate coffee, but how can I refuse?

I am completely comfortable with him. Words tumble out of me effortlessly when we talk. His voice is unhurried, languorous, flowing like a smooth, slow river. However, my contribution is undulated, one moment leaping in smooth arcs in the air like a dolphin as it breaks the surface every two minutes before submerging again. The warm aroma of coffee, the gurgling of the cappuccino milk frother, and the hum of the voices around us envelop us like a warm cocoon, to help incubate our interaction. I ask him about himself.

'I am a marine biologist, working mainly in Australia, but here at the moment to help set up part of a university training programme,' he says.

I am impressed but also immediately depressed, because I know that he is bound to be much older than me. Instead I tell him that his accent doesn't sound Australian. He laughs.

'Oh, I'm English, but I've lived in a variety of countries throughout my life.'

'What made you do that?' I ask, bonding immediately.

'My father was in the army, so we moved around a lot throughout my childhood,' he says, 'but unlike many of my contemporaries, I didn't go to boarding school – I stuck close to my family. We finally came home to Exeter when I was about sixteen, and then I wished I had boarded, but it was all too late, of course.'

I tell him all about my travels but not about my difficulties in settling.

His presence is intoxicating, and my whole body tingles as our eyes frequently collide. I notice how sensuous his mouth is, and I long to stroke the back of his hands with my fingertips.

'I know this is rude and not a question you should ask, but how old are you, Maya?' he asks.

'I'm nearly eighteen,' I lie, but he seems to believe me.

He gives a big sigh.

'I'm afraid that I'm much too old,' he says, and I can see that he is flirting with me, daring me to disagree.

'I like mature men,' I say, rising to the bait. 'How old are you?'

'I'm not sure if I want to tell you,' he says, keeping up the banter, 'but I can't resist a question from those shapely lips. I'm nearly thirty. Now are you ready to write me off?'

I have to admit that I am nonplussed, but quickly I reply that of course I don't want to write him off.

He laughs and keeps looking at me as he talks, genuinely admiringly. He is warm and interested and is amused by my account of my methods of study as well as my anecdotes about school, as I am taken in by his humour and his accounts of his weekly game of rugby, or when he tells me about some of his work experiences.

Emboldened by his warmth and intoxicated by the environment, the pace of flirtation increases, and I ask him if he has a girlfriend. He hesitates.

'I'm married,' he says, 'but we're separated at the moment.'

My churning gut arrests, and the pounding of my heart suspends mid-beat.

'I married Marie, my wife, three years ago,' he continues, 'but we've had difficulties in our relationship.'

I continue to say nothing, but he elaborates anyway. 'I was uncertain whether to marry her, but she was such a good friend, and I thought that life without her would be difficult. After all, I was at a crossroads. Should I end a perfectly good relationship, which was comforting and caring, for the possibility of nothing, or should I make the best of what I had? As you can see, I'm a coward. I settled for the latter option because it was easier, more comfortable, but it hasn't really turned out to be all right.'

He looks at me, full in the face, and I can see the anguish in his eyes. I don't really know what to say. It's all too grown up, too deep a pool of treacle for me to swim in, and I know that I am floundering.

'Do you love her?' I ask, and then I curse myself for asking such a trite question.

He doesn't answer me directly. Instead he says, 'I can't believe I'm talking about this, but I will. I want you to know the truth, even though we've only just met. I'm not really sexually attracted to her, and we haven't had sex for over two years. In fact, I've had the best few months I've experienced in a while recently, whilst I've been here and she's remained in Australia. Maya, I feel so bad saying this, but the sense of freedom I experience when we are apart is indescribable. I feel constant guilt about letting her down when we're together.'

I have stopped listening, although I think a part of my brain is working on its own accord, mopping up his words, searching for some comfort and hope. I try to stand up, ineffectually.

'Mark, I think I better go,' I say. 'Thank you for the coffee, the compliments, and the lovely afternoon.'

His gaze clouds over. 'Maya, I know why you want to rush off,' he says gently, 'and I don't blame you. All I can say is that I've never done this before. Please, will you stay?'

I nod and sit down again. I am trying to gather my thoughts, manoeuvre my way around what he is saying.

A part of me was crying in the corner.

He touches my hand, and weirdly a spark of static electricity ignites for a millisecond through our fingers.

'Please, Maya,' he says, 'don't be sad.'

We arrange to meet again tomorrow, in the same place, at the same table if possible. We kiss before we say goodbye. It is my first kiss: so tender and gentle, the brush of a powder puff against my lips. Do I initiate it, or does he? I think I close my eyes and tilt up my chin when he leans close to me.

I'm in love, and it's wicked.

In Suffolk

3 August 2006

It was well into the morning when PC Reeves finished examining all the evidence. He pushed back his chair and rubbed his eyes wearily. On his table were two drained cans of Red Bull and three empty mugs of black coffee. He felt jittery from the caffeine but also from his discovery. He got up from his desk, his muscles aching from having been still for such a long time. He tidied his desk and stacked the dirty mugs in the sink.

'I'll be in around about one,' he said to the officer at the front desk. ' I need to catch up with a few hours of shut-eye.'

He sleepwalked to his flat and got into bed without brushing his teeth. His rest was fitful, since he got up twice to go to the toilet.

When he got in to work later, he had a couple of discussions with his fellow officers.

'The victim was a voyeur and possibly a blackmailer,' he reported, 'small time and not connected with the bombings. He tapped the phone lines of his friends and listened to their calls. He also had little spy cameras fixed in their rooms. Looks like he was a student and he filmed his flatmates and his girlfriend mainly, and there is one tape of a lecture. I think he was obsessively possessive and this was his way of keeping tabs on the people he was close to.'

'Hey, Alan,' said one of the officers, 'that girl Maya you wanted me to get hold of, well, I've got her address. It's in London.'

'Great,' said PC Reeves. 'I know it's unorthodox, but I'm going to ask the boss if I can pay her a visit, in my own time if I have to. I know quite a bit about her. Let's see what she has to say.'

Chapter 17

Lighter than Air

Maya, 1997

The next day, with so much to say, we are both at the coffee shop half an hour earlier than we had agreed to meet. He looks so handsome in a deep-blue rugby shirt with jeans, his hair ruffled as though he has spent half an hour running his fingers desperately through it, which he later tells me he has, because of his worry that I might not turn up. It has taken me over an hour and a half to dress. I have deliberated for ages on what outfit suited me, and I have finally settled for a casual top and black jeans. I have my hair loose, since it makes me look older.

He has with him some flowers: a small bunch of pink sweet peas. I have never had anyone give me flowers before. We kiss before we say anything to each other; it feels the most natural thing in the world to do.

> *I don't care how this is going to end. I just want to enjoy the moment.*

Several months pass by, and we meet not only at the coffee shop but in the park and the cinema. I am totally intoxicated by him. One day he invites me to his home, and I walk hand in hand with him along shady avenues and past a large park covered in crops of summer flowers and new leaves, to his flat. It is small but stylish; masculine in white, grey and black; and just a little untidy.

My whole being tingles as though I have stuck my finger in a plug, and I feel very alive.

We spend ages just talking, so that when he leads me to the bedroom, it seems the most natural thing in the world. We kiss for what seems like a long time, his kisses trailing a pathway from my mouth to my eyes, my ears, my neck, and my throat. He is tender and gentle when he undresses me, lingering over each button of my top, slowly pulling down my trousers. I let him do the work. He pulls off his clothes rapidly, and I am amazed at the warmth of his body, the smoothness of his muscles, and the creamy caramel texture of his skin.

I should have been more restrained, but I didn't want to think at that moment, and I still don't.

He cries after we make love, I don't know why, but I hold him and comfort him, and he tells me how fearful he has been of being unable to perform sexually, because that's how it has been with Marie.

'Maya, you're wonderful,' he says. 'My body loves you. Look how it's responding yet again.'

I am triumphant. Even inexperienced women like me appear to be able to score in bed, and I am happy that I can provide Mark with something that Marie apparently cannot.

We are a pair – we are meant to be.

I abandon my studies in my final year at school. I keep this secret, since I know Mark and my parents will disapprove. I don't really care about how well I fare in my work anymore; being with Mark is so much more fulfilling. I move from having tried to intellectualise my emotions to wanting to emotionalise my intellect. When I sit for my final examinations, for the first time in my life, I am not sure of many of the answers. I look at the test papers and see a pink glow around them. The examiners will know I am in love; it will be infectious; they will be pleased. I have to stop myself from drawing two entwined hearts in the column, with the initials M and M.

I continue to liaise with Mark throughout my exams, and the days drift by effortlessly, quite different from my usual high-stress exam days. I sometimes catch my mother looking at me peculiarly. With a woman's instinct, I wonder if she can sense a difference in me, but since she is not confident in talking to me, she cannot bring herself to ask what might be encasing me in a glow of phosphorescence, particularly when her mood is black. Like potholes on a well-travelled road, she keeps falling into phases of depression as she tries to move on. Her current obsession is yoga, which she attends every day, and she also practises every morning for at least an hour at home. My father is pleased for her but also puzzled.

'I'm at home at lot more now,' he says, 'since my job specification changed. Yet Diane is never here to join me.'

Neither of them asks me about boyfriends. I don't complain. I certainly don't want them to know about Mark. On Mark's recommendation, I go to a family planning clinic and start on an oral contraceptive. I am amazed at the number of young girls I see in the waiting room. I meet up with Nora fairly soon after I have been to the doctor's. I haven't seen her in ages. She stares at me.

'Maya!' she exclaims 'Who is he?'

'How do you know?' I ask, surprised, and then, with little invitation, I launch into the whole story. She looks at me critically.

'Well, I hope you know what you're doing,' she says. 'He sounds cool but really old and a bit weird, and his situation is crap.'

'He's caught in a terrible trap,' I tell her. 'He's waiting for Marie to come over to tell her about us. He doesn't want it to be on the telephone, long distance. He wants to be with me, I'm sure of that.'

Nora shrugs her shoulders. 'Nothing between men and women lasts,' she says, 'because all men are traitors and all women are insecure. Rather you than me, Maya. I don't want a *relationship* at any cost.'

I say nothing. 'Are you sleeping with Mark?' she demands. I am taken aback by her directness but answer her truthfully.

'Yes, I am, Nora. Do you think that's bad?'

She doesn't appease me. 'What about your views on sexual relationships Maya?' she asks. 'How come they've changed so radically? Remember *Frigidity?*'

To be with Mark is wonderful. To be with him is to belong. I feel safe and cared for, and nothing else matters.

'I don't know,' I say truthfully. 'But Nora, please don't tell anyone.'

I continue to have my clandestine meetings with Mark, and soon it's my seventeenth birthday. My parents ask me what I want as a gift, and I just shrug. After all, I have the best birthday present: my first boyfriend. My parents accept my response. We are not a demonstrative family, and my mother has no enthusiasm for shopping for others anyway. However, they surprise me by informing me that they would like to give me a gift of a course of driving lessons.

On the morning of my birthday, I receive a birthday card from my father's parents (my first ever card from them), congratulating me on my birthday. Enclosed in it is a twenty-pound note, which my mother immediately takes offence to. I also receive a card from my aunt and uncle. In it my uncle has written, 'Here's wishing a beautiful girl the best of things to come.' *The creep,* I think violently. The card also has a little note from my aunt, stating that she is pregnant. Their first baby is due in a few months' time. My mother is convinced that the good wishes bestowed upon me from my father's family are due to this: wishes from my aunt because it is one way she can break the news without having to have any direct contact with us, since she has not been in contact with my father since her last visit; wishes from

Grandparents de Silva, because they can now afford to be gracious, since there is to be another grandchild. I receive nothing from my mother's father, since without Grandma to remind him, he no longer remembers birthdays. This upsets my mother even more. Forgetting me equals forgetting her.

The news about my aunt's pregnancy makes me feel uncomfortable, but I am too caught up with Mark to think too much about it.

Mark knows when my birthday is, and he has made special plans. When I go over to his flat in the evening, he gets me to close my eyes and takes me to his study. When he permits me to open my eyes, I can only gasp in delight. The room is filled with helium balloons, silver and gold, whilst a vase with eighteen roses stands on the table. Eighteen small presents nestle in a box – little things that he has remembered I like: a silver jewellery box, a pocket-sized dictionary, my favourite type of chocolate, a small teddy bear, a locket, and a ring are amongst them. I have tears well up in my eyes. No one has been so thoughtful to me since Grandma died. He gives me a hug. I cry also because I feel guilty, since I have received one extra gift and because he thinks I am one year older.

A lie can't be a good start to a relationship, can it?

'Happy Birthday, Maya,' he says.

We go out to a special meal that night, after we have had a champagne celebration at his home and make love in the room full of helium balloons. I have told my parents that I am going to Nora's to celebrate and that after that, I will be sleeping over at her place. She is in on the plan, of course, and willing to provide me with an alibi. We eat voraciously, both of us finding food an erotic prelude to what we know will follow. Once we finish dinner, we go back to Mark's flat and make love again. I surprise myself with the urgency I feel within me, the yearning I have for his touch and for his kisses, so I am suddenly surprised when I tense up as he touches my thighs, and I'm shocked by my startled, aversive response. Then I cannot let him touch me at all. It makes me feel uncomfortable, just as when he first cupped my breasts, I recoiled.

I love Mark, and he loves me.

I let all other feelings that don't accord with this sentiment float up to those balloons that look down upon us, so that when I finally drop off to sleep that night, I feel lighter than air.

In Suffolk

Early July 2006

The television was never turned off in the room. He stared at the shows that were aired on a particular channel listlessly all day. They were always reality shows. Big Brother *was the most on, minute-by-minute accounts of a social experiment broadcast to millions of viewers. Occasionally it would be* Survivors, *or* The Fear Factor, *or* 'I'm a Celebrity – Get Me out of Here, *but if* Big Brother *was showing, that trumped all. The interest he showed in the programmes was selective. If you asked him the names of the participants, personalities, or any individual features, you would draw a blank; they simply didn't register as distinct. What he did note were collective features: how people ate, how they slept, how they interacted, how they thought. They were TV lab rats that you could spend all day with, so that you never felt alone. You never felt without, because they were your company – illusory family and friends, non intrusive inhabitants. It was a torpid existence, but that suited, because no interaction was required. Instant intimacy was available that was never threatened or threatening.*

A while ago, voyeurism, exhibitionism, and promiscuity were considered deviant behaviour. Now they were celebrated publicly. It was so much easier to make connections today – upfront and speedy. The fact that they were virtual was even better – no shame, no pain.

No shame, no pain. The phrase orbited around his head, ran round and round and didn't budge, even when he shook his head violently. He didn't mind his carousel of thoughts; they were like reruns on TV. Thinking the same thing was comforting; he didn't need to process it; it just circulated. Just like the reality shows, it didn't matter what time you tuned in, the content was much the same. How they were packaged was inconsequential; all the shows were about one thing: a longing for connection.

He smiled. He had total possession, all by remote control. He had total control.

Jackson and Freddy

10 July 2005

Jackson first got the idea after the London bombings.

'I know how to lay my hands on cheap ingredients that make up an explosive,' he told Freddy excitedly, 'and Tony down the market has contacts who need this kind of stuff. If we can get into it, man, we are into megabucks.'

Freddy looked at Jackson. It wasn't often he saw his friend so excited. 'Tell me again. What's the idea?' he enquired.

'Well, if we can sell some of the ingredients that are needed for bomb making, we can make masses of money,' said Jackson patiently. 'Take the make-up of the bombs that went off on the seventh. They were cheap but effective.' Although they didn't kill the bastard who was supposed to die, *thought Jackson to himself.*

The answer to Jackson's determination to make money was simple: so he could rescue his mother from her situation and pay for a hit man to bump off the Bastard. That was his first thought on waking and his last thought at night.

His gaze rested momentarily on the large scar on his forearm. Against his wishes memories flooded back about the one before the last incident. It was a Friday, just before his sixteenth birthday and he had come back from school to find her sobbing by the ironing board in the kitchen.

'Mum, what's up?' he had asked, rushing up to her to give her a hug.

'I think he's having an affair,' she sobbed.

'Leave him, Mum,' encouraged Jackson. 'Let's go now.'

He ran to get her coat and some money and then stopped short when he heard the front door slam. Ray was back home early. His mouth set in a determined line, Jackson went downstairs to his mother.

'Oh, Jackson,' she said, smiling weakly, 'thank you for offering to take my coat to the cleaners. Make sure you tell them to do a good job.'

Jackson took a deep breath. 'Mum, come with me,' he said. 'Come on. Let's go together.'

Ray stood at the kitchen door with a cup of tea and a ham sandwich in hand. 'What's all this, then?' he asked, eyes darting from mother to son.

'Jackson's just taking my coat to the cleaners,' said his mother, still smiling. 'Let me warm up your dinner, Ray, Yorkshire pudding and sliced beef today.'

Jackson stood his ground. 'Come on, Mum,' he pleaded in a low voice.

'Fried onions too – your favourite, Ray,' continued his mother urgently.

Ray strode over to Jackson. 'You waste of space,' he snarled, 'I know what you're both up to. Think I'm stupid, do you?'

Jackson didn't see Ray swing his arm, giving him a powerful uppercut to his chin; he didn't feel the kicks that Ray aimed at him or the punches he threw at his body when he was on the ground. What he did feel, however, was the burning hot iron that swung in the air and landed heavily on his forearm, branding him for ever.

Chapter 18

What Goes around Comes around

Maya, 1997

My first night at Mark's house, the night of my birthday, is branded by a dream.

> *I dreamt that I was running through an empty, desolate street because I was scared. There was a cold wind, and the smell of sulphuric acid was in the air. I think I was being chased. I looked down at myself, and I saw that I was naked. Initially I was unashamed, but then the streets started to get busy, and people began to point and jeer at me. I kept running. Then in the crowd, I saw my grandmother, but she had two heads, one her own and the other my mother's. The heads looked at me and were sad. 'We have been let down by you,' they said. 'You have failed us.' I then tripped and fell down, and down, until I woke up with a cry, bathed in sweat and anxiously clutching at the bedcovers.'*

Mark is not next to me in bed. I sit up to check where he is, and I hear his voice in the next room, on the telephone. I look at my watch. It is three o'clock in the morning. Who could he be speaking to at this hour? I carefully creep out of the bed and make my way nearer to the bedroom door, so that I can hear him in the hall. His voice is very distinct from where I am standing.

'I'm looking forward to seeing you,' he says. 'What a nice surprise. Eight o'clock, did you say? Well, I'll be there.'

I know instinctively that it is Marie that he is speaking to. Who else would he speak to at three in the morning? I hear him winding down the conversation and drag myself back to bed. My feet have bound themselves to the ground, leaden with the weight of my fears. I say to myself that my dream has been a premonition. Something malevolent is around the corner, and I am going to be exposed as having no shame. Punishment has to come my way for what I have been doing. I expect no retribution.

He comes back into the room and knows from my face that I am aware of the situation. He moves over to put his arms around me, but I shrug them off; I cannot bear to be touched just at the moment.

'That was Marie, sweetheart,' he says unnecessarily and a little too loudly. 'She has decided to pay a surprise visit. She arrives at the end of the week.'

He looks upset, worried, puzzled: a mixture of emotions. He doesn't respond in the right way for me. He stays distant and awkward and doesn't rush to console me or to say the words I want to hear him say.

I need to know that he loves me and that he wants to be with me. That if I'm patient, he will tell her all about us once he sees her, and from then on, we'll be together.

He says nothing. The mood between us is broken. The ghost of the past and the ghost of the present are with us and send their icy fingers down my spine and poke their long fingernails through my heart.

I say to him, 'I'd better clear out any stuff that I may have left.'

He nods miserably, nonverbally negating his comment about there being no hurry. Then he looks at me and then looks away. 'I'm sorry,' he mutters inaudibly.

'What are you sorry about?' I retort. 'You didn't know she was going to visit so soon?' I hesitated before saying, 'Or did you?'

He shakes his head. 'I'm sorry the timing is so bad. I wanted your birthday to be special.'

'It has been!' I exclaim vehemently. 'It has been.'

I get up and go to the kitchen to make myself some coffee. For someone who hates the stuff, I am not doing too badly. I wander over to the drinks cabinet and pour some brandy into it. I gulp it fast when it's lukewarm and shiver as the brandy batters my chest and stomach. It's about five o'clock in the morning.

I collect my clothes, my presents, all of those eighteen wonderful gifts, and leave at six. Neither of us has slept for the past three hours. I am exhausted and light-headed, and when I close the front door behind me, I feel like I am the skin of an orange, peeling myself off my centre, leaving juicy segments behind, taking thin peel away.

'Maya.' He is plaintive as he opens the door. He calls down the road as I leave, 'I'll contact you once I know what Marie's plans are.'

'Of course,' I utter, and then to myself I say forlornly, 'I hope you will.' I start walking back home.

Now I know what 'stabbing pain' means.

'Maya?' he calls out again and I turn, hopeful that he is going to tell me what I want to hear, finally. 'Do you know of anyone who may want these balloons?'

I take one with me as I walk down the street, tears streaming down my face, but not before I tell him acidly that his good wishes to me can be recycled as a welcome-home present for her. I can see from his eyes as I say it that the idea had not crossed his mind, but that he is not averse to it.

I seek the solace I am thirsty for in Nora. She is awake at six o'clock in the morning and answers my call promptly. She invites me over straight away, and when I arrive, she is at her front door to usher me into her room. At a time like this, I need Nora, a creature of order, rules, and method – someone to whom dogged persistence is a way of life.

Her room is monastic in its simplicity. Gone are some of her indulgences: no more videos, very few current CDs and books. The walls are bare but for a cross hanging by the side of her bed and a new painting.

*   *   *

I am interrupted by the telephone that I have forgotten to turn off. However, I am for once pleased to answer its strident command, because I only realise now that Nora's room change also depicted a change in her after treatment. Not only was she more controlled, but that new painting disturbed me for a long time, although I never spoke to her about it. The painting was of a rounded woman serving a strange platter of two breasts presented with a feather between them. I play around on the Internet to find out more, based on remembering the name of the artist, Cariani. I find that it is of St Agatha, who was made a third-century Sicilian saint because she rejected the love of a Roman governor and was therefore thrown into a brothel, where she endured various forms of torture, including the removal of her breasts. Her endurance of pain and her compliant offer of her body bestowed upon her the status of a saint. Was Nora's femininity up for offer on a plate too?

I am unsettled by this image and decide to immerse myself in going back to that time.

*   *   *

Nora laughs when she sees my eyes focus on the cross.

'I've put that there for effect,' she says casually. 'My family think I'm a loony, and that's there to frighten them even more. It makes them leave me well alone.'

I cannot help but smile at her rebellion, even though my facial muscles are tense and hard. The brandy churns in my gut and makes my head feel like a paper doily. Nora chuckles as she opens a drawer to show me a large bible.

'I got this when we were last at a hotel,' she says, a wicked glint in her eye. 'I put that out with some bookmarked pages when they get too nosey and start checking. It works better than garlic for the devil. They leave me and my room well alone.'

I am impressed with her struggle back from the jaws of death, and by her sheer determination to survive in the way she wants to, and to not give in to either internal need or external pressure.

> *Nora made me sit on her bed whilst she told me off. Her bed is so solid – an extra hard mattress with a plank of wood under it. I am reminded of a bed of nails, for this is surely what anorexia is, an amazing feat of mind over body to endure starvation, discomfort, and pain, and to paradoxically convert it into something noble and self-effacing.*

She pulls up a chair to sit opposite me.

'His wife has come back,' she states matter-of-factly. 'Or is on her way back?'

I nod, miserably.

'Well, you knew she was in the background – he never denied it. Why are you so upset?'

My voice is a croak. 'I didn't expect her to be here so soon.'

'What does it matter when she arrives? The fact is, she would have arrived at some time, and now that she has, he can tell her and get it over and done with. It's so much better for you.'

My voice rises to a wail. 'He didn't tell me that he would tell her. Nora, he didn't reassure me. He just sat there and said nothing. Nothing about how we will be together soon.'

For someone who has never been in a relationship and doesn't want to be in one, Nora is wise. 'He's probably in shock and can't verbalise it,' she says. 'Let him figure it out. Don't push him.'

'What should I do in the meantime?' I ask her piteously, pathetically.

'Why don't you try to get some sleep?' she suggests. 'Then let's go for a walk by the river this afternoon. I have to go to the hospital for a while today. We can meet after that and talk more.'

I realise that over the past few months, I have been so wrapped up with Mark that I haven't checked on how she's been doing. Maybe I've also wanted to avoid the weight I've felt every time I've seen her. I ask her how she is faring, and she shrugs.

'So, so,' she says. 'I'm eating because I don't want to repeatedly end up on that medical ward with tubes down my nose, but I know I won't ever be able to relate to food the way they want me to, and I hate my body, especially now that it looks grub-like and fat. Look at the rolls on my stomach – and the dimples on my thighs – ugh!'

There is no point in contradicting her, although her stomach is concave and her legs sticklike, because all this will do is cause an aggressive denial. In addition, she will feel let down that I have even noticed her anatomy. So instead, I show her the gifts that Mark has given me. She is unimpressed.

'Why so many, and why such small things?' she asks.

I shrug my shoulders, unconsciously aping her manner. 'Guilty conscience, maybe?' I venture, not wanting to spoil what I have held so precious, and yet wanting to lash out at Mark for betraying me.

We talk a little more over two double espresso coffees. I am grateful for mine, because the alcohol is still having some effect on me. I note that she has hers extra strong, almost treacle-like in its consistency. When I ask her why, she shrugs.

'I like it,' she says evasively.

* * *

The current me stretches as I hobble around the room to get rid of a cramp in my leg from sitting awkwardly. I now know why Nora imbibed such strong coffee, since I have read that this is often a trick in anorexia. The caffeine is a stimulant, and in such a strong dose, not only does it provide energy that is lacking from food, but it also helps one to feel less hungry and substitutes for a meal. I shake my head. I was so blind and self-absorbed then. Would it have made a difference if I'd known? Perhaps I could have kept a better eye on her? I know that when she was told to cut down on her caffeine, she really suffered; I would have liked to have prevented her some of the pain of withdrawal.

* * *

When I am finally ready to leave, Nora gives me an awkward hug as I head towards the door. Physical contact doesn't come easily to her, but I am beyond observing. Something in me has shut down. I walk back home, still holding my balloon, now somewhat deflated. I leave some of the gifts at Nora's house, to be collected later. Parting with them is not easy, but I don't want to arouse any suspicion in my mother.

When I get back, I find Mummy rushing around, spring cleaning the house, vacuum cleaner in one hand, a duster in the other.

'Morning, Maya,' she trills. 'I've been cleaning the house from seven this morning after my yoga practice, so you're not to make a mess.'

This is an unnecessary comment, and it annoys me, but I stay quiet. She continues, 'I'm going to sort out all our old photographs today and clean out my wardrobes. I may also tackle the kitchen cupboards if I have time.'

She whirls like a dervish around the house. If she has this much energy after yoga, which is supposed to be calming, what will she be like without? When I was little, I used to call her yoga mat an 'ogre mat' – although it was a mispronunciation maybe there was something in it? I do not trust myself to speak without my voice breaking, so I just nod. As I turn to make my way upstairs, she addresses me again.

'Did you have an enjoyable evening?' she asks, and for a moment, forgetting the lies I have told her, I stare at her in panic, until I remember that I am supposed to have had an evening celebrating my birthday with Nora.

'Yes, it was very, er, enjoyable,' I reply.

'Rather childish, the balloon isn't it?' she asks as she heads upstairs, duster and furniture polish in the ready for action.

I take a shower and then sit in my bedroom, sorting through the little love notes and the letters that Mark has written to me. They are so passionate, and they sound so genuine. Perhaps Nora is right, and I am overreacting. I will believe him and let him sort out things with Marie first, before demonising him.

Cheered and suddenly ravenous, I wander down to the kitchen for some tea and toast. I read the newspaper aimlessly. My mother comes in and, unusually for her, reminds me that my examination results will be out next week. I have not even thought about them, but I keep up my silent vigil and nod in acknowledgement.

My mother goes upstairs again, and then she comes back into the kitchen within half an hour. 'I've sorted out some of the photographs, but it's getting a little boring,' she says. 'I'm going out.' She has put on some make-up, and her hair is tied back. She collects her handbag and goes out shopping. What is it that makes people consume, no matter the substance, when they are unhappy? Have we lost our self-sufficiency? I wonder for a brief moment if I should join her. Being with Mark has awakened in me an interest in clothes that had died with my grandmother. I change my mind and wait, in case Mark does what he never has and rings me at home. I daydream about him and his response when he next sees me – how he will declare undying love and we will be together forever.

I wonder how my parents will react to Mark. I think Mummy will like his blondness and his good looks, but what will she say about his age?

I leave at three o'clock in the afternoon to meet up with Nora. We walk along the river, past moored houseboats with predictable names like *King of the Waves* and *Poseidon*, some of their decks and windows made appealing with window boxes full of flowers and plants. Some well-fed ducks and moorhens bob along the water, and a myriad of people sit on the benches along the river, reading or talking to one another whilst others wander the banks with their young children, who throw large chunks of bread to the ducks, adding more debris to what is already floating there. There is only a mild wind, but Nora has on a number of layers of clothes, and a scarf that covers most of her face. She says that her hands are freezing, even though she sticks her hands in her pockets. I suggest going into some tea rooms nearby to cultivate my newly found vice of coffee drinking and to help her warm up. She insists we walk more first. She can make no allowance for what she sees as proposed inactivity and indulgence, unless she feels she has worked for it.

'Has Mark rung yet?' she enquires, even though she already knows the answer. She is our go-between, the person with the mobile telephone he will call to convey a message to me.

'No, he hasn't,' I reply, equally unnecessarily. 'Not yet, anyway.'

Unusually, Nora talked about her eating today.

'I feel sick after I eat, Maya,' she tells me.
'Why, Nora?' I ask.
'I don't know – it just comes up. I must be eating too much.'
I dredge up my newly acquired knowledge of eating disorders. 'You haven't been making yourself throw up, have you, Nora? I read

somewhere that if you throw up often enough; the food comes up on its own accord because of the damage you inflict.'

There is a pause.

'I just can't bear looking the way I do now. I just can't," she says. 'Yet, I have to keep to this stupid eating programme and continue to be weighed. They make me go to the toilet every time I am weighed, you know, and they take urine and blood tests to make sure that I don't water-load. Throwing up makes me feel a little more at ease.'

I remember the time I tried to throw up the biscuits I ate at my grandmother's house the day after she died. How much better it would have made me feel to get rid of something I felt so guilty about consuming.

'Nora, it'll cause a great deal more harm,' I say.

'Who cares?' she retorts. 'There's too much damage done now anyway.'

She tells me about a trip to Germany that she will be making soon. She's very excited about it.

'Father has a conference in Frankfurt, and he's suggested that I might like to come and spend some time with him, taking it easy whilst he presents his papers and attends the various symposiums,' she says. 'I'm so nervous. We've never done anything like it.'

They are following a suggestion made by the family therapist at the hospital, who has proposed developing some quality time between father and daughter.

I would love to spend some time with Daddy, but I'm no longer his little girl, although he still is the three kings rolled into one to me.

We have finally walked a distance that is to Nora's satisfaction, and she permits me to drag her into some tea rooms, where she orders some strong, black tea whilst I have a milky one. I notice that they now serve chai, tea laced with cinnamon and cardamom and sugar. So much for me being shy about eating curry at school, when not only do traditional tea rooms serve chai, but supermarkets now even sell tandoori chicken pizza and curried ketchup. Nora doesn't eat anything, and since I feel awkward munching in front of her on my own, I refrain from ordering the slice of lemon cake that sits tantalisingly in the display cabinet in the counter.

She tells me about her academic progress. Nora never returned to our school after her first hospitalisation. She felt too much loss of face, and so she started at another school.

'I'm struggling but determined to do my best,' she says.

I tell her that I have stopped caring about my academic achievements. A look of disbelief crosses her face, and she grabs me by the shoulders and shakes me.

'Maya,' she says, 'no one is worth giving up your studies and your future for. Mark may be great, but Maya, you're greater. You're the brightest girl I know. Please promise me that you won't waste all your hard work and brilliance.'

My results arrive in the post a few days later. I haven't wanted to pick them up from school. I open the envelope warily and then stare in disbelief at the printed page. The results are a bombshell. My grades are mediocre, not even meeting up to the criteria of my conditional acceptances to the universities of my choice and well below my predicted grades. Contrary to what I have said to Nora, whilst I have been upset, even devastated by my experiences in my relationship with Mark, there is no comparison to what I feel now.

There is nothing special about me anymore.

I stare at the sheet of paper for a long time. I know that I want to react in some sort of violent way, but I can't express any emotion. Something within me has frozen completely.

My parents are shocked, my father in particular. He asks me if we should get the results checked. Surely there must be a mistake. I shake my head. I know there's no error. There, on paper, is confirmation of my preoccupation with Mark. The examiners were not taken in by the rosy glow of my love. The disappointment in my father's eyes is visible, but he blames himself. I hear him talking to my mother that night.

'We shouldn't have let the school talk us into letting Maya take her examinations a year early,' he says. 'It obviously didn't leave her with sufficient preparation time.'

I don't hear my mother's answer; perhaps she doesn't answer him, in the same way that I ignore people when I disagree with their view.

'I'll talk to the school tomorrow,' he says, 'and I hope that they'll offer Maya the support she needs to re-sit her exams.'

* * *

Reading this chapter of my life makes me realise why I always set myself such impossibly high standards. That feeling of failure was crushing and is something I never want to feel again. The only part of me that I have accepted and been proud of has been my ability to apply myself to academic work. To lose this part was devastating. I felt I had lost the best bit of me.

* * *

My misery over my results is amplified by my preoccupation with the absence of Mark.

Mark still hasn't called.

I decide to start reading again, and as I look at my bookshelf, my copy of *Anna Karenina* catches my eye. I take it off the shelf, and out of its pages fall the sweet peas that Mark gave me on that first day we met. I had forgotten that I had pressed them. The flowers are brown and translucent, the smell off-putting as the plant cells decompose. I sit down and write a poem.

The Flower

*I am like the flower you hold in
Your hand, my friend,
just blossomed from its bud.
It's pure, white, and lovely,
But –*

*It has only a few more hours to live,
To keep its beauty before it dies,
All curled up and withered,
unrecognisable to all eyes.*

*Then,
Who will remember how soft*

*the petals were?
Who will remember it's very
special fragrance?
Who will remember how innocent
It looked?
Who will remember?*

*My life is like that flower
My friend,
At the peak of its bloom.
But soon, I too will wither or die.
Life ends so soon!*

Then,
Who will remember who I was?
Who will remember
My life?
Who will remember my
Joys and woes?
Who will remember?

My mother knocks on my door. Nora is on the line. I shove the poem under my pillow as I hurry to take it. Mark has called Nora to say that he will meet me at the coffee shop tomorrow. Hurray!

I go back to my room and take the poem out from under the pillow and slip it into my poem folder. It no longer carries the same significance. In fact, how self-pitying it sounds.

I'm suddenly ravenous and go to the kitchen to make myself a sandwich. My father is downstairs, cleaning the oven. He's surrounded by various cans of cleaner, and his hands are smeared with grease and soapy bubbles.

'Maya, I'm pleased you've come down,' he says enthusiastically. He is sorry I had to see the disappointment in his eyes over my results.

'I'm starving, Daddy. I need a sandwich,' I say, and I potter around getting together some wedges of cheese and bread.

'Well, I'm pleased to hear that,' he says. 'We miss you at the dinner table these days.'

I do something I haven't done in a while: I go up to him and put my arms around him. 'I'm fine now, Daddy. Really, I'm fine.'

He kisses the top of my head, something that he hasn't done since I was six or seven years old. I stay close to him and feel his comfort and strength. My mother comes into the kitchen and looks at us strangely.

Mummy isn't a very cuddly person.

I now know how it is to yearn to be close to the person you love, to let your eyes lock discreetly in the company of others, to let the tips of your toes touch in bed, to let his warm breath fan your face as you sleep. I can't wait to see him again tomorrow. I know all will be well in my world after that.

In Suffolk

4 August 2006

The current case was making PC Reeves or Jack Reeves reflect on various matters he hadn't thought of for a while. All was well in Jack's world until just over two years ago. Up to then, deducting the time he had spent away when training, Jack lived at home with his parents. He loved them both but adored his mother. She was kind and caring and had always been fair to his sister and himself. A social sciences teacher, she became a full-time mother after Jack's birth. Jack's parents had a loving and caring relationship and bestowed upon both of their children a good sense of value about themselves and the significance of relationships. John Reeves was also in the police force and was well respected by his colleagues. He was Jack's role model in many ways.

I wish my parents had met Susannah thought Jack. He knew that his mother would have loved her and her choice of films, just as much as Susannah would have loved his mother's cooking and baking. His father, on the other hand, would have appreciated her feisty spirit.

The tragedy happened just over a couple of years ago, when his father died in his sleep of a heart attack. The irony was that he had never had any major illnesses in his life, and his records at his doctor's comprised half a sheet of notes. His mother had pined so much that six months later, she too was gone. The old fashioned saying,' died of a broken heart' only made her further elevated in Jack's estimation. As a consequence, neither parent saw Jack graduate from Hendon Police College, but Jack knew they were there in spirit. They were always there with him in his thoughts, just as they had always been there to share in his ups and downs when they were living. He just wished they'd had a little longer together, so that they could be part of his life now.

Jack looked around his office at work; it was a little different from his father's but still decent. He stared out of the window at the summer flowers and remembered how his mother loved this time of year although she also loved autumn when she would go and jump on the crisp brown leaves with him. I wish, *thought Jack,* death hadn't been so greedy in its haste to exclude my parents from me.

Chapter 19

Pink Elephants and Bearded Goats

Maya, 1997

> *Today is one of those bright and clear days. The morning sky is cobalt blue, and birds, lulled into a sense of security about good weather ahead, are awake early, composing their shrill melodies. The trees are clad in their clothes of green and ochre; reminding me of the changing colour of Mark's eyes. The trees have haemorrhaged dried blooms on the road in the night, their spill now being mopped up by a lone and diligent road sweeper.*

Since I experienced my first major panic attack, I've become somewhat superstitious. I've started having my own little predictors of good and bad luck. I'm ashamed to admit how trivial some of them are. For example, if the towel in the bathroom had fallen on the floor in the morning, it means it will be a bad day, just as if the top letter in the daily post is face down instead of face up. I use no scientific theory of predictability for this. They are random generations of a fearful mind. I decide that the sighting of a lone sweeper predicts good luck. He is sweeping away the past and making way for a new future.

I take hours getting dressed. I know that Mark likes me in black; my mother doesn't. Strangely enough, neither did Grandma. As always, just the thought of her makes me feel sad, but at the moment, my emotions are still on super-freeze, and so the sadness is cerebral, a fleeting thought that I miss her. I own very few black outfits, but I rummage for my one pair of black jeans and a lilac top. I spray myself liberally with the perfume that Mark gave me (one of the eighteen gifts) and then decide that it might make my mother, who is at home, too suspicious, and I end up having a shower and starting all over. I wear the thin silver chain with the locket he gave me too, with no photographs in it yet, tweak my hair this way and that, and check that I have worn my matching black underwear.

The birds sing even more raucously as I depart. I decide to take in a deep breath of fresh air, and I end up coughing and spluttering instead when a motorcycle zooms past me, injecting a dose of carbon monoxide into the already polluted air. I have managed to avoid seeing my mother, saying goodbye when I know that she is having her morning shower after her morning's 'ogre' practice. I have told her that I am going to school to discuss options, which I do hope to do later in the day, after Mark.

'After Mark,' I whisper to myself.

I skip to the coffee shop. I am about half an hour early, so I go into the newsagent next door to buy myself a magazine. I do not want to look like I am loitering with intent.

The shop says, 'Patel's Newsagents', and Mr Patel or his son is behind the counter. It is a typical little corner store that smells of a mixture of mothballs, incense sticks, and cough sweets. It is packed full of goods. Displayed on one shelf are the traditional bar upon bar of chocolates and sweets, whilst on another shelf there are biscuits, some packets looking distinctly past their sell-by date but are not, just shopworn and tired from having been thumbed by various schoolchildren, who all end up buying individual sweets from the 'Pick and Mix' bottles instead. There is a shelf of mixed stationery, string, Blue Tac, scissors, and envelopes on which stands a sign saying, 'I sell stamps here' and another stating 'Brighten up someone's day, send them a letter.' A counter is weighed down on one end by a variety of magazines, whilst on the other are some basic groceries, coffee, tea, sugar, bottles of Marmite, and tins of Golden Syrup. There are condoms on the back wall, next to scratch cards and lottery slips.

The irony is not lost on me: all chance items together. There are old-fashioned greeting cards with sickly sweet messages, and bookmarks with verses of equally vomit-inducing sentiment. There are flea collars and rubber bones for dogs stacked together with garish gold and silver bracelets for kids. The variety is huge, a veritable Ali Baba's cave. Asian underground music or bhangra, popular at the moment, plays in the background.

I browse through the magazines and pick up a packet of extra-strong mints, still dawdling, when the man behind the counter decides to chat to me. He first says something in Punjabi or Gujarati, and I shake my head, indicating that I don't understand. He smiles and switches to English.

'What's a pretty girl like you doing around here?' he asks. He must be Mr Patel's son, since he looks young on close inspection. I tell him that I am waiting to meet a friend, wanting him to ask me if it is a boyfriend so that I can reply affirmatively. I want to shout, 'I'm waiting to meet my lover, my friend, my boyfriend', but of course I don't. He looks at me and surprises me with his next question.

'How old are you?' he asks.

I decide to flirt, because he makes me feel uncomfortable. 'That's not a question you should ask a woman, is it?' I say, fluttering my eyelids at him. 'Why do you want to know, anyway?'

He looks at me seriously. 'I have a sister who looks like you,' he says. 'Not as attractive as you, but she looks about your age. She's nearly sixteen. Are you bunking off school?'

'Of course not!' I exclaim, adding for good measure, 'I've just finished my A levels.'

He shrugs, not in the least perturbed. 'Sorry,' he says, a twinkle in his eye. 'Well, have a good day, young-looking one, and come and buy more things from my shop any time.'

Some of the air from my happy balloon escapes. The implication that I am underage makes what I am doing appear seedy. I shiver as I get in touch with the same uneasy feelings I did after my encounter with my uncle. I hurriedly buy two magazines and some sweets and leave the shop.

I enter the coffee shop five minutes before the meeting time and scan the people sitting at the tables. No Mark yet. The café isn't particularly busy, but I scan it again just to make sure that I have not missed him. I can feel the start of butterflies in my stomach, a tensing of my chest muscles, and a light coat of perspiration on my brow.

Breathe in and out, I command myself: *slow count in for six, hold, slow count out for eight.* I practise a few times; until I can feel my heart gradually slow down. I go up to the counter, order a hot chocolate, and sit down with my magazine. I try to look unconcerned as I flick through the pages. I scan articles titled 'Life after a baby' and 'Making the most of a small kitchen.' I realise that during my uncomfortable interaction with the young Mr Patel, I have 'accidentally' picked up a magazine my mother would have picked.

I look at my watch and then scan the clock on the wall. Five minutes past. Mark is normally never late. I have a moment's anxiety. I hope this is the coffee shop he wanted to meet in. I try to quell my anxiety by studying the black and white photographs on the wall of famous cities and their landmark buildings. Next to them are some famous quotations, each one handwritten and then framed. My eyes rest on one that says, 'If you want to know the value of money, try and borrow some. – Benjamin Franklin' and on another, 'All you need in this life is ignorance and confidence, and then success is sure. – Mark Twain.' The coffee machine bubbles in the background, whilst one of the baristas behind the counter vigorously grinds some coffee beans – the fresh aroma enveloping my senses.

My eyes stray to the clock again. Ten minutes past, and I am now getting very edgy. Is he not going to turn up after all? Then suddenly the sun shines and the room is bright. I see his familiar figure push open the door, and his face looks around worriedly and then breaks into a smile as he sees me.

I try to act cool and smile back, but I have to fight the urge to get up off my seat and rush up to him so that I can fling my arms around him. He comes up slowly towards my table. The coffee grinder is applause in the background, the milk frother the happy gurgling of my heart.

'Why, hi there,' he drawls. 'Sorry I'm late.'

'Hi there to you too,' I say. He comes up to me, hesitates slightly before he gives me a light peck on the cheek, and then sits down.

He looks tired. There are fine lines around his eyes, or is it that I have just not noticed them before? He doesn't kiss me, but I gulp in his features with my eyes, draw in deep breaths of his smell.

'Would you like something to drink?' he asks, and then sees my full cup. 'No? Well, excuse me whilst I get something.'

I watch him as he walks over to the counter. I note that his hair is just that little bit too long and that this makes it curl up around his collar. He is wearing one of my favourite shirts, and I hear the low timbre of his voice as he orders himself a coffee.

He is back with me soon, and I keep looking at him, studying every detail of him, as intently as I would memorise my work in the school library.

'What news of your results, then?' he asks.

I shrug. The pain of failure seems to have a way of melting my frozen emotional state as quickly as the application of a blow torch to snow. I wince as I say that they are not good. He is too kind to ask me for a breakdown of the grades. Instead, he takes my hand and squeezes it.

'Never mind,' he says consolingly, 'you can always retake. I repeated mine.' That reassures me immensely.

I ask him how his time has been with Marie. He's hesitant. 'Let's catch up first,' he says.

I can't fathom whether this is a good sign or bad, and I clam up instantly. It doesn't seem to matter, since he fills the space. After ten minutes, I can't bear it any longer and repeat my question, but phrased differently. How has Marie been since her arrival in the UK?

He sighs. 'I don't know how to say this,' he begins, and my heart starts a drum roll. 'I have broached the subject of the two of us.'

My heart lifts again. If he has broached the subject of the two of us, then things are looking up. I then realise that the 'two of us' that he is referring to is the two of *them*. The drum roll erupts again. His voice breaks.

'I'm sorry, Maya, my lovely Maya, but I just can't completely end with her. She wants us to try to give our relationship one more chance.'

As I listen, a well-worn little assumption about me immediately comes into play. 'I don't belong,' it says. 'No one wants me.' How could I have been so presumptuous to believe that this experience would be any different from anything else in my life?

He picks up one of my lifeless hands and gently rubs it. 'Maya, I truly am sorry,' he tells me earnestly. 'I just never thought that Marie would want to give it another go. It's been over for me for at least a year, and the last few months with you, well, they've been the happiest ever. I've felt so free, but Maya, I've got to give my relationship one more chance if I'm going to stop feeling guilty about it.'

I nod, I can't trust myself to speak. He continues, speaking almost to himself. 'I can't explain how not being able to respond to her has made me feel, and when Marie suggested we go to some marriage counselling, something she's never done before, I had to agree.'

Through the haze of filtering in the implications of what he has just told me, and using the coldness within me, I reply sarcastically that of course, he must think of himself and his marriage, it is only right in a situation like this. I wish him all the best and then excuse myself. I have important things to do, like going to school to discuss my future. I even shake his hand before I leave, and as I exit, I can feel the ice that is within me crack, piercing shards of icicles through my heart.

Contrary to what I hope for, he doesn't try to stop me from leaving or follow me. I start walking, blindly but speedily. I want to put as much distance as I can between my unrealistic hopes and sense of defeat.

I walk for ages. I pass neighbourhoods I know, and then I walk in territory that is completely unfamiliar. I trudge past rows of townhouses, closely set together like teeth in a crowded jaw, and then I get to more run-down, spread-out terrain, on which large tower blocks loom, spaced out, like prehistoric monsters. The pavements have not been cleaned, and a piece of stray chewing gum lodges itself on the sole of my right shoe, which I continue to stickily walk on. London's never-ending traffic passes me by, but by this time, it is thinning out, like the hair of the balding man in front of me. I pass small shops selling hardware, plastic goods, another Patel's newsagents, a run-down Indian restaurant with an equally run-down Chinese takeaway next to it vying for trade, and a small petrol shed, the side of which is stacked with hundreds of old, disused rubber tyres.

It doesn't really matter where I am; I am disconnected with what is happening outside of me. I feel as if I have taken in a whole load of gas and air, which is neither pleasant nor unpleasant. I come to a vast building site, and I find myself looking up at the great iron structure, foundations around which another ugly building will soon emerge, and wonder what it would feel like to be at the top. Would it be high enough to jump from, and what would the descent feel like to a wingless Icarus like me? I am calm and cut off when I contemplate this; there is no long-term thinking that accompanies it, no one else's perspective but mine.

My numbed senses decide that all this thinking is tiring and that I need to rest – but where? So I walk on aimlessly, dragging my feet, until I come to a pub. It is garishly painted, with bright green outer walls and yellow roof tiles. It is named, rather ridiculously, as is the vogue for many pubs, 'One Pink Elephant in a Tutu.'

* * *

The current me grins wryly.

I remember a project we did at school, when I was about nine years old, about local buildings of interest and about how public houses had been given their names in the past. We learnt that behind every traditional pub name was a story based on its history or geographical area. So 'The Dog and Fox' or 'The Bald face Stag' referred to hunting that may have been carried out in the area; 'The Castle' was so named because of the proximity of a castle in the area; 'The Brewery Tap' was because of an association with a local brewery; 'The Lion', 'The Sun', 'The Swan', and like were associated with various heraldic symbols of rulers, and names like Lord Palmerston, King Edward, Henry the V, and others obviously referred to individuals of importance at the time.

So what about the Pink Elephant? I think it typifies the perils of losing an identity through change – just like me?

* * *

It is lunchtime, and the pub is busy. I go up to the counter and order myself a drink and look around for somewhere to sit. Although I have never done this before, it all flows very smoothly. There doesn't seem to be a chair available, but I find a comfortable spot against the bar, which props me up quite nicely. I then order a drink and then another when the person behind the bar doesn't ask me for any identity. In half an hour I drink four glasses of wine and leave the pub rather unsteadily. I have eaten nothing today, but the wine leaves a warm glow in my belly. I can understand why my mother is so attached to it; after all, mothers know best, don't they?

I keep walking. I think I'm heading back in a homeward direction, because the scenery looks familiar: more tall, grey buildings, more rubbish on the streets. There is the same air of desolate abandonment, of people who are too tired to maintain their environment, the burden of life weighing too heavily down on them to think of spending any extra energy on aesthetics. It is starting to drizzle slightly – spit down, we used to say as schoolchildren, as though the sky gets something out of mocking and deriding us. It certainly has cause to mock me now. I, who have been so foolish as to hope.

I see another pub. This one is more traditionally painted in maroon and gold, but with yet another silly name, 'The Pickled and Bearded Goat.' I decide that I should go in there to avoid being insulted by the rain. Somewhere in the recesses of my memory, I also conclude that I need to relax. I think that has been the intention of this journey. I go in with confidence and order and drink two whiskies. They go down quickly, particularly for someone who has not even smelled the stuff before. I am amazed that again, no one challenges my age. I hate the taste of the whisky, but I like the after-effects. I drift off on a small, white cloud of my own. What bliss! Why has this secret been kept from me all this time? I no longer need to sit; I can just float. Is this what is meant by levitation?

A man in the bar tries to chat me up. I can hardly focus on him, and his attention does not scare me. I tell him that I am otherwise engaged at the moment but politely thank him for his attention – several times, just in case he misunderstands. There is no need to lose one's manners just because one is drunk, is there? I obviously handle it well because he buys me another drink.

After about three quarters of an hour, I sadly say goodbye to the Pickled and Bearded Goat, since I've only a few pounds left on me. I leave the premises, admiring the ornate gold sign with a picture of a goat in the front. The goat looks rather like me in the picture, bewildered and lost, and so I go back in to compliment the barman on the aptness of his pub sign, ignoring the expression on his face as I weave my way out again. Leaving seems much harder the second time around, but I don't mind.

Once outside, I try to stop a taxi that passes by, but he shakes his head when my fumes collide with his face. I find this hugely amusing and stand on the pavement laughing for quite a while whilst watching the back of the cab disappear into the distance.

I spot a bus stop and stagger to it and sit on one of the seats. It takes me a while to figure out how to sit on the seat, since it has a frightfully clever spring mechanism, which makes it lift up every time I lower myself onto it. I finally manage to make it work, and I am terribly pleased with myself.

It's not a very busy time of day for buses on that route, and there is no one else at the stop. What a shame, since I could have helped them with working out the seating technique. I'm serene and pleased with myself. I look at the bus timetable, but it's all a bit too complicated for me to figure out, and the letters are blurry – wet in the rain, I suppose. I guess that if I get in a bus with the driver with the friendliest face, I'll be safe.

When the next bus stops, I get in. I can't really decipher if the bus driver's face is friendly or not, since it floats in and out of focus. How clever! I should find out how that's done.

'Where to?' she asks impatiently. It's a woman bus driver. I don't know, but I reply, rather grandly, 'the end of the line, please.'

I've heard this line being used in the movies, so it must be right. It takes me a while to count out the coins for payment, and in the end I just hold out my hand, and she helps herself to the right amount.

The bus starts off with a jerk, and I'm just able to sit on a seat before I fall on the floor. I fumble around for my seat belt and am very confused when I can't find it. I wonder if I should draw the bus driver's attention to the absence of this, but I am distracted by what seems to be some graffiti on the seat in front. I think it says, 'If you can read this, you are too close, if you like to get even closer, call me.' A telephone number is also written. I squint to read the number, but I find my eyelids closing on me instead, and I fall asleep.

I wake up when the bus comes to a juddering stop. 'End of the line,' calls the bus driver.

I find that I can focus a little better, but my head hurts and my mouth tastes awful. My tongue feels heavy as I try to speak.

'Where are we?' I finally ask. When the driver tells me, I can't believe it. I'm miles from home. I burst into tears. The driver, thankfully, is sympathetic.

'What are you doing drinking, a kid like you?' she asks, 'I knew it when you got on the bus, and although I'd usually refuse, I thought you'd be safer in here than out there until you sobered up. You girls are all the same. I've a daughter about your age – smokes like a chimney, and not just tobacco at that, mind, and hangs around with a whole load of good-for-nothing folk. Now, where do you want to go to?'

I tell her, and she shakes her head unbelievingly. 'You're miles away,' she says. 'Tell you what, you can use that call box over there by the depot to call your folk and get them to pick you up. It's probably the easiest thing to do in your state. Here, I'll come with you.'

I gratefully go with her to the call box and dial Nora's number. 'Can you come and pick me up?' I whisper, trying not to move my head. 'I need you to come and pick me up now.'

Nora's voice is sharp. 'Maya, where are you? What's happened?'

I rapidly pass the telephone to the bus driver. I hear her giving Nora details of the location as I rush to throw up in the bushes. I vomit until my body feels empty, a poor, and beaten rag. The bus driver wanders up with some tissues and some water. 'See what happens when you drink?' she says. She has become an unlikely guardian angel.

'Now sit over here, and your sister will be here to pick you up within the hour,' she continues. I open my mouth to correct her and then think of what a warm glow that statement gives me instead. So I close my mouth, nod, and then regret the movement.

'Don't go wandering anywhere, now. I've got to go, because I'm late for my next schedule,' says the angel as she gets back in her red chariot. 'Don't forget to think of how you feel today when you go out drinking again – at this time of the day, too.'

I thank her before I sit down at the bus stop and close my eyes again. I've no idea how long I sit like that, but I'm not uncomfortable, because the quieter I am, the less I do and the less I think, and this helps my headache and nausea. I doze intermittently, and I'm finally woken by Nora, who arrives in a taxi. She ushers me in and says nothing as I continue to sleep the whole way back. When we get to her house, she guides me to her room and fills a bath for me. She gives me water to drink and then gently undresses me and helps me into the bath. The water is warm and inviting, and I sink into it gratefully. I sit there for a long time. The warmth spreads like two comforting arms encircling me, and I decide that it's as good a place to sleep as anywhere else. I let myself slip under the water.

Nora comes into the bathroom, and I gasp as she pulls my head up from under the water for the second time. She slaps my face and shakes me like a dog.

'Stop it,' she hisses. 'Stop it right now.'

She gently washes the stale smell of vomit off me, and lifts me out of the bath – heaven knows how, with her fragile frame. She doesn't bother trying to struggle with putting my clothes on. She just wraps a bathrobe around me and puts me to bed.

When I awake, it's dark outside. I'm in Nora's bed. I sit up and clutch the bathrobe I'm wearing, as it opens to reveal my nakedness. The robe is soft and comforting and smells of a washing powder that is unfamiliar. As I tie the belt, I have vague memories of warm water and the feel of bubbles on my face. The face of some unknown woman telescoping in and out of focus also passes through my mind. I clear my throat and call for Nora. She's there in an instant, her lovely, warm smile spreading through her face. She sits on the bed, and I put my arms around her. I can feel her ribs as I gently squeeze her.

'How are you feeling, Maya?' she asks.

'I'm fine,' I answer. 'Tell me what I can't remember.'

'Well,' she says, 'I'm not sure of some bits myself, although I can guess. You were going to meet Mark in the coffee shop this morning, all happy, and then this afternoon, I came and picked you up, dazed, drunk, and covered in sick, from a bus stop miles away, after you were rescued by a woman bus driver.'

I'm suddenly awash with memories: Mark's tortured face as he told me he had to give his marriage one more chance, my visits to the garish pubs that in some way were connected with animals, my discovery of the effects of alcohol, and then the throwing-up of my innards in the bushes. I give Nora a potted version of events. Surprisingly, her fury is directed towards Mark.

'He's so weak,' she says. 'What does he mean by having to give his relationship a chance? If it's dead, it's dead. He obviously can't make clean endings from people.'

I rush to his defence as usual, but Nora is not having any of it. It turns out that she's equally furious with me.

'Why do you always have to put yourself in the position of second best?' she asks me.

I am startled by this revelation.

Do I think I'm second best? If I do, how does that influence keeping me on the outside?'

She continues, 'Prioritise yourself, Maya, and soon. You do things for others and not for yourself. When are you going to get it into your thick head that you're deserving of the best?'

I bristle and then try to shrug it off, but she catches me by the shoulders and shakes me hard, making me wince as the pain behind my temples drives nails into my head.

'I mean it,' she hisses.

I find out that when I called her to come and collect me, she had been about to go with her father to the airport for their Germany trip. According to her, he had been extremely understanding and had rearranged her flight for tomorrow.

I'm profusely apologetic. She commands me to be quiet and says that she's pleased that she has been able to help.

'Do you think this is all about helping you?' she asks me quite seriously. 'Maya, this is as helpful to me as to you, because it makes me feel real, able to do something, to define myself as a friend. Otherwise, all day, every day, I am Nora the pathetic anorexic.'

She tells me that she has also had a chat with my parents. I catapult out of bed.

'What?' I exclaim.

'I can't have you here and not let them know, Maya,' she says. 'I rang them and gave them a different version of the story. I said that you'd been anxious about going to school and so had a few drinks beforehand for some Dutch courage, but then got very ill on alcohol.'

I stare at her and panic. I've blown my cover.

She smiles. 'They were great Maya,' she says. 'They understood.'

'Are they upset that I didn't come home?' I ask.

'I told them that I encouraged you to stay with me,' she says, 'because I wanted Daddy to check you out. They were fine about it.'

I remember feeling something cold on my chest when I was partially asleep and a light shining in my eyes. I look at Nora, and she nods.

'Yes, Daddy did check you out before he left,' she says, 'and said that you were fine and just needed to sleep.'

I can feel tears prick at the backs of my eyes, and I marvel at what I've done to deserve such a kind and considerate friend. I give her a big hug, and she returns it. Nothing more need be said. We both know what we mean to each other.

Since Nora is to go to Germany the following day, I reluctantly go back home that evening. I would be lying if I say I'm not apprehensive on the journey home with my father, but he just gives me a huge hug and remains silent as he drives. Not surprisingly, my body reacts in its usual way to stress by making me start a period early, but this hardly bothers me, so anxious am I about what lies ahead.

Daddy didn't say a word on the way back home. I wanted to apologise, but I didn't know what to say.

Startlingly, my mother comes rushing up and puts her arms around me. I immediately dissolve into tears, and then I worry that I am overburdening her.

'It's all right, Maya,' she says. 'We're not cross.'

I wait in the comfort of her arms for a while longer before breaking free. I find physical contact with my mother awkward.

'I'm sorry,' I say.

'We're sorry too,' says my father. 'We should have realised the impact of your exam results on you, and we didn't.'

I felt so guilty that they were taking the blame, but it was also so comfortable that I didn't want to spoil it with the truth.

My mother clears her throat and looks really nervous as she speaks. 'It's not just our lack of acknowledgement on the impact of the exam results, Ruwan,' she says. 'What about my depression, my drinking, and my apathy?'

My father moves towards her and puts his arms around her as she burst into sobs. I have never seen my mother cry or turn to my father for comfort.

I saw Mummy in a different light today.

My mother continues, 'I've been afraid of you turning out to be like me, Maya, and so I've done everything within my power to detach myself from you, with the hope that as your closeness with your father grows, you'll become more like him. It's worked, because I've seen the similarity in intelligence, kindness, and ability to adapt to people and situations. However, I now see how limited I've been. I can't deny the part of me that's in you, and I need to take responsibility for that and permit it to grow.'

My father is the first to break the silence. 'Why don't I make some tea for us all?' he asks.

I suddenly felt so tired that all I could do was snuggle on the sofa.

I hear my father bustling around in the kitchen, making tea, and then I hear him making me a hot chocolate. He makes the same sound that Grandma used to make when she made me those hot, steaming mugs of comfort, and I burst into tears. My mother nods.

'It's Grandma's sound,' she says knowingly.

My father comes in with three mugs on a tray. We sit there in companionable silence as we sip our hot drinks. Corny as it sounds, I know that this evening will be etched on my mind forever. It's the day when something very fundamental shifts in our family. I may have lost Mark, and for that I will probably be sad for a long time, but through this experience I have gained my family, and for that I'm grateful. I drop off to sleep before I finish my hot chocolate, and when I am asleep, I think that I dream of both my parents kissing me gently on my forehead before they go to bed.

Freddy

October 2005

Most nights, Freddy dreamed of what it was like to die, and every morning he woke up disappointed. Until Freddy met Jackson, his life was all about planning an effective ending. Freddy had tried to kill himself in as many different ways as most people had hot dinners. His very first attempt was swallowing two Paracetamol tablets. He was about six years old at the time, and having swallowed them, he lay in bed with his eyes closed for what seemed like a very long time, peeping from under his eyelids from time to time to see if he had arrived in heaven yet. When he realised that getting to heaven was not that easy, Freddy doubled his efforts. He progressed onto eight Paracetamol tablets, and then onto twelve. He tried drinking disinfectant, but he threw up whatever he managed to get down. It seemed that whatever he did was never enough. He tried to tie his dressing-gown belt around his neck, but he just couldn't find something effective to tie the other end onto. He walked along exposed train tracks, but it seemed that trains never ran down those tracks when he was there. He gave up eating for two weeks, but hunger was too big a contender. He took as many recreational drugs as he could tolerate, sometimes possibly enough to kill a full-grown horse, but with only the odd bad trip or lost day to show for it. After the London bombings, and when the loneliness of being on his own after Jackson went away to do some work gnawed at him, he travelled on every tube train and on every tube line he could get himself on. So when stations were empty, just full of the fear of people, Freddy was there. Line after line, he got to know the distances to most places, and which part of the platform to stand on so that the carriage stopped furthest from an exit. He came across a variety of different people, but he never confronted a bomb. He was fed up with his body. He wanted to leave it, but it rebelled against dying. He felt weary and disillusioned by the world. In a place that was so savage, why did violence shun him?

Freddy couldn't understand why everyone around him wanted to live. Since life was purposeless, the idea of taking a huge risk was not daunting. If it meant that he died in the process, that would be exactly what he wanted. If he were put in jail instead, well, perhaps he could do something there that would speed up his death. Freddy was familiar with prison films. They were full of guards who were ready to shoot. He would just goad them.

He had no worries at all about encouraging Jackson to start putting their plan into action; as far as he could see, he couldn't lose. Succeed, and he would have loads of money to ensure that he could afford a foolproof plan to kill himself or arrange to be killed. Failure would keep him longer in the same shit hole of a place and that would surely only encourage him to obtain his life's ambition to die?

In Suffolk and in London, on the phone

6 July 2006

'Hi, is that Maya?'
    'Oh, my god! It can't be. Yes, it's you.'
    'You still remember?'
    'Of course. How are you?'
    'Well, so-so.'
    'Look, I feel really bad about this, but I've been meaning for ages, I mean, since it all happened, to explain.'
    'No, really, you don't have to.'
    'Yes, I do. I'm so—'
    'Come on, Maya, don't spoil it all. Tell you what – shall we meet? Then you can tell me.'
    'Er, I don't know. I'm really not sure about meeting.'
    'It would be good if we do, Maya. I've something extremely important to tell you.'
    'Really? After all this time?'
    'Yes. Really, really important.'
    'The thing is, I'm kind of busy these days. Can't you tell me over the phone or give me an idea of what sort of importance?'
    'Well, it's about Jamie.'
    'Jamie?'
    'Yeah. Something that could affect him really badly.'
    'Oh, really? How come you know something about him?'
    'There are lots we have to catch up on. It's too serious for me to explain on the telephone, but be reassured you'll be relieved to know this. Also you said you wanted to explain your side of things – that's two birds you can kill with one stone.'
    'Well, time is hard to free up, but okay. I'll meet up, but just for a short time.'

'You'll really help him out, Maya. Now, you have to come to Ipswich.'

'Ipswich? Why?'

'That's where I live. I'm disabled now. I can't travel.'

'Disabled? I'm so sorry. OK how about the twenty-fourth? Give me your details. I'll be there.'

Chapter 20

Friends

Maya, late 1990s

I've been chuckling about the pub experience that happened as a result of the ending with Mark that I wrote about the other day. I would definitely like to read more but have to leave it for when more convenient, since this weekend I've visited my parents, a task I have been putting off subsequent to my mother's mission to inform me of my father's health. Discussion is staggered and I notice that we hover on neutral topics. I am aware that I can't embark on a frank discussion with my father, and I'm angry that he doesn't tell me his news. I am further irked with my mother that she doesn't assist me. The guilt I feel over avoiding facing bad news dictates my behaviour with them, so that I'm over solicitous and spend more time than planned. I'm late for my dress fitting as a consequence, and the French seamstress makes no bones about showing me her disapproval of my tardiness. 'Rush, rush, rush – that's what my life's all about at the moment,' I mutter to myself as I head back home through the traffic. What was it Shakespeare stated? 'To climb steep hills, you need a slow pace at first'? The chance of me attaining my goal is obviously bleak, given my current acceleration. I pick up my diaries once I'm back, they help soothe me.

* * *

When I wake up the morning after my drunken excursion, my neck and back are stiff and sore. I have slept on the sofa throughout the night. Yesterday is like a dream, and I stumble to the toilet to relieve myself, unsure of what really took place and what I might have imagined. I look at my watch. It's 8.00 a.m., and both my parents are still asleep. This is amazing, since my mother is usually awake, sometimes as early as four in the morning, a 'lie-in' being treated as a heinous crime. Perhaps last night did happen after all. Out of habit, I look out of the downstairs window and have got to smile to myself when I see the solitary road sweeper out there again collecting petals. Well, my prediction of how lucky a sight that was didn't go exactly to plan. I run through Mark's meeting with me again in my mind and wish the outcome could have been different. I wonder what he might be doing now and feel a pang at the thought of Marie being with him.

I ring up Nora to wish her a good trip. She's breathless when I ring, having just come back from a jog. I've never spoken to Nora about her exercise or weight, but I wonder if I should. I'm afraid of losing her as my friend, and yet I know that I'm not a true friend if I permit her to remain stuck where she is.

* * *

I'm interrupted from my writing by a telephone call from my mother. Apparently one of the websites has a list of helpful hints for relatives of someone suffering from Parkinson's disease, and it's all very depressing. I placate her as she works herself up and feel drained as I put down the telephone. I scan what I've written and suddenly make a relevant link. I've stepped in to be a carer and a rescuer to my mother from a young age, but I never challenged why she has constantly needed that care. You only need to rescue someone if they are in danger. If they constantly, compulsively hurl themselves into destruction, should I keep rescuing them, or should I point out their compulsion to them so that they can make the change themselves? Have I also stepped in as a carer for others not only because it's a familiar role but because it gives me a sense of value and belonging?

* * *

I do something that I have never done before. I make my parents tea in bed, and when I knock on their bedroom door, they are both awake, looking rather sheepish. Being a woman of the world these days, I can see the tiny visual signs and smell the aftermath of sex in the air, and I'm not sure how to react.

I tell them that I have been giving my studies some thought and that I would like to retake my examinations but that I would also like to explore other degree options. They are both pleased and ask me if I would like them to come with me to school when I go to discuss this. I say that perhaps I would, and we all look somewhat surprised.

Mrs Noland-Smith, the head, is a matronly, bespectacled woman who carries herself as upright as if she has been in the army. She is feared by most of the girls because of her explosive temper and regarded uneasily by many parents because of her rather ungracious, frosty manner. However, at our meeting today, she is charming; she even smiles.

'Well, Maya, this is certainly a turn up for the books,' she says. 'Definitely not what we'd expected, but knowing what a conscientious girl you are, the results are the biggest punishment, I'm sure, so nothing more needs to be said about what's happened. Let's focus on solving the matter.'

My mother clears her throat. 'This has been a stressful time for Maya,' she begins. 'Her grandmother died not so long ago, and—'

Before she can continue, I have broken in by saying that perhaps I did not apply myself as best as I could have, and that's what I want to do now.

Mrs Noland-Smith smiles at me. 'Well, that's what I was hoping you would say,' she replies.

I can't believe Mrs Noland-Smith thinks I'm okay.

I eagerly await Nora's arrival back from Germany. When I see her, I am shocked, because even though she has only been away for a week, she has lost more weight, so that she looks, if possible more frail and gaunt. She has brought me some children's books by a German author, Helme Heine. They are titled *Freunde* or *Friends*, the English translations of which I have read as a child. My school German is enough to translate the heart-warming text of the books, and I impulsively give her a little hug.

'How was your time in Germany?' I enquire.

'I managed to have a good time,' she smiles. 'I spent the daytime on my own, but my father and I were together in the evenings, usually reading or playing a game of Scrabble. We also spent some time visiting various galleries and museums, and we went to the opera to see *La Bohème*, which we both really loved.'

I don't know what prompts me to ask her the next question, but it's out of my mouth before I can stop it. 'How did you find eating out with your father?' I ask.

She looks evasive as she replies, 'Well, I ate early, usually.'

I can hear the voice of her eating disorder speak.

'And the throwing up?'

She gives me a tight little smile. 'Why the interrogation?' she asks, but she goes on to say that the German toilets are better than the English ones for people with eating disorders, because they are constructed in a way so that you can see what you have thrown up. I cannot bind into the conspiracy of her illness any more, and emboldened by Helme Heine's wording about friends – 'No way was too stony, no slope was too steep, no curve was too dangerous, and no puddle was too deep' – I gently ask her if she hoped ever to break away from the destructive nature of her illness.

She's desolate. 'You've let me down, Maya!' she exclaims, and then adds, 'You've always been on my side, but now you've crossed over to the other side where everyone else I know stands, and from where you all conspire to make me fat. I'm so disappointed in you.'

'Nora, I assure you that I have no plans to take away your illness, but I would like you to see that there are many other things that make you precious, especially to me. I've been so unsure about whether to talk to you about this, but you are my best friend, and I don't want you to get worse.'

'But I *do* eat,' she says, 'and I *am* fit and well. I mean, I get less coughs and colds than you. I can't understand why there's such a fixation by everyone, including you, on my weight.'

'I've no fixation, Nora, although if I'm honest with you, it looks as though you've lost weight since your break in Germany. If you really want to know, what I worry about is your inability to move away from restriction, your need to throw up, and your need to harm yourself.'

She stares at me. 'What do you mean?' she asks, wide-eyed, and that look makes my heart jolt. I realise that what I mean by harming herself through vomiting and starving is not what has made her react. I grab her arm and pull up her sleeve. A mass of cuts, some superficial, others much deeper, is clearly visible. The same is true on her other arm. Almost all the cuts look newly inflicted.

'Maya!' she screams, trying to pull her arms away, her voice high. 'Leave me alone! Oh, why did I ever confide in you? I hate you! I hate everyone who just can't leave me alone!'

I've never seen Nora emotional.

The rawness of her feelings resounds around us, but I know that this time, she too knows how far things have gone, so I put my arms around her. She initially resists my contact, and I sense that she wants to kick or head-butt me, but then her body softens, and she leans on me as her emaciated frame shakes. She weeps dry sobs.

Nora never cries.

'Nora,' I say, 'you've seen me at my lowest point, drunk and with vomit in my hair. Please don't be ashamed. You have to face your illness, and if I say nothing, I'm colluding with it and not being a good friend.'

She's dry-eyed but still shaking spasmodically. I think low weight often acts like an emotion-numbing drug. The lower the weight a person, the less the emotion they show. It's as though the brain takes over basic functions, keeps the body alive, and cancels other, complementary functions, like emotional well-being. Given Nora's difficulty in reacting to herself, I am pleased that at least something has shaken her out of her apathetic state.

We talk for a little longer before I leave. Awkwardness hangs in the air. I don't tell Nora, but I'm shaken by the sight of the cuts on her arms. I keep going over how they look. She has told me that she uses a Stanley knife, the sharp, retractable-bladed knife that is used to cut carpets, to inflict the cuts, and the thought of that frightens me. Does she dislike herself so much that she uses another, even more radical technique to destroy herself?

> *I thought that Nora was better, but worryingly her* anorexia *may now be mutating into featuring some of the aspects of its twin sister,* bulimia.

Nora promises me that she will confront her need to harm herself in her individual therapy, and that she will do her best to stop cutting herself. I try to shelve my concerns about her as I start revising, and I am pleased with my ability to learn new information just as efficiently as I always have.

'I'm going to do my very best not to think of Mark.

Maya the academic robot re-emerges, and I permit all else in my life to fade into insignificance whilst I devote my time and effort to revision.

Chapter 21

Mata Hari

Maya late 1990s

My time and effort at the moment solely focuses around my diary and my wedding. My dress is nearly ready, and I'm both excited and nervous to try on the nearly completed gown.

'Make sure your florist complements the design when putting together your bouquet,' says the strict French seamstress, and I nod acquiescently.

'Also, the person doing your makeup and hair should know what it looks like,' she continues, and I nod again.

Tomorrow I go with Bella and Nora to have a trial makeup session and hairstyles; sometimes I marvel at the fuss before a wedding. Keeping the whole process a secret from my man is equally hard, since I am used to sharing most things with him, but it also adds to the excitement of this first formalised step of establishing our future together. Time is precious at the moment, but I pursue my journal writing with renewed vigour whenever I can.

* * *

I re-sit my examinations a few months later, and this time I'm ready. I march into the room with confidence. I realise that I'm relaxed, because I note the size of the room, the number of examiners, and most importantly, I understand and know the answers to the questions. I put my knowledge to the test, and when I finish, I know that I'll fare well. This is later confirmed by my results, since I achieve all grade As. After my many months of gloom over Mark and my own performance, I'm ecstatic.

I wish I could ring Mark and let him know.

It's soon my eighteenth birthday, and I celebrate it in an understated manner. To my immense joy, I get a small second-hand car as my birthday present from my parents. I spent the summer learning to drive, and to my amazement, I passed my driving test the first time round, but I never once thought I would own a car of my own so soon.

'I hope that this might ensure that you drive down to see us from university more frequently,' says my father as he hands me the gift-wrapped car keys, a twinkle in his eyes.

As a celebration, I decide to take my mother with me in the car for my first drive. She looks surprised when I ask her, but she consents to coming. I drive slowly and carefully down our road and along the many mini roundabouts to the busier section of town.

Mummy was so nervous in the car today. She had little beads of sweat on her upper lip and she clutched her hands together on her lap very tight. For some reason, I found myself remembering the times she didn't come to see me on prize-giving day at school or when I took part in the school plays.

I turn into a quiet road and stop outside a house. 'Are you nervous Mum? Do you want to go home?' I ask.

'No, no, not at all,' she says hurriedly. 'But I do have tasks to catch up with at home, so let's not be too late back.'

I've been really panicky today. In fact, I've been awful this whole week. I wish I could see Mark.

My birthday is also the anniversary of my break-up with Mark. When I am alone in my bedroom, I take out all eighteen birthday presents he gave me. Looking at them brings a lump to my throat. He was so kind and caring.

I must move on and focus on new relationships. I must also not let myself get too close to anyone – never as close as I did to Mark.

My grandfather phones, and I say, as I always do, that my mother is unavailable.

The last time Grandfather telephoned, Mummy asked me to say that she was out.

Unusually, my grandfather sends me some writing paper for my birthday, which, out of duty to my mother, I put in the bin since she says that it is definitely something that was bought by Rhona. My mother has not seen him for over a year, ever since she heard of Rhona moving into his house.

I also receive a card from my father's parents for my birthday, this time with no money enclosed in it. My father is puzzled until we realise that this card says, 'On your nineteenth birthday.'

My mother gloats. 'They don't even know Maya's age,' she says.

Enclosed in the card is a photograph of a baby, my cousin Anita. My paternal grandparents have not visited us for over a year now. Grandmother de Silva makes a telephone call to my father.

'We're busy sorting out our retirement so that we can look after Anita,' she says. 'You know, your sister needs all the help she can get. What with the NHS only giving six months of paid maternity leave, it's even more vital that we spend time with our granddaughter. We don't really have time to make the long journey to see you at the moment.'

'That's all right' says my father in his courteous way, but my heart bleeds for him, because I can sense the heartbreak behind his voice, the difficulty he has in understanding why such a difference is made between his sister and himself. I am uneasy when confronted with the photograph of the baby, in the same way as when I heard of her impending birth.

> *When I close my eyes, I can still picture the beads of sweat on his upper lip and hear his heavy breathing as he stroked my legs. I shudder when I remember how he felt my breasts. I know that I didn't make up what happened, but did I do anything to invite that response? Maybe I was provocative in some way?*

I try to ignore the other rational voice within me that says that even if I had worn something to provoke a response from him, what I would have wanted would have been some attention, flattery from someone who was older, so that I could recognise my blossoming maturity, not what he offered.

My thoughts tarnish me with apprehension and guilt and pose a dilemma that drives me to have a number of sleepless nights. Do I have a responsibility to warn my aunt to protect my young cousin, or am I overreacting and going to ruin a perfectly good father-child relationship, maybe even family situation, by admitting to something that is not really very significant?

I decide to present my dilemma to Nora. Her reaction is instantaneous and volatile.

'You have to stop child abuse,' she says instantly. 'If he did it with you, he'll do it again. He's got to be stopped.'

The term 'child abuse' sticks in my gullet, like thick porridge. This throws me into further despair. I am very afraid of being accused of overreacting or, worse still, of lying. I am also apprehensive of being outcast again. The shame of admitting to any form of abuse, even if mine is mild in comparison to what usually happens, is huge.

I tell my mother and father that I would like to see my new cousin before I go off to university. My mother is appalled, even betrayed, by my request. My father is noncommittal but I think, in a way, excited about a possible family reunion. Finally, my mother agrees to the request, but only if we invite them home to us.

'We're not going to force ourselves on them,' is her response.

We write and tell my aunt of my good news regarding exam grades and acceptance to university, and we invite them to tea with Anita. The invitation is accepted, together with a footnote to say that my grandparents will also be coming. I am jittery with nerves. I don't really know what I am going to do, but I would like to see them all before I decide.

The decision has been made. I wonder what the future will bring.

Meanwhile, I continue to talk to Nora about her self-harm.

'It's a recent happening, Maya,' she reassures me.

'Why now?' I puzzle. 'When everything seems to be getting better, and when you have had and are continuing to have so much treatment?'

'I really don't know how to describe it, except that it makes me feel connected with myself and it also makes me feel alive,' she says.

I find this a difficult idea to understand. I remember once hitting my head hard on a door when I felt humiliated and frustrated, when I had moved to a new school and someone had said something nasty about me. At the time, that head bang had been because of frustration that I felt over the situation and a solution to something that I could not verbalise or resolve. It was a way of experiencing controlled pain created by myself, in response to a situation that had caused uncontrolled pain. I have never done that again, and at the moment, I find it hard to imagine myself ever doing it, certainly not deliberately or repetitively, as Nora does when she cuts herself.

I have taken to asking her to show me her arms. This feels awkward, because I am now policing a friendship, but within me is a huge fear of Nora accidentally causing herself a fatal injury. I also cannot bear to see her deface herself in the same way a graffiti artist defaces crisp, new walls.

> *I think that Nora is worried about something in her family as well as hating her treatment. She says that her brother is doing very well at university and is not visiting home as much, so I don't think he is the reason. When I ask her how things are at home, she clams up and says, 'Oh, much the same as always.'*

Seeing her injuries has a curious affect on me. I start to have recurring nightmares in which someone close to me is injured. The dreams are vivid and full of blood. I often wake up sweating and with my breathing erratic and disturbed. I find myself becoming more sensitive to newspaper reports of injuries sustained by others: muggings, accidents, it doesn't seem to matter. I cannot watch hospital programmes on television, and I start avoiding them. I worry about Nora's future and what the future holds in store for me. My over protectiveness towards my mother recommences, and I repeatedly start checking her medicine cupboard to note decreasing medicine supplies.

As I check through her items, I sometimes come across things I don't want to know about. For instance, I find rows of bags filled with unworn, new clothes shoved into the corners of her cupboards. They replace the empty bottles of alcohol I used to find before: a secret presence of guilty consumption. I'm often shocked by the sheer magnitude of her expenditure and waste, but I say nothing and find my own way of forgetting. I'm scared, because I know that she's still not well.

> *I'm feeling very out of control. The responsibility of making sure that Nora doesn't hurt herself is proving to be so hard. I wish I could tell someone without breaking her confidence.*

After much soul searching and several sleepless nights, I decide to visit Nurse Taylor at school. I find her in the sick room, catching up with her notes.

'Maya,' she says, her eyes lighting up, 'I'm so pleased to see you, and congratulations on your results.'

'Thank you,' I say, thrilled that she has taken the trouble to find out.

'Well, what can I do for you today?' she asks.

'Nurse Taylor, my anxiety symptoms have started again, although they are much better than they were. I can't understand it, because things are so much better.'

'Well, tell me what's happening in your life at the moment,' she asks. I run through a list, and she tells me that change, whether good or bad, can trigger anxiety, because adapting is stressful.

I hesitate. 'Um, what do you think I should do if I know of someone who is self-harming?' I ask her.

'What sort of self-harm?' she enquires.

'Um, I am unsure of betraying a confidence by telling you more,' I reply hesitantly.

'Well, my policy on breaking confidences is only when I feel that someone is putting their life or someone else's life at risk. If you think that by withholding the information you have, you may be aiding someone to put their life at risk, then you should think about breaking the secrecy,' she says.

I take a risk with her and tell her about my discovery of Nora's self-harm. She is, as expected, non-judgemental.

'I'm really grateful for the information, Maya,' she says. 'I know the nurse at her school, and I also know that she has a good relationship with Nora. I'll have a discreet word. Please don't worry because I promise that I'll handle the situation with total discretion, and there won't be any reference whatsoever to information that I've received from you.'

Although I know that I can trust Nurse Taylor, I am conscious now of what it feels like to betray someone, and I hate it. Nora is right. I have crossed to the 'other side.' I decide that I have to avoid facing her for some time; my conscience is heavy, and I am too cowardly.

I am relieved, however, to read a leaflet that Nurse Taylor gives me about post-traumatic stress disorder. The relief of knowing I am not going mad is invaluable, and I am yet again grateful to Nurse Taylor, who also suggests that I may be helped by seeing a clinical psychologist.

'Talk to your general practitioner first,' she says. 'Of course, I'll be pleased to liaise with him or do whatever is necessary about the referral too.'

When Nurse Taylor suggested to me today that I should see a psychologist, I thought I'd let everyone down.

'May I think it over?' I ask, trying to control a sudden tremor in my voice and not let my deflation show.

To ask someone else for help is so weak.

Nurse Taylor is quick to read my mind. 'Maya, what I'm suggesting is a strong thing to do – to learn new ways of dealing with situations and people. It will be about adding to what you have, not about taking anything away from you.'

I promise her that I will think about it, and I return home, pensive. There is a lot to reflect on, and a part of me is keen to leave it all behind me here at home and start afresh at university. I'm sure I can reinvent myself. After all, I am Maya, and I'm used to doing that.

Jackson and Freddy

July 2005

'Hey, Jackson,' said Freddy, 'I'm all for our change, reinvention from rags to riches. Listen to what this book says, mate. "Explosives are chemically or otherwise energetically unstable. The initiation produces a sudden expansion of the material accompanied by the production of heat and large changes in pressure, with typically a flash or loud noise called an explosion."

'So what?' said Jackson, in a bad mood. 'That's just a definition. We need more than that.'

'Explosives have to be sensitive,' Freddy continued, "Sensitivity is usually divided into the following measures: impact, friction, and heat."

Jackson took down his backpack from the shelf. 'I'm off to train,' he said, putting the heavy pack on his back, 'Twelve miles today with this pack on, just to see if I can cut my time down by at least two minutes. Learn something useful by my return, won't you?'

'Wait, I've got it,' said Freddy. "Explosives are usually of two main forms of composition. They either have powder components or are chemically pure compounds such as TNT and nitro-glycerine."

Jackson opened the front door in preparation for his jog. 'Have a list of ingredients together with costs and suppliers, when I'm back, then,' he called, and he set off, initially slowly, and then speeding up as he warmed up.

Chapter 22

Hot Air

Maya 1998

> *It's so strange preparing to go to uni. I'm worried about leaving my parents, and I'm worried about being on my own. It's so silly, but – will they forget me? Will I become less important? I hate all of this. Wish I could just go to sleep.*

I become moody and unpredictable. I argue with my parents at the slightest provocation. I avoid seeing Nora. I convince myself that home life is constraining and that where I live is provincial and that my friends are all small-minded. I tell myself how pleased I am to be going away. I take long walks and occasionally pop into a pub on my own for a quiet drink. When I am there, I feel at peace. I try writing, but the flow of words within me is like a river in the drought.

Once, when I go to a pub not too far from the coffee shop where I used to meet Mark, I think I see him: a brief glimpse of a thatch of blonde hair and tall, muscular build. I don't stay to find out, especially in case he's with Marie, I turn away and leave as fast as I can.

The summer flows with tepid ease in this way, until the day of the visit of my aunt and entourage. The week leading up to this visit is full of unease for me. I don't sleep well, and neither do I eat. I know that I look pale and drawn. My parents have made their usual preparations in honour of the visit and our three up, two down, semi-detached property gleams like teeth after a visit to the hygienist. I refuse to involve myself in this domesticity, and instead I go out for a long walk and then to the cinema.

I have such a pounding headache. I've literally had it up to here.

I settle into my seat at the cinema, the smell of popcorn comforting, as are the rustling sounds around me of people opening their bags of sweets or slurping their drinks. I close my eyes and, lulled by the womb-like warmth and darkness of the auditorium, fall asleep.

I wake up when the film is finished and people around me are starting to stumble out in the partial darkness when the film credits are showing. Their progress out of the cinema is slow, since their eyes are still mesmerised by the screen.

I feel more refreshed. My headache is better. My throat is furry and dry, as though I have been crying in my sleep. I stumble out of the cinema, my eyes taking a while to adjust to the contrast of emerging from darkness to light. The sharp teeth of apprehension continue to gnaw at me. I glance at my wristwatch: it is five minutes before the visit. I look down at what I am wearing: grubby jeans, a sweatshirt, and my hair in a ponytail. Due to my headache, I am wearing my glasses instead of my contact lenses. I smile to myself. There is nothing remotely wanton or attractive about me today.

When I get home, I can see their silver Mercedes parked on our drive. I have an irrational urge to let down the tyres or run my house keys along the immaculate paintwork. I stick my hands deep into my pockets as I walk past. I take in a deep breath as I open the door and find that the extra oxygen does nothing to help my anxiety, and so I pretend to fiddle with hanging up my jacket before I go into the living room, so that I can regulate my breathing.

They are all sitting formally on our buttercup-yellow sofas as I walk in. My parents have recently repainted our living room a royal blue and then hung yellow and blue drapes and colour coordinated the sofa to match. It is a bright and happy room now, and my first thought is that all of these visitors are in discord with it.

My grandparents look older. Retirement does not suit Grandfather de Silva, and he has lost his air of authority. He reminds me of a tortoise with his wrinkled neck protruding from his white collar and his dark-rimmed glasses. He holds a favourite china cup of my mother's in his hand and is in the act of coordinating bringing the cup from lap level up to his mouth. Grandmother de Silva retains her air of authority and control. The only concession she has made to retirement is that she is dressed in a velour tracksuit. I have never seen her look informal, and it is somewhat shocking for me. She looks like a real person instead of some two-dimensional cardboard cut-out character, but rather grotesque. Casual clothes do not suit her – imagine Margaret Thatcher in a tracksuit. I focus on them first as I go up to greet them: a quick handshake, no hug.

I turn to my aunt. She looks tired and more worn than when I last saw her. She has on her lap my little cousin Anita. I crouch down and awkwardly pat Anita's head and then smile in greeting at my aunt. I finally, very reluctantly, turn to see my uncle, who has stood up to greet me. He looks the same, but his hair is even darker than before. *Out of a bottle, no doubt,* I think spitefully, and then rather childishly I wish that like Roald Dahl's Matilda, I could mix his hair colour with peroxide so that it would bleach his hair orange.

'Maya,' he says, 'how lovely to see you, and how proud we are to be here to congratulate you on your achievements.'

He hugs me, crushing me tightly against his chest. I move away from him as quickly as I can, and my legs tremor as I move. My mother stares at me, willing me to assume my usual role of helper. I don't respond but instead sit, resembling a small, dark thunder cloud on the piano stool, since this is the farthest seat away from my uncle, and because it makes me appear to be taller than the others.

Grandmother de Silva dominates the conversation. She talks only about two things. The first is the impact of retirement, and the other is my cousin Anita. No small detail of Anita's accomplishments has escaped her beady eye or left her memory, and we are all held ransom by her repeated accounts of these. 'Do you know what Anita did today?' she asks, or, 'Do you know what Anita said today?'

My aunt says very little when Grandmother de Silva holds court on these matters. She sits on the chair like a stuffed doll, and I wonder why she is so apathetic. My mother has completely clammed up and sits on her chair, staring at the wall, making no pretence whatsoever about her tedium, yawning now and again and not bothering to cover her mouth.

I look at Anita, and I know that I will confront my aunt and tell her about my uncle today. I sit on the stool in a daze, running through what I will say in my head, and when and how I will say it. Shall I tell my parents first? Will they try to stop me from carrying through with my plan? If I find some way of blurting things out, will they be offended that I haven't told them first? I feel the beginnings of my headache again.

I realise that a question has been addressed to me and that I don't know what it is. Everyone looks expectantly at me.

'I'm sorry,' I say, 'I have a terrible headache, and for a moment I lost my concentration. What did you ask me?'

Grandmother de Silva sniffs disapprovingly. Her whole body conveys its lack of approval for how I am today: untidy, dishevelled, and selectively deaf.

'I just asked you,' she retorts, 'how excited you were to have another cousin.'

I stare at her uncomprehendingly. I really don't know what she's talking about. My mother breaks in, realising this. 'Your grandmother's asking what you think of the good news of Auntie's second pregnancy,' she says. 'The new baby is due in two months' time.'

I stare at my aunt. I can see now that she looks bloated and swollen, her skin distended and tightly stretched around her, like a pair of small tights on an extra-large woman. Any further progression of my thoughts and actions has been efficiently executed.

'Er, I'm pleased,' I say. 'Congratulations!'

My anxiety deflates. I stare at my uncle and imagine I can see a glint of triumph in his eyes. I get up and excuse myself.

'I'm sorry,' I say, 'I really do have an awful headache, and I think I should go and lie down. I would hate it to be something infectious.'

I dutifully bend down and give Anita and my aunt a light peck on the cheek, shake hands with my grandparents, nod to my uncle, and leave the room. I make no eye contact with my parents.

I take some Paracetamol and lie on the bed. My head and neck muscles are in paroxysms of movement; a drum is beating some primitive rhythm in my head. Lying down is too uncomfortable, so I make myself get up and sit down on the rocking chair in my room, the very same one that my mother is supposed to have sat on to breastfeed me all those years ago, and I rock myself to sleep.

I had such a strange dream. I was in a hot-air balloon. It was drifting in the wind. There was a man heating the air below me, but he was making it too hot, and I was drifting far, far away into the sky. I asked him to stop, but he took no notice, and I knew then that the man was my uncle. I started trying to cool the air by blowing, puffing out my cheeks and filling in my lungs to their fullest, but there was nothing I could do. The man below me straightened as I drifted away. He was laughing, and I recognised the sound of the laughter instantly. The man below was not my uncle. It was Mark.

I wake up thinking that I have tears streaming down my cheeks, but my cheeks are dry. My mother is in the room with me.

'Maya, wake up,' she says. 'You were having a bad dream, because you were struggling in that chair, which I was afraid would tip you over.'

My head is light, as if it has managed to drift away from those tight muscles that held it captive a while ago.

'Is your headache better?' she enquires solicitously. 'I brought you some medicine and something to drink.'

'It's gone,' I say brusquely. I don't want her here. I want to be left on my own. My voice sounds like it does after I've cried for a long time and yet I've not been crying. I repeat, 'It's better.'

My mother sits on my bed. 'Maya, why did you want to see your aunt?' she enquires.

'I wanted to see Anita,' I reply gruffly, mouthing the words into my sweatshirt.

She stares at me, and I notice with a pang that my mother's magnificent thatch of hair is thinning out on the sides.

I wonder if Mummy has stopped using her recipe for luxurious hair.

'It's just that you've been acting as though you don't want to see anyone at all recently,' she says, 'not even us. So I'm not sure why you wanted to see Anita.'

'That's different,' I say, squirming. I don't like the direction this conversation is going in, so I take it on like a charging bull, ready for attack in the same way as I have been responding to many conversations these days.

'She doesn't pester me with questions like you do, and anyway I thought you'd be pleased that I wanted to see my father's side of the family for once.' Here I get my poison arrows out: 'It does convey a better impression since they seem to think the worst of us.'

My mother bridles. 'Are you implying that they have a poor impression of us because of me, Maya? You'd better watch what you say. You're becoming very insolent these days.'

I lapse into a morose silence. My mother's voice goes up a few decibels. 'Are you listening to me, young lady? You'd better get that sullen look off your face and learn how to communicate if you're going to make friends at university.'

Her comment hits my Achilles heel, and I snap back. 'I can't wait to leave home. I can't wait to find new friends and leave everything connected with my dismal life – especially family life – behind.'

As the words leave my mouth, I am sorry. My mother spins around and leaves the room. My stomach shakes with unaccustomed emotion. I hear my mother moving downstairs in the kitchen; she is noisy, putting away dishes and cups in the dishwasher with unnecessary force. Then suddenly the front door bangs behind her as she makes her way to the gate. I stare out of the window furtively. She is dressed in her running clothes, and as she gets to the gate, I see her shift gear and take off.

As she sprints down the road, a detached observer in me watches and thinks nothing of the desperate rhythm that her training shoes pound on the pavement, the catharsis of converting fury into physical energy. A wave of nausea envelopes me, and I run to the toilet. Although I retch, nothing comes up, and I stare down the toilet, thinking of Nora's comments of being pleased about being able to see what she had thrown up. The physical feeling of ejection in my chest reminds me of the last time I was sick, and I contemplate going out to a pub again. I had so enjoyed the initial state of numbness alcohol had afforded me.

I wonder where my father is. He must have gone out somewhere fairly soon after his family left. It is a Sunday, a day when he tends to potter around, fixing things in the house. I think of telephoning Nora, but I haven't called her for a while, and I don't want to just use her when I am needy. In a trance, I dial Mark's telephone number, using a blocking code before I dial so that he can't trace the call. I hear his voice.

'Hello,' he says, and then again, after a moment, since I remain silent, 'Er, hello?'

I am flooded with memories of the two of us. I remember running my hands through his hair, the way he would kiss me on the top of my head when we went out together, and his coffee-smelling breath after our café assignations. I replace the receiver and restlessly sit down to write, but nothing emanates. I check my purse and find that I have no money, having spent my last few pounds on the cinema ticket.

I poured myself a large brandy from the bottle that sits in the kitchen cupboard. I took the whole bottle upstairs with me, as well as the large balloon glass I had filled.

I take another sip of brandy. There is now a large bonfire burning in my belly, travelling up to my chest, and warming my breasts. I sit on the rocking chair and am just about to take another large sip when my father knocks on my bedroom door and enters immediately. I leap off the chair whilst attempting to camouflage the glass I am holding, and at the same time kicking the bottle on the floor somewhere out of sight. Of course, I am successful with none of these manoeuvres and end up slipping off the rocking chair with the glass upturned on my lap and the bottle in full view.

There is a moment's silence before I scramble to my feet, my jeans soaked. My father says in a quiet, controlled voice, 'Maya, change out of those wet clothes and come downstairs immediately. I'll be in the kitchen.'

I rush to the toilet, my heart pounding. The soft alcoholic veil that had started to descend is no more. I change my clothes, brush my teeth, and gargle with a mouth freshener, sickened by the taste and the smell of the brandy as the fire within me is doused by apprehension and shame. I find myself chanting the lines of an old prayer, something I haven't done since Grandma died. I know I've let myself down, and there's no going back.

Suffolk

Early June 2006

He had made his plans very carefully, since there was no going back once they were put into action. He didn't know how the idea had germinated – it might have been after the repeated listening to his tapes or the viewing of the TV programmes. He didn't really care; all he was concerned about was that he was never going to permit the feeling of loss in his life ever again, and so he had to take effective steps to ensure an incontrovertible outcome.

He knew that she had to be made to feel bad, so bad that she changed her decision. It also had to be strategic, because if he got to know, it would all collapse. Most of all, it had to be precise.

Over the next two weeks, he carried out several different types of research. The first was on the effects of several over-the-counter medicines and their interaction with antidepressant medication. The second was on the average time taken for ambulances to answer emergency calls on weekday afternoons. The third was her time schedule, and the fourth was on average journey time from the station to his home. He often caught himself humming a little tune as he worked out the details.

I feel happy, he thought to himself in amazement. After such a long time, I'm finally happy. This is what it feels like when you do the right thing and when you are in control.

Chapter 23

Confession and Atonement

Maya 1998

My father is on his own when I go to see him in the kitchen. He keeps his emotions well under control. My mother is still not back. I stand silent, staring down at my feet. My father indicates that I should sit and pours me some black coffee. I gulp it down quickly, not wanting to say that his manner and being found out is as sobering as any substance. His first question takes me by surprise.

'Why, Maya?' he asks gently. 'What's today been about?'

I would prefer anger, scorn, and rebuke. I want to feel guilt, and I want to pay penance in a big way. 'Tell me,' he insists, and since there is no way out, I tell him the truth, slowly and falteringly. I tell him about my anxiety about seeing his family, my desire to have confronted my uncle because of my need to protect my little cousin, my altercation with my mother and my fears for her safety, and finally my refuge in a bottle.

I told Daddy what happened with 'Lester the molester' today. He was so angry. I had to beg Daddy not to call him straight away. He agreed only on the basis that I talk to Mummy.

'Stop worrying about your mother,' Daddy says. 'She's fine – just letting off steam. I passed her on my way back home, and we had a little chat. She's gone to the sports centre to calm down. She wants to be able to talk to you about things, Maya. She'll be understanding – just try her. What I can't understand is why you have chosen drink to contend with your upset when you know, from seeing how it is with Mum, that it's no help whatsoever.'

I nod. I do know, but can't explain to him how impulsive I am when I feel certain emotions and how quickly I want to assuage them.

He continues, 'I now understand your distance from us, but why have our interactions been so volatile and intense recently? What else have we been doing wrong?'

I shake my head.

'Maya,' says Daddy gently, 'do you think it will make leaving us easier if you pretend we're an irritation?' He continues, 'Come to think of it, I think I did that too before we left Sri Lanka, and then I was puzzled why I missed everyone and everything so much.'

I am, as always, in awe of my father's perceptiveness. We watch a television programme together until my mother comes back.

'I'm sorry,' I say to her, 'for saying what I said. I didn't mean it.'

We give each other a hug. After she has a shower, she comes into my room. She is a bit surprised that I have all the windows open (to get rid of the smell of brandy, which my father hasn't told her about) but says nothing. She sits on my bed.

'Maya, Daddy has told me about Lester,' she says. My face colours instantly. 'Is that all he did?'

I nod speechlessly.

Mummy will hate me for what I have done.

'Are you sure, Maya?' she repeats.

What is she asking me? Am I sure it happened? Am I sure it was abusive? Doesn't she believe me? I fight very hard to overcome the urge to cry.

'Maya,' she says gently, seeing my face, 'I believe you when you say it happened. I just want to make sure that I know all that he did so that I can be absolutely sure of my facts when I face that bastard.'

I nod firmly. 'You know everything.'

'Well,' says my mother, 'Daddy says you want to wait until after the baby to tell your aunt.'

I nod again. 'Well, I think there's no time like the present,' she says, 'but I respect your wishes. We'll find a way of discussing it with her after the baby is born.' She turns to leave and adds, 'I'm sorry that it happened, Maya.'

Mummy doesn't hate me.

I wake up the next morning feeling tired but resolved to sort out important relationships before my departure. I telephone Nora, and we arrange to meet. When we do, there is no awkwardness between us. Our relationship does not need continuity. We are always the best of friends, taking up where we left off. There is no reproach or recrimination from her.

'I'm so pleased that we are friends,' I tell her impulsively.

She looks at me with one eyebrow raised. 'What's the reason for this confession, then?' she asks gruffly.

'Oh, I suppose I'm going away and I want to make sure that I'm not forgotten,' I joke.

She smiles. 'Shall we watch a movie?' she asks gruffly, and we shuffle off together to watch a film on the big screen. In the cinema, cloaked by the protective mantle of darkness she says, 'You know, Maya, I'm pleased that we're friends too,' and I reach over and gently squeeze her hand.

We spend more time together before I leave for university. She helps me pack, and we tour some of the more picturesque sites in our hometown and visit some shops and galleries. Just before I leave, she gives me a bracelet made of beads.

'These are called tiger's eyes,' she says as I stare at the brown, yellow, and amber beads. 'They're for confidence, if you believe in that sort of thing.' I slip the bracelet on my wrist and vow not to take it off unless I really have to. I wear it throughout my years at university. I still wear it now.

* * *

I pop in to see my parents again and find my father on his own, pottering around in the garden as usual, absent-mindedly pulling out plants as well as weeds.

'Maya, how lovely to see you,' he says. 'Do you think we have ordered sufficient alcohol for the wedding?'

'It'll be fine, Daddy. We've done all the calculations,' I reassure him.

'Are you sure? Because if not, I can order some more,' he starts to say, and I reiterate that he shouldn't be concerned about the amount of food and drink.

'Well, if you're certain,' he repeats and goes back to his weeding. He stops mid-pull and looks up. 'Maya, have you sorted the car or should I see to that? How many hotel rooms are you booking?'

I gently take his hand and make him sit down. 'Daddy, there's nothing more to be done for the wedding,' I say. 'Do you think you might be worrying about something else?'

He looks at me, his eyes full of anguish. 'Mum told you, didn't she?' he asks, and I nod, my eyes brimming with tears.

'I don't want to let you down on your special day by not being able to walk,' he tells me, and there is a break in his voice as he says it.

'Of course you'll be able to walk,' I say with confidence I don't believe, 'and if we have to take it very slow, then that's what we'll do.'

He shakes his head sadly. 'I can't believe it,' he says.

'It may never get any worse than it is now, Daddy.'

'I know,' he says, 'that's what my consultant says too. Apparently my presentation is atypical, and so I may not even need treatment.'

'Well, we've got to be positive,' I reassure him, but I have witnessed fear in my father's eyes, and it terrifies me.

Chapter 24

Moving in Circles

Maya 1999

> *I like university life, especially the lack of structure. What I now have to decide is which lectures I want to attend.*

I have a room in the Halls of Residence. My building is old. Large gothic scrolls and figures sit on the roof outside, darkened by time. My room is small. I have space for a narrow bed, a desk and chair with a shelf above it, and a single wardrobe. The desk is rickety, and the chair creaks when I sit on it. I wedge a piece of paper under one leg to make it more stable, and I add more wedges of paper under the feet of the table. I have on the shelf some of my favourite books and then some space for the textbooks I will be using, most of which I have on rotating loan from the library. On the desk are my writing books, some pens, and two photographs, one of Nora and the other of my parents. I also have a small television balanced rather precariously in the corner, and next to it is a bright pink radio alarm, both of which I have brought from home.

I have also brought with me my amethyst paperweight, my little wooden clog from Amsterdam with my name on it, and my two teddy bears and scruffy soft dog that I have owned since I was a few months old. A recipe book holder that was Grandma's now props up the latest book I am reading. I have my little jewellery box covered in mirrors, within which sits the necklace Grandma gave me when I had my first period and the locket from Mark.

The bed is hard and makes me itch. When I write about this to my parents, I get sent a large parcel with a mattress protector, some fresh sheets, and the washing powder we use at home. They also send me a tube of cream from the pharmacy. It helps, but even with the itching sorted, I find it hard to sleep, and I twitch and twist around frequently, my bedclothes often ending on the floor.

> *Having to share the shower is horrible. I woke early today so that I could be the first. The water from the shower comes out either scorching hot or icy cold.*

I learn to take a bag of clothes to the launderette and to sit there with a book, watching the clothes go round and round. It is mind-numbingly boring, and the fact that many other students see it as a potential meeting place makes it tedious at best. I take to wearing my jeans a great number of times before I wash them.

> *Jeans were invented for field workers in China and I've read that the durability of the fabric is increased by dirt.*

I wear, in rotation, three different types of sweatshirts that don't need ironing. I can't believe how my standards have slipped. I also struggle with the cold. My circulation doesn't handle extremes of temperature at the best of times, and the unaccustomed frosty atmosphere, digs its fangs into me. I carry a frozen block of ice within, which spreads its lattice of glacial fretwork through me. I am an Arctic maiden.

> *I find mealtimes strange. I have a sandwich for lunch and a packet of soup in the evening, which I make in the communal kitchen. Most of the students eat two or three chocolate bars for breakfast. I eat fruit. Sometimes my parents send boxes packed with treats in the post – muesli bars, Japanese rice crackers, and unusual cheeses. I keep them fresh in a plastic box that I leave on my window sill since I don't trust the shared fridge.*

I observe what everyone wears and modify my clothes accordingly.

Body piercing is becoming popular. So are bindis, a beauty spot placed decoratively in the middle of the forehead. According to a book I read in the library, the original positioning of the bindi was between the eyebrows, since this was seen as the seat of latent wisdom, said to control various levels of concentration through meditation, so that the bindi could be the outlet of this potent energy. In Asia, a red bindi signifies life, whilst black bindis are placed on children's foreheads to avert the evil eye. Amongst some university students, bindis in all colours prevail, as do tattoos on most parts of the anatomy. The working-class associations they once had are no more. They are now high fashion as well as an individual statement.

Gradually, I start to identify some faces from out of the vast sea of students. Variety with regards nationalities, hairstyles, individuality of attire, and range of 'normalcy' is huge, and for once, I do not feel different. Difference at university is celebrated, the more individual, the better. I start nodding to certain people I see whom I recognise from either my block of flats or from various lectures. They nod back. Sometimes we exchange smiles. I falter at lunch, not sure who to sit next to at the refectory, and then one day, I sit with my tray next to a boy who attends some of the same lectures as me and who is very good looking.

He initially only acknowledges my presence with a nod, since he is focused on the plate in front of him with immense concentration, as he shovels down the 'all-day breakfast' menu that he has ordered: two eggs with bacon, baked beans, fried bread, tomatoes, mushrooms, and chips. Once he has washed this all down with a pint of orange juice, he sits back and gives me a wide grin.

'Hi,' he says, 'how are you settling in?'

'Fine,' I answer. 'I'm very well, actually. And you?'

'Oh, you know, so-so,' he says with a twinkle in his eye, adding, 'I'm Jamie, by the way.'

We sit next to each other at the next lecture, and he introduces me to his friends. Later, we go for a drink at the student bar.

My parents write to me frequently. I am sad every time I receive a letter from home, even sadder when I speak with my parents on the telephone. I hadn't expected to miss them as much as I do.

Nora writes to me too. She sends me beautiful art cards and sheets of delicate writing paper, all covered in her tiny, neat script: rows and rows of perfectly formed, even letters, as if they have been typed. There is never one mistake, one scribble, or one inkblot. Does she draft everything first and then write it neatly? She tells me that she has started studying in earnest for her A-level exams now and is enjoying schoolwork a lot more. She has also been referred to a new therapist for individual work, and she gets on well with her. 'For the first time,' she writes, 'I feel there is a reason for getting better.'

She also writes that her parents have now separated and that her father has moved into lodgings of his own. Her mother will move to a smaller house soon. As usual, she tells me nothing about how all of this affects her.

I pine for all things familiar that first term. I remember trivial things from home – an old money box I keep on my bedroom shelf, a set of little Chinese masks on the kitchen walls, the way my mother absentmindedly curls a lock of her hair around her finger when she reads, or how my father taps to the beat of the songs he likes on the steering wheel of the car, and I then have to control a sudden welling of tears in my eyes.

Money, or the lack of it, is also restrictive. My parents have usually given me adequate pocket money for my needs, and the sudden economic deprivation is a shock. I decide that I need a job, and I get one being a waitress in an American-style diner, which I spread over two evenings a week and alternate weekends. I find the work hard, particularly dealing with difficult customers. I also struggle to balance homework assignments and extra reading.

I meet Jamie and his friends most days. They like to watch or play football at the weekend and go out drinking towards the end of the week. He's so lucky. He stays with friends from the year above in his own accommodation.

I tentatively try to make friends with a girl called Rebecca who is in my building.

'Do you know, I cry every night because I miss my boyfriend back at home so much,' she lisps, her eyes filling up with tears. 'I want to give up and go back to him.'

'Can't you see him in the holidays?' I puzzle.

She looks at me pityingly. 'Do you have a boyfriend, Maya?' she asks, and when I blush, she sighs, 'Well you won't understand, then.'

I stop seeing Rebecca after a while, because my impatience grows with each statement she utters. I hear the same litany from her lips. I avoid other girls too and hang out with Jamie and his mates instead.

I'm still not sure where I fit in.'

Jackson and Freddy

15 July 2006

Jackson looked around their new large and airy penthouse apartment overlooking the River Thames. It was in stark contrast to where he had ever lived, and it certainly was an unimaginable leap from the cardboard boxes in doorways that Freddy and he had shared. Freddy caught his eye and gave a triumphant whoop. 'We're in,' he said, 'Jackson, we did it!'

Jackson nodded. His heart was beating fast, and his throat felt dry but he knew it wasn't because of their move. It was because of what he was going to do next. The time was right for him to telephone his mother and invite her to leave the Bastard and come and live with him. He couldn't wait to hear the lilt in her voice and visualise the happiness in her eyes when she knew that finally, she could leave all her pain behind.

He went into the guest bedroom for the third time that day. He had decorated it in the colours she liked and made it very comfortable. He could see that her clothes would probably only fit into a small space in the existing wardrobes, but he planned to take her shopping once she arrived. Harrods food halls, he thought. She's never seen them, and she would love the experience. We could go in a red London bus. Maybe I could get her a cashmere sweater from Marks & Spencer – Maxmara would scare her – and a blue scarf to match her eyes? Also, she'll love the Albert Memorial, the Tower of London, and Camden Market, and then I could book tickets for the theatre. She will like a musical. Just thinking about spoiling her made him smile. It didn't cross his mind that these were all experiences he hadn't given to himself either; they were bits of information he had absorbed and stored as marking accomplishment in life.

He went back into the living room and picked up the telephone. He dialled the number and instantly put down the receiver when he heard his stepfather's answer-phone message. He wouldn't leave a message; he would call later. He just couldn't wait to hear her voice.

Chapter 25

Brown Snow

Maya 1999

I can't wait to go home for Christmas. To my surprise, nothing has changed. Even my room has been kept as it was when I left.

> *Why am I homesick when I'm at university and university sick when I'm at home?*

We spend a quiet Christmas Eve together. When Grandma was alive, she and I would go to midnight mass together, but now there is no one to carry on that tradition.

I decide to go for a long walk on Christmas morning before I go back to help my father with making lunch. Gone is my excitement to be back. Instead I am troubled by having to fit back into old, established relationship patterns at home. I resent having to give up my new identity as an adult to be the junior person at home.

> *I went for a walk in the morning. It was a cold, crisp, clear morning, and my breath formed dense vapour balloons ahead of me as I breathed out. The temperature was exhilarating. The paths were damp with melted morning frost, the leaves on the trees glistening as though they had recently been polished with spittle and Mr Sheen. A feast of poinsettias provided brilliant seasonal colour along the path. The town was all lit up with glittering fairy lights, even in the morning; the lamp posts were entwined with garlands and hanging Christmas lanterns. The shop fronts were inviting, with beautiful evening gowns for New*

Year's Eve parties in the windows of some, overcoats and smart suits in others. The streets were deserted, since everyone was either sleeping late after midnight mass or preparing for the family festivities of the day.

Christmas has always been associated with Grandma for me. I remember her worrying about the Christmas menu two months in advance. Should she make duck according to a Danish Christmas recipe she had read, the thighs only, boiled first and then roasted, covered in thick layers of its own fat and salt? Or should she order a goose and stuff it with a recipe of spicy gooseberry compote? Then would the flavour of the meat be to everyone's liking, and did she really want to go and queue at the butcher's to make the order and then queue again to collect it? Grandfather would probably refuse to go and pick it up, especially if the premises were crowded with other eager Christmas carnivores. Perhaps she should stick to turkey, but embellish the usual recipe, using some spices in the gravy – but would that deviate from the traditional festive spirit? Once she had come to some decision about the meat she would serve, she would then apply the same complicated process of decision making to the accompanying vegetables. Should she serve parmesan roasted parsnips again, or should she serve little florets of broccoli with garlic and Stilton instead? Should she make the traditional roast potatoes that my father loved, perhaps sprinkled with cumin and black pepper this time, or mini noisettes of potatoes that we could have fun making together?

During these times I was expected to remain quiet but attentive. She appeared to want help in coming to a decision, and yet she would get very short with me if I did voice an opinion.

Once the main meal had been decided on, we would then shop together for ingredients for the Christmas pudding.

* * *

I put down my pen with a sigh. I am looking forward to reading this, but I am also apprehensive about how it may make me feel. Making Christmas pudding was such a special activity that since Grandma died, I have been unable to eat any. As a point of fact, I felt betrayed when my mother decided to make some last Christmas. I had fruit instead, which offended her terribly, but I didn't care. I haven't been able to listen to 'The Holly and the Ivy' either, and when the children's choir sang it in church, I had to walk out, since it was Grandma's favourite carol and she would sing it at the top of her voice.

* * *

Making Christmas pudding with Grandma is one of my favourite tasks. We stir, dice, and beat, the smell of nutmeg blending with the fumes of Grandfather's best brandy that she insists on using to marinate the ingredients of the cake. I often finish the whole process reeling, inebriated by the fumes, since we take turns to hand stir the cake, making a wish each time we swap places. I love licking the bowl and the spoon of leftovers, and Grandma joins me, sticking her fingers in the mess with gusto. She always makes two Christmas puddings: one for Christmas Day, in which she includes a ring, a pound, a thimble, and a button as tradition dictates; and a second, little secret one for the two of us to share towards the middle of February, when she says everyone needs extra comfort food and cheer.

Thinking about my grandma as I make my festive walk makes me pensive, as always, and I wonder if I should start making my way back home. I have asked Nora to come over to our house at about five o'clock in the evening, and I am really looking forward to it.

A snowflake drifts onto my nose, and I then see a swirl of them gently start to come down. I am as excited about the icy flakes as when

I was a child. It snows so rarely and lightly in London. I lift my face to the sky, opening my mouth and letting the odd flake drift in, tasting the sharp taste of powdery ice in my mouth.

Reluctantly, I start heading the long way home, unclear why I am delaying my return. Halfway home, I pass a garden in which a tree laden with berries spreads some of its branches over the road. On impulse I pick a branch of twigs; looking around furtively to make sure I've not been spotted, I scuttle back home.

As I open the front door, I am greeted by the aroma of the turkey and potatoes roasting, the smell of thyme, basil, and oregano combining with the smell of poultry fat. My parents have started their preparations without me. I pop into the kitchen, expecting it to be a hive of bustling activity, but it is empty, although the oven light is on and the food is browning nicely within.

I take a vase from out of one of the cupboards, put the twigs in it, and take it to the table where we will have our Christmas meal. The table looks warm and inviting. It has laid on it a white tablecloth with a holly pattern in forest green and gold, and some dark green plates with gold serviettes. There is a Christmas cracker on each plate – two on mine, a concession to my youth. There are wine glasses on the table, together with red and white grape juice to go in them, since my father is happy to encourage my mother's continued abstinence.

I wander into the living room, thinking that perhaps my parents are watching a Christmas broadcast, but there's no one in there. I sit on one of the sofas and thumb through the *T.V. Times*, noting that one of my favourite sitcoms is about to start, and I decide that I will make myself something hot to drink whilst I settle down to watch it. I hear hurried footsteps upstairs as I fill the kettle. I leisurely make myself some coffee, wander back to the drawing room, and settle comfortably on the sofa again. It's certainly luxurious to be watching television at home, in contrast to watching television in my icy little room, wearing my football socks to keep warm.

I notice that my parents have got a newly framed photograph of me on the shelf next to the television. I take it as a sign that they have been missing me. My programme starts, and I settle comfortably on the cushions to the opening lyrics of the theme tune. I am hungry and wonder if my parents will be cross if I make myself some microwave popcorn in the break. Intermittently I hear footsteps crossing the landing upstairs and the noise of someone flushing the toilet.

My father's voice cuts through the programme just before the first break.

'Maya,' he calls. 'Maya, can you come up here, please? I need you.'

'I'll be there in the break,' I shout.

He calls back more insistently this time, saying that he needs me now. I make my way slowly and reluctantly up the stairs.

Why do my parents assume that they can command me as and when they want?

A scene of chaos hits my eyes as I get up to the top step, and I am instantly awake, doused by a bucket of ice-cold trepidation. There are sheets on the floor on the landing, a trail of linen making its way to the upstairs toilet. My parents' bedroom door is wide open.

I rush into their room. My mother is lying on the bed, motionless. There are no sheets on the bed, but there is a stench of vomit and alcohol in the air. My father looks up when I come into the room.

Mummy drank a bottle of whisky and took four Paracetamol tablets today. Apparently Grandfather called from the Bahamas to let her know that he got married to Rhona yesterday.'

I go into action mode and make sure that the room is aired and that there is some water for my mother to drink. I switch off the oven and make my father a cup of tea. I carry the laundry down to the utility room and load the washing machine. I bring my mother clean sheets and crackers to eat.

My mother looks at us, ashamed. 'I'm sorry,' she says. 'I don't know why I'm so impulsive. As if I care what he does anyway?'

'It's okay,' says my dad. 'Shall we settle for having Christmas lunch soon?'

We have our meal at four in the evening, on trays balanced on our laps, in my parents' bedroom. My dad has done us proud with the food, although none of us savours it. We are about to start on dessert when the doorbell rings, and we all stare at each other, puzzled. I suddenly realise the time and jump to my feet.

'It's Nora,' I say. 'We invited her – don't you remember?'

My father wants me to tell her that my mother is unwell. I escape feeling guilty that I am pleased to be getting away. Nora looks like a matryoshka doll on the steps. She is holding an armful of Christmas gifts and is wrapped up well for the cold, since it is snowing outside. I put on my 'television screen' face, the one that says, 'Look at me, and be entertained.' I kiss Nora as she comes in and then offer to hang her coat. She peels off layer after layer of clothes, and I wonder how much of her is within the ones that she still insists on keeping on.

'It's very quiet,' she exclaims as I usher her into the living room. I tell her that unfortunately my mother has one of her migraines, but that my father will be joining us.

'Am I in the way?' she asks worriedly, immediately sensitive.

'Not at all,' I say definitely. Lowering my voice, I say, 'Actually, I'm delighted you're here. It's so strange to be back at home.'

After I've got her a mineral water and poured a lager for myself, we settle down to chat about university life.

'What's it like?' she asks me.

'Relaxed,' I say. 'I start attending lectures around eleven in the morning – '

'Why so late?' she says, interrupting.

'They start then,' I tell her. 'That's early. Students come in much later, if at all.'

'What about the work?' she asks. 'Is it hard?'

'Some of it is,' I say, 'and some of it is a recap of what we have done for our A-levels, with a bit more detail. The coursework assignments can be tough, though, but it's your choice how much you want to do.'

'That's brilliant,' she says. 'Not like old Ratty Bags, who insists on giving us tonnes of homework every day.' This was an irreverent nickname for Mr Ratsberg, my old maths teacher.

'What about the lecturers and the students? What are they like?' she wants to know, and I give her little character sketches of some of the students, including Rebecca, whom I mimic unkindly. 'I soo, soo miss my boyfriend. You soo, soo don't understand,' I say dolefully, and she bursts into giggles. I tell her about Mr Major, a middle-aged lecturer who is rumoured to usually end up sleeping with some of the female students by the end of the second term; and Ms Cappati, who's terribly butch, with a tribal tattoo on her left shoulder, which two female students have already copied. I tell her about my room and the communal facilities and leave out details of how uncomfortable they are. I want my student life to sound romantic, not uncomfortable and lonely.

She fills me in about herself. Apparently her father has moved out and is living with another man. I am so surprised. Her mother, whom she lives with, is proving to be an impossible companion. She is currently with boyfriend number three.

'I can't tell you the number of times I've opened the toilet door and found them having sex on the floor, or in the shower,' she says. 'I once even surprised them in the garden shed. When all is well with the men in her life, she's happy. When they leave her, she comes crying to my room at all hours of the night, wanting to talk, and once even wanted a cuddle – ugh!'

'What about your brother?' I ask.

'Oh, he does whatever he does at med school and, I believe, sees my father from time to time. I try my best to see my father too, but I make sure it's not when it coincides with Nick.'

My father interrupts our discussion as he makes his way downstairs. 'Hello Nora,' he mutters. 'I'm sorry, but Maya's mother is – '

I interrupt him. 'I've already told Nora about Mum's migraine,' I say with a warning look.

He looks at me gratefully and heads towards the kitchen. 'Would you like some Christmas lunch? We've got loads left over,' he asks.

Nora hesitates, and I immediately come to her rescue by informing my father that we had been hoping to go for a walk before it got too dark. He nods absentmindedly; he's not really listening. It is dark already, and why would we want to go for a walk anyway, especially when there is a layer of snow out there?

I gesture to Nora to come to the door with me, and I wait until she dons all her layers again. We slowly walk down to the end of our road and find a low wall to sit on, after I gallantly brush the snow off it with my glove. We sit there for a while in companionable silence. I apologise for my father's insensitivity in offering her food. She shrugs.

'Don't be,' she says. 'Anyway, my goal today will be to have something with you, perhaps some turkey and salad.'

I have to learn to stop being overprotective of Nora. I'm sure she can look after herself. I have to learn to let go, even if I worry about her ending back in hospital again.

With my newfound wisdom, I hesitate to ask her about her self-harm, but she spontaneously offers me the information I need. Apparently it stopped the day her father moved out of her family home and has not occurred since. She can now look at the cuts and start to be horrified at the scars.

'I've been told that I'll need some skin grafts on two of the scars to make them look less noticeable,' she says, 'and I hope that the others will fade, because in the summer I would like to wear some clothes that show a little more of me.'

I am delighted with my friend's progress on her road to recovery. She has never mentioned an interest in clothes, and certainly she has not showed any inclination to wear revealing clothes.

She hesitates. 'I worry so much about looking different,' she says, 'of not belonging and of never belonging.'

I look at the snow on the ground in the dim light. It has already started to go slushy around the edges, so that brown snow sits on the margins of the white. An old feeling envelops me, and for a brief second I hear the playground taunts I often heard about me.

'I'm brown snow,' I want to say to Nora. 'It's my destiny to sit on the margins of the white, not yours.'

We stay another half an hour. When we go back, I am frozen, and I stand next to the radiator in the hall. Surprisingly, my mother is downstairs and greets Nora warmly. I am pleased that she has made an effort and is dressed well. Her hair is neat, and she has made up her face carefully. We finally settle down to celebrating Christmas as it should be celebrated at about 9.00 p.m. We open the gifts that Nora has brought us all: a beautiful shawl for my mother; a recent autobiography of a famous politician for my father; some poetry books, a new leather-bound diary, a teddy bear, and some perfume for me. We eat a light meal later, which Nora suggests we make ourselves, thus avoiding any awkwardness about food preferences.

We finished the day by playing some board games and aimlessly watching television.

Nora stays over at our house for the first time, and we end up sharing a bed. We are intimate and chatty, as girls are, but I sense that Nora is anxious. I guess that this is because she worries about sharing her personal space, and so I leave her on her own before I join her to sleep. When I wander back into my room, she doesn't hear me enter, and I see her doing sit-ups on the floor. She is lost in her own world of counting, and so I discreetly leave her for longer. When I go back, she is still carrying out her routines, this time in the toilet, brushing her teeth, and then prolonged scrubbing. I leave the room again and hang around downstairs on the pretext of tidying up, and it is after about an hour when I go back upstairs. She is wearing a pair of my old pyjamas, ones that I wore when I was twelve years old, and she still looks lost. She sits on my bed, and I can see that she is shivering.

'Good night, Nora,' I say.

'Good night, Maya,' she repeats obediently, and she looks around helplessly as I change quickly, go to the toilet, which looks sparklingly clean (has she polished the taps?), turn off the light, and then get into bed. I pretend that I am not awkward and purposefully close my eyes. To my surprise, I drop off to sleep quickly, uncomfortable as I am about squashing her. I don't think she finds it that easy to sleep, but for once I am not over-solicitous. I am tired, and it's been an eventful day.

PC Reeves

August 2006

PC Reeves was tired by the events leading up to the near completion of his report. His station was unusually busy with a rush of theft, unrest, and general chaos following the terrorist attack which he had been unable to avoid being dragged into. He worked intermittently on his report and found that he continued to be strangely affected by the details he was putting together about the deceased's life. All evidence pointed to a man who had lived a reclusive life but who had desperately wanted to be totally enmeshed in those he had got to know, to the point that he had been invasive. The piles of surveillance tapes, diaries, and meticulously kept notes attested to this fact.

PC Reeves' thoughts went back to the crime scene. He thought of the neat and ordered flat, like a hotel room with regards tidiness and décor. The kitchen cupboards had rows and rows of neatly stacked cans of baked beans, tuna, and spaghetti hoops, although the fridge was stocked sparsely. Out of context in this setting had been the two television sets, one in the bedroom, the other in the kitchen, both set on silent, and both on a television channel that showed reel after reel of reality TV shows.

PC Reeves completed his profile of the man. Wealthy father and good education, he scribed. Estranged from parents who were divorced. The deceased's mother had laughed when PC Reeves had made a visit to inform her of her son's death.

'I'm relieved,' she said to PC Reeves. 'I know you'll think I'm heartless, but he was a thorn. I couldn't get rid of the waster from home. He kept checking on me like he was my gaoler. Preach, preach, preach, that's all he did, and threaten people in my life. There was no way of getting rid of him, so this is a turn for the books.'

The father was equally dismissive. 'Not seen him for a few years,' he curtly informed PC Reeves. 'I haven't wanted to, either. Was *diagnosed with some mental health problems a while ago, but whether he had treatment or not, I don't know and frankly don't care. He kept making written contact, though – you can have the letters he wrote. They're all about how I should get on with my life. How he got the information, I don't know, but it made no difference to me anyway. Never close to him. He was a whiny child and effeminate teenager. He spent too much of his time with his mother. She's to blame for how he's turned out, if you ask me.'*

PC Reeves sighed. The highly made up mother, wearing clothes more appropriate for a teenager, and the well dressed but equally disagreeable father made him feel a twinge of empathy for the dead man who had tried to live any life other than his own. He made time to go see his chief. He had checked on travel to London and wanted to go there in the next few weeks to complete the final pieces of the puzzle.

Chapter 26

'Man Ahoy!'

Maya 2000

I'm using the beautiful diary that Nora gave me for Christmas. Life is certainly puzzling and eventful enough to make good use of it.

I start my preparations for going back to university. My mother, over this short time, has become a twilight shadow of herself, a diluted watercolour instead of the dramatic oil painting that is her, but she says that she has decided to accept my grandfather's lack of motivation to involve her in his life. She thinks that we should go, if we are invited to his wedding reception. She is determined not to let him witness the effect he has upon her.

I ask my father, when we are on our own one day, cleaning the patio together, why we have not had our traditional visit from his parents before Christmas, and he reddens as he responds to my question. Apparently he visited my aunt after she had her second daughter and, seizing an opportune moment, told her about my uncle.

'She was alternately upset and angry, but in the end she thanked me for the information, apologised for any impact it may have had, and said that she would deal with it accordingly,' he says. 'I made sure that she knew it didn't affect my feelings towards her, and I also offered to support her in any way that she might find helpful,' he continues. 'Unfortunately, she contacted our parents instead.'

I insist that he tell me his parents' reaction.

Daddy told me he had received a telephone call from his parents about a week after he told his sister. His mother was on one line and his father on the other. They berated him for his conversation with her, since she had wanted a trial separation from 'Lester the molester' to think things through. Apparently, they were both furious.

My father didn't tell me at the time the full details of that discussion, especially how my grandparents questioned my honesty and integrity.

'Maya is a manipulative girl with no morals,' Grandmother de Silva had said, 'just like her mother.'

'How dare you say that both Maya and Diana have no morals?' my father had retorted angrily. The long silence on the other end of the line further exasperated him. 'Maya is a good and honest girl. It's just convenient for you to ignore the wrongdoings of the son-in-law you evidently put above us all.'

'Ruwan,' Grandfather de Silva had intercepted, 'Maya probably needs your attention, with an alcoholic mother to contend with, and what better way to get it?'

My father had stuttered in his rage. 'Please leave Diana out of this. Why are you maligning her when your son-in-law is a child abuser?'

'Well, this is where you're being deliberately short-sighted, and don't slander,' Grandmother de Silva had shouted. 'Lester is a good and decent man with an impeccable family background, no family history of mental illness or instability, and no flighty reputation like your wife. Why do you think we try to arrange for a good match of caste and family background in our culture, which you so conveniently have forgotten? It's to rule out these family insanities as much as anything. You're deliberately trying to ruin the very good marital relationship that your sister has because you're jealous, since your relationship is so terrible.'

It was then that my father decided, amidst their vitriolic tirade, that there was no point in trying to explain or justify his view; their minds were made up about him, and there was no changing that.

Grandfather de Silva had the final word. 'We're no longer going to call you our son,' he'd said, 'given your manipulative intent to harm your sister. We also disown your daughter, since she has obviously inherited the worst of both of you. Don't forget that it was at your request that we made the visits we did to your house, and now see how our goodwill has been paid back? We never should have permitted your sister to have dealing with you.'

I'm sad that Daddy has lost the little bit of family he has, through me.

'I'm sorry to have caused so much bother, Daddy,' I say contritely.

'Maya, you're not to blame. It's not your fault, but theirs, for being so small minded,' he replies. However, guilt weighs down heavily on my shoulders, and like a bullock yoked to a heavy load, I feel it, and it adds to my fear of my potential for evil. It is made all the worse by the knowledge that there is no going back for me on what has been said, since it is out there now in a defined, crystallised format instead of a hazy memory in my head. I repeatedly question the wisdom of what I have done. I try to comfort myself with the thought that I have acted in the best interests of my cousins, but I only feel a hollow echo of righteousness. What prevails instead is the refrain of my mortified conscience insisting repetitively in my head that I have deliberately ruined multiple relationships.

I slink ashamedly back to my room, unsure of what more I can say or do to repair my father's feelings. I don't ask him about my mother's reaction; I'm too scared to find out. It's all too great a responsibility to take on, and I want to escape back to student life and the confines of my cell-like room, which helps me to limit myself and my deliberations.

* * *

I go for another long walk, trudging up and down the muddy paths, since it has been raining. I know that I want to feel at peace with myself about the whole 'Lester the molester' experience. As I let the monotony of my pace and the journey soothe me, I realise that by writing what happened, I can be more objective about the Lester experience. I can see that it wasn't about me; I could have been anyone; he just had the opportunity with me, and he took it. What I worry about more is the impact it has had on my father and his family relationships. His parents still don't speak with him, and we no longer endure their visits. I give my father a telephone call as I walk.

'You know, Maya,' he says in his usual calm way, not in the least surprised at my questioning him on a matter so out of context, 'sometimes things happen to make you realise your priorities. My needs from my current family – Mummy and you – trump my needs from my past family – your grandparents. I've got what's most important, and I've let go of what I can't have.'

* * *

My holidays are soon over, and this time it's much easier to leave. I drive fast to the university, only stopping once at a service station en route. The first time I made this journey, I had to pull up on the hard shoulder of the motorway to calm my breathing, and today as I drive, my mind wonders whether I might have a panic attack behind the wheel, and what the consequences of that could be. As I feel the familiar tightening of my chest that accompanies these fearful thoughts, I do my best to dismiss them through rational self-talk, and after a while, the symptoms subside and I involve myself in listening to the radio and to observing the changing scenery around me.

I ring Jamie immediately I get back, and I love hearing his familiar drawl on the telephone.

'Come over,' he says. 'We are just about to have some beers and a couple of joints.'

I go over to Jamie's home after I have unpacked my car. I leave my room window ajar to get rid of stale air and dismiss the empty feel of the room.

Jamie's place is, as usual, in disarray, even though his flatmates have only been there a few hours. There are dishes and dirty mugs in the sink, stubs of cigarettes and joints in overflowing ashtrays, and empty packets of crisps and chocolate wrappers littered on the kitchen top. They are all starting to settle around the television with cans of lager when I walk in, and I am greeted with great enthusiasm. I help myself to a can and make myself comfortable.

As I catch up with everyone's news, someone new walks into the room from the bathroom. He has just had a shower, and he has a towel wrapped around his lower half. His torso is bare.

Drops of water clung to his hair and the backs of his shoulders. Tendrils of damp, dark chest hair clung to his chest as though caressing him and one rivulet ran down his finely toned chest and down to his stomach.

A momentous shiver runs right through me as I let myself drag my eyes away from the droplets of water to meet his eyes. As I do, I am instantly and totally bewitched.

'Hi, Rob. Meet Maya,' says Jamie casually, flicking an arm in my direction and then vaguely in the direction of the vision in the towel.

He's very relaxed, even though the towel barely covers him. He walks towards me and looks me up and down before stretching out a hand. 'Hi, Maya, good to meet you,' he says.

His hand is warm, and his grasp is not too firm but not too gentle, either. I remember reading an article once about a person's handshake and how you could judge their character from it. Was it some psychology undergraduate student's 'not particularly useful for understanding human behaviour but will generate media interest' research project? I'm mesmerised by the damp hairs that cover his thighs, and I do my best not to look. He is still holding my hand, and I hesitantly take it away and then sit back on the chair, trying to look nonchalantly non-aroused. Dazed, I take a huge swig of my lager and, absentmindedly, a large puff of Jamie's joint, as Rob heads towards his room to change. Sadly, he doesn't re-emerge from that room for the duration of my stay that evening, and finally, terribly disappointed I stagger back to my room, unused to the high state of arousal, the large quantity of drink, and the dope. Jamie accompanies me back as protection, although neither of us is in any state to defend ourselves effectively, should we need to.

I hang around Jamie and his mates most of that term.

I really want to meet Rob, but he's strangely elusive.

I find out that he is reading law and that he is at a different campus. He appears to be a diligent student; if rumour is to be believed, he attends all his lectures and hands in all his coursework assignments on time. He never joins us socially.

I dreamt last week that Rob talked to me. We were both wearing small towels.

I start having cold showers in the mornings, much as I detest them, to suppress the longing in my body. Sometimes there is nothing I can do to make me less restless. I take to running every morning before lectures and sometimes in the evenings too. I think of nothing when I run, only push myself further and further.

Help! I'm turning into my mother.

One evening I go out drinking with Jamie and the boys (still no Rob) and purposely get completely drunk. Jamie takes me back to his room, since I am incapable of putting myself to bed. I vaguely remember stumbling up his stairs with my arms around his waist and murmuring that I should really brush my teeth. I take off my make-up, saying something like, 'Leaving make-up on makes you get spots,' before passing out.

I wake up in the middle of the night, desperate for the toilet, and unsteadily make my way there and back. Getting back in bed with Jamie, I am overwhelmed by desire. Why is Rob so elusive? He is so close – in the next room – and yet so unattainable. Still partially drunk and therefore completely uninhibited, I rub my body against Jamie's, and he moves closer. We stay still for a while, our bodies touching, whilst I enjoy the warmth of him. Then our bodies gradually awaken to each other, until we are slowly and then fiercely moving to the same rhythm, aiming for the same goal. Due to the steady build-up of need I have been experiencing for Rob, I climax quickly, but Jamie, suddenly awakening fully and coming to his senses, leaps away from me.

He sits up in bed and puts on the side light. 'Christ, Maya!' he exclaims. 'I'm so sorry.'

He looks hugely distressed, and I drowsily sit up. I can't think in a straight line. 'Doesn't matter,' I mumble, before dropping back off to sleep.

He shakes me awake, and I desperately clutch at my sore head. 'It does matter,' he says. 'I should never have taken advantage of you whilst you are in this state. I'm really sorry.'

He's so sweet. I gently pat his face, although my hand seems to have trouble reaching the exact place I want to touch. 'Itsh okay,' I slur. I will say anything for an easy life at the moment. 'Got to go to shleep now... ' And given that my body is finally empty of desire, I roll over and go back to sleep instantly.

When I awake, it's eleven o'clock the following morning, and I find myself in an empty house, since everyone has, amazingly, gone off to their various lectures. I sit up in bed somewhat confused, and then immediately I feel shame about my actions, particularly in involving good and decent Jamie in a situation where he is only a pawn. It frightens me how out of control I can get after I drink alcohol.

I make my way to the toilet and then decide to have a quick shower before I go back to my room. If I hurry, I will probably make it to the last lecture. I help myself to one of Jamie's clean towels and then decide to have a bath. This is a luxury not available in my accommodation, and I take my time, luxuriating in the warmth and making sure that I am clean and completely awake when I step out of it. Wrapping the towel around me, I make my way back to Jamie's room and then stop as I hear someone's key in the lock. The door swings open, and Rob walks in. He has on a pair of black trousers and a black, heavyweight leather jacket, and his hair is all tousled. He looks surprised to see me, and then he nods briefly before continuing to make his way to his room.

'Jamie okay?' he asks, looking towards Jamie's room as he passes by me, and I suddenly realise how it must look to him. Desperate to make him see that Jamie and I are not a couple, I mumble, 'No, no, he's at a lecture. I just wanted to freshen up for the morning after last night.'

I stop as I realise that this sounds even worse. Before I can say any more, he has gone into his room. Shivering, I go back into Jamie's room to change, and I wrinkle up my nose at the smell of stale tobacco clinging onto my top. The trousers are not as bad. Hoping Jamie won't mind, I dig into his wardrobe again and pick out a rugby shirt and put that on. It feels comfortable and smells freshly laundered. He has obviously done the same as me and brought back a load of washed and ironed clothes and linen from home. As always, I feel warm at the thought of Jamie and scribble a quick note to him, thanking him and letting him know that I have borrowed his shirt and towel and will clean them both and return them. I prop up the note on his bed, which I hurriedly tidy, and make my way to the front door to let myself out of the flat. I have just started making my way down the stairs when the door opens behind me and Rob starts making his way to the exit too. I notice that he takes in the fact that I am in Jamie's top, with my hair wet and uncombed, before he rushes off, barely acknowledging my existence.

Damn, damn, damn! I don't see him for weeks when I've made an effort with my make-up and clothes, and then he sees me in the most compromising of situations, looking like a wreck.

I go back to my room, change, and rush to the next lecture. I catch up with Jamie in the afternoon. He is awkward and withdrawn. I give him a hug and thank him for helping me the night before. I also tell him that we must forget our nocturnal adventure. He looks at me imploringly, and I nod very firmly.

'Are you sure?' he asks. 'I just don't know what happened. Maybe I was having a randy dream.'

I don't enlighten him with the fact that since I met Rob, I've been constantly having randy dreams. I squeeze his arm in reassurance.

*   *   *

My telephone rings, disturbing my writing. It's my father, wondering if I want to meet up to chat more about what we last spoke about. I assure him that all is well, and after we've chatted, I spend some time reflecting on these first impressions of Jamie.

Jamie is one of the sunniest people I've ever met. He usually will be able to see the bright side of something before I do – how does that happen with some people and not with others? Jamie usually laughs when I ask him.

'I don't know how,' he says, shrugging his shoulders. 'It's not such a big deal.'

Maybe not for him, but it is for me, because it gives me a sense of stability, security, and predictability that I couldn't start to put a price on.

I love Jamie's family. His parents, Louise and Jonathan, seem to enjoy each other's company, as they do Jamie's and his sister's. They show him, in a multitude of ways, how much they care for him, and they are there to support him when he needs it.

Jamie's mum once said to me, 'Parents are there to give you roots when you're young and wings when you grow up.' It's not an original saying, I think, but is that what they've done to enable him to be the wonderful person he is? How important are the foundations we have?

*   *   *

After this episode, Jamie and I resume our friendship, feeling even closer to each other, but we are both careful about going out drinking together. I increase my evening waitress shifts out of desperation for more money, and this provides me with the added restriction of depriving me of meeting up with Jamie and his flatmates at the bar.

Soon my academic abilities are tested with the first batch of coursework being due, and I find that I have got good marks in two assignments. I'm delighted. I've jumped my first academic hurdle.

Before I know it, another term is over.

It's time to go home again.

Freddy, London

23 July 2006

Freddy entered his new home that morning laden with bags. He usually spent most of his money on 3 Cs – chocolate, cocaine, and comics. When he was little and he lived at home with his parents, he found that reading comics helped to obliterate the sounds of his parents' arguments and the throwing of furniture. He also had his own cartoon sketches, which he kept in a sketch pad under his bed. One day, he would publish his own series of comics.

When he was transferred into care after his father fractured his arm and ribs for the third time, he took his comics with him and read them even more voraciously. They helped again to block out the sounds of homesickness and fear, the screaming and rushing of the hyperactive, and the despondent tread of the carers.

Freddy was about eight years old when he started reading Batman, Superman, and Spiderman. It was then that his life changed. He knew that one day he would be a superhero; after all, they were lonely, troubled souls with no families, like him.

Chocolate was his passion. When he was on the streets that was what he survived on, a bar or two of chocolate. It was a quick fix of cheap energy and he loved the taste. Cocaine on the other hand was a vice he had developed since last year. It helped him, like the other 2C's to block out despair.

When he arrived back at their penthouse apartment that morning, he was in excellent spirits. He had finally achieved superhero status. In various shopping bags, he carried a dozen boxes of Lindt and Godiva chocolates (since he had been told these were the best chocolates to buy and he felt he could now afford them), a collection of vintage Batman model toy cars, and in his pocket was a gram of cocaine.

He rushed to his room, and once he was there, he flung his new acquisitions on his bed and lay on it, turned on his CD player, and gazed fondly at the framed superhero pictures on his wall. Two more Cs to add to my collection now, *he thought,* champagne and CDs – I'm the king of my castle. *He turned up his music and settled comfortably in bed, reaching over to pop a chocolate in his mouth. He had finally got what he wanted and he hoped his friend would too once he saw his mother tomorrow.*

Chapter 27

Eat As Much As You Can

Maya 2000

'You look awful,' sounds out my mother as I walk through the door, 'far too thin, and your hair needs a cut.' Before I can say anything in my defence, she adds, 'I might as well tell you my exciting news now. I've decided to enrol on a degree course to read law.'

When Mummy told me about her course, one part of me was excited for her, but another part of me was jealous. I wish I could be cool about it.

As much to deal with this as to keep myself occupied, I take on a holiday job at a large bookshop in the high street during the break. I am particularly bored since Nora's away. I visit her new house before I find out about this, and am surprised to be faced by her mother instead of their housekeeper.

She looks gaunt and pale although immaculately dressed and made-up. 'Nora's with her father in Boston,' she informs me.

'Oh,' I exclaim, taken aback. 'Nora didn't mention anything about going away to me.'

'Well, her father is on another work trip there,' she tells me, 'and Nora decided at the last minute that she wanted to join him, even though she knew that I don't think it's a good idea.'

I hesitate on the step, not knowing what to say. She doesn't invite me in, and yet she seems to want to talk. I don't want to say anything that sounds supportive of her, because that would be disloyal to my friend, and I don't want to say anything in favour of Nora, because I can see the distress in her mother's face.

'Er, please tell her I called over,' I say in the end, turning around to go.

'Well, she did promise me that she would revise out there,' her mother continues, talking to my back, and I swing around to face her again. My heart sinks, because I can see tears in her eyes.

'Maya?' she asks me imploringly. 'Do you think she's maintaining her weight? I really don't think she's well enough to be having long breaks away from her treatment programme.'

She's stating my concerns too, but instead I awkwardly try to reassure her. 'I'm sure she'll be fine. Um, yeah, I'm sure…,' I can't finish my sentence gracefully, so I impulsively put my arms around her and then turn around and run away before I burst into tears.

* * *

I'm surprised to read this. Nora has always depicted her mother in a two-dimensional way, as someone with no space for anyone else but herself and as someone with an insatiable sexual appetite. At times she has been described as the pampered wife with nothing to do but amuse herself by cooking. Never has she said that her mother might have concerns about her, and yet it would seem, if this diary entry is anything to go by, that Nora's mum did worry. Was it nourishment that Nora couldn't take in, or was it something her mother couldn't feed her?

* * *

Work is mind-numbingly boring, but I need that staff discount for all the books I want to buy.

One day, when I have been allocated the task of sorting out teenage fiction, I hear a familiar voice behind me. I swing around, nearly toppling off the small ladder I'm on, and see Mark with a well-toned, tanned blonde whom I assume to be Marie. She has a book list in her hand, which she is pointing out to Mark. My heart speeds up instantly, and I immediately turn back to the shelf, wondering what I should do, and then decide to make a quick getaway. I am edging towards the exit when she asks me whether we have a particular book in stock. I have no option but to look at her and Mark, and I direct them towards the section she is looking for. Mark's eyes meet mine for a brief moment before they move away.

I had such a rush of rage towards Marie. I would have liked to have said that I knew her man intimately and that my body had made his work again. That we'd spent many afternoons together and that I had a drawer full of presents from him.

I stay in the toilet for ages and finally make my way back to where I've left my ladder, and I start sorting out books at breakneck speed. After about twenty minutes of this, my curiosity gets the better of me, and I make my way towards the book section I had directed them to, drawn by some magnetic pull, wanting to check if I could catch one more glimpse of Mark, but they're gone. I check the cash desks nearest to me, but they're not there either, and so, rather disappointed but also relieved, I go back to my sorting.

I don't see Mark at work again, although I find myself dressing just that bit smarter for the rest of my time there, and before I know it, holidays are over. I go back determined to aim for a first-class honours degree. Somehow the matter of my mother completing a degree has unsettled me more than I could have predicted. Our roles have been reversed. She's been the weaker one, the one needing protection and care. Suddenly she's fighting back, and I'm not sure if I like it.

* * *

I rub my eyes wearily, and I lay down my pen and stretch myself. I've been writing frantically, and my neglected cup of tea is now cold. *What goes around, comes around,* I think. My obvious reluctance for my mother to compete with me in academic work sounds much the same as her reaction to me when I first started private school. Do we both vie for the same thing, and if we do, what is it? I hobble to the kitchen, shaking pins and needles from one leg, and make myself a sandwich and a fresh cup of tea. Sighing, I pick up my pen.

*   *   *

The next term swirls by, and I'm caught up in the carousel of academic work and part-time restaurant work. I barely have time to register that Rebecca (the having problems in separating, 'I miss my boyfriend' girl) has left, unable to put up with her separation or insecurity, whichever it may be. I spend all my time with Jamie.

I've decided to give up on Rob.

It's soon Jamie's birthday, and I'm invited to celebrate it with him and a group of friends. He suggests that we go to a Chinese restaurant and then onwards 'to paint the town red.' He warns me affectionately, in private, that he'll be keeping an eye on my alcohol consumption. He doesn't want any 'extra' birthday presents.

My shift at the restaurant needs completion before I can meet them. I've asked for an early slot so that I can meet Jamie and friends on time. I rush around, serving the 'early bird' diners, and then I change at work into my casual clothes. I've decided to be practical; 'painting the town red' probably means a pub crawl.

I wear a pair of trousers and a casual shirt, and since there's a breeze, I put on my leather jacket. I tuck up my hair so that from a distance it looks short. The boys usually tease me when I put on make-up, so I keep my ministrations to a minimum; spray myself with some perfume to take away the smell of burgers, onion rings, and chips, an inevitable hazard of work; and start on my way.

I make sure that I've got Jamie's presents. I've bought him a computer game that I know he's been wanting for a while and some chocolates, as well as a rude birthday card. I'm running about a quarter of an hour later than planned, and so I hurry.

The streets are full of evening shoppers, people hurrying home from work, and many young people out for a good night's entertainment. The Chinese restaurant that Jamie has chosen is very popular with students. It has an 'eat as much as you like' policy for a standard amount – an open invitation to waste, as it appeals to people's greed and mistaken idea of value for money. The entrance to the restaurant has a line of people queuing to get in, and I hope that Jamie has managed to arrive in time to get a table. I walk past the queue, experiencing some stares, and make my way into the restaurant.

'I'm meeting up with a group of friends,' I say, and then I catch sight of William and Garfield, two of Jamie's flatmates, and wave wildly at them.

'I can see my friends,' I say, rather obviously, to the seating host, and she nods me on.

'Maya,' they scream joyfully as I come up to them, and I'm enveloped in several big hugs until I get to the end of the table where Jamie is, surrounded by a bunch of red balloons with 'Chin Chow Chinese Restaurant' printed on them in gold letters.

'Happy birthday, James, my dear,' I say, producing his gift from my bag and giving him a hug.

'Thanks, Maya, Oh, I do hope it's another porno movie,' he says jokingly, tearing off the wrapping and then looking really pleased.

'Look, guys,' he exclaims, waving around the computer game and the box of chocolates, 'real presents, not like yours, you perverts, all condoms and blow-up dolls – all except for yours, of course, Rob.'

I look at the person that he's addressing, who has been hidden from view until now. It's Rob. I've become so used to him not being at any of the social gatherings that it hasn't even crossed my mind that he might have been invited. I'm instantly conscious of what I see as my masculine appearance.

'Hi, Maya,' he says. So he remembers my name.

'Hi, Rob,' I reply huskily. I've rehearsed this line so many times on my own that as I say it, I have a sense of déjà vu.

Everyone clatters around, getting ready to go up to the buffet table to help themselves to food.

'Come on, Maya,' Jamie requests, 'just dump your bag and then start getting stuffed.' Jamie is interrupted as he is dragged to the buffet by his friends, whilst I look rather awkwardly at Rob and then move towards an empty chair next to him. Rob looks amused.

'Get stuffed isn't usually what I would say to my girlfriend,' he chuckles.

I see a golden opportunity to put him right on some facts. 'Well, as just another friend of Jamie's,' I say, 'there's never any elegant treatment for me from him, or from any of them, come to think of it.'

His eyes meet mine, and I drown in their treacle depths. He smiles very slowly, and my legs immediately turn to jelly.

'I'm very pleased to hear that, Maya,' he murmurs, 'very pleased indeed.'

We walk together to the buffet table, and I serve myself in a daze. My vision is strangely altered, and everything consumable suddenly, embarrassingly, takes on sexual overtones. The sweet and sour prawns look glistening and moist, like kissable lips, and the spare ribs, phallic.

'Do you put MSG in your food?' I overhear a customer ask, and I giggle deliriously.

Not sure how I can eat anything when my stomach is doing cartwheels, I shuffle back to the table with a mixture of food on my plate, and then I sit down to make small talk to Rohan sitting next to me, whilst I wait for Rob to return with his plate. When he does, we eat in silence whilst everyone laughs and jokes around us. The focus on sexual innuendo extends into the conversation.

'Hey, Jamie, do you know what an Australian kiss is?' someone asks.

'No, mate, tell me,' says Jamie. There is a lull in the conversation around the table.

'It's like a French kiss, but down under.'

I find myself going deep, warm claret. I usually let the boys' humour drift over me, and sometimes I can tell a rather racy joke myself, but whilst Rob is next to me, I'm conscious of every statement and every movement.

Halfway through his meal, Rob turns to me. 'How are you finding university?' he asks.

'Oh, good,' I mutter inanely, searching my brain for some scintillating conversation, but the left hemisphere of my brain is experiencing a drought.

We converse intermittently, most of the time stopping to listen to the others. Once we are finished, the boys suggest going on a pub crawl in the red light district. I can see Jamie looking at me uncomfortably, and I hesitate. Surprisingly, Rob comes to my rescue.

'Jamie,' he says, 'I can't stay up too late tonight. I can walk Maya back if she likes.'

I see Jamie hesitating, and I falter too, not certain that I've heard what's just been said. If my eyes have been playing tricks, so could my ears. Jamie looks at me and then makes up his mind.

'Thanks, Rob, that's great,' he says. Bending over to kiss me on the cheek, he whispers, 'Are you okay with this, Maya? Else we can change plans.'

I nod vehemently – so hard that my head hurts. We part ways at the entrance to the restaurant. There's a faint drizzle as we leave, which then turns to a heavy downpour. Rob and I run for cover and stand underneath the awning of a shop front. I'm breathless, and I pretend it's from the run. The rain doesn't look like it's about to cease, and small puddles start forming on the road.

Rob hesitates before saying, 'I think there's a wine bar around the corner. Should we make a dash in there?'

We run madly, the rainwater splashing up on our trousers, the muddy droplets making our legs look like they've developed chicken pox. My hair comes out of its confines and clings in tendrils to my face and along my back. There's a drop of water at the end of my nose, which I blow at as we run.

I see the bright lights of a wine bar and dash in there, Rob next to me. He stands on the step and shakes like a terrier. Rivulets of water run off his coat and his wet hair, and it reminds me instantly of our first meeting. He takes a cotton handkerchief from his pocket – the only other person I know who owns proper handkerchiefs is my grandfather – and first dabs it gently on my face and then, terribly intimately, uses it to clean his own face. A tremor runs down my spine, and I know that it's not because I'm chilled. We push open the swing doors and enter. It's all glass and chrome and is packed full of people. All the seats are occupied, and the air is hazy with smoke. The noise level is high. Rob looks at me with lifted eyebrows as though asking me if this is acceptable, and I nod. He mimes having a drink, and when I agree, he pushes his way to the bar. Once we have ordered our drinks, we make our way to where there's a huge suspended radiator and stand by it to dry out. Whenever we want to talk, we have to put out heads very close together so that we can hear. I'm conscious of having eaten both onion and garlic, and I hope that my breath smells acceptable.

We start talking about our respective courses, but then we veer towards our personal lives. I ask him about himself, all the time conscious of the sexual spark between us but trying my hardest to stay on a neutral course of conversation. He is reticent, and I have to coax him to disclose information about himself.

'It took me a while to make up my mind whether I wanted to do this degree,' he says.

'Why?'

'Oh, boring family money issues, but it's all sorted out now.'

'Well, it's great you're finally here,' I say, and he smiles.

'I'm beginning to realise that too,' he replies, 'especially after today.'

I chatter on to cover my embarrassment. 'Rob, why are you never around the flat?' I ask.

'Oh,' he answers, looking a bit put out, 'you've found out my dark secret, Maya.' Then, because I look at him, uncertain whether he's joking or not, he adds, 'I have a driving job most evenings and weekends, and I also do some bookkeeping, since I need the money.'

Rob is amazing for being so committed.

'Now it's my turn to ask you about your deep, dark secrets, Maya,' he says, and my heart briefly arrests. 'Are you and Jamie just friends, or have you been a couple at any time?'

I relax. 'Jamie and I have always been good friends,' I say.

'What about that occasion at the flat when you slept the night?' he asks.

'Oh, Jamie rescued me that night when I was far too drunk to be on my own,' I say, as I draw a veil in my own head about the subsequent happenings of that night. I notice that Rob is very contained with his drinking, and it's not difficult for me to follow suit. The attraction between us is headier than a whole bottle of brandy, and when we leave the wine bar, I feel drunk on our magnetism.

He walks me back to my flat, and we kiss very gently under the oak tree near the entrance. His breath is warm and gentle on my face.

'Good night, Maya,' he says. Then hesitantly, 'You're sure you're not Jamie's?'

'Good night,' I reply. 'I'm not anyone's, Rob. Look forward to seeing you tomorrow.'

*   *   *

Revisiting the past is such a strange thing. Here on paper is my attraction to Rob, how he mesmerised me, and how I fell for him. I am ashamed that my attraction to him was so physical, but as Beck, a modern-day psychologist, says, 'There's more to the surface than meets the eye.'

In Suffolk

21 July 2006

The plan was set, and he ran through it in his head every night before he went to sleep. He had even written down, minute by minute, how he expected it to go.

It was simple, really. He wanted her back, and he would get her by showing her how important he was to her. No one else compared, and she would realise that when he showed her. Some people needed evidence before they realised. He didn't; he knew she was the only one for him, and he always had.

His plan was foolproof. He would write her a letter letting her know how much he loved her and saying that he couldn't live without her. He had already arranged for her to come and see him, and when she was on her way, he would take the mixture of drugs he had collected over the past few weeks, timing it absolutely accurately, including the small margins of time variation. He knew she would come when he told her what he had to show her, and because she always kept her word, he knew that she would save him, because she was an angel, and she was meant to be with him and no other.

Then nothing more would be necessary. They would finally be together, but if she needed a little more convincing, well, he could certainly do that.

He crumpled up the paper that had the minute by minute plans and threw it in the bin. He smiled and realised how rusty those muscles were. I need to smile more *he thought,* and I will be soon. Life will be sweet. Yes, very sweet indeed.

Chapter 28

Misfit v. Miss Fit

Maya 2000

Two days, which seem like two years, go by before I next see Rob. We have brief, bittersweet moments of meeting, wedged between his various part-time jobs. This becomes our pattern: little morsels of snatched moments, passionate but hurried. He works long hours. I've never come across anyone as dedicated to the application to work, apart from my father. Spurred on by his activity, and as a way of distracting myself, I too start to apply myself to my academic work and to earning extra money.

We meet every two or three days. During these times, our encounters are intense sexual interactions, hours of suppressed longing merging into short bursts of time. I am totally swept away, like the heroines in the novels I read as a child, but I'm also cautious. I continue to check about potential others in his life, although he is never very forthcoming on information about himself. He is, however, very demanding of information about me.

'Who have you seen today?' he asks me, or, 'Who are you planning to go out with this evening?'

It is standard that he questions me on what I plan to wear if I'm going out.

Rob asked me not to wear high shoes with a short skirt and suggested that I wear trousers instead. It's so sweet he cares.

If I do go out, he telephones me first thing in the morning and asks me who I sat next to and, if it was a man, what we had spoken about all evening. He wants the information verbatim.

'Did you tell him you have a boyfriend?' he demands every time. I always reply affirmatively rather than incur his wrath.

I feel cared for by Rob's questioning, and I never tire of reassuring him of the fact that no one else is attractive to me but him.

His most-asked question, however, is whether I have seen Jamie, and since I know it upsets him when I do, I start seeing Jamie less and less, although I miss him terribly. I sit next to various girls at lectures and lunch, but I find that we don't share much. After a while, I stop seeing the girls, since Rob questions me about them too.

'Do they sleep around much?' he asks. 'Are they straight?'

I start spending hours in the library, poring over journal articles and the latest publications. As a result, my essays are the best researched and the most up to date. I stay in my room, much as I hate it, and when I'm not revising, I stare at the television, not really interested in the programmes, just letting them become a colander of time.

When we are drawing to the end of the first academic year, I receive a letter from Nora. Within it is enclosed another letter in a sealed envelope. I recognise the writing on the envelope instantly. It's Mark's. Nora's letter states that Mark has contacted her on two occasions, asking her how I was and requesting a contact telephone number. She writes: *I refused to give him one, not knowing if you would want him to have it or not, and to test his keenness, I told him to write to you instead so that I can pass it on. Imagine my surprise when the following day, there was a letter addressed to you, care of myself, through my letter box. Well, here it is, and remember you don't have to open it if you don't want to.*

I smile, acknowledging her fierce protectiveness of me, and skim the rest of her letter quickly. She writes that she hopes that I'm well, and adds that she has just completed her examinations and is awaiting the summer holidays, when she is hoping to work as a volunteer in a children's home in Spain. Would I like to join her? If not in the summer, perhaps in the Christmas break, since if she likes it that is where she will plan to go again. I don't process her suggestion any further, since I'm in too much haste to read the enclosure.

I open Mark's letter with shaking hands. *Dearest Maya*, it begins. Dearest? Surely that's an intimate way to begin a letter to an ex-girlfriend. *Although I've not been in contact, I've never stopped thinking about you. Neither have I stopped regretting the decision I made to try to make my relationship with Marie work. You will, perhaps, not be surprised to know that things between us have not changed significantly, even after a number of sessions of couple therapy. I suppose I've been cowardly and clutched at straws. However, I was trying to convince myself that I had to stay with my decision, until I saw you in the bookshop the other day. Maya, my heart leapt, and I felt a myriad of feelings that have been completely dormant since I last spent time with you. You looked adorable balancing on that ladder, with the sunlight from the fanlight above illuminating your hair, and that thoughtful expression you have when you are all absorbed in something.*

I put the letter down, my hand shaking. I am finding it hard to breathe. When I regain my composure, I start reading again: *I tried to avoid contacting you immediately after that day, because I felt so guilty about the surge of feelings within me, but also because I didn't want to cause you any more pain. However, after three weeks, I couldn't go on any longer and had to give in and browse around the section I saw you stacking books in. Do you know, I worried that I might be mistaken for a child molester, so often did I visit the junior book section, but I realised after a while that your holidays must have finished and that you had gone back to university. So, Maya, this is why I'm contacting you now. I'm unable to get you out of my thoughts,*

I live and breathe you every day, and I would really like to see you again, perhaps in the summer holidays, if you are coming home? I am enclosing my telephone number. Please ring me whenever you can. Of course, I'll respect your wishes if you don't wish to make any contact, but I do so hope you will. Yours truly, Mark.

> *I can't believe what Mark wrote to me. He still loves me. Why am I so excited? I'm totally in love with Rob, aren't I? Mark is over.*

I telephone Nora. She's not surprised to hear from me. It's not often that we talk on the telephone to each other, but having forwarded me Mark's letter, she knew I'd call. I summarise the contents. She is, as usual, her cynical self, and she answers me with the dogged scepticism that so characterises her.

'Don't believe any of it,' she commands. 'Ignore him, Maya, and concentrate on Rob since he sounds too good to dump.'

I agree and guiltily put away Mark's letter in my trinket box with my other treasures, even though Nora has instructed me to throw away the letter and not to memorise the contact telephone number. I determinedly focus on Rob when I next see him, worried that my face might be illuminated with the joy of receiving Mark's letter. Usually Rob is very good at sniffing out potential disloyalty. Instead, he is edgy and in need of comfort about his academic performance. His anxiety makes him short-tempered, and the intensity of our meetings is now interspersed by small rows, usually initiated by him.

'Rob, I'm worried about our summer break away from each other,' I confide in him. He is the most available, the most comforting of me when I'm like this, imploring and anxious.

'We'll write to each other,' he assures me. 'Who knows, I may even come and visit you.'

'I'm not sure if I believe you,' I say, 'but I'll remain hopeful.'

'Can you remain faithful to me whilst we have our break?' he asks me. He asks me this question repeatedly.

'Of course I will, Rob,' I say, a little too vehemently each time. 'There's no one else – there could be no one else in my life but you.'

To my ears, my voice sounds brittle and untrue. Mark is lodged in my brain.

I'm sure that major punishment awaits me just around the corner, over my lies and wickedness.

I'm over-passionate with Rob that evening; is it guilt, or is it dormant passion over Mark? I can't tell, and although I try to block my unease, I'm not as efficient as I usually am at doing this. The tight packaging that I usually keep around myself is starting to come apart at the sides.

The term draws to a rapid close, and on two occasions I ring the number that Mark has given me. On both occasions, I put down the receiver when I hear his voice. My behaviour splits me in two. One part, like an ex-addict, is obsessive about Mark, doesn't want to accept an ending, and wants to pursue him. The other part is totally in love and committed to Rob, and worries about the separation from him.

Jamie calls me, but I don't answer the phone. He unfailingly invites me to various parties. I accept but then don't turn up. I'm too embarrassed to tell him why I'm avoiding him. I'm also too apprehensive to turn down the invitations, in case, in his discerning way, he asks me why. I try to avoid bumping into him at lectures, and when we do meet, I'm awkward and monosyllabic. I often see him staring at me with a hurt or puzzled look on his face, and I wish I could see him again, because I miss him, as I do the camaraderie of his group of friends and their complete acceptance of me, but I also know that it won't be worth fuelling Rob's possessive control over me. It'll not be worth the hours of questioning, his angry accusations, and the lengthy pacifications I'll need to make.

* * *

I put down pen and diary and stretch. I don't like reading about this part of my life. It makes me out to have little substance and to be completely controlled by men. I also reflect on my emotional strategies. I know that I dealt with not seeing Jamie by resorting to an old denial technique that I used as a child every time we moved. I detached, not just from the person but also from myself.

* * *

The stress of balancing Rob and my secret feelings for Mark, and the energy invested in avoiding Jamie, make me start to lose weight rapidly, and Rob begins his questioning of me again – why am I attempting to 'diet' before I go home for the break? Do I want to make myself attractive to someone else? I do know, don't I, that he likes slim women? Why am I making myself so desirable to him when he can't be with me?

The term soon ends, and I go home full of anxious trepidation. Rob and I promise to write to one another and telephone each other whenever we can. I'm a little concerned about my parents' response to the knowledge that I have a boyfriend. I'm not sure if I have negotiated the change in our relationship from child to adult yet, or indeed whether I want to.

The first comment my parents make is about my loss of weight. They're worried about the dark circles under my eyes and the fact that I look tired and drawn. I rather enjoy their attention, but I pretend that I think they're fussing too much. I'm edgy, wired, as if strong espresso courses through my veins. Although I pretend that I don't know what this restlessness is about, every atom of my being is alert to the possible course of action that I can take concerning Mark.

My father tells me that he's been promoted at work again. It's a very senior post, and he'll now no longer be travelling abroad. He sounds sad when he says this, and I suddenly realise that my father is getting old. His thick, dark hair is naturally highlighted with fine silver now. There are lines on his forehead and under his eyes. He looks thinner. There's a catch in my voice when I comment on his loss of weight to him, and he gives me a little grin.

'Two of a kind, aren't we, my lovely?' he says, and the endearment makes me catch my breath. It's so long since I've heard it, but it's there, in the attic of my childhood, and I brush the cobwebs off the endearment and savour it greedily.

My mother, on the other hand, is looking exceedingly well. She's wearing a pair of jeans that are new, and they reveal curves in all the right places.

'You look well, Mum,' I say reluctantly.

'That's because I've started on a new form of yoga that strengthens the upper body,' she says. 'It's more strenuous than an hour of aerobic activity.'

She's now vegetarian – well, a 'Western vegetarian,' in that she has fish but no flesh. She says the word 'flesh' with the morbid relish of a new convert.

'I'm really enjoying my course,' she babbles on.

I pretend to be interested, but the word 'course' embeds itself and lies like a straight metal rod alongside my spine, stiffening it, pulling me away, so that my mother and I are like the South poles of two bar magnets. I curb any further discussion with her and politely excuse myself early. There are stirrings of a cobra of envy deep within me, lifting its hooded head and waiting for the opportunity to strike, accurately and venomously.

I settle back at home uneasily. Nora is in Spain, and I long for her company. I telephone Mark's number a few times again, each time saying nothing and hanging up. On one occasion, he's obviously in a restaurant, since I can hear raised voices and the clatter of plates and cutlery. After that call, I decide not to call him again; it's a window into too much painful intimacy.

I speak to Rob every day. He says he's uncomfortable being back at home. He sounds very low. He also sounds distant, and I panic. Does he sense my deception? I become extra attentive towards him.

'The atmosphere here is not good,' he says. I have an image of a polluted home, where he needs to wear a filter over his nose and mouth to keep out noxious elements. He casually asks me about my day whenever I call him, and I'm always careful to describe in much detail but leaving out any social contact I may have had.

My telephone conversations with him leave me unsettled. He's able to arouse passionate sexual feelings within me that are hard to quench, and so I take up running long distances.

I receive a postcard from Nora. She says that she's enjoying the time she's spending doing volunteer work, although the living conditions aren't the most comfortable, and the life stories of the children she's working with are distressing.

My father suggests that we all go on a short holiday. I don't want to go away with my parents, but I am hard pressed for cash, so I accept gratefully. We fly to Southern Italy. We are away from the hordes of tourists that usually frequent in the summer, but the area is full of Italians enjoying their summer break. I love the sun, and I particularly love the people, their culture, and their warm hospitality. I have a short flirtation with a very handsome waiter who works in our hotel.

What's wrong with me? I'm so out of control.

I write to Rob every other day when we're on holiday; seeing so many handsome men emerging from the sea and swimming pools can't help but bring back sensuous memories of him and of our first encounter. I telephone Mark just once, but I still can't bring myself to speak to him.

On our journey back, I decide that I will definitely contact Mark. By the time we've landed at the airport and on British soil, I've reversed my decision. My newfound confidence on holiday vanishes, and I'm back in a pit of indecision. The remainder of the summer drags by, and I start to regain the weight I've lost but exercise produces a very toned me. I don't mention any of my body changes to Rob. I know he'll disapprove, but secretly I'm pleased.

I look good at the moment, and I like it when I attract looks and whistles. Mostly I like it because now I know I look better in my jeans than Mummy.

PC Reeves

August 2006

PC Reeves put on his jeans and looked excitedly at the file on his dining table. The frantic aftermath of the bomb in town had left him, together with his colleagues, depleted. He had been forced to witness scenes of tragedy far worse than he had come across in his training, and his thoughts focused on some of the desperate stories he had heard, some running like a film spool in his head, often disrupting his sleep. He was therefore particularly pleased that the chief had granted him permission to travel to London. What's more, as a treat, the hotel and the journey were booked, compliments of the case and as recognition for the hard work invested over the past few weeks.

Before PC Reeves told Susannah about their impending time away, he made some arrangements. First he called the hotel and made sure that he paid for an upgrade to a suite.

'I would like there to be champagne and flowers in the room the day we arrive,' he informed the helpful receptionist.

He also asked to be put through to the hotel spa, where he paid for a half-day pamper package for Susannah. He made this the day he hoped to visit Maya, so that she would have something of her own to do. He called the Old Vic Theatre and booked tickets for a play – a murder mystery, of course. He had to pay premium price, but he didn't care, and then he called the Curzon Cinema in Mayfair to check on the demand for tickets for a new thriller. His last reservation was for the Sherlock Holmes experiences: a visit to the museum in Baker Street and a Sherlock Holmes tour of London.

When he put down the phone, his heart beat fast, and he felt heady with excitement. He then called Susannah.

'Hey, Suz,' he said, 'guess what? I'm not working next week.'

He waited until Susannah's squeal of pleasure died and then continued, 'For the first time I'm making full use of the fact you have *the summer off from work. I've got the okay to go to London, and if you would like to accompany me, I've just made the most amazing list of things for us to do when we get there.'*

Chapter 29

A Walk in the Park

Maya 2000 - 2001

I start making lists to help organise my return to university. In the middle of one of these list-making episodes, we receive a telephone call from my aunt. My mother answers the call and immediately passes it over to my father, a strange look on her face. The conversation is short but obviously serious. My father listens very intently to what my aunt is saying, and on one occasion he glances at me briefly before looking away.

'Do you want me to come over?' he asks, and my mother raises her eyebrows immediately.

My father arranges a date to go over and meet my aunt, and he ends the conversation by telling her to look after herself, and that she can count on his support.

Of course my mother and I are eager to be updated on the discussion.

'Well,' says my father, looking upset but elated at the same time. 'You're not going to believe this, but Lester has been reported to the dental regulatory board for malpractice. Apparently he's been accused of "inappropriate patient contact," and it seems very likely that he'll have to give up practising. Two of the patients who've complained to date are teenagers.'

> *I've heard people use the expression about having the wind taken out of their sails, but I swear I literally felt the breath leave my body for a brief moment before my mind started working overtime.*

My mother voices some of the thoughts that are swirling in tornado fashion within me.

'Well,' she says, 'I think that completely absolves Maya of any part she may have played, contrary to your parents' view. What a pervert! I hope he gets a prison sentence, as hard as that may be on your sister and the children.'

My father nods, absorbed in his own thoughts. 'Nisha's going through with a divorce for definite now. She wants me to be there when she talks to our parents about accepting her decision.'

'Make sure you don't get used and blamed again, Daddy,' I say anxiously, and he nods.

* * *

I smile wryly to myself when I remember this. Of course Daddy did get blamed by his parents, who still hold onto the view that my mother and I somehow contributed to the breakdown of Nisha and Lester's marriage. I get on really well with Nisha, and my little cousins will be the flower girls at my wedding. My grandparents have said they will not attend.

* * *

As a reaction to the news about Lester, I feel that I need to shake the clouds of the past out of my head, and I tell my parents that I am going out for a long walk and then to listen to some jazz at the new pub by the river. They too are going out this evening, to dinner with one of my father's work colleagues at a venue several miles away, and they won't be home until very late. I head towards the river. There is a long walk ahead of me, but the sun is shining, and I have all the time in the world. I take a notebook with me, and a bottle of water. I have stopped writing poems, but I think I would like to put some thoughts to paper. I wear a short skirt and a small top, revealing a part of my midriff. The triad of rest, healthy eating, and exercise works well, and I know that I look good.

The weather is glorious, and I inhale the smell of honeysuckle and jasmine, peppered by the heated smell of foliage and warm air, as I walk briskly towards the park, through which I hope to cut through to my final destination. I pass couples pushing their babies in their pushchairs and children rollerblading down the side roads, some with their dogs running alongside them, others sucking ice lollies that leave little coloured puddles on their clothes. It has been a while since I walked this route, and I look at the changes in some of the houses I pass: which houses have their exteriors painted a different colour, which have new fences or new landscaping, and which have got 'For Sale' or 'For Rent' signs outside.

I get to the park in good time and make my way to a shady spot, having bought myself a large ice cream. I haven't had a *Mr Whippy* with a flake for a long time, and so I savour it as I make long, slurping licks. There is no one in the near vicinity, and I am uninhibited in my enjoyment. Some of the ice cream melts and runs down my hand, making my fingers sticky, and I rummage around my bag with one hand whilst still holding the ice cream cone with the other, desperately trying to find a tissue.

Someone runs past me and then stops, retreats back, and flings himself next to me. I look up, startled, and see Mark's beautiful green-brown eyes staring at me. I gulp and wildly look around me, not knowing what to do with the offending cone, now dripping stickily everywhere. I fling it over my shoulder, rub my hands on the grass, and clean my mouth on my sleeve in an undignified way.

'Hi,' he says.

'H-hi,' I respond.

He looked fantastic, his blonde hair even further bleached by the sun.

'Did you get my letter?' he enquires.

'I did.'

'And? No response for me?'

'You can't just write to me out of the blue, Mark, and then expect me to get back straight away. Not after how you ended things.'

He is taken aback by my vehemence, but he nods.

'You're right, Maya, and I'm so sorry. I really wanted to do what I thought was for the best, but Marie and I are really struggling. I haven't been able to think of anyone else but you all this time.'

I stare at him. Reflected in his eyes is my projected image of Rob. As I look on, the image gets smaller and more distant and is lost completely.

It is an ineffective statement that emerges from my mouth, but I voice it anyway: 'I've a boyfriend now, Mark. I've tried to get on with my own life and forget you.'

He nods seriously. 'I know, and I realise that contacting you again, and what I'm asking from you, isn't fair.'

I wish I could make myself less easily available, but I succumb and permit myself to be drawn into the depths of his eyes, into the depths of him. He stares at me for a few seconds before he moves close to me, and we kiss. It is a passionate kiss, the Sleeping Beauty variety that could wake anyone from a torpor.

How could I have responded to Rob so passionately? I just can't understand myself.

He gently rubs some dried ice cream off my nose and kisses that too. His face is serious as he puts his arms around me, and I rest my head against his shoulder. We spend the rest of the afternoon in the park, catching up. He tells me about the treatment that he and Marie have embarked on. He's despairing of himself.

'I'm fond of her when I'm with her, but not in the least sexually aroused,' he says. 'She's like my sister or my best friend.'

I refrain from telling him too much detail about Rob and our explosive sexual relationship.

I've just realised that my relationship is a mirror opposite of Mark's relationship with Marie: great sexually, and not so good in closeness. When I thought Rob cared for me, I was wrong. He was just jealous and possessive and wanted ownership.

The evening suddenly envelops us, and with it comes a mild wind. He puts his arms around me since I haven't a jacket, and I suggest that he walk back home with me since my parents won't be home.

'Are you sure you want me to?' he asks, and I nod.

The roads are quiet now. It is twilight, and the streetlights glow a warm red before they turn amber. We pass a few houses where people have decided to take advantage of the good weather by having a barbecue, and the smell of charcoaled steaks and sausages wafts in the air. We make our way slowly back home.

I felt so shy when I let him in.

We say very little to each other. Instead I gently take him by the hand and lead him to my bedroom. It is the start of another chapter for us, and I have all but forgotten Rob.

* * *

I put down my pen to think things through. One of my goals in collating my diaries and going through them myself has been to try to make sure that I can maintain a long-term relationship. I don't like the fact that I can be so fickle. Do I move around relationships because moving is what I'm used to, or is there something in me that just can't connect?

* * *

I feel like I've swallowed a fizzy pill of joy.

I see Mark every day. My parents comment on my absences, but I am at a stage when I don't really care if I am 'found out.' If given a choice, I would like to carry a sandwich board, like the walking advertisement man on Oxford Street, proclaiming to the world that Mark is back in my life.

I don't think of the difficult task ahead of me when I go back to university. For the time being, I abandon myself completely to Mark. He too is happy, and he tells me that he will be ending with Marie very soon – when she comes back from her current business trip. He promises to visit me as much as he can during term time, although his work will provide him with its own gruelling schedule.

'*I'm no longer bothered about my mother.*

She goes out on her own three evenings a week. She has started learning Ceroc dancing, a type of French jive, with some of her friends on the course. When my father suggests that they learn it together, she shrugs her shoulders indifferently.

'I would prefer to learn it with my friends, Ruwan,' she informs him quietly but firmly.

I notice the hurt in my father's face, but I don't respond. I am still a bubble in my effervescent world.

I'm scared that distress is contagious, and I don't want to feel sad.

My father involves himself in helping his sister sort out her marriage and with breaking the news to their parents. He struggles to achieve harmony with them but is pleased to be close to at least one family member.

I don't want to leave Mark to go back to university. I have said so many goodbyes over the years.

Mark gives me a mobile telephone as a gift. 'Call me,' he says. 'This time we are not going to lose touch.'

* * *

I meet up with Nora. She is still annoyed with me for having asked her to be my bridesmaid.

'It's not because I don't want to share in your big day,' she assures me. 'You know I hate any focus on me.'

'The focus will be on me, not on you, you vain creature,' I tease her.

'You know what I mean,' she says seriously. 'I mean, I'm grateful that you've let me choose the clothes that I want to wear, but the photographs, and the duties, and the walking behind you in the aisle between rows and rows of people… Maya, I don't know if I'll be able to do it.'

'You'll have to do it for me,' I say. 'You have to take your special place at our wedding, Nora, you have to be there on hand to calm me down.'

'Well, let it go on record that I'll never do this for anyone else but you,' she says, and I give her a hug to show her my appreciation for what she's doing for me now, but also for what I know (and have confirmed in the recent days of writing) she's always done for me.

We spend a lazy afternoon lounging around at home. Later, I tell her about my father.

'That's absolutely awful,' she says, sympathising. 'If something like that ever happened to me, I wouldn't want to live.'

'I don't agree,' I say. 'Part of life is to adapt to whatever it decides to throw at you, and anyway there are worse illnesses than Parkinson's.'

'True, but it involves a loss of control over the body. How could I put up with that? You're so much stronger than me, Maya. I really am a pathetic human being.'

I look at my friend. She is still thin, and she still battles with her food demons, but she has pulled through the worst of her illness. She continues to see a therapist, but she no longer has crisis periods, and at times she almost seems normal in her behaviour towards food. She remains on her own, and I think her next battle will be to deal with her ambivalence about intimacy.

'Strange,' I say to her, 'you say you couldn't put up with a chronic illness and a loss of control over your body, and yet that's exactly what you have done with your eating disorder. You now have to learn to be in a long-term relationship.'

She clears her throat nervously, and I look up in surprise. I'm not used to Nora being nervous or hesitant.

'Actually, Maya,' she says, 'I was going to ask you a favour. Um, do you think I could invite a friend to the wedding?'

I am stunned. A friend? What sort of friend? I feel a pang of jealousy. She wants to ask a new friend to my wedding? How important am I?

'Who... um... who is it? Anyone I know?'

She blushes a deep rose.

'It's someone called Josh,' she says, and I feel instant relief.

'Josh!' I exclaim. It's the first male name I have ever heard Nora mention. 'I would love to meet him, you dark horse. Of course he's welcome. You were the one who said you didn't want a "plus one" on your invitation.'

'Maya, don't make too much of this, will you?' she pleads. 'He's just a friend.'

But I know it's different, because I know my friend. 'He must come,' I say decisively.

'Thanks, but I mean it, Maya. He means nothing significant, okay? I don't want any fuss.'

'Okay, Nora,' I say.

As I get up to go to the kitchen to make some coffee, she says, 'Do you think I'm going to look all right? Maya, do you think he'll find me more attractive in trousers or a skirt?'

Jackson

20 July 2006

Jackson kept ringing his mother's telephone number every day for a week; every time, the phone was picked up by the Bastard's answer phone message. He tried ringing at different times of the day, still with no response. He didn't ring late evening, because that was the time the Bastard was there, and he didn't want to get his mother into trouble. He tried to think of what might make her not pick up her phone. They couldn't be away on holiday, because they never went away together. The Bastard would go for golfing weekends with his friends, and a few times on holiday with them too, but he never included his mother. Remembering that, Jackson decided that he would take his mother away for a break. He couldn't think of where she might like to go. Culturally she wasn't very sophisticated, and she wasn't used to shopping. He couldn't imagine her enjoying the beach.

On impulse he stopped off at the travel agent's the following day and explored several options. He finally decided that he would like to take her to Amsterdam. She loved flowers and water, and he remembered long cycle rides that they had both enjoyed before the Bastard came into their lives. He made a note of hotel names and was warned by the travel agent that booking early for certain times of the year were essential.

'I'll let you know by next week,' Jackson assured her.

When he couldn't get through on the telephone the following week, Jackson started to worry. Images of the Bastard hitting her crossed his thoughts. Could she not speak at the moment because he had hurt her in some way? There was no other way to reassure himself but to visit his mother.

Chapter 30

Hostage

Maya 2000 - 2001

I speed down the motorway away from my parents, my little car packed again for another year of study and independent living. I no longer feel disoriented when I get to my destination. One year of student life has left an indelible stamp on me.

I have been unable to find shared accommodation and so, with great difficulty, have managed to negotiate for one more term in the Halls. I settle back in another small and uncomfortable room, no different from the one I had before, except it is more vulnerable to noise from the dining area. I hesitate, wondering whether to add a photograph of Mark, which I took in the park, to the rest of my collection, and then I decide against it. I look at the photograph of Mark laughing up at the camera, before I clasp it against my chest briefly and place it in the wardrobe with my clothes. I decide to go out and check on whether Rob has arrived. The dread of having to break bad news lies heavily in my lower body, making my bladder weep frequently and copiously in anticipation.

As I wander outside, I hear someone calling my name and turn around to see Jamie looking bronzed and relaxed from his break. He gambols up to me and gives me a huge hug. The distance between us, created by me before the summer break, is forgotten. I instinctively hug him back, hugely delighted to see him.

'Have you had a good summer?' we ask each other simultaneously.

'Yeah, after a great family holiday in Barbados, I've been fruit picking in France,' he says.

'That means relaxing in the sun. Well, it explains your heavy tan.'

'It wasn't relaxing,' he retorts indignantly. 'It was hard work but satisfying at the same time. Here, look at my muscles,' he says playfully, rolling up his sleeves.

They ripple in the sun, coiled bands of thick, elasticised rope, tightly winding themselves around his arms. I run my fingers along them and pretend to shiver in ecstasy. He gives me another hug.

'Hey, you look great.' He teasingly pulls at my curls. 'You look like you've been kissed by love.'

I instantly tense and move away. Is it that obvious? I don't want it to be when I confront Rob.

'Perhaps being kissed by the Italian sun equates to the same thing,' I tell him lightly, but he knows I am moving away, and he frowns.

'Maya...' he begins, but he never gets to finish what he was going to say, because Rob is suddenly there. I turn to him with a smile on my face, but I know from the look on his face that he has seen my intimate interaction with Jamie and that he is displeased. He moves very close to me and grips me tightly, one of his hands pressing hard into the small of my back. He bends down and kisses me briefly but possessively, and then he nods at Jamie. He keeps pressing hard and my back slowly but painfully starts to throb.

'How are you doing, Rob?' drawls Jamie. 'Did you have a good summer?'

'Great and you?' asks Rob, similarly laconically. The hand on my back is pressing down so forcefully now that I bite my bottom lip hard drawing blood, to stop myself from crying out in pain. It is, no doubt, a warning to me, and I am duly apprehensive of his reaction that will follow. They exchange a few more pleasantries before Jamie says goodbye. His eyes flicker warningly at me before he goes.

When Jamie is out of sight, the pressure on the small of my back reduces, and Rob swings around to make eye contact with me. His face is black with rage, the pupils of his eyes pinpoints of fury. His body shakes, as does his voice.

'So, Maya, is this it, then? Is it? Are you finally going to admit to me that our relationship is over?' he hisses, and I am taken aback by the venom in his voice, but also by the heartbreak I see in his eyes. My heart turns over. What I want to say to him, I no longer can. Not now, and not under these conditions. Not with him thinking it is Jamie.

I pacify him. I hold him tight, even though he is rigid and resists my contact. I hold onto him until I can see some of the pain in his eyes dissolve, and I reassure him repeatedly, even though there is a break in my voice, that Jamie is a friend. I ask him not to spoil this meeting that we have both waited all summer for. I have tears in my eyes from the sheer desperation of protecting Jamie, and the effect of them is positive, because Rob finally relents.

Rob is like a smouldering firework, ready to go off at any moment, and I don't want to be around the explosion when it happens.

We go to my room and end up having sex. My body works in complete isolation from my emotions, and Rob is finally convinced that I am totally his. I have a sudden realisation about him. He doesn't know to love; he only knows to possess.

'I've tormented myself all summer, convinced that you'll want to end our relationship when we meet up again,' he says.

'Why are you so negative, Rob?' I ask.

He shrugs. 'I can't see why you would want to be with me,' he says. 'I want to believe it, but I can't. I believe that ultimately, everyone is unfaithful.'

I ask him if that applies to him too, and he smiles. 'Of course not,' he replies illogically.

I wonder whether this is true. Does he project his own fears of unfaithfulness onto others, or is his belief in himself so low that he can't accept anything good for himself?

Knowing what has happened between Mark and me, I also wonder if perhaps Rob's theory is correct, but somehow I know that it isn't.

I want to prove to Rob that he's wrong not to believe in relationships and loyalty, and at the same time I know that what he believes is a prophecy that I will prove true.

Perversely I ask what he would have done had his fears been true, thinking again of the hard hand against my back. He shrugs.

'I can't think of life without you,' he says simply, and I feel a shiver start at the base of my spine and slowly make its way upwards.

'What do you mean?' I ask sharply, angrily.

He stares back at me, his eyes flat, without reflection, like a spider just about to contemplate eating its mate.

'Just what I said, Maya,' he says, and the look in his eyes silences me.

Soon the term is back in full swing, and I resume my attendance of lectures and my solitary social life. After the encounter with Rob, it is as though Jamie knows, and he keeps out of my way, although he is always warm in his welcome when we pass each other. Rob starts his study-work schedule again, and I get myself another part-time evening bar job. A few weeks into term and into my job, I meet up with Rob, and I know immediately that something is wrong. He is cold and indifferent, and I am instantly guilty, worried that he has found out that I have been making late-night telephone calls to Mark, or writing him long and involved letters. He is rough when we make love, and for the first time, I turn away from him immediately after.

I feel sick at this pretence.

He immediately grabs me by the shoulders and turns me to face him.

'Stop it, Rob!' I say sharply.

His pressure on my shoulders increases and his pupils become pinpoints of ebony. He wrenches me around to face him.

'What is it then, little Miss Hoity-Toity? Ready to move on to someone else, are we?'

I am infuriated and snap back at him. 'Stop it, Rob. Stop all these accusatory comments about my leaving you. You're forcing me to leave you by being so rough and careless of my feelings.'

He turns so rapidly that I don't see the hand that rises rapidly to slap me. I put my hand to my cheek. I am too stunned to speak. No one has ever hit me.

'*Me* careless of *your* feelings? You bitch!' he shouts. '*You're* the one working in a bar every evening. *You're* the one flirting with all the male customers, flashing those dark bedroom eyes at them, giving them that come-hither look. *You're* the one who has not cared whatsoever for my feelings, gallivanting around with Jamie and openly stroking his arms. I know you're a cheat and a liar.'

I am too stunned to speak. I realise that our communication is running on wildly divergent lines.

He continues, 'I'm not forcing you into anything, you little tart. Don't blame me for an outcome that you so obviously want to orchestrate. Well, it's fine with me. If you want to sleep around, let's call it a day, shall we?'

He moves to the end of the bed and flings on his clothes. I lie there, stunned, bemused that he has hit me. I cannot believe that I'm having this conversation with him. He strides back towards the bed, infuriated by my silence, and I shrink back.

I was terrified. He seemed so out of control.

He sees the fear in my eyes and backs away, banging the door behind him as he makes a hasty exit.

I sit up in bed, shivering. I turn up my little heater and put on an extra jumper, but nothing helps. I just sit there, my mind in a whirl. A part of me tries to comfort myself by saying that I have achieved the ending I wanted. He has done the dirty work for me, but the knowledge of that is not really comforting. I am not sure what to do.

I want to talk to Jamie.

After my avoidance of him, I'm too embarrassed to pick up the telephone to call Jamie. There is a knock on my door, and I start to hyperventilate. I don't want it to be Rob. I'm afraid of further confrontation and of possible attack. The door opens, and Rob comes back in. His face is streaked with tears. His hair is all tousled. He looks as if he's nine years old. He sees me sitting up in bed, my hand still on my reddened cheek.

'I'm sorry your cheek hurts,' he says. 'I'm sorry you feel so bad.'

Rob never apologises for his actions, just for their consequences. It subtly shifts the blame onto me for not withstanding his onslaught.

I nod, preoccupied with trying to gasp in air and trying to stop my muscles from shaking.

'I don't want us to end,' he says. 'Just stop working nights at the bar, Maya, and all will be well again. Please, for my sake. Will you?' When I nod imperceptibly, he grabs my arms and showers kisses on them, starting from my hands and fingertips and moving all the way up to my shoulders.

He talks in between each kiss, each statement, a gasp for air.

'I've been so low that I visited the doctor to get some antidepressants during the holidays. I think they make me go a little crazy at times, you know. Today I took five more than I'm supposed to, I was hoping it would calm me, but I think it's made me more agitated instead. Maya, darling Maya, you make me so happy. I would take all of my prescription and more if you weren't in my life, you know. You will stay with me, won't you? Yes, Yes, Yes?'

I am a wax effigy that he has moulded to acquiesce. I melt into agreeing. I am too afraid of the consequences of not, and anyway my ability to assert my independence is vapour somewhere in the atmosphere.

He is passionate in his goodnight embrace. I let actions fill the void that has been left by the desertion of speech. Violence lends intensity to the communication, or the lack of it, as it stands between us.

I cried myself to sleep last night.

In the morning, everything seems better, but it lasts only an instant. Fleetingly I wonder if I had one of my vivid dreams last night, but then I know from the soreness of my cheek that it was real.

Inside of me, I know that things have changed within my world forever. I feel a little like after Grandma died.

I grieve for the sense of invincibility that I have lost, for the ardent romantic in me that has been abandoned.

I get dressed and collect my books together. I have started my stress bleeding again, something that has not happened for years. As I stare at myself in the mirror, I marvel at what lies underneath my surface, since none of the debris floats above visibly. I am on automatic pilot as I walk into the morning's lecture and then to the next and the next. I want to overdose on the soothing quality of words, on the structure of the lesson, on the familiarity of the lecturer's tone of voice, his pace and delivery, on the hum of the students' voices. It is a rhythm that is soothing and comforting, like the beat of a mother's heart heard in the womb, and I let it wash over me. When I go back to my room, it's night time, and on my way I realise with a shock that it's one of my nights at the bar. I wrestle for a moment with the idea of not calling in sick, of not calling in at all, of disappearing off the face of the earth, but years of training to 'do the right thing' take over, and I find my fingers dialling the number and hear my voice making the apologies.

'I'm sorry I'm not there,' says my voice, 'but I've come over with the most awful nausea and sickness. I'm sorry for the late apology and for leaving you in the lurch, but it's sudden.'

The manager's voice is abrupt, fed up by the lack of commitment from students, by their lackadaisical attitude. She says she is sorry to hear that I am ill, but she has to remind me that I haven't followed the sick-leave procedure for part-time staff. Since I have given her less than the required numbers of hours of notice, I will have to take it as unpaid leave. I am humble. I go out of my way to placate her and assure her that of course, I realise this; I would accept no less. For myself, I am pleased to be punished for my behaviour. That sits right. Once I put down the telephone, I compose a resignation letter and drop it in the post-box.

I skip dinner and make myself go to bed early. I sleep fitfully. It's difficult to find a comfortable position to lie in, especially since resting on my sore cheek hurts.

Rob meets up with me the following day. He's loving and affectionate, as though last night didn't happen. He asks me if I'm going to work, and I tell him that I have given in my resignation.

'I believe you,' he says rather weirdly, and then he hugs me again.

We go out and see a film together. He buys me a large container of salted popcorn, my favourite, and he holds my hands throughout the film. He has rebounded from the vortex of emotions experienced recently.

I too continue with student life as though nothing momentous has happened. I ignore Jamie whenever I see him, because I know I'll not be able to maintain my pretence with him, and yet I long for his comfort and strength. I start either skipping meals or eating lunch and dinner on my own to avoid any other social contact. I ignore the telephone and the messages I can see collecting in the voicemail box, only to be automatically erased without ever being heard, after three days.

The evenings start to get dark earlier, and a chill enters my room. I wear more layers of clothes in an attempt to keep warm. My weight has plummeted again, but I no longer care. I am in retreat. I have run away from reality and from myself.

* * *

I look at the last sentence I have written. Is this what Nora tries to do: to run away from reality and herself? Does my mother do it through exercise and shopping?

* * *

One evening, there is a gentle knock on the door of my room. I am revising, and absentmindedly I open the door before checking who it is. It is Jamie.

'How are you, Maya?' he enquires as he enters the room.

His eyes are warm, and his concern is so apparent that it cuts through my self-imposed exile like a hot knife through butter. I dissolve into tears and find myself enveloped in his arms, and I cry for what I have lost and for what I have longed for and never had.

We spend a long time talking that evening. He is perceptive and has made the right assumptions about Rob. He is encouraging in his support of me and in my moving on to make an ending with Rob. He assures me that he'll be there to help me through the break-up.

For the first time, I feel lightened of an emotional load.

I drop off to sleep whilst we are still talking, my head on his shoulder, as we sit on my bed. When I wake up the following morning, I'm tucked in bed, and a little note lies on top of my revision notes. 'Smile,' it says, and it works.

I have a shower. I'm embarrassed to admit to myself that I've even neglected my personal hygiene recently. I clean my room and then check the text messages that have accumulated over the weeks. There are three from Mark. The first is a loving communication wondering whether I've lost my telephone, since I haven't been answering his calls. 'Please ring,' it says. The second sounds more concerned. Where was I? Why wasn't I calling him? Was I in some way angry with him because he still had been unable to let Marie know about us? I shake my head, disappointed, when I read this. The third text from Mark is desperate. He has told Marie about wanting a separation. She's taken it hard, but he's been adamant, and so they are to have a trial separation starting from next month. Apparently it is difficult, because she sees it as a time apart to get a different perspective and 'to make things work,' whilst for him, it's no different from 'constructive dismissal' in a relationship context. He's leaving. Please, can I call him? He doesn't really understand why I'm being so indifferent, but there are so many things to discuss, and he misses me so much.

I'll call Mark tonight after I've told Rob that all is over between us.

I owe my newfound courage to Jamie and his gentle support. I can no longer be hostage to Rob's demands. I telephone Jamie.

I asked Jamie to help me find a way to end with Rob when I called him today.

I arrange to see Jamie at lunch. He's having his 'all-day breakfast' as usual, and I watch fondly him as he speedily and methodically eats his way around his plate. We say little to each other during this time, but I am on edge and can't help myself from looking around the canteen. I tell Jamie that I hope to tell Rob this evening, and he nods.

'Where will you meet?' he asks, as though unconcerned, and yet I know this is an important question. It's his way of making sure he can keep an eye on me.

'I thought that I might suggest meeting at Ed's Café,' I say.

Ed's is a student café where Rob and I often meet. It's smoky and busy, and usually it serves a range of well-priced and wholesome food to line student stomachs. I hesitate. 'Jamie, I'm nervous,' I say impulsively, and he nods as he takes my arm.

'I'm not surprised,' he says comfortingly. 'Why don't you come over to the flat, so that we can have one more chat in preparation for this evening?'

I cling to him. I hope rehearsal will help to calm the fluttering of a million butterfly wings in my stomach and the meringue that is my heart. We go to the next lecture together and then set off for his flat. I feel like a prisoner condemned to the guillotine.

Jamie's front door is ajar when we get there, and he frowns. 'I wonder who forgot to lock it,' he mutters as he pushes it open. All is tidy and in place when we enter, and we are relieved that no opportunist has taken advantage of the lack of security. The living room is as cosy as ever, and I seat myself on the comfortable sofa with a big sigh. I have missed sharing in Jamie's life. He goes off to the kitchen to put the kettle on and then goes into his room to throw his jacket on his bed.

'Maya, come here,' he says, and the urgency in his voice is unmistakable. I rush to his room, and we survey, in silence, the scene in front of us. His cupboards are open, and all the contents are on the floor. On top of his clothes is a pile of my clothes and with it, my photographs, including the one of Mark. Something hard (a boot?) has been thrown at the mirror, which is now cracked. His shoes are piled on his bed, his pictures skewed on the walls. I know with certainty that this has been done by Rob, who I can see has also somehow managed to get into my room to take my things.

Jamie is white with fury.

'That idiot Rob's mad!' he exclaims. 'Maya, you've been going out with a fucking maniac.'

We look at each other, and then, with the same thought, we both turn and move to Rob's room, but it is locked. We then search the flat and find Rob, pale and lifeless, in the bath. Jamie rushes to telephone the ambulance, whilst I throw up in the sink. When I am able to look at Rob, I see that in his hands are several packets of pills. I'm too scared to see how many he has taken or to check the effect of the damage, and I am relieved when the ambulance men arrive. I don't know where Jamie is, and I long for him to be by my side. They take Rob to hospital, and Jamie and I follow. Rob is kept in for observation, and since Jamie and I are so shaken, we are told to go home and return the following day.

Rob didn't die that day. He had his stomach pumped and was then transferred onto the psychiatric ward. Jamie and I are both questioned by the liaison nurse for psychiatric services when we go back.

'What do you know about Rob's circumstances?' she asks. 'Do you know why he might have attempted suicide? Has he talked about it with either of you? Did he leave a suicide note?'

I want to be seen to be guilty. It gives me some sense of control over the situation.

I tell her that I'm Rob's girlfriend but that things had deteriorated between us since the beginning of the term. I describe his moodiness, his aggression, and his single-minded jealousy. I tell her that I had been on my way to break up with him and that he might have sensed this.

I then wait for them to bring in the verbal handcuffs, but instead the psychiatric nurse asks me what I know about Rob's family. I say that I know very little, but surprisingly Jamie is better informed. He says that Rob's parents have been separated since Rob was fourteen years old and that Rob had grown up with his mother and her various boyfriends. Apparently Rob had told him that she had never stayed with a partner for more than a month. Rob's father was a mysterious figure whom Rob rarely saw, but when he did, he was supposed to be violent, authoritarian, and dismissive. He had been a successful lawyer in the city but had recently lost his job and moved back to live at home with his mother, with negative consequences. Neither of Rob's parents supported his decision to read law at university, and so Rob was financing himself.

A number of pieces of the puzzle fall into place for me. No wonder Rob has no trust in me; no wonder he doesn't know how to love.

I'm completely trapped. I can no longer leave Rob. That means I only have one option. I have to break up with Mark.

So I exist as a watered-down spirit in the land of the living. In time, I make the most difficult call of my life to Mark and in addition write a number of letters to him, trying to explain myself. He says he is devastated at my decision to end things between us, and he keeps me awake by ringing me at night and even threatening to come down to see me, which I implore him not to do, because to face him in person will be just too hard.

Rob seems to have recovered quickly. He's gone back to his studies and his part-time work. It's a month since his overdose, and he is on the waiting list to start psychological treatment.

Rob moves out of Jamie's house and never discusses the events leading up to his overdose. I stay silent too, although the sense of invasion I feel by his having broken into my room smoulders within me.

I stop seeing Jamie again and wander through life wearing a deep-sea diving suit of depression. I grieve for Mark and for Jamie and for the life that I have lost, just as much as I grieve for what I have lost through my experiences with my uncle, and miss my friendship with Nora and my beloved grandma. The comfort of bed beckons with every day that passes the warmth of its cocoon-like comfort and its potential to anaesthetise emotions. Some days I'm able to challenge the spell it weaves on me, and on these days, I drag myself to attend my lectures; but on others, I give in and spend most of the day asleep. The latter occurs more frequently, since I experience a tiredness I find hard to describe. Even my bones seem to ache for sleep.

The weather starts to change outside. No longer are there flame leaves and warm autumn fruit. Instead the trees are, as though acid has been thrown on them, burning the branches of their foliage and exposing a desolate bareness.

Jamie calls me on several occasions, and I find that the easiest way of avoiding his searching questions is to pretend that all is well between Rob and me, and that I am deliberately avoiding lectures. I implore him to remain distant until I work things out with Rob.

Things between Rob and me are awful. I wish I'd never met him, because I'm now permanently snared.

My depression lowers my libido so that it is virtually nonexistent. Every time I refuse sex or seem disinterested, Rob is volatile and accusatory. My appetite for food varies, so that I swing from periods of starvation to periods of bingeing when, for a short time, large quantities of food act as tranquillisers that soothe away the sharp edges of what I feel. Of course, the binge-and-starve cycle starts to effect my weight, and I soon start hating the variability of my body for its expansion and contraction, and this further contributes to my withdrawal from Rob.

'You've gained weight, haven't you?' Rob remarks acidly or: 'Maya, you should start watching what you eat.'

If I attempt to shrug off the weight gain, he gets a weighing scale.

'Stand on this, then. Let's see,' he says and I burn with embarrassment as I climb on it reluctantly and hear his crow of triumph. 'You've put on three pounds, you greedy thing.'

Better are the days and weeks when I have been apathetic and not eaten a morsel. Then he says, 'That's better – half a stone lost in three weeks. You're finally starting to listen to reason, I can see.'

I know of no response except to shrink further into myself. My skin, which until now has never caused me any difficulties, erupts in spots; my complexion is pallid and pasty; my eyes have dark circles under them. Due to my fluctuating weight, my breasts lose tone and sag, and I notice, with a pang, that I have tiny stretch marks on the tops of my thighs. True, they are barely visible, but to me they are further proof of my deterioration.

I'm so ugly.

Whilst I yo-yo in my management and evaluation of my physical self, I manage, by a hairline, to keep my coursework up to date, although my ability to concentrate is seriously impaired. My marks are often average, sometimes even low-average, and I then chastise myself about my academic performance, sometimes despairing about the lack of being able to achieve my true potential, at others convincing myself that this is what I am: an average sort of person, with no real talent or ability.

One day, after a week of lying in bed, I drag myself to a lecture. I sit on my own, head pounding, forcing myself to listen. I make no eye contact with anyone. Jamie deliberately comes and sits next to me during the break.

'Jamie,' I whisper, 'Remember our agreement, please.'

'No, listen to me, Maya,' he tells me. 'I'm fed up with watching you deteriorate in front of my eyes. There's no point in making yourself a martyr over this whole situation. You have to take charge.'

'Jamie, I just can't. He's better but not well enough. I can't go through another episode like the last one.'

'Yes, you can, Maya. No relationship based on emotional blackmail is worth it. It doesn't matter how good a minder you are – you won't be able to prevent him from carrying out whatever action he wants to, if he's really determined.'

'But I'll be the cause, Jamie, and I just couldn't live with that.'

'You won't be the cause, Maya. Why can't you see that? This whole scenario isn't about you. It's about him and his pride and his needs. It's not about how much he cares for you and how devastated he will be when you leave him. It's what you represent to him that's become his obsession.'

'I don't know what to do for the best, Jamie. I really don't,' I burst out. 'I'm the person who decides his future.'

'Give up that responsibility,' says Jamie, 'and look after yourself first. Please? For me?'

I love Jamie. He just gets me every time.

Jamie clinches the argument by suggesting that I may also want to do it because, if I do, I can move into one of the spare rooms in his house, since he now had two rooms free, Rob's and another friend's, who has moved in with his girlfriend. My housing situation is pressing. I need to move out, and the idea of sharing with Jamie is both comforting and appealing.

'I know you're right, and I'll do it, I promise,' I say.

'I also want you to promise me that you'll go to the doctor and ask for a referral to see someone you can talk to,' he says.

*   *   *

Jamie values talk. Having got to know his family, I can see why. His mother is very responsive to both her children, and they turn to her to share in their worries and hopes. I remember being startled by his parents' relationship with one another when I first met them. They are not restricted in conveying their feelings towards each other, often making out like teenagers, even though they met at university and have been together for what seems to Jamie and I like aeons. When they first met me, it seemed the most natural thing in the world for his mother to give me a hug, and it only took a few meetings before I was included in family meals and holidays as though I was one of them. I have hoped that Jamie's sister, Hannah, will not be displaced by this, but it would seem that the worry has only been mine. She will join Nora and Bella as my third bridesmaid, and I know she has been linking up with Nora in planning my hen night, which is to be soon. It's all so exciting; I can't wait.

*   *   *

I leave breaking up with Rob until the last week of term. The time I choose is when it's two weeks before Christmas and the environment around me is weeping water and ice. We meet in the café, as previously planned.

'Rob, things are no longer working out between us, and I want out,' I say bluntly.

The first thing that strikes me is that he doesn't react in the way that I think he will. He is silent for quite a while. I suppose he has been preparing himself for this from the time we started our relationship. Maybe he is marshalling his resources, preparing for attack. I can't bear the tension, whatever the reason, and so I repeat, 'Rob, I'm sorry, it's over.'

'I heard you the first time,' he says, and then, matter-of-factly, 'I suppose it's predictable. It's what I expected.'

'It's only predictable to you,' I want to shout. *'This is all you ever prepare yourself for. How can any relationship of yours expect to survive, when you're so busy preparing for the ending before you've even begun?'*

I've never had the opportunity to get close to Rob, because he's so suspicious. He alienates me, because the intimacy that he wants, he can't get. He wants a closeness that has no space, that is a complete overlap of him and me, where I am a mussel to be enclosed in his shell.

I don't say anything confrontational. I mutter instead, 'I'm unable to form relationships, Rob. I'm sorry, but that's me, and my past proves it. You know that I've told you that I don't fit in, that I don't belong, and that I never will. I've moved from half-caste to outcast.'

He looks at me penetratingly. Do I see a dawning look of relief on his face? I press on hopefully. 'Rob, you need someone less insecure about herself.'

The strange thing is that as I say all of this, I know that something within me has shifted and that I no longer believe it. These are ideas belonging to an old me.

'Well,' he finally responds, 'you're an elusive person, Maya, and that makes you irritatingly distant, you know.'

As I predicted, there's no acknowledgement on his part about his contribution to the relationship. Seeing my advantage I stay silent, pleased that I haven't yet triggered his explosive anger or his impulsive behaviour. He scrutinises me very intently as he asks me the next question.

'Is there anyone else? Are you lying to me to make me feel better?' he demands, and I flinch as I see tension build up in him instantly.

'There's no one else,' I assert vehemently.

He suggests that we remain friends, and I decline the suggestion, because I know that friendship is not something that Rob will be able to offer me. Some relationships can only remain frozen in one form; they don't translate into another. I kiss him gently on the forehead before we say goodbye, and I squeeze his hand. He doesn't respond.

I've come to realise that I'm a rescuer.

So I choose to ignore the note of pathos in his voice, the beseeching look in his eyes. I choose to walk away without my automatic response of concern and care, although anxiety reverberates within me from my unfamiliar response. This, then, is my goal: to make the unfamiliar familiar.

I balance on a tightrope of suspense over the next few days, awaiting bad news. Not surprisingly, the suspense brings on my panic attacks, but they don't bother me. I know their source, and so I am able to accept them when they happen. I sit and await crisis news of Rob. In my waking hours, I imagine a variety of scenarios where Rob is found either nearly dead or dead. In my dreams, I float viewing and reacting to scenes of tragedy and crisis. Alternatively, I await him surprising or threatening me. After a week of not hearing anything and of not seeing him anywhere around, the suspense becomes too unbearable, and I contact a friend of his to find out how he is. The friend sounds surprised.

'Oh, I thought you knew,' he says. 'Rob had to go home early – some family crisis, he said.'

I meet up with Jamie to express my concerns. Has Rob really gone home? Who was going to keep an eye on whether he was going to attempt suicide or not? Has he already tried? After all, the last reaction had been immediate. Should I ring his home to check?

Jamie calms me down. He'll reach relevant parties and find out how Rob is, but meanwhile I am to make no direct contact with Rob whatsoever. The relationship is severed.

Jamie keeps telling me that I mustn't worry about Rob's reaction.

True to his word, he contacts me shortly to let me know that Rob is at home and well.

I thought I would feel better ending with Rob, but I feel so sad. I know why. I had to convince myself how awful the relationship was so I could end it. Now I'm flooded by a vast ocean of fond memories.

To say that I am pleased to get away from university for the break and to bury myself in something completely different with Nora is an understatement, and as I leave to lose myself in charity work, I experience an element of near ecstasy in mood at putting distance between me and all relationships. As with all things that I enjoy doing at the moment, however, it carries with it an element of guilt. Should I be feeling relief, getting excited and looking forward to something, when I am causing so much pain to someone else?

I am delighted to see Nora. We haven't seen each other for a while, and I am pleased to note that she looks thin but not unhealthily so. Her face looks aged, however, etched lines of suffering or starvation, repeated loss of electrolytes affecting the consistency and elasticity of her skin. We are instantly comfortable with each other. No catching up is needed.

'You look awful,' she tells me. 'You're not developing my illness, are you?'

I shrug. 'You're right, Nora – men are not worth the bother.'

What I have forgotten, until I am with Nora, is her ability to cut off from the emotions that she doesn't want to engage in. What I have also forgotten is her ability to infect me with this skill of dissociating, and not for the first time, I am pleased about this contagious habit, because I am almost instantly soothed into forgetting and focussing on the trip ahead of us. So we travel together, to another place, where we can both stop thinking about ourselves. We are fleeing, but it's acceptable and companionable. We don't mind how transient it may be; we hail the relief of cutting off from reality.

Jackson

24 July 2006

Jackson hailed a taxi once he arrived at the station. He felt jittery and on edge. He wanted to get things over speedily; coming back to Bastard territory freaked him out.

He took an early train so he could avoid the rush hour and got there just before the streams of commuters started their daily ritual. Traffic was congested due to road works, however, and the taxi took three quarters of an hour for what was usually no more than a fifteen-minute journey. Jackson welcomed the extra unplanned-for time, since he prepared and rehearsed what he wanted to say as he nervously looked out of the window of the cab. Soon they were in territory he knew like the back of his hand although he marked the changes that had taken place over the time he had been away, and through to the trellis of small roads, one of which was where his mother lived. The street was quiet as they drove up to the house.

'Stay for me, please,' said Jackson to the driver, 'I won't be too long, and even if I am, just keep the meter running.'

He walked up the path, noting that his mother's well-tended flowerpots were no longer there. He knocked on the door, and when he had no answer, he rang the doorbell. Obviously no one was home. Motioning for the driver to remain, Jackson walked towards the neighbouring house and knocked on the door. He thought he heard a voice calling, but just then a car pulled up on the drive. It was the Bastard returning home from a workout at the gym. Jackson spun round and walked up to the car. The Bastard got out, scowling.

'Well, look who has turned up after all these years and to what do we owe the pleasure of this visit?' he asked.

'I want to talk to my mother,' said Jackson.

'Want to talk to her, do you?' said the Bastard. 'Well, you can't.'

'*I can bloody well do what I want to now,*' said Jackson. '*I'm no longer your punch bag, you pathetic old goat and I'm not going to let my mother stay with you a moment longer. Now tell me where she is, and we can part company forever.*'

The Bastard laughed. '*Let me think,*' he said. '*Hmm, she could be a little busy at this time, or she could be not – most probably not, I think.*'

'*What do you mean?*' asked Jackson, feeling the hairs on the nape of his neck bristle. '*Where is she? What have you got her doing for you now?*'

'*She's dead,*' said the Bastard flatly, opening his front door. '*She died two years ago. Kept looking for you all the time you'd gone and then kept asking for you on her deathbed, but you'd buggered off for good of course. I took pleasure in pointing out to her that her so-called fucking wonderful son that she couldn't stop caring for, didn't care a shit about her but it made no sodding difference, she still loved you.*'

There was a sudden explosion far away, but the whole earth seemed to move. Jackson remained turned to stone, but the Bastard stumbled and fell on his knees, and the taxi driver ducked in his car.

'*Fuck, what was that?*' yelled the Bastard. Jackson remained very still.

A minute passed, and the taxi driver got out of his car. '*Don't like the sound of that,*' he said, looking shaken. '*Sounded like a bomb somewhere local. I wonder if it was in the train station.*'

Jackson came to life. With a roar, he flung himself on the Bastard and started to punch him in the face. '*You killed her, you murderer!*' he screamed, tears pouring down his cheeks. '*You killed her!*'

It took the taxi driver and a nervous neighbour several minutes to control Jackson, whilst the Bastard, looking distinctly worse for wear, bolted into the house and locked the door.

'*Come on, mate,*' said the cabbie soothingly. '*Not worth taking on someone like that. I know the type. My old man was the same, and* he got his comeuppance in the end. He was dead at the age of sixty, killed by a so-called friend in a pub brawl. Let's tune into the news in my cab and see what's happened. It sounded like the bloody bottom dropped out of the world.'

Chapter 31

Kicking Butt

Maya 2001 - 2002

Rob has dropped out of the course. I heard through his tutor that he's decided to take a year out. I feel so guilty and yet so relieved. Maybe one day I'll get the chance to apologise to him.

Spending Christmas with Nora has been a healing experience, and I have come back refreshed and relaxed, having eaten better and rested.

In the early summer, when the trees start dressing again after their long period of nudity, Mark telephones me. Our conversation is stilted, carefully controlled.

'How are you?' he asks me: such a mundane question.

'I'm fine,' says the restrained me, whilst I curb the urge to rush to where he is.

We continue our uneasy conversation, just focussing on content, our emotions catatonic. He is going away for three months to Australia; nothing can begin now; we both know that. Neither of us mentions Rob or Marie, nor do we mention the future. We keep our discussions in the present: it's safer.

When I enter my third year at university, it's with no attachments, but with expectations and preparation for a less tumultuous time. Being the only girl where I live affords me a variety of privileges, such as a longer time in the bathroom and a special corner of the sofa, all of which I hugely appreciate. In addition, Jamie and I spend most of our time together.

There's masses of work to cover for my finals.

Our theses demand intensive application, as do the large amounts of academic work. There is little time for anything else but the ingestion of work material, and my tutor, sensing the change in me and observing the remarkable recovery of my application to coursework and rising grades in various tests, takes it upon himself to further encourage me.

I make some new friends, a cross-section of female and male, but surprisingly it is the increase of female friendships that gives me pleasure. I find myself enjoying the company of women, their gentleness and insightfulness, their shared support. I still find what I interpret as their innate competitiveness difficult, but I also learn to acknowledge that this is because I'm unused to it, rather than because it reflects my inferiority.

Best of all, my panic attacks become shadows of themselves, devoid of the power to affect me in the way that they have done in the past.

I sit for my final examinations apprehensive but also challenged, supported by the knowledge that there are hundreds of other stressed, sleep-deprived, apprehensive final-year students, all joining me to put ideas, both learnt and original, onto paper. Our shared flat becomes a smoke-filled, finger-tapping, hair-pulling place where emotions rocket from one extreme to another. Some of us walk around memorising facts and formulae by muttering them repetitively to ourselves, chanting inanely like Hare Krishna converts, whilst others give imaginary lectures to themselves. Jamie huddles in a corner in a foetal-shaped ball, the only movement he makes being the occasional turn of a page of the book in front of him whilst he learns facts his way. He uncurls himself out of this position only two or three times during the day, so he can shovel vast quantities of toast with butter and Marmite into his mouth, before curling up in the corner again. We are so absorbed that we barely acknowledge each other's existence.

Study times also vary. Some revise throughout the day and then go out and relax in the evening, whilst others learn through the night, imbibing cup after cup of coffee to prop open tired eyelids, only to sleep like weighty boulders, awakening in the afternoon to venture out of their bedrooms with the heavy tread of slothful dormice.

I heard that some students wrap wet towels around their heads to keep awake throughout the night.

Nights blur into days as I digest three years of facts into meaningful and memorable material that can be regurgitated. Finally, the exams begin, and I recall, explain, and compose answer after answer, my writing hand aching at the end of the day. When they are finally over, I am shell-shocked after the last paper. Whilst many go out to celebrate, I drag myself to bed and get in, fully clothed. I am asleep before I even cover myself up with the blanket – usually a necessity for me. It's my first proper period of sleep in months, and I wake up at three in the afternoon the following day and find that Jamie has followed a similar pattern. We finally stagger into the living room semi-awake and slump on the armchairs, still depleted. Suddenly Jamie comes out of his daze and gives a war whoop as he lifts me off the chair and twirls me around.

'Hey, Maya, we've finished! We've finally finished!' he yells, and I cling onto his shoulders as he whirls me around.

'Yes, it's over! It's over!' I shout back, the joyous news making me effervescently ebullient, and we gyrate madly like whirling dervishes around the living room. Finally exhausted, he puts me down on the sofa and flings himself next to me. We are both out of breath and laughing.

'Three cheers!' I yell, and I slump against him, my head on his shoulder, whilst I fling my arms around his waist.

'Three cheers!' he yells back, but more subdued, and his arm around my waist tightens. I notice that he's no longer laughing.

Instead, he's looking at me intensely, passionately, and I suddenly halt in my tracks, the laughter that has been welling up in my throat trapping itself somewhere near my epiglottis. I catch my breath as, inexorably, his face descends close to mine, and I instinctively close my eyes as he kisses me full on the lips.

It was a gentle yet passionate kiss. It was wonderful.

I push him away. I can feel myself shaking. My first and only thought is that he is precious and that I can't lose him.

'Maya,' he begins, and I gently place my finger against his mouth, silencing him with it, and with the look in my eyes.

'No, Jamie, listen to me first,' I say. 'There are things about me that you don't know.'

'But –' he begins, and I silence him again and tell him, for the first time, about Mark and about him being in Australia at the moment, but how I hoped we could make things work when he gets back. I am vehement and so involved in my own story that I fail to notice the light go out in Jamie's eyes.

Jamie is my very best friend and I don't want to lose him.

Our moment of joy and celebration is now well and truly dampened. Having provided Jamie with all the details, I no longer know what to say.

'Maya,' he says insistently, as though he has something important to say, and I am unsettled by the assertiveness in his voice. I quieten him again. I don't want him to speak right now. I know he will try to absolve me of the guilt and the uncertainty I feel over my conduct in relationships, and I want to remain penitent for longer.

'Let's go out to see a movie,' I suggest. 'Let's just not do any more thinking. My brain is taxed already. Please, Jamie, let's just go and relax.'

I see his shoulders slump, or do I imagine that?

'Yes, let's go out and, er, celebrate, Maya,' he says. So this is what we do, and the moment of intimacy between us is forgotten, or rather I convince myself that it is.

Leaving university is a watershed, and I don't know what to do with myself. All my life I have followed a structure, a routine, and a plan. Having your life mapped out is comfortable – until now, I have not appreciated how comfortable. I am left with an abyss of time, and I panic. I don't know if I have the skills, the knowledge, or the determination to move on. Adult life looms ominously larger than the pinnacle of Mount K2.

I go back home, outwardly a hero with my first-class honours degree, but inwardly a fool with no practical skills, no planning ability, and no idea of what I'm going to do and how.

My mother greets me with blonde streaks in her hair. Gone is the use of her 'recipe for luxurious hair' she now visits Michele, the upmarket hairdresser on Broadway, every six weeks, where she has her hair highlighted and cut. She is super-slim and wears very trendy clothes. I notice that she has two earrings pierced in one of her earlobes.

'I'm on a special diet now,' she tells me proudly.

She is, apparently, wheat and lactose intolerant. She tells me that since the diagnosis – for which she was tested by a number of people with confusing titles, whom she seems to consult regularly – she has been fantastic. I open the fridge to find Soya milk in cartons, and strange-smelling and even stranger-tasting yoghurt and cheese.

Today Mum served sticky rice pasta mixed with unflavoured chunks of what I initially thought were cubes of goat's cheese, only to spit it out after tasting, since it was plain tofu. Never having been a creative cook, or indeed been interested in cooking, Mummy was so proud of her culinary efforts that we didn't have the heart to complain. She didn't seem to notice that Daddy and I left our food virtually untouched on our plates.

'You should get yourself tested for gluten intolerance,' she tells me. 'It does wonders to your gut and digestion. As for your father, well, seeing what his health is like, so should he.'

My father retreats behind his newspaper. His long-suffering air makes me think that this is not the first time he has heard this.

This morning, I went to make myself some coffee. All I found were some tea bags labelled Ayurvedic tea and some chicory powder in a jar. They both tasted vile. I then tried to make some wheat-free toast, but it burnt easily in the toaster and smelled (and probably tasted) like mouse droppings. There was no butter to make the toast any less dry. Mummy suggested I spread some Manuka honey. Apparently it's great for your immune system and sex life – too much information, Mum.

My mother comes downstairs as I hungrily search the fridge and cupboards for something to eat. 'Mum, where's the small jar of coffee I brought back from uni?' I enquire.

'Oh, I threw it in the bin. Noel, my nutritionist, says that coffee is Satan's vomit.'

'What a charming man he must be, Mum.'

'All his clients have given up coffee, with excellent results,' she exclaims.

'I bet he's on coffee manufacturers' hit lists. He's now certainly on mine,' I mutter darkly.

My mother has not only acquired new eating habits, she also has a new vocabulary. She talks about her qi, *which has been rediscovered; she detoxes and has colonic irrigation. She knows what her chakras are, and she has 'feng shui'd' our home.*

My mother is a stranger, and the gulf between us widens. She is as unavailable to me now as when she was drinking. I wonder if I should talk to my father about it, but then, as time passes, I shrug off the need.

I miss Nora, who has started at university. My only consolation while I am at home is the fact that Jamie telephones me frequently. We agree to meet one Sunday, and I suggest a pub down the road. I don't want him to visit my peculiarly unconventional home. My mother is hardly here, and when she is, she often has a retinue of friends. There are friends from her law course, friends from her yoga group, and friends from her women's group. Whilst some of her law friends appear normal, her yoga friends and women's group friends I mentally, narrow-mindedly, label as strange, eccentric types and give them a wide berth.

One day when I come home, I hear an unfamiliar male voice in the kitchen and curiously push open the door and enter. I see a tall, thin man, clad in chinos and a chequered shirt, sitting at the table, sipping a cup of Ayurvedic tea. His hair is long and curly.

'This is my daughter, Maya,' says my mother, waving her matching cup of what I mentally rename 'Ah, you wee'd in the' tea.

'Maya, this is Noel, my nutritionist and my general health advisor.' She beams at him fondly, and I instantly hate him.

'Hello,' I mumble as he eagerly jumps up and proffers his hand. His grip is slight: effeminate, I think, uncharitably.

'As you know, Noel has turned my life around for me,' gushes my mother.

'Besides turning life upside-down for us,' I retort, not caring if I am rude.

He beams. My anger is lost on him. 'I'm so pleased,' he says, and I glare at him.

'Noel, following your eating plan is doing me so much good,' says my mother, 'but I'm really hungry all the time.'

Noel smiles benevolently. 'Hunger is good,' he says sagely. 'Experience hunger, and welcome it. There's nothing to fear.'

I bang the cupboard door. 'Just trying to find a sick bucket,' I mutter under my breath.

'Bad digestion creates nausea,' babbles Noel. 'It would be my pleasure to carry out a dietary analysis on you at any time.'

'I don't think that'll be necessary,' I say. 'I enjoy my unhealthy lifestyle too much to make a change. Why, I couldn't exist without my morning egg-and-bacon sandwich on white bread, and my double espresso – sorry, Satan's vomit.'

'Oh,' he says, taken aback for the first time. 'Well, time yet to make a change, I suppose.'

I walk over to the sink to get a glass of water to drink and then change my mind, knowing that drinking water will probably be commended. Instead, I head towards the fridge, take out an old can of beer, and deliberately open it in front of them. I wish I had a cigarette I could light up too.

Noel reads my mind. 'I can help you kick butt too,' he says obtusely, and for a moment all I can do is stare at him uncomprehendingly.

'Oh, Noel, you are a scream,' says my mother in a loud voice. 'Kick butt – how catchy is that? Is that how you market your new giving-up-smoking campaign?'

He beams back. 'So pleased you approve.'

I can take no more. 'Well, see you around,' I say as I head towards the door and up the stairs, shelving my inclination to kick some butt.

As I head out of the room, I hear my mother whisper to Noel, 'Touchy teenagers trying to integrate back at home, sorry,' and Noel's response: 'I sense much hostility there, yes, and an ocean of rage. It's all to do with the stomach and colon, of course. Impacted, you know.'

Even crosser, I kick open my room door and devour two bars of chocolate before I can think straight.

* * *

I have to chuckle when I remember my first meeting Noel. His 'Kick Butt' campaign has been a huge success for him. He has been on a variety of television shows demonstrating his formula for success and has set up his own practice called 'Butt Out' in Central London. The steely determinism and business acumen that has been demonstrated in his success, and even his macho practice name, is in contraposition to his epicene façade.

* * *

Noel soon becomes a fixture in our house. He is my mother's right hand and is always there, first for afternoon tea, after which he stays on to dinner; and over the weekends he even comes early, so that he can have lunch with us. The only advantage to these visits is that he teaches my mother new vegetarian recipes, so that we sometimes lunch on bean casserole or roasted vegetable salad with couscous. The food tastes surprisingly good, but wild horses wouldn't drag an acknowledgement from me. Instead, I occasionally present myself at the table when I think that my father is looking under strain. At these times, I find myself possessed by an impish intent beyond my control. I bring chips and sausages from the chip shop to the table, or get a pizza delivered, which I then share with my father, who happily participates in this rebellion with me. Often I ask my father if I can finish off the meal with a large brandy, and to my surprise, he obliges. I can see my mother desperate to admonish my father at these times, and I eagerly prepare myself for conflict, but she says nothing, and when I leave these gatherings to go upstairs, I am strangely deflated.

Sometimes I wonder if my mother and Noel are having an affair, but I find him peculiarly asexual, and I dismiss this thought from my mind. Increasingly my father absents himself from home, and I attempt to follow his example, as I try to motivate myself to apply for a job.

When Jamie and I finally meet, I am exasperated with life at home. I ignore acknowledging to myself how much I have missed him even though I am delighted to see him. We spend a wonderful day walking along the river, having lunch, and then while away the evening chatting in a pub. When we are there, Jamie clears his throat.

'Maya,' he begins, and my heart suddenly sinks in negative anticipation.

'Don't tell me,' I implore desperately, but he does, nevertheless.

'I've been offered an engineering job that will take me to Saudi Arabia for a year, maybe longer,' he informs me. 'It's a wonderful package, and I've decided to take it.'

I felt sick when Jamie told me today he was going to Saudi Arabia.

'When will you go?' I ask, trying not to let my voice wobble.

'Before Christmas,' he says.

'But that's just around the corner,' I whimper plaintively, and he gives me a hug.

'Come and see me out there,' he responds. I wind my arms tenaciously around him when we say goodbye.

Does everyone who is important to me leave me?

I lounge around the house for a few days, and then, spurred by Jamie and by what I see as an unbearable situation at home, I start sending off job applications in earnest and visit recruitment consultants. I have made up my mind that I too have to get away.

* * *

My mother telephones me in the evening. I'm having a quiet night away from my journals and my writing.

'You haven't convinced Daddy,' she hisses in a low voice.

'What do you mean?' I enquire, knowing fully well what she is referring to.

'Maya, don't be difficult!' It's an exasperated exclamation. 'I wanted you to talk to Daddy and convince him that he'll be well at your wedding. I don't think he's assured.'

'He'll be fine, Mum. Just leave him alone,' I respond. 'He just needs some time. He's still in shock.'

She sighs. 'I hope you're right. Now, what about those awkward bridesmaids of yours? Have they practised walking gracefully?'

'They're fine, Mum. Everything's fine. Look, I can't talk at the moment.'

'Why not?'

'Oh, I'm, er, trying to finish a last-minute project that I couldn't complete before I left work.'

'Well, make sure they pay you something extra for it. Doing it in your own time, too. Call me when you've spoken to Daddy.'

'Yeah, okay, Mum. Bye.'

In Suffolk

23 July 2006

He had always admired the character of Sisyphus in Greek mythology. To him, Sisyphus was crafty and clever. On one occasion he betrayed Zeus's secrets, and when Zeus ordered Hades to chain Sisyphus in hell as punishment for his treachery, he managed to trick Hades and escape. The second occasion was when Sisyphus tricked Persephone into letting him out of the underworld so he could cheat death again. Cheating death for the second time was the ironic part, because this was what the current plan entailed. 'Like hero, like me,' *he thought as he lined up tablets and water and the goodbye note.*

He opened his cupboards for the tenth time and made sure that all his clothes were ordered neatly. He did the same with the items in the kitchen cupboards. He looked at the bookshelves and made sure that the books all had spines facing outwards and that there were no titles to be ashamed of. He checked that his secret stash was still secret and wedged firmly under the bed. What he wanted discovered, he wanted to be proud of; everything else was to remain untouched.

I'm all set, *he thought to himself, and excitement filled his body so rapidly that he felt light-headed and shaky.* I'm ready to put my plan into action. I'm going to win.

Chapter 32

White Noise

Maya 2002 - 2003

I'm not winning any time to maintain this journal regularly, but I'm going to try.

I've got my first job. I'm going to be spending some time in Holland, in the head office of a large engineering firm, before I transfer on to some far-reach destination. I'm not too fussed about the potential my new job offers, but at least Mummy and Daddy are proud of me. Daddy offers to keep up the insurance payments on my car whilst I am away, but I'll get a new car with my job anyway.

'Tell me what your job is all about,' asks my mother, and I give her the briefest of replies.

'I stayed in Amsterdam for about a year on my travels,' she says, but I don't respond to her attempt at friendship. When Noel drops by, he too tries to chat to me, but I am even briefer with him.

Instead, I busy myself with my move, shopping and packing and keeping my mind off the anxiety I feel about the new stage in life I am embarking on. I try to contact Mark before I leave, but I get no reply from the numbers I have for him. I decide to drop him a postcard updating him on my news, together with leaving him a contact number. I also let Nora have my details and then write to Jamie to let him know. I don't ask him about new friends and relationships, even though I am curious. I want to leave 'the Jamie issue' alone; it carries with it a pain I don't understand and don't want to feel.

I fly off to my first proper job with my new set of suitcases and my even newer briefcase, which is a gift from Nora. Settling abroad comes easily to me, and I find out, to my relief, that things have changed since I was a child.

Thank goodness for a multicultural society.

I try to develop my social life. I remember, all too well, my mother's loneliness when we lived abroad. I enrol in regular evening dance classes, and I use the company gym every morning and strike up some friendships with some of the regulars there.

Occasionally, I have a short-term boyfriend who takes me out to dinner or to the theatre or who provides me with the 'authenticity' required to receive invitations to dinner parties and other social occasions where even numbers fit better around the table. There is no major passion in any of these relationships for me, but they help keep loneliness at bay.

I am happy when Nora occasionally visits. She looks better and says that she is enjoying her degree. She has no boyfriends; anorexia remains her suitor.

'It's not as big a part of me anymore,' she tells me, 'but it supports me through difficult times and is always in the background, like white noise.'

'That's what my current boyfriends are to me,' I tell her.

'How's Mark?' she asks, and I tell her that I've had no news of him. Do I imagine it, or does she look pleased? We discuss men; she's always inquisitive about the men in my life, and I generally don't mind discussing them with her, all except for Jamie, whom I categorise as someone different and special and not to be gossiped about.

Nora told me today that the thought of sex with a man is still foreign to her. I felt sad that there was so much she still missed out on.

When Nora goes back, she leaves a space behind, which I endeavour to fill with a whirl of work and social life.

I got a letter from Mark today.

'I am en route to the UK for a short time and would like to meet up,' he writes. I deliberate whether to contact him, but for only a minute.

I'm crazy – why did I suggest we rendezvous in Paris?

We meet in a new restaurant, *Chez Albert*; its cosy, with dim lighting and a string quartet playing discreetly in the corner. He looks older, graver, but still so very good-looking. It is the first time that I have seen him in a suit: charcoal grey with a grey and blue tie. He is already at the restaurant when I get there, and his eyes light up when they see me; his face creases up in a big smile. We kiss, and it's as though we met and parted yesterday. He holds the key to the steel casing around my heart. We eat, but I don't remember what, and then we walk for ages along the river, our arms entwined around each other's waists, our desire for each other palpable in the air. I know we should talk about what has happened, about our respective situations, about us, but I am possessed by a strong physical urge that blocks out any coherent thought. It appears to be the same for him, since he too is quiet, his kisses insistent, his hands exploratory as they wander my body.

We walk with one step to my hotel room and make love in the dark, pressed against the door. Our desire permits us no further initially, but later I lead him to my bed, with its fresh cotton sheets, and this time we are slow, languorous, and tender as we make love again. He cries in my arms, a reminder from the past, and I hold him tight until he drops off to sleep.

The following day, our desire spent, we talk. I hear with some trepidation about Mark's relationship.

'We've spent some time apart and tried the friendship and companionship angle,' he says. 'I thought about us all the time I was with her, about how much I missed you, and particularly about Rob and you, and I felt sad and jealous.'

I look at him hopefully. 'Things are over between Rob and me,' I begin, but I stop when I see a certain look in his eyes. 'How are things between Marie and you now?' I ask warily.

He runs his fingers through his hair, tugging at the ends in the endearing way I remember.

'Well,' he says, and then he hesitates. 'Marie begged me to follow through with an IVF programme last month, since she's desperate to have a child.'

I stare at him in amazement. He continues, not noticing my reaction.

'She's older than me, you see, and her biological clock's been ticking for a good few years now. I said to her, to have a child, you have to have sex, which we don't. I don't want children anyway. I remember once, in the early days of our being together, she thought she might be pregnant, and I absolutely panicked. Luckily, it was a false alarm. Anyway, she asked me – no, she begged me to go through at least one cycle of IVF with her. She insisted that this did not have to mean any commitment from me towards her and that she would be prepared to go through with the process whatever the outcome of our relationship, and that she wanted my help and involvement in the early phase of treatment only.'

I can bear the suspense no longer. 'What was your response, Mark?' I ask.

'I told her that she was mad to contemplate such an action and that I wanted no part of it,' he says, and I look at him, suddenly hopeful, but I see no joy in his eyes, and a feeling of déjà vu sweeps over me. He senses it too and turns to hug me, but I purposefully move away.

'I know that I'm a coward, Maya,' he murmurs gently, sadly, 'but I feel so guilty when it comes to Marie. I've wasted her life with my uncertainty, and I just can't refuse her request, as irrational as it sounds. She knows I don't love her, not in the way I love you, but I care for her and for her well-being and future. She's a large part of my history, and I don't seem to be able to let it go.'

I didn't know what to say, but then out of the blue, I thought of Jamie. I remembered his undivided loyalty to me, his clarity in his commitments to people, his belief in what is right and wrong. Then I knew that to continue with Mark, without thinking about myself, would be wrong.

'What now, Mark?' I ask.

He looks sheepish. 'Well, Marie and I went for a number of tests, and apparently we're both fertile, so Marie has started on the hormonal treatment required. When the process is successful, then I won't be needed.'

I gaze at him in disbelief. 'Why did you want to see me, Mark?' I ask.

He shakes his head slowly. 'I love you, Maya, and whilst it's all wrong, I wanted to let you know how important you are to me. I know it sounds mad because I'm doing this IVF nonsense with Marie, but I've never felt so separate. With you, I'm whole, and yet I can't let her down, even when I know with all of my being where I want to be.'

I can't understand his logic, but then I realise that I've never really understood him or his relationship with Marie. What is more important, I've never given weight to my own needs in relationships.

In my desperation to belong, I haven't prioritised myself.

'Can you wait?' Mark asks, 'I know we'll work – I've just to cross the last hurdle.'

'No, I can't, Mark,' I say. 'It no longer works for me, nor will it ever.'

We say goodbye, and tears stream down his face. My eyes are dry, and as he leaves, I feel suddenly, surprisingly, free. I no longer personalise the break-up. Jamie has shown me that I am important, that I can be cared for because of me, and that I can be included – if I want to be.

I ring in sick and arrange for some days off work and then contact the clinical psychologist who was so helpful to me through my final year of college and arrange to go and see her. On my flight to my appointment, I know that this time I have to finally put to rest my feelings towards Mark. I have three really useful sessions with her, and I accept that I've been repeating a pattern of behaviour in relationships based on my belief about my unacceptability. I've been trying to get myself included in the most difficult of situations where I know, really, that inclusion is unavailable. I have been trying to attain the unattainable as a way of perpetuating and maintaining my beliefs.

I can't deny that Mark has been important to me. Neither can I say that I haven't loved him, totally and completely.

Yet I've always known about Marie, always been exposed to his dilemma of duty of care and loyalty towards her, versus his feelings towards me and our relationship.

I wanted to win so that I could feel special and omnipotent. I wanted to be the only one who could make a change in his life and be what others couldn't be for him. I thought I could make him commit.

How disillusioning it is to realise that I have been pursuing an old programmed need in me, rather than being able to see Mark and the situation for what it is. I can also see that he has mirrored some of my needs. To attain what he desires has to come from him and only him, not from someone like me who charges in and wants to rescue him.

I fly back to Amsterdam sadder and wiser. I apply myself with diligence to my work, and I also spend time and effort on the building of new friendships and start to avoid short, dead-end romantic liaisons, which are heady yet unfulfilling. I worry that I may have become boring, just as I worry about my weight, my single life, and my financial flexibility. Guilt is a constant companion, although I practice spending money on myself. I start having regular beauty treatments, I buy expensive shoes and clothes, I travel to exotic places, and I also sometimes drink too much.

Life is good. Best of all, I have started to write again: poems and short stories. This makes me truly happy. I have found a part of myself again.

I find that I miss my friends and family far more than before. I remain irritated by my mother, but I think about my father frequently, and I wonder how he deals with the various changes at home on his own. I also keep in touch with Jamie.

I was really sad today when Jamie told me that he had met an air stewardess called Cathy and that they are dating.

'Is she attractive?' I find myself asking him against my will, when we next speak.

'Gorgeous, with legs to die for,' he replies, and the green-eyed monster stirs within me. 'What about men in your life?' he asks.

'Oh, a few,' I reply defensively. 'Mark's been in touch.'

'Really? After all this time? Is all well?'

'Absolutely,' I respond vehemently, feeling unexplainably sick. 'All is well, Jamie.'

In the summer, I decide to visit home. I haven't seen my parents for at least six months. My father insists on coming to pick me up from the airport, and we talk on our journey back. He tells me that he has developed a love of archaeology and that he has started attending various courses on this subject. He has also booked himself on some archaeological tours, and he invites me to accompany him on one the following week. I tell him that I can't imagine anything more enjoyable than accepting his offer. My mother comes to the door to greet us when we get home. She has even shorter gelled and highlighted hair, and her face is beautifully made up. She has lost more weight and could pass as half her age in her tight jeans and baseball shirt. She puts out her arms to cuddle me, and I awkwardly step aside as I enter. I notice that my parents do not exchange any pleasantries.

Dinner that evening is a sombre affair. My mother remains a vegetarian, and we all eat our nut roast with rice in silence. I note that my mother's cooking has improved significantly. I have bought some continental chocolates as a gift, which we eat as dessert. Just as we finish, my mother clears her throat.

'Have you kept in touch with Nora?' she asks.

I am surprised. She never asks me about my friends.

'I have,' I say. 'She's doing really well.'

'That's good,' she replies, lapsing into silence again.

'How's Noel?' I enquire back politely.

'He's well,' she says, 'very successful. He's been on breakfast TV, talking about toxins found in food.'

'Very interesting,' interjects my father dryly.

My mother looks at him. 'Well, it was your choice to watch it,' she retorts.

'Oh, of course,' he responds. 'I never said that you made me.'

I've never heard anger expressed between them, and since I feel uncomfortable, I change the subject.

'How's Grandfather?' I ask, knowing that by introducing him into the conversation, my mother will have another target on which to vent her anger.

'I don't know too much,' says my mother crossly. Then she cheers up. 'I did hear that Rhona and he are having difficulties.'

'What sort of difficulties?'

She is gleeful. 'Oh, well, apparently Rhona entertains lavishly all the time and spends a lot of money. She has also had building work carried out on the house, and now having completed it, wants to move to bigger, which your grandfather doesn't want. I hear she has also restricted his golf hours.'

'I suppose the house looks very different to when Grandma was there,' I say wistfully, a picture of my grandmother's bedroom in my head, the smell of homemade jam from the kitchen drifting into my thoughts, together with the smell of lavender and rose from her garden.

'I expect so.' My mother is dismissive. She is the reverse of me, not attached to the departed but very much wanting to be attached to the living.

There is no more to say after this, and we clear up the dishes and settle to watching the evening news. Before I go to bed, my father clears his throat.

'Maya is coming with me on my next archaeology tour,' he announces to my mother. 'Next week.'

'Oh, good,' my mother replies, almost as though she is not listening.

I go to bed troubled. I dream of the undertaker's, a dream I haven't had for ages. I dream of being tied to the railings and of people throwing tomatoes at me. In the crowd is my mother. I can see that she is the distributor of the tomatoes. She is selling them, and to those who cannot afford to buy, she is giving them free. 'Tomatoes for the traitor,' she chants. Suddenly, the railings are those in front of my grandparents' house. I walk down the drive and open the front door and see that the hallway has been converted into a funeral chapel. Tall candles are lit, and the smell of incense fills the air. I float into the main hall and see a number of coffins and then search for the kitchen. When I find it, it's unrecognisable, because it is now where the corpses are prepared for embalming. My mother is there, beside a bubbling pot from which the smell of formaldehyde emanates. As I walk in, she turns to me and smiles. Her teeth are rotted; her breath is foul. 'I hope you've come to help me, traitor,' she whispers.

In London

August 2006

PC Reeves felt he was a traitor to his place of training. He was in the offices of New Scotland Yard, wanting to be helpful but feeling very out of place. This was the first time he had been back in London since his training days, and he already found himself overwhelmed by the hustle and bustle of the city and the abrasiveness and cynicism of his London counterparts.

He was exhausted but at the same time elated. A few final pieces of evidence to pick up, and he could file away the case that continued to puzzle him as closed.

He was so excited about spending time with Susannah in London. So far things couldn't have gone any better. She loved the hotel and they had thoroughly enjoyed the champagne he had arranged to have ready in the room when they arrived. They had walked around the local streets and she had been enthralled at the fashion boutiques that nestled in the small but exclusive roads around the hotel. Today Susannah was having her spa day today and thoroughly looking forward to it.

He picked up the telephone, dialled a number, and asked to speak to Maya. It was her mother on the other end who said that Maya was just about to leave for an appointment relating to her wedding. Could the call wait? He was insistent, and then finally he spoke to the person he had been building a profile of over the past two weeks. He introduced himself.

'Do you know a Mr Robert Langford?' he asked.

'Yes,' said Maya. 'We were at university together, but then he left in the second year.'

'When did you last see him, miss?'

'Strange you should ask that, officer. I had no contact at all with him until about a month ago, when he called me, saying he had something important he wanted to discuss with me.'

'What was that miss?'

'Is there a good reason for this, officer?'

'I'm afraid there is, miss. Please tell me what he said.'

'I never got to find out, unfortunately. We had a telephone conversation in which he was terribly evasive, and he then suggested meeting at his home which we arranged for the twenty-fourth of last month due to the travel restrictions based on his disability.'

'He had no disability, Miss.'

'I can't believe it. He tricked me. Anyway, I agreed to meet him, because I've always wanted to apologise for how things ended with us, but it was the day of the Ipswich bombings, and I was on a train that was half an hour after one of the trains that got blown up. I had to disembark and make my way back home. I tried to call him to let him know why I hadn't come but couldn't get through, all the telephone lines were down. I reckoned he'd put two and two together and call me sometime, since frankly I was dreading seeing him, but he never got back.'

'I'm sorry to give you bad news, Miss,' said PC Reeves, 'but he died that day. Would it please be possible to arrange a meeting? I've some things to show you that might be of interest.'

Chapter 33

The Best Thing since Wheat Bread

Maya 2003

I've only got one more diary to complete reading and then I will be ready to add the last bits of my life from memory and finish. I am under pressure to complete since I have little time left before my wedding. I am still reeling with surprise over the information I've obtained from my meeting with PC Reeves. There's not a lot to say about Rob, really. I suppose I always suspected he would come to a sad end. The police officer was really sweet. I still find it hard to believe that Rob spied on me and on Jamie. No wonder he was so up to date with information. I thought that I might feel angry, but all I feel is sadness when I realise the true extent of his paranoia and the futile nature of his need to be part of my life.

Its peculiar – Rob always talked about Sisyphus and what a hero he thought he was. I don't think Sisyphus was a hero at all. He only escaped death twice because he was a trickster, and as a punishment for his trickery, he was blinded and compelled to roll a huge rock up a steep hill, but before he reached the top of the hill, the rock always escaped him, and he had to begin again. It's interesting that the gods deemed futile and helpless labour to be the biggest punishment of all. Rob's need to control was 'Sisyphean'; how can you regulate the sun rising and setting or waves falling or rising? Rob was like Sisyphus and wanted to control the uncontrollable – love, loss, even death.

The police officer told me that Rob had never intended to die. He had been plotting and planning ways of getting me back, and after the ending of a brief relationship with a girl he'd met at the last mental health unit he was at, he put his plan into action. He called me to make me believe that he not only had something to tell me that was important about Jamie, but also that he needed to hear my apology. He lied about being disabled, so I would travel to his home. His plan was to take just the right amount of an overdose minutes before I got there, so that I would find him and 'realise' how much I cared for him, and once I had called the ambulance and he was 'saved', we could have a reconciliation. He invited me to visit him at a specific time, and when he heard a knock on the door, he took the overdose, thinking it was me and that I had arrived earlier than expected. It wasn't me of course, because I was stuck in a train that couldn't get through to the right station because of the bombs. It was his neighbour's estranged son at the door, who was visiting his mother whom he hadn't known had died, and who was making some enquiries. He then shouted for me to come in, because he had left the door unlocked, and he waited. He waited a few minutes, and then, when the explosion in Ipswich town went off and I still hadn't come in, he tried to call 999. The impact of the bombing shut down telephone lines in the area and affected the network for mobile phones. He couldn't call anyone, and by then it was too late: he couldn't coordinate his movements to get help.

*   *   *

My father and I leave for his archaeological dig feeling excited. We potter around dusty ruins and after hard days of travel and discovery have quiet evening meals in little restaurants together. We catch up with lost conversation, especially about my mother.

'I'm pleased Diane is no longer depressed,' says my father, 'but ironically I don't like the happy her. What I miss the most is being able to talk to her. She has become an unknown quantity, a newfangled woman who talks of Reiki and of taking Spirulina supplements, in combination with world politics and the injustices of the legal system in South America.'

As I comfort him, I am reminded of being the adult talking about a difficult teenager.

'She's just finding herself,' I say. 'She's so happy about becoming a lawyer that I'm sure the rest will work out all right.'

He shrugs. 'I can give her time to find herself,' he says, 'but what I object to is her finding it with idiots like Noel.'

I look at him and hesitate. 'Dad, do you think they're having an affair?' I ask.

A look of pain crosses his face. 'I don't think so,' he says. 'I don't think the man is testosterone-filled enough for your mum. He's just an available male she can manipulate, but,' He hesitates before saying, 'Maya, I have a confession to make. I've been seeing someone else, only for companionship, because I've felt so lonely. Before we left for this weekend, I told her it needed to stop.'

I'm so unhappy. I don't want to believe that Daddy has had an affair.'

'I can't believe it,' I say out loud, and he smiles wryly.

'I've let you down, haven't I, Maya?' he says. 'No don't deny it, because I feel I've let myself down too.'

'What happens now?' I ask, dazed.

'Well, I hope it will free me to start again with your mother,' he says.

'Will you tell her?' I ask, and he nods.

'There can't be lies in our relationship,' he says seriously. 'I know it works for some, and that your partner doesn't have to know everything, but I've never kept secrets from your mum until now, and that's how I want it to be.'

'Will she accept it?' I ask worriedly, and he shrugs his shoulders.

'I don't know, but if she doesn't, I know that my task will be to persuade her to do so, because I love her too much to lose her.'

I'm angry then because he has betrayed her, but more than that, he has betrayed me. He has included someone other than me in his life and has made her special.

'Why didn't you tell me?' I demand.

It is his turn to be angry. 'How can I tell you anything? You haven't been around, remember. You don't ever call, or write or visit.'

He's right. I have purposely cut myself off from my family, especially over the past year, so I can establish my independence and give a wide berth to conflict.

'I've kept away to avoid you and Mum,' I agree, 'particularly Mum.'

'I've found it hard too,' he says, 'and I suppose it's been my way of absenting myself. What I now acknowledge is that I can't keep doing that. I have to face the problem head on and come to some sort of resolution. Too long have I avoided facing her excesses, be it alcohol, or money expenditure, or her tendency to take on New Age ideas.'

I stare at him with respect. I suppose I had never thought he would acknowledge what I have thought are Mum's secrets, and therefore mine.

'Maya, I'm accepting responsibility for the hardships you've suffered,' he says. 'I've let you get on with propping up Mum and looking after her, whilst I buried myself in work. I know you've always accepted my behaviour, but it's been a flight, and it's not been fair or right to you.'

I am embarrassed and appalled. My wonderful father saying he has been wrong? Never! However, he persists, and in my heart of hearts, I know that although I have made my mother the bad parent in this situation, my father has, through his avoidance, also been a contender in aggravating issues. Reluctantly, my idealised view of him is dismantled. It's a painful process, because I want to continue to revere him and see him as my knight in shining armour, but instead I see him for the difficulties he has in dealing with emotions as much as for his strengths.

When we go back home, I have recovered from feeling shocked about my father's confession.

In a way, I am honoured that Daddy took me into his confidence.

The anxiety that remains is knowing that he will confess to my mother on our return. I decide to become a tourist in London, to keep out of the house. Every time I get back home from these outings and put my key in the front door lock, I hold my breath, not sure what to expect, but nothing eventful happens, and then I start to feel resentful towards my father for maintaining my suspense. I make no eye contact with either of my parents. I feel as though I'm betraying my mother by having information that pertains to her relationship, and I feel anxious for my father and for the potential crisis and change he faces.

'Just three more days before I leave,' I think to myself gratefully as I undress to go to bed one evening. As I settle into watching some television in bed, I hear a knock on the door.

'Come in,' I say, rather surprised, and I sit up when I see that it is my mother.

She comes in and sits on the end of my bed. Her face is strained and pale, and I can see that her jaw is set very tight.

'Maya, Daddy's told you about his affair, hasn't he?' she asks me abruptly, and I instantly blush, as though I have been doing something criminally wrong.

'Well, er, um, he did, um, mention a brief relationship, er, that he had finished, when we went away together, that, er, he was going to talk to you about,' I mumble, fixing my eyes on the television screen, unable to make eye contact with her.

'He told me a few days ago,' she informs me, 'and, well, I don't know what to think.'

I steal a look at her. Her jaw is still very set, her face hard in the dim light of my room. My heart sinks, and I experience a wave of panic. Do I have a responsibility to be my father's envoy?

She says, 'That's not true. It has made me think. Every minute of every day since he told me, think, think, think – that's all I've done.' There is a sudden break in her voice, but she still looks withdrawn and holds herself together rigidly.

'He was lonely and confused,' I say.

She looks at me. 'He missed you, Maya. He missed you when you went to university, and then he missed you even more when you went abroad. He loves you so much, and I suppose I felt jealous. I wanted him to love me too, and so I tried to make him miss me. All that going out with Noel and my friends, it wasn't really because I enjoyed their company so much. It was my way of trying to make myself elusive except I didn't understand that that was what I was doing, and he didn't understand it either. He thought I was discarding his company and our life together, and now look at what's happened.'

I continue to stare at the screen, but I can feel anger stir within me.

'Are you saying that it's my fault that this has happened?' I ask in a carefully controlled voice. 'My fault that he had to seek the solace of someone else?'

My mother winces and looks at me. 'Oh, no, Maya. No, that isn't what I'm saying at all,' she says. 'It's my fault for not being able to ask for what I want. I didn't resent him missing you – I missed you too. I resented him not loving me enough, or thinking that he didn't love me enough. That's nothing to do with you.'

I finally make myself look her in the face. She stares back at me and suddenly bursts into tears.

'I'm just hopeless at communicating,' she sobs, 'just hopeless at trying to say what I mean and asking for what I want.'

I move up and gingerly put an arm around her shoulders. 'You can't always be self sufficient,' I say. 'You have to let yourself be vulnerable at times.'

I realise, as I say this that I do this too, but that I have friends, true friends like Nora and Jamie, who have seen through this façade and have forced me to change. We sit in silence for a long while.

'What a mess,' my mother sighs. 'I just don't know how to sort it.'

I look at her. 'What have you told Daddy?' I ask, and she looks downcast.

'Nothing,' she mutters inaudibly, and I take her hand.

'Mum, you have to sort out your relationship,' I say. 'Go and talk to him now, and tell him what you've just told me. He wants to make things work. I know he does.'

She looks at me hopefully. 'Are you sure?' she asks. 'I can't believe he would want to, after how I've behaved.'

'He does,' I say definitely. 'He wants to resolve things, and the best way is to start talking now.'

I just couldn't sleep last night. I kept thinking of Rob and of Mark, and I now know for sure that I'm over both of them completely.'

I go down for breakfast filled with trepidation, uncertain of what sort of reception to expect. I find my parents sitting down and having some toast and tea. The atmosphere is quiet but not strained.

'Good morning, Maya,' says my mother.

'Morning, Mum. Morning, Daddy,' I say, making my way to the kettle to put it on.

'Would you like some toast?' asks my mother, and I look at the pack of bread on the counter.

'But this is normal wheat bread!' I exclaim, and my father chuckles.

'I know. I went and bought it this morning, together with some rich roasted coffee and butter,' he says.

The three of us make eye contact, and we suddenly burst into laughter. My mother laughs the loudest.

'Of all the rebellious acts I've carried out,' she says, 'this has been the most ridiculous,' and I feel comfortable enough to go up to her, put an arm around her shoulders, and give her a squeeze.

'Daddy and I have talked and talked,' she says, looking at him and smiling.

'We've both decided to try to work on sorting out our communication,' my father adds, 'and that includes me saying that I love having normal toast with lashings of butter and proper coffee, as a start.'

> *I'm not going to keep my diary anymore. I will leave my diaries to gather dust somewhere safe, until maybe one day I will be brave enough to read them all, but for the moment, I will put them away and try to focus on getting through the challenges I have in life in a practical way.*

I say good bye to my parents and head back to my apartment and job in Holland.

Jackson and Freddy

January 2007

Jackson and Freddy looked at the challenge posed by the prospectuses spread out in front of them. They had been reading them for the past hour, and now it was time to exchange ideas. The proposition of furthering their education had come to Freddy out of the blue, and as far as he was concerned, it had been a stroke of genius. Jackson had sunk into a major depression after he had learned about his mother's death, and for a few months it hadn't mattered what Freddy had said; Jackson had remained catatonic in his receptiveness. One day when Freddy was completing another of his comic characters, this time sitting in the living room with his sketch pencils and pad rather than in his bedroom, he voiced his idea.

'You know, mate, I've had an idea of possibly going to art college, you know – may help me with drawing and things,' he mumbled, going a bright red as Jackson looked up at him for the first time.

'Show me,' commanded Jackson, and for the next couple of hours, he pored over the sketches that Freddy put in front of him, was enthralled by some of the stories he read, and even managed a travesty of a smile at some of the jokes. Finally he looked up and met Freddy's gaze.

'You're right,' he said. 'You should develop these – they're bloody fantastic. I love the sketches – like graffiti but even better.'

Freddy blushed again. 'They say a story,' he said.

'Yeah,' agreed Jackson, 'a story of hope, of building oneself, block by block.'

'You should try it.'

'Nah, I'm no bloody good. I used to spray the walls of the station with my mates. We wanted to make a mark, but I was never the artistic one. Made a different mark now, haven't we? Even though I don't want it now there's no Mum.'

Freddy twitched in his chair. He felt worried that this comment could change the slowly developing improvement he could spot in Jackson by reminding him of his loss, but Jackson continued to speak.

'I think I'd like to learn a science subject – always been interested in chemistry. We had a good teacher. He made me feel like someone in the class. I could be a teacher, Mum would have liked that.'

'That's what I like when I sketch. I have the power to make things work, and when it's finished; I am someone – the person who made characters come to life. That's pretty amazing.'

There was a pause and then Jackson said, 'I wonder if it was some of our stuff that was in the make-up of that last explosion or whether it was a coincidence and that other people had also cottoned onto the same idea?'

'I've been thinking that too,' said Freddy. 'That's why I want to do something different. Superheroes build, not destroy.'

The two men grinned at each other. 'Well, looks like we've found something else to pursue,' said Jackson. 'This should keep us out of trouble and with our feet on the ground.'

Freddy laughed. 'I'm ready,' he said, taking out the application forms. 'Shall we begin?'

PC Reeves *En Route Back to Suffolk*

August 2006

The train thundered along the English countryside, liberated from its originating confines at Kings Cross Station in London. Jack sat in one of the carriages, getting hotter and hotter as he thought of the task ahead. Well, it wasn't just a task; it was the most important goal in his life to date, and he didn't want to blow it. Sleeping comfortably, resting her head on his shoulder was Susannah. He stared for what seemed like the millionth time at her face and marvelled at its perfection. He loved the fine, downy hair just under her chin, the way her nose curled up just that tiny bit at the end, and her perfect ears. He now knew why love was so inspiring.

He glanced up at the parcel shelf above them and smiled as he saw the shopping bags. Selfridges, John Lewis, Marks & Spencer, they had spent a wonderful day in Oxford Street after he had spoken with Maya.

This case had affected him strangely. It had made him reflect on the nature of relationships far more than any other case. That poor sod Rob. What a sad but skewed example of unrequited love.

He had a little conversation in his head with his mother. Thank you, Mother, *he thought.* Thank you for providing me with security, love, and respect.

He felt in his trouser pocket for the box, and as his fingers came across it, a little grin started on his lips, which then spread along his face until he was smiling broadly.

'I'm going to ask her, Mother,' he whispered, 'ask her to move in with me and to marry me. I can't wait to hear her say yes.'

Chapter 34

Outside (Inside) In (Out)

Maya 2006

Inside Out?

Tomorrow will be my wedding day, and I just can't wait. Everything is as I've always dreamed of. How strange, when there was a time when those dreams seemed so far away. I have just the last bit of my writing to finish. I'm so pleased I've nearly completed me.

* * *

When I get back to Amsterdam, I look around my beautiful apartment. It's furnished to a high standard with every modern convenience I could ask for. I wander up to the bookshelf and see that the cleaner has been in, because there is a note propped against one of my photographs, asking me to buy some more furniture polish and toilet freshener for when she next visits.

I look at the photographs on my shelf: my parents on the induction day at school; the photograph of Grandma and I in front of the museum, now in a frame; Nora with me in Spain, when we worked in the children's home; a photograph of my final year at university, and Jamie and I at our graduation. They are snapshots of my life, snapshots of happiness, and as I view them, I finally admit to the huge ache that's within me.

Impulsively, I pick up the telephone and dial my travel agent. I book myself a flight to Saudi Arabia for the weekend. Whatever Jamie's situation is with Cathy, I need to go out there and see him.

Having made my decision, I experience my best night's sleep in a month.

I fly to Jamie's territory over the weekend and book myself into a hotel. I am as nervous as when I sat for my A-level exams, maybe even more so. I make myself have some breakfast and then dial Jamie's home number. My fingers tremble as I push the keypad. 'Please don't let Cathy pick up the phone,' I mutter to myself, and I feel a wave of relief when I hear Jamie's familiar voice on the other end.

'Jamie,' I say.

'Maya, hello,' he exclaims. 'How are you and how was your trip to see your parents?'

'It was good, very, very good, Jamie,' I reply. 'Anyway, guess where I am at the moment?'

He chuckles down the line. 'In the bath?' he asks jokingly, and I laugh too.

'Actually, I'm in a hotel a few blocks from where you live,' I say.

I hear him say, unbelievingly, 'You aren't. How come?'

'Oh, passing by,' I say inanely. 'Can we meet up today?'

'Maya, we meet up now. Right away,' he says. 'I'll brush my teeth and put on something decent and be with you in the next half hour.'

I flee to my room, brush my teeth again, and then deliberate on what to wear. I change four times before I am satisfied. I fiddle with my hair and wish I had taken some time to blow-dry it after my early morning shower, when the insomniac in me couldn't find anything better to do. I look at my nails and wish that I had manicured them. As I hesitate, not very satisfied with myself, there is a knock on the door and in walks Jamie, who looks wonderful. The Saudi sun has tanned him a golden brown, and he has obviously been working out in a gym, because he looks rippled and toned.

'Jamie,' I screech, and I fling myself into his arms.

'Maya,' he replies, and he squeezes me tight. We don't need to elaborate; we both know the mission of my visit. As Jamie's lips descend towards mine, I know where I finally belong.

*   *   *

Outside In?

Well, very little is left to say, since it's all in my collated journal. I know now that I am not alone in my need to belong and that being different can be positive as well as negative.

Of course it is Jamie that I am marrying; there is no doubt whatsoever in either of our minds that this is what we want, and there is little reason to delay being together and publicly declaring this intention. It turns out that Cathy was not significant after all.

We have set up home back in the UK, where Jamie and I can pursue our careers. We will face life's challenges together, and I hope we will pull through them, as we have done up to now. Meanwhile, the lesson I have learnt is not to be afraid of my underground world, and that to go about my over ground life, I need to acknowledge what lies underneath, for it shapes me and propels me to destinations where I need to travel so that I can feel complete.

'To bear the unbearable, I have had to bare the *unbareable*,' says my diary, and this is what I have done.

Maya is my name. 'Illusion' is it's meaning, but I am not an illusion. I am real, and by moving my inside out, I have shifted from the outside in.

The End

Acknowledgements

I would like to thank the various people I have encountered in my clinical career who have shared their inside worlds with me and taught me about the common fears and hopes we hold. Thank you to Philippa Pride whose invaluable help was available from the time the idea for this book germinated to its completion, and to Elizabeth Crossley and Kez Kendall for editing help. To my parents who provided me with the most loving and stable of outside worlds and nurtured my inner development, I owe my heartfelt appreciation. Thank you Natasha, Litza, Jodie and Lara, for giving me the opportunity through you to discover in amazement my potential to create. My special thanks to you John, for being my inspired beginning, passionate middle and happy ending.

Dr Nihara Krausé is a practicing Consultant Clinical Psychologist and lecturer with significant clinical experience in working in adolescent and adult mental health. She is an advisor to the media including TV, magazines and newspapers. This is her first novel.